The Kingdom
on the
Edge of Reality

The Kingdom on the Edge of Reality

Gahan Hanmer

TWO HARBORS PRESS

Two Harbors Press
212 3rd Avenue North, Suite 290
Minneapolis, MN 55401
612.455.2293
www.TwoHarborsPress.com

ISBN-13: 978-1-937293-62-8
LCCN: 2011942363

Distributed by Itasca Books

Cover Design and Typeset by Steve Porter

Printed in the United States of America

For Amanda and Karol

Chapter One

"Of course there is nothing illegal about what you did," said the sheriff, "keepin' in mind that it could've got you killed."

"I'm sorry about what happened, Sheriff. I lost my temper." And I *was* sorry to be making trouble for myself in the state I was in.

"Those men should not have been using your house like that without permission. But it had been vacant for a number of years. And according to what we heard, they were trying to clear out of there when the trouble started."

"The trouble started when they stopped me in the road with guns and searched my car."

"Oh, yes, that can be annoying, I know. We have been trying to discourage that kind of behavior. But the militia serves its purpose here, if you want my opinion. Things being how they are, it's good to know who is coming into Marysville, and if possible, why. So I'll come right out and ask you what brings you to our quiet little town? You don't have to answer me if you don't want to. It's just a friendly question. We want everybody to get along and be happy here."

So what was I supposed to tell him? Did I even know? The bottom had fallen out of my life, and I needed to regroup somehow. I needed to find some balance, some reason to carry on. I had been clinging to a fantasy about a little house that I had inherited years before in the boondocks of New York State, a house I had never seen. I thought if I could just get there, I could cool my brains a little, soak up some nature and sunshine, and maybe start feeling a little better. It wasn't anything I was going to try to explain to this sheriff.

"I came to take possession of this house."

"Well, you did that! But Tom Herman has got such a bad sprain, he couldn't go to work today."

"It was an accident." Herman had to have been the militiaman who had gone over the card table covered with moldy fast-food garbage and militia leaflets on his way out the door. It was sort of an accident. That yahoodie had enjoyed pointing his shotgun in my face while they were searching my car and questioning me. When they found out that I was actually a property owner in Marysville, then according to our quaint customs, he wasn't allowed to point his shotgun in my face anymore. What's more, I was also allowed to throw them and all their stuff out of my house abruptly and rather tactlessly because they had been trespassing and using it for a militia H.Q. and fast-food garbage dump. It's funny how fast things can change sometimes. Or perhaps I should say instead that it's sometimes funny how fast things can change, and sometimes not, as you will see.

I wasn't happy about what had happened. If I had it to do over again, maybe I would have more sense. It frightened me that I hadn't any better control over myself than that. The sheriff was certainly right when he said I could have gotten myself killed. I didn't know who I was dealing with, and there were certainly enough weapons on hand.

So now what? Everybody in that little town would have heard about it by now. I was off to a hell of a start in

Marysville! But the worst thing about it was feeling afraid of my own state of mind.

"How long are you planning to remain in Marysville, if you don't mind my asking a friendly question?"

"I don't know, Sheriff. I just need a little peace and quiet right now. I need to work some things out. I don't have any definite plans."

"Well, all right, I won't pry. I just wanted to stop by and have a look at you after what happened. Just one more friendly question, Mr. Darcey. What exactly do you do?"

"I'm kind of betwixt and between right now, Sheriff."

"What did you do before you came here?"

"I owned a little theater, but it . . . well, it burned down."

"A movie theater?"

"No, the other kind."

"A playhouse?"

"Yes, that kind."

"Oh! Well, I don't suppose there would be much need for one of those in Marysville." He tried to say it pleasantly enough, but I think if I'd said I used to own a transvestite bar, it would have made about the same impression.

"I'm not planning to build one here."

"I just don't think there would be much interest in such a thing." The sheriff looked at his watch and hitched up his belt. He looked over his shoulder at his police car and gave me a grim smile and a nod. "All right, Mr. Darcey, I won't take up any more of your time. I will say that it would probably be just as well if you didn't tangle with the militia. Just a little friendly advice, that's all."

After the sheriff was gone I walked up onto my little porch feeling tired and confused. I sat down in a rickety chair and leaned back against the wall. I was off to a pretty bad start in Marysville, but I was pleased with my little house. It had a stove. It had a fridge. It had a toilet and a shower and a bed. I had everything I needed for the time being, and maybe after awhile I would even have a life again. Okay, I have a little bit of a temper, and it was not the first time in my life it had got me into trouble. But I supposed the trouble would pass in time. Peace and quiet was what I needed, and that would be abundant in this tiny country town.

So there I was, minding my own business, sitting in my rickety chair, my arms dangling limply, soaking up the sunshine and the gentle rhythms of the rural countryside, when I had another visitor; this one drove up in a Rolls-Royce Silver Cloud and parked under the maple tree.

It was the sound of the car door closing that made me open my eyes, so I must have been dozing. There was the Rolls, just as if it had appeared from nowhere, and there was this man who had probably seen the last of his twenties. Four or five inches over five feet tall maybe, he was nicely built, well-proportioned, and very bold in his fashionable and expensive duds. He took up his position at the bottom of the steps, very still and composed, not tilting his head back to look up at me, but keeping his chin level and looking out from under his brows. It made a businesslike, even sinister impression and it made me smile to myself to see this man taking himself so seriously, Rolls-Royce and all.

"Jack Darcey?" he said, and that surprised me very much because I hadn't told a soul where I was going. Looking this man up and down, I couldn't find a clue as to who he might be and what kind of trouble he might be bringing with him, so I chose the voice of a country hayseed from my actor's bag of tricks and said, "Nope, not me."

That caused him to smile a little ghost of a smile, and he said, "Well, if you know where I can find him, I've got some good news for him." The accent was hard to place. Cleveland? Detroit? It made me think of professional gamblers, the prize ring, and the track, and that made me nervous. I had made a couple of shady loans to create my little theater, and I was planning to make some provision for them; unfortunately, I hadn't gotten around to it yet. Could that be it? I didn't believe for one second that anybody had chased me all the way to Marysville to give me good news.

"Nope," I said finally, using the same hayseed persona. "Nobody by that name lives here in Marysville, mister."

He put his head a little over to one side and continued to regard me with the same ghost of a smile for a few moments. Then he reached inside his jacket, and I had a strong impulse to vault the porch railing and make a break for the woods. But instead of a weapon, he produced a photograph; and after glancing at it, he walked up the porch steps over to where I was still leaning against the wall in my rickety chair and held it out to me. I hadn't much choice but to take it, and there before me was a clear and recent photo of myself loading stuff into my car; in the background was one corner of my little theater, or what was left of it after the fire. I had been completely alone at that moment, very much alone, because every single person who had been part of that enterprise had scattered to the four winds of heaven since there was nothing to hold them any longer. In that moment I had felt as alone as a man can feel, and so I wondered very much who could have taken that photo.

When I looked up, the man had put his hands behind him and he was leaning comfortably against one of the porch posts. The ghost of a smile was gone, but his attitude said he would be content to wait as long as need be. He could have been a process server, or a private investigator, or a cop, or a goon. But driving a Rolls-Royce Silver Cloud?

"Okay," I said finally in my own real voice, "who are you, and what do you want?"

"My name is Rudy Strapp. An old friend of yours, Albert Keane, sent me down with his car to get you and bring you up to the old homestead for a little study break."

Now there was no disguising my surprise. "The old homestead" was the Keane family nickname for one of the largest country estates on the eastern seaboard; "a study break" was a weekend away from private school. Those were words from my distant past; I hadn't seen Albert Keane in over twenty years. I did, however, happen to know that his parents had both died in a plane crash, and that he was now a stupendously wealthy man.

In my memory I could see that neat quadrangle of buildings around a grassy lawn: classrooms at one end, dining hall for four hundred people at the other, dormitories on the sides. All heavy red brick edifices in the federal style, with oak trim and tall white pillars, everything well maintained and in excellent taste: The Chesham School, a bastion for the careful breeding of the privileged few.

Beyond the quad were the athletic fields; beyond that a meadow and a thick border of trees. A lane of blacktop ran you out to the front gate, the highway, and the edge of a tiny and boring Connecticut town where most of the girls had either married or run away by the time they were sixteen. If you'd been a good boy (according to some stiff institutional definitions of what that meant) and weren't on restrictions of any kind, you could walk into town on Wednesday and Saturday afternoons to sneak cigarettes or try to get a feel off some town girl in the movie house or out in the fields. The rest of the time you were confined within the perimeter of the institution, and the teachers did their best to see that your parents got their money's worth.

6

Children wound up in such schools for two main reasons. Some parents were anxious to make lawyers or doctors or corporate superstars out of their kids and were willing to pay for the huge advantage a school like Chesham provided. Other parents, for a variety of reasons, couldn't keep a real home for their children, and were willing to pay other people to take over their responsibilities. My parents were in show business and they were as nutty and unstable as show business people usually are. When I was thirteen or so, they were going through a screaming, cut-throat divorce, and I was languishing around Hollywood with a rowdy set of friends, trying out the new drugs and getting into fights. My parents saw the writing on the wall and tried to do the best they could for me. Somebody knew somebody who knew the headmaster of this particularly good school. Arrangements were made, a small wardrobe of appropriate clothing was selected to replace what I was accustomed to wearing, and off I went to New England.

"So you work for Albert, do you?" I asked my visitor.

"Yeah, you could say that."

"You're not his chauffeur."

"No, no. I drive him around sometimes, but I'm not his chauffeur. Mr. Keane doesn't have a chauffeur."

"Are you his bodyguard?"

Instead of replying, he gave me an enigmatic look, as if the answer might be both yes and no.

"What do you usually do for him?"

"Whatever needs to be done."

"You're a man of many talents."

"You could say that."

"Did you take that photo of me?"

"No, that was taken by a pro."

"Why would Albert send someone to take a photo of

me?"

"Why don't you ask him? He'll tell you anything you want to know. If you want my opinion, you're very lucky he's interested in you."

"What's he interested in, exactly?"

"Ask him. Maybe he wants to be your friend."

In the beginning it had been Albert who needed a friend. According to a peculiar boys' school prejudice, he was what was known as a rich bitch. He was the only child of a family that was so astronomically wealthy that he was already, in theory, set for life; to boys whose parents had sent them there to sweat the climb to the highest pinnacle of success or die trying, it looked like he had it made from the start. That he was a natural straight-A student; that intellectually there was no one in the school more committed to the life of the mind; that he had his sights set on Harvard and would doubtless be accepted when the time came not only for his scholastic achievement but also for his impeccable character—none of these factors gained him any favor. He was still a rich bitch who already had it made.

He was not a social climber; he was not an athlete. His upper-class manners, which were so stylized that they came off as affectations, made him seem aloof when he really wasn't at all. And the aspect of his personality most infuriating to his peers was that he didn't seem to realize or care that he didn't fit in. He went back and forth to his classes completely absorbed and fascinated by everything he was learning, and he was always polite to everyone in a manner that was cordial and delicate. He was an oddball, he was a rich bitch, and he was alone.

Meanwhile, I was also doing a good job alienating myself from my peers at that school. I had grown up believing (thanks to my bohemian family) that if anybody had scads of money, they had probably acquired it through the exploitation of all the helpless and innocent lambs that my parents felt sorry for. These exploiters, basically the entire upper-class of America except for a handful of rich artists who had acquired their wealth *ethically*, were by definition callous and heartless; good people, soulful people, did not have them over for dinner unless perhaps it was necessary for business reasons.

In any case, that was my childish interpretation of what my family thought. And so, in looking for a more salubrious environment than the streets of Hollywood for me to spend my teens, my parents had overshot the mark a trifle by plunking me down in such an upper-class school.

Somehow, and don't ask me how, I understood that it was to my advantage to stay in that strange and alien place where boys wore white shirts and jackets and neckties to class and were required by the oddest of all customs to eat fried chicken with a knife and a fork. Somehow I understood that I could make a more stable and healthy home for myself there than the one literally flying to bits in vicious, drunken fights in California. I could pass the courses and follow the rules. I could get what was known as a good education and start to make myself a life. But I couldn't allow myself to bond or even connect very much with my upper-class and upper middle class schoolmates. That was too much of a stretch. In order to feel even marginally good about myself in those awful teen-age days, I had to remain loyal to my parent's ideas, such as I understood them, and that meant keeping myself separate from rich people and also social climbers, who were incipient rich people and for some reason were supposed to be even more detestable than the ones who had already made it.

So although I decided to remain at that school and put up with the insane rules and the impossible load of homework, I stayed on as the resident bohemian, a gadfly, and a judgment against the whole class that the institution represented, and I too, was alone.

"Do you like to ride horses?" That was Albert Keane talking to me outside the evening study hall. "*I* do," he continued when I didn't answer right away, "but it's ever so much more fun when you have someone to ride with."

I did like to ride. There was a ranch at the lower end of Griffith Park in the Hollywood Hills which rented horses quite reasonably, and I used to spend many pleasant hours weaving my fantasies as I rode the trails above the city. Los Angeles, from that vantage above the permanent curtain of smog, looked like some lost city of the future where no one lived anymore because of the radioactive cloud that had poisoned it.

"Sure, Albert," I said sarcastically, "let's go right after study hall."

He laughed at that. "Oh, I don't mean *now*." He had a jolly laugh, bubbly and uncool. Everything he did was uncool, like paying sincere compliments to people without hedging them in sarcasm or irony the way the rest of us did.

"I do like to ride," I admitted. "We could ride old Mr. Stookins if we could find a camel saddle."

Albert waggled a finger at me. "Mr. Stookins is a brilliant teacher, and we're all very lucky to have him." Albert was a very funny duck. No other student in the school would have reacted that way to what I'd said, for we were as cruel and bitchy as any other group of American kids that age. To stick up for a teacher? That was really strange.

"But if you like to ride," he went on, in the same pleasant tone he'd used to reprimand me, "what I'm suggesting . . . Maybe you're already busy. It's kind of short notice, I guess, but I hope you're not. You see, I'm going home next weekend, and if you'd like to come too, Mother says it will be all right, and we have horses."

"Out of the road, rich bitch!" That was Guy Hawke, the class bully, shoving Albert out of his way. Albert staggered, and he might have fallen except for bouncing off the doorjamb.

"Watch who you're shoving, Guy," I told him, and then I thought, *Oh, God, why did I have to say that?* There was no reason for me to stand up for Albert, except that I'd been born with a bit of a temper, something I've never been able to mend, and that temper had gotten me into trouble pretty consistently over the years.

Several other boys had heard the exchange, and their own conversations came to a halt. Fear came gushing up along with the adrenaline, for there would be no way to brazen this out with words. I would have to fight him now, or kiss his ass, and I had already made up my mind which it would be.

Guy Hawke was not your average hulking bully. He was tall and lean and almost graceful in the way he slowly turned and walked back to where I stood. But when he shoved his face right down into mine, I could see how impatient he was for an opportunity to hurt someone.

"What did you say?"

"You heard me."

"You want to make something of it?"

"Yeah, I do."

"Meet me behind the studio in fifteen minutes."

"I'll be there."

Guy Hawke seemed pleased. Giving me one last baleful stare, he walked away. It was a frightening look, very powerful and predatory; it made me sorry once again that I'd gotten myself into this mess. But there was nothing to do now but go through with it, so I went back to my dorm to change out of my good clothes.

Albert followed me upstairs. "You're not going to fight with him, are you?"

"Sure, I am."

"Why?"

"Why? What do you mean why?"

"Don't you know why?"

"Get out of here, Albert. I have to get ready."

"Is it a matter of principle?"

"I don't know, Albert. I hate people like that. I always wind up fighting with people like that. It doesn't matter why."

"Do you think you have to save me from him?"

"Huh?" I was looking for my high-top sneakers.

"You told him to quit shoving me."

I had forgotten about that. "It isn't about you. A person like that, he's . . . Let's talk about it tomorrow, okay?"

"Tomorrow may be too late. Everything we do, Jack, spreads out in ripples to the edge of the universe, and then comes back to touch us with good or ill."

That made me bark with laughter. "Albert, will you give me a break?" I had broken my shoelace. "You're going to make me late for this fight. I don't want to be late. I want to be early so I can get myself set."

"You don't have to go through with this."

"Are you crazy? Of course I do."

"You can inform him that you've decided not to stoop to his level."

"If I did that, he'd be lifting his leg on me all year!"

"There's no need to be vulgar. We could go to him together as a united front. We could embarrass him with the smallness of his behavior."

"Albert, I've got to hand it to you. You are a real maniac."

12

Grabbing my sweatshirt, I bounded down the stairs.

The studio, where art and music classes were held, was off by itself between the quad and the gym. There were strict rules about fighting in the buildings or on the quad, but hey, boys will be boys, and there was a tacit understanding that the disciplinary machinery would overlook a fight behind the studio if nobody got seriously hurt.

When I got there, a lot of boys had already gathered to watch the fight. In a dull place like a boys' prep school where life is mostly classes and studying, news of anything interesting spreads fast. Guy Hawke wasn't there yet, so I had a chance to catch my breath and look over the killing ground. It was just a bit of lawn covered with dry autumn grass, a couple of big trees at both ends of the studio, and a hedge of blackberry bushes running below the windows in between. The lights were off in the studio but there was some spill from the lights in the gym. Coupled with a bright moon, there was plenty of light for me to get my ass kicked that evening.

I felt good. I was a little afraid of getting hurt, but I was excited too. This would be my first serious fight at that school, and I wanted to make a good showing while I lasted. One good fight with someone bigger than you fixes you right up with a reputation even if you lose; then in the future, anybody who might think to give you a hard time is more likely to pass you by for someone who won't fight back.

Boys kept arriving but they all kept pretty quiet, because if they attracted the attention of the teachers, the fight would be broken up before it started, and nobody wanted that. Now I couldn't wait for Guy to get there, because I'd decided to give them all a surprise. Instead of the usual preliminaries with insults and shoving, I was going to go at him with everything I had the second he stepped onto the grass. I could still remember that strange and awful look he had given me outside the study

13

hall, and I wanted to get right into it before I lost my nerve.

Well, there he was, in jeans and sneakers just like me, and walking between some of the boys he liked to hang out with, big boys who were on the football team. My body gave a little hop in the air, and then I was charging. Guy crouched with his fists up to meet me and his friends jumped to either side; and suddenly, there was Albert. Damn him! I don't know where he came from, but he was right in my way and I had to pull up short or else run him down.

"Albert, get out of the way, I mean it! You're going to get hurt if you keep this up."

"Don't do it, Jack. You'll only regret it, I assure you. And as for you," he said, turning to Guy Hawke, and moving right up under the point of Guy's beaky nose, "you may think you can intimidate people with your size and strength. But I'm warning you in your best interest that *God is watching*."

That made all the boys laugh. Still, there was a certain hesitancy in the laughter, I suppose because nobody was completely sure that God *wasn't* watching. Whether we believed in God or not, nobody wanted to get into trouble.

Guy Hawke was furious. It was frightening to see the veins swell up in his neck, the insane look that came into his eyes. What he was thinking I have no idea, but he brought his arm back across his body and dealt Albert a hell of a backhand crack that sent him sprawling flat on the grass. A little gasp went up from the crowd at the viciousness of it; a split second later there was another gasp because I had moved in on Guy while he was distracted and nearly dropped him with a solid punch right under the left eyebrow.

I went right in after him, trying to land a few more, but he got his guard up and was suddenly charging me in his fury. I jumped back and then started to circle him, looking for another opening.

I had gotten very lucky with that first punch, for his eye began immediately to swell, and in no time at all it was closed completely over. Now I was circling, circling to the right, into his blind side. At first he tried to rush me, but I was fast in those days. I hopped back and came right in on his blind side again. He was roaring now in his frustration, and the crowd of boys had forgotten how to be quiet in their excitement. Guy Hawke had made enemies. There were plenty of people there who would be glad to see him lose. On the other hand, I was not particularly popular myself. So anybody's blood would be welcome in that fight, and the boys cheered us on.

He charged me again, but this time I dodged wrong and circled right into the blackberry bushes. That was a bad mistake, for suddenly he was on me, punching with all his strength, knocking the wind out of me, splitting my lip. The best I could do was to grab him by the shirt and yank him into the thornbush with me, and a mighty thorough scratching we got trying to get to one another after that!

A sharp command from one of the teachers brought the fight to a halt. He looked us both over in the beam of his flashlight, and then took us both to the infirmary where a doctor was called in to look at Guy's eye. Then we were sent to our rooms and told to stay there until they decided what to do with us. The fight had been too bloody to overlook.

"Well, you are an amazing sight," said Albert when I walked into my room. There was a mirror on my dresser and I went to look at myself. My lip was split and puffy. It would be tender for a while but it would heal up fine. My face was scratched from the thorns, but that was nothing. My sweatshirt was flecked and smeared with blood. That was kind of neat.

"You should see Guy Hawke," I said.

"So what do you think that proved?"

"Look, Albert, I feel pretty good right now, so if you're going to start up again with that faggy crap, why don't you just get out of here."

To my surprise he got up and left. In the doorway he stopped and said, "I suppose a fight now and then isn't so bad. But there's no excuse for that kind of language."

A few seconds later he came back in. "I think we should wait a few weeks before we go to my house. I can't introduce you to my parents looking like that. It wouldn't make a good impression."

"Okay, Albert, whatever you say." What a maniac! I hadn't even said I wanted to go. Did I want to be associated with a fruitcake like Albert Keane? Could I go out to some big estate and take tea on the knee with the super-rich? Wouldn't that be some kind of a betrayal to my parents and the things we believed? On the other hand, I was really itching to get out of that school for a couple of days, and the idea of having a horse to ride was very tempting. I could go once, I thought, just to say I'd done it.

At that moment I felt like I could do anything I wanted. I had just gotten the best of someone who was a lot bigger than I was; he even had to see the doctor! I was high as a kite. While we had been sitting on opposite benches in the infirmary, with me holding a guaze pad against my lip, and he with a great bag of ice over one eye, Hawke had whispered hoarsely, "You hit me when I wasn't looking, you little runt. And I'm going to get even with you if it takes me the rest of my life." I gave him my best puffy-lipped smile as if to say I was ready anytime. Anytime at all.

"Okay, Rudy, here's the scoop. You get back in the Rolls and go back to the old homestead, and tell Albert that I'm very touched he was thinking of me, and I'll give him a call

16

in a few weeks. You can leave me his number." I was actually feeling something akin to nausea from all those old memories. I was looking forward to getting Rudy and the Rolls back on the road, and then treating myself to a nice long nap.

Rudy looked a little put out. "Oh, come on, Mr. Darcey, don't be like that. Why don't you just get a few things together and let me drive you out there? Mr. Keane is going to be very disappointed if you don't show up."

The last thing I wanted was an argument about it, and I was trying to be polite to this man who had driven all the way from Massachusetts for nothing. "Look, Rudy, just tell Albert it's square business, okay? That means I promise to call him soon. Going with you today is just out of the question, that's all."

He reached into his coat again and handed me an envelope. I opened it, and on some expensive stationery was a note from Albert.

Dear Jack,

I would like you to be a part of something that is happening. Please do not be stubborn and balky. Be guided by our long friendship and not by any subsequent separation, and please come right away because time is a factor. I will explain it all when you arrive.

Your dear friend,

Albert

"Do you know what this is about?"

Rudy gave me a long look and shook his head.

"Is it important?"

He gave me a shrug.

"I think you know what this is about."

"If I did know, I couldn't tell you."

"Well, leave me Albert's number, and tell him what I said." I went over to the stairs, and gestured with my head toward the open road. We walked together to the Rolls, and he opened the door but didn't get in. Instead he got a pair of gloves from the pocket of the door and started to draw them on. I remember they seemed kind of thick for driving, but I wasn't paying much attention. I was thinking instead about how much I was going to enjoy my afternoon nap.

"Mr. Darcey, can I tell you something?"

"Sure, Rudy, lay it on me." *Anything so long as the next thing is goodbye.*

"You're not doing so well. You lost your theater. You lost all your money and then some. You're living in a dump in the boondocks, and you don't have the slightest idea what to do next. Am I right?"

I just looked at him.

"Okay, well, somebody is trying to do you a big favor, and I am also trying to do you a favor by telling you that you are being very stubborn and foolish. Now why don't you do *yourself* a favor, and go lock up the house, and get in this car. You don't even need a toothbrush."

"Thanks for telling me that, Rudy," I said, stifling a yawn. "I'm sure it's very good advice, and I promise I'll get in touch with Albert in a week or two. Now please just get the hell out of here and give me a break."

I was very relieved when Rudy suddenly relaxed and grinned at me; all the energy had gone out of him. He shrugged and said, "Well, that's that. You can't say I didn't try." He winked at me, and I smiled back, glad that it was finally settled.

Then he did a curious thing. He bent down as though he wanted to pick something up from the ground; and at the same time he made a beckoning gesture with his finger as though he wanted to show me something. So I started to bend over also—like a chump—and the last thing I saw was his fist in that heavy leather glove coming up at me all the way from the ground.

Chapter Two

When I came to, I had no idea where I was. There was a pillow under my head, and I was tucked up in a soft blanket. There was a soothing, vibrating sensation but no noise. Very faintly I could hear a clock ticking. Otherwise it was silent.

My jaw ached. There was something I wanted to remember that seemed vaguely important, but I was quite comfortable and a little groggy. I just wanted to sleep a little longer.

Suddenly I sat up. I was in the back of the Rolls-Royce. That little bastard had coldcocked me, and now he was hauling me off to Albert's! There he was behind the wheel, cool as a breeze. I would wring his head off like a chicken!

But the thick glass partition did not respond to my tugging at it; and when I rapped sharply on it with my knuckles, Rudy didn't even bother to turn around. It was just a quarter inch of glass and I was sure he could hear me rapping. If he thought he was going to get away with this, he didn't know Jack Darcey! I looked around for something solid to bash the glass with, but there was nothing. I didn't even have a good shoe to work with. I was still in my old beat-up sneakers.

I sat back against the seat. It felt ridiculous to keep tapping at the window. What time was it? I found the clock by its gentle ticking, a lovely and expensive timepiece set into the armrest. It was early afternoon, and the best I could figure was that I'd been out for about an hour. That little rooster had put me out for an hour with one punch? I thought about those gloves he had slipped on. Now I could see them clearly in my mind's eye, padded across the knuckles with a little pillow of lead sand. Sap gloves they were called. What a sap I was not to have noticed! And the way he set me up, smiling and winking. What a chump I was! It should have given me a good laugh at myself, but I didn't feel like laughing.

Where were we? We were humming down some turnpike that could have been anywhere. From the position of the sun I guessed we were headed east. This was kidnapping, wasn't it? I was being kidnapped, a federal offense! It didn't *feel* very much like a federal offense, with me sitting in the back of a Rolls-Royce with a pillow and a comfortable blanket. But it was, goddammit!

This time I pounded on the partition with the side of my fist and shouted, "Rudy, you better listen to me, buddy, if you know what's good for you!"

"No need to shout, Mr. Darcey, I can hear you just fine." The voice came from a little speaker above the partition.

"Turn this car around, Rudy. Take me back home."

"Aw, Mr. Darcey, why don't you make yourself a cocktail and have a nice snooze. We'll be there in a couple of hours. You'll have a good time, I guarantee it. You like to ride horses, don't you? Mr. Keane said to tell you he has a really fine horse for you that is the spittin' image of Phoenix."

Phoenix was the horse the Keane family used to keep especially for me to ride, as though it was my own horse. Of course I'd like to ride a fine horse; how could I say otherwise? And that wasn't the point.

"Listen," I said. "Horse or no horse, you have no right to do this. This is kidnapping, understand? A very serious offense. You take me back home, or I will see you sitting in a cell!"

"Be a sport, Mr. Darcey. How would you like it if Marya Randall had put *you* in a cell?"

21

Marya Randall? I couldn't believe my ears! What did he know about Marya? She was an old lover I hadn't seen in ever so many years. He had to be referring to that time back in college when I kidnapped her and took her off to the mountains to have sex with her. It had all been very playful and as much her idea as it was mine; a novel and exciting way for us to begin our relationship. But what was I supposed to say now?

I was starting to feel very confused. Leaning back in the seat, I closed my eyes. Was I being stupid? A spoilsport? Maybe so, but I still wanted to have some say over what I was going to do or not do.

Then it occurred to me. We would have to stop somewhere. There had to be a traffic light or something between there and the old homestead. I could just open the door and jump out and then I could make my way back home. It wasn't a very heroic plan, but it gave me some feeling of being back in control. Isn't that what we all want, the feeling that we have at least a little control over what happens to us in our lives?

So I relaxed a bit, and started to enjoy the lush summer landscape dotted with farms and little towns, waiting for some kind of delay that would give me the chance I needed. But when I began to look for the door handle, just to be ready when the time came, I couldn't find one. There was no handle, no lever, no button, nothing that would open the door or even the window. Maybe it was very cleverly disguised to blend in with the decor, or maybe it was all controlled from the front. Now I was fuming again, and my mind was filling up with dark thoughts about what I would do to that little bantam when I got my hands on him.

On the outskirts of some little burg, we picked up a cop who jumped on his motorcycle and took off after us. I put my nose against the partition and tried to see the speedometer.

Eighty-five miles an hour! It certainly didn't seem so fast in that smooth-rolling Rolls. Anyway, it would get Rudy pulled over, and perfect timing too, because that little town was sure to have at least a bus station. Once again I relaxed. I decided I really didn't care about the whole kidnapping business and trying to get Rudy in trouble. Best just to think of it as a joke and forget about it.

The cop turned on his flashers, but Rudy didn't even slow down. Instead I saw him punch some numbers into a mobile phone. What he said into the receiver I couldn't hear, but a minute or two later the cop pulled around in front of us with his lights still flashing and gave us an escort all the way to the Massachusetts line. There he pulled over, touched his helmet in an informal salute, and went about his business.

In the meantime, something had snapped and all the fight had gone out of me. I was on my way to Albert's for a little study break, and what had I really been fighting against anyway? My own embarrassment, mainly. I didn't want to go face someone who knew my whole history, feeling like a failure and a drifter who had forgotten where he was drifting, someone who had had every opportunity in the world, and wound up wasting them all. In my old jeans and sneakers, with no luggage and no toothbrush, I was going on a visit to see a man who had somehow earned such gracious solicitude from the New York State Troopers.

"Rudy," I said, "where are the cocktail fixings in this dream machine?"

A small but well-stocked bar, quite a marvel of engineering and cabinetry, unfolded itself and slid into place. When this graceful transformation had completed itself, I had to laugh with admiration.

You don't even need a toothbrush. "Thank you, Rudy," I said. "Where are my clothes?"

A drawer slid open, and there, beautifully folded without so much as a wrinkle, was a complete outfit, casual but in impeccable taste. Everything fit me perfectly, even the shoes. I put my old clothes and ratty sneakers into the drawer, and it quietly swallowed them and disappeared.

Better prepared in my fashionable clothes for a journey in a Rolls, but also feeling disoriented and somewhat unreal, I poured myself a brandy and gently rocked the liquor in the bottom of the glass, sipping from time to time as I gazed out the window. The idea that I'd made a mess of a perfectly good life kept recurring, and that made me feel sad and blue. On the other hand, sitting in that Rolls with a brandy in my hand, I also had the comforting sensation that life was really just an amusing dream. It made for a kind of balance, and I wasn't suffering as we hummed along through the Massachusetts countryside.

It didn't seem long at all before I began to recognize Albert's neighborhood, the big estates with the rustic names like Oakbridge, Briarthorn, and Overknoll. This was fox hunting country, and Albert and I had ridden to hounds in some of these very same estates. It was quite a wild and nutty sport, all that was left of the noble hunts of ages past. Everyone had booze in their coffee in the morning to get them in the mood, that is reckless as hell, and then you rode until your ass fell off. Someone was always breaking his arm, or almost breaking his neck, and that was one more thing to crack jokes about. When we all finally straggled back out of the woods and fields, exhausted and giddy, there would be a huge dinner, and everyone would get really plastered and finally stagger off to bed. It was very expensive and rowdy fun.

Albert's mother and father did not participate in fox hunting, though they were both accomplished riders, and Mrs. Keane had a jumper she was very proud of. Actually they disapproved slightly of fox hunting. I heard her refer to it once in private as being *déclassé*; but they didn't mind if Albert and I went occasionally. They understood that since we were locked up in school most of the time, we had to blow off some steam.

When we got back to school, back to the classes and books and endless papers and tests, life at the old homestead seemed like a half-remembered dream. I would go back to pestering people about liberty, justice, and human rights whenever I began to worry that I was starting to blend in too well with my upper-class surroundings. I persuaded myself that my trips to Albert's home were in no way inconsistent with my ideals. There was a time for classes and studying and bandying ideas about, which was most of the time; occasionally there was an opportunity to have fun. When I was having fun, I told myself, I was entitled to make the most of it.

Anyway, the enemies, according to my teenage ideals, were people obsessed with making money, and who made it by exploiting people, that is by lying, cheating, double-dealing, and card-sharping the innocent and helpless. Albert's parents couldn't have cared less about making money; they were not in any way sly or venal. On the contrary, Albert's father was always running off to some meeting about some hospital or library he was founding, and his mother was often busy with charities. And if they occasionally forgot to say thank you to elevator operators and doormen, they were very friendly to their own servants and let them take home all the leftovers.

From our first meeting, the Keanes were very nice to me. When Albert told them that my family was in show business, I saw Mrs. Keane raise one hair on one eyebrow about a tenth of a millimeter. But except for that one moment, I always felt completely accepted and welcomed as though I was a member of the family. In addition to the horse they kept especially for me to ride, I also had my own room with my own closet and bath. I had a particular chair in the dining room where I always

25

sat to eat. And when it was time to head back to school, Mrs. Keane always reminded me that they wanted me to think of the old homestead as my own home.

Mr. and Mrs. Keane were glad to see that Albert had a friend. He was their only living child, and he had been more than a little sheltered. I understood that. They were also a little short on kids. Albert's older brother had died young, and Mrs. Keane, for some medical reason, could not have any more children. I understood that too.

What I did not really understand was that they genuinely liked me just for myself. Like the majority of young people, I hadn't yet learned to like myself very much. And my own family had sent me away. So it puzzled me and made me uncomfortable sometimes to be treated so well by these people.

What I also did not understand at all was what an inestimable blessing it was to have the patronage of such a powerful family. A lot of parents who sent their children to prep schools went down on their knees every night praying that Junior would find a friend with a family as rich as the Keanes. Such parents told their children right up front that they were being sent to school to make friends in influential circles and never to forget it.

I didn't understand any of that at the time. I don't think anybody ever explained to me what I was doing at that school. The first time my parents approached me about going there, I said no way in hell. The second time they talked to me about it I said oh all right. That's all I remember. I was tired of horrible fights and breaking glass keeping me up until all hours of the night, so I let them talk me into going. Whatever they may have said about it being for my own good, I disregarded as typical adult lies and subterfuge and forgot about it. Anyway, I had no clear notion of why I was being sent there, and mostly

I felt like they just wanted to get rid of me.

When the Keanes took me in, I was very touched and grateful to have another home. I took what they gave me and thanked them for it. But I didn't know that it would have been normal and acceptable for them to use their influence to help me make my way in the world; and I never would have dreamed of asking them for anything.

I never ever told my parents about Albert and his family. I was afraid they would think worse of me for consorting with the enemy.

Now I recognized the northwest corner of the fieldstone wall that bordered Albert's estate, and about two miles down the road, there was the impressive fieldstone arch, two hundred years old at least, that framed the entrance road. And I was *very* surprised to see, on one side of the arch, very bright and garish and out of place, a sign that said: AUCTION TODAY.

We started up that familiar road that wound through lovely woods that all belonged to Albert now, and my stomach began to churn with a whole ragbag of emotions: nostalgia and envy and a kind of dread at having to admit to this friend from my past that I had done nothing really worthwhile with all the years since I'd seen him last. Time had passed me by; I didn't have any answers to life's big questions or anything to show off. I'd just wandered from one thing to another and one place to another and let it all slide. I was wishing now that I'd been more creative about escaping from the Rolls and making my way back to my cottage in the boondocks. Not for the last time!

When we arrived at the mansion, a monument of fieldstone and oak, all gables and dormers and diamond-paned windows, the grounds were so crowded with cars and trucks that several men with orange batons were busy trying to keep them organized. They waved the Rolls by, and we drove across the west lawn to the house.

Rudy came around and opened the door for me. With my new clothes on and a couple of brandies inside me, it seemed like a long time ago that he had knocked me cold and kidnapped me; I hardly felt I could hold it against him. Maybe he had done me a favor. At this point I wasn't sure.

One of the side doors opened, and a woman came over to the car. I guessed she was a year or two into her thirties, and her casual jeans and sweatshirt did nothing to disguise her world-class beauty.

"Welcome, Jack," she said with a smile that brought a lump to my throat. "We're so glad you could come. I'm Jenna Yumans." She gave me a handshake that was both warm and firm. "Everything in the house is bedlam right now, but we're having something to eat in the kitchen. Won't you join us?"

I nodded and followed her into the house. The way her dark brown hair glistened with auburn highlights in the sunshine, the graceful, alluring way she walked . . . Ah, here was trouble.

"So," cried a familiar voice, "it's you!" Hélène Hardricourt, big-bosomed and silver-haired, made for me across the kitchen, folding me up in a hug that made me gasp for air. "Where have you been?" she wanted to know, as though I had just come back from playing outside and was half an hour late for dinner. "You had a fight with Albert, okay, these things happen. But you don't write? You don't call? You don't have anything to do with the people who love you? Oh, Jack," she cried, impatiently wiping the tears out of her eyes, "it's so good to see you, but you should be ashamed of yourself!"

"I'm sorry, Hélène, God's truth I am. But this is America, you know? It's a big country and it's easy to get lost."

Hélène was the Keane's cook, one of the family of servants that went with the house. She was married to Émile, the butler, who took his turn next, shaking my hand and embracing me with tears in his eyes. Then their daughter Maxine, who had been a child when I last saw her, embraced me and kissed me and introduced me to *her* daughter, who embraced me and kissed me, and then they all cried again. They are French, so they behave that way. I'm a yank, so I hide my feelings; but inside I felt very moved to see them again.

What Hélène had said was true. When Albert and I had parted ways in anger so many years ago, I had pushed the whole household out of my mind, out of my heart. I didn't know any better.

Now Hélène heaped up a plate for me, and I fell upon her delicious cooking just like I had in the old days. Hélène sat and watched me eat, but Émile was antsy and excused himself. With so much activity going on in the house, he was not comfortable unless he was keeping an eye on things.

"What's going on?" I asked Hélène. She replied with a series of emphatic French gestures, but said nothing. So I looked questioningly at beautiful Jenna Yumans, whom I had been pretending to forget about while I was eating.

"We're having a huge auction, Jack, as I'm sure you can see. But I think Albert would like to be the one to tell you what it means."

"Where is Albert?"

"I don't know. The auction upset him. I'd be surprised to see him before tomorrow afternoon when this will all be over. In the meantime," she said, running her fingers back through her hair and shaking it out, "he asked me to make his apologies, and to see to your comfort. Do you like to ride?"

I tried not to swallow, but I couldn't help it. "I love to ride, Jenna."

"Then that's what I think we ought to do after we finish eating."

"You're not auctioning off the horses?"

"Not all of them." The smile was enigmatic, teasing. *Oh, Albert, hurry up before I do something I'm going to regret!*

An hour later, dressed in borrowed jeans and boots, I swung myself into the saddle of a big brown stallion named Pollux. He was spirited and required quite a tight rein at first. That was all right with me. I would give him his head when the time was right. Jenna had changed into a light blouse, some kind of a cross between shorts and a skirt, and tennis sneakers. She was riding a roan mare named Cassie. We took a trail straight into the woods from behind the stables. Soon the droning of the auctioneer faded away, and we were alone among the whispering trees.

"Are you a good rider?" I asked her.

"Are you?"

"I think the main thing is not to break your neck."

"I heard you used to ride to hounds."

"Albert and I used to do that sometimes on a break from school."

"It's hard to imagine you at one of those schools."

"It was kind of an accident that landed me there."

"I didn't think you looked very comfortable in those clothes you arrived in. You look more relaxed now."

"They weren't my clothes."

"I know. They were in the drawer in the car."

She was still talking to me in that teasing manner that made everything she said seem like a little puzzle to be solved. I was very intrigued by her. I was also making the pessimistic assumption that she was Albert's girlfriend, and that I was a damn fool to be falling for her. "Whose clothes are they?"

She looked at me, and her lower lip made a little pout. She didn't want to talk about clothes. She wanted to flirt. "They're your clothes," she said. "They were bought for you."

"They fit me very nicely."

"Of course. Why would we buy you ill-fitting clothes?"

"But how did you know my size?"

She shrugged. The pout became more pronounced. She seemed a little offended. What had I done? We rode in silence to the edge of a broad meadow.

"Actually I think all clothes are stupid," she said. "Do you mind if I take mine off?" And she did, without bothering to get off the horse. First the blouse went flying. Then, with the sound of ripping Velcro, the skirt went flying after it. And there she was quite irresistibly buck naked in her tennis sneakers.

"Are you a good rider?" she asked.

It took me a moment to find my voice. "I have had a compliment or two in my time."

"Then let's see if you can catch me." Snatching up the reins like some crazed and exquisite Amazon, she whacked her heels into Cassie's flanks, and shot off across the meadow like a vision in a dream.

With a whoop, I gave chase. If anything I had underestimated Pollux's spirit, for he was mad for a gallop. In a few seconds we were bounding across the meadow after Cassie and Jenna, whose flying hair and callipygian rear had suddenly become the focus of all my energies and desires. My mind was blank, the past was gone.

It is very difficult to think while you are galloping, especially over rough terrain. Why was I chasing her? I didn't know. What did I expect to achieve? I didn't care. I was just a crazy centaur chasing another crazy centaur across the crags of the timeless past.

I chased her across the meadow, but she disappeared down another trail. I chased her down the trail and saw her plunge into the trees. I chased her through the trees, and when

31

she splashed across a stream I splashed after her. Now we were back at the meadow, and I chased her in the opposite direction. We were both wet from the stream and whiplashed from the branches. Was she planning to go streaking through the auction?

No, she veered onto the trail toward the waterfall, and suddenly I was gripped with fear. It was not a good place to be reckless. The trail there turned into a twisty and steep dirt road that switchbacked down through a narrow canyon to the bridge in front of the waterfall. I knew it well, for it had made a hair-raising course for a Flexible Flyer when the snow was deep. On a galloping horse it would be suicide.

"Jenna, don't! Jenna, no!" I knew it was too late. At the top of the grade, I reined in sharply and looked down. Her horse was out of control. It was too steep to stop, and she would never make the last turn before the road curved down to the bridge. Far below were the big boulders of the streambed.

Someone was screaming now. Was it me? No, it was Jenna screaming at her horse, screaming Cassie up to top speed, lashing the animal with her voice. She was lying low on the withers, one hand tangled tight in Cassie's mane, the other arm gripping the horse's neck. Suddenly I saw what she had in mind.

On the other side of the canyon the road jutted out from the hill. Jenna was going to try to make it across the gorge. It was all up to the horse now. I saw Cassie break a quarter stride as she measured the distance. She knew what she had to do to survive.

Please God give that horse wings, please God don't let her fall, please God, oh please God, please! The horse was in midair now, straining every nerve, the forelegs reaching out, the hind legs tucking up, all time compressed into one second, one beat of my heart. Now a rasp of rocks spun out

32

into the gorge as the hooves found a few inches of purchase on the other side. Cassie was stumbling, went almost to her knees, caught herself and stood up straight, stamping in the road. Jenna was still lying flat against the horse's spine, her hand tangled in its mane.

Slowly she sat up, slowly she rolled a leg over and slid to the ground. Dropping to the grass, she wrapped her head up in her arms.

When my heart stopped pounding so desperately, I rode the short way back to the meadow and retrieved Jenna's clothes. Then I picked my way along the road past the bridge, and tied Pollux up near Cassie. Jenna accepted the clothes and pulled them on without comment or coyness.

"I'm sorry if I frightened you," she said finally. She seemed annoyed with herself.

"I'm glad you're all right, Jenna."

"I have to do things like that. I can't help it."

"You did that on purpose?"

"Well, no, of course not. But throwing my clothes off, behaving wildly . . . It's just that life gets so boring sometimes, don't you think? And when you try to liven it up, things often end badly. Why is that?"

"I don't know, Jenna. I don't know anything about life, except that it's easy to get it all screwed up, even with the best intentions."

"Do you think I'm crazy?"

"Oh, yes."

It was not the answer she was expecting. "Oh? Well, I'm sorry I asked."

"I think everybody's crazy. I don't see any way around it."

"But you don't think badly of me?"

"I think you're a hell of a rider."

"Would you like to kiss me now?"

"Where do you fit in around here, Jenna?"

"Wherever I want."

"Are you Albert's girlfriend?"

"I don't belong to Albert or anybody else."

"But are you Albert's girlfriend?"

She turned angrily away. "Oh, you are so bourgeois!"

We rode home without talking. The auction was winding down for the day. After we had turned Cassie and Pollux over to the stableman, Jenna said, "I think that unless Albert comes back, we will dine out on the terrace, just the two of us. Will that be all right?"

"I'd like that, Jenna."

"Let's eat at seven. No need to dress."

"I have only that one set of clothes anyway."

"Look in your closet," she said over her shoulder as she walked away. "You'll find a few other things."

Sure enough, there were several changes of clothes in the closet of my old room, all my size and very thoughtfully chosen. For dinner on the terrace I chose slacks and a light sweater, but when I came downstairs, there didn't seem to be anyone home. The house seemed empty and hollow after the ravages of the auction, which was obviously not just the kind you have to clean out the attic. No, this was the hardcore, going-out-of-business kind of auction: everything must go! What wasn't already gone was rolled up, stacked up, or lined up on its way to the block.

I could see where some living space had been temporarily improvised, like a mini-living room consisting of a table and a few chairs near a nice window in the corner of a large and empty room. But mostly it was a ghost mansion now. It echoed; and the shades of Albert's ancestors slipped from room to room shaking their heads in dismay.

Dinner had been served on the terrace, and sat waiting on a candlelit table. It seemed a little spooky to me, like a magic dinner in a fairy tale. I was sipping a bit of brandy when Jenna finally appeared. She floated in wearing something that was a mixture of evening gown and negligee. It was very silky and looked like it would be easy to slip off.

I held her chair as she sat down, and she smiled at me coyly over her shoulder. When I was seated she began to serve me; every time she leaned forward she was showing me her perfect breasts nestled in the silky folds of her dress. After she served me, she stole things back from my plate and fed me little bites from hers. She poured my wine and then took sips from my glass. It was very exciting. She transformed eating dinner into a silent conversation about sex, and she did it with grace and style and humor. She was melting me down.

"The house seems very empty," I said.

"Yes, I thought all the servants could use a night out."

"Jenna, everybody is going to know."

"So what?"

"Well, they're Albert's servants."

"And?"

"Do you want Albert to know?"

"Jack, don't spoil everything. Aren't we having a nice time? I told you I don't belong to Albert, and that's the truth. Also, Albert doesn't *want* to know, so no one is going to tell him, don't you see?"

"But . . ."

"No, Jack, no buts. Now for the rest of the night we're not going to mention Albert's name, do you understand?"

I could have gone upstairs and locked myself in my room

until morning, but I didn't. I was having a wonderful time with this beautiful woman, and it was easy to convince myself that the pleasure would outweigh the consequences. I had at least one thing in common with Jenna: life often seemed boring, wasted, pointless. To reject such an exciting encounter for the sake of a scruple seemed ungrateful, like throwing away a gift from the gods. Reality, I chose to let myself dream, had been suspended indefinitely. The night would last forever, and we would live happily ever after.

"Darling?" she said, lifting her warm, moist lips from my tingling body. We were upstairs in her candlelit suite, lying on satin sheets in her canopy bed. Beyond that was the gentle night, the moon and stars. There was no stress or strain, no poverty or violence, no lack or need. All undesirable things had been remedied and healed. There was nothing left in the world but luxury and happiness and Jenna. It was one of those moments in life that almost make up for the rest of it.

"Yes?" My voice sounded very far away.

"Do you love me?"

"Yes, Jenna, I love you very much," I said, and I meant it. I also felt a little fear, for when you love, you have something to lose. But as long as dawn never came, everything would be all right, and dawn would never come.

"Darling?"

"Yes, Jenna?"

"It's dawn."

"No, dear," I said, "there will never be any more dawns. It was simply a mistake in the original creation, and the mistake, at my request, has been corrected. Stupid mundane day with all its pointless cares has been cancelled and replaced by endless luscious candlelit night."

"How poetic! But, darling, it really is dawn, and the servants will be up and about soon."

36

"So?"

"Well, I don't think it would be a good idea for them to see you leaving my boudoir."

"Don't be crazy. I left them a note on the mantlepiece saying that you and I are in bed together. If they see Albert coming, they're to ring the silver dinner bell three times."

"The silver dinner bell already went to auction. And this bed is going today. Things are going to get busy very soon around here."

"This bed?"

"Yes, dear, isn't that awful? So you see . . ."

I held my head tightly in my hands. Reality was like the sudden onset of a migraine. What kind of a world was this? You have a few hours of joy, and then they come and auction the bed right out from under you! And what about Jenna? Did she really care for me? "I don't know when I've ever had such a magical night," I said, reaching out to her.

"Yes, it was wonderful," she said, covering my neck with little kisses. "You're a very gentle lover, Jack."

Was that a compliment? Did she really mean wimpy? Unimaginative? I was feeling very desperate all of a sudden. Jenna got out of bed, found my shirt, and began to help me on with it. I wanted to cling to her, but I knew that wasn't the thing to do. I was supposed to get dressed and make a cheerful exit. *Until next time, Cherie!* When would that be? For competition I had her zillionaire boyfriend who might be arriving at any moment. It was his house. It was his bed. And I was his guest.

"Listen," Jenna said. "It's Albert."

A jolt of adrenaline hit me like a blow. Where was he? What had she heard? I expected him to come bursting into the room, and all I had on was a shirt. "How do you know?"

I whispered.

"Can't you hear it? The helicopter?"

Sure enough, I could hear the whop, whop, whop of the rotor off in the distance. I had a little time then. My clothes were all over the floor where I'd dropped them, the landmarks on a treasure map leading to a canopy bed. I watched Jenna as I dressed. She looked a little hurt, a little puzzled. Her words came back to me: *I have to do things like that. I can't help it.*

My shoes were in my hand now, my silk scarf draped around my neck. When I went to kiss her she gave me a frightened look, but grabbed me around the neck and kissed me wildly.

"Goodbye, Jack," she panted. "Thank you so much. Oh, here, don't forget your sock."

So with shoes in hand, I sneaked guiltily across the mansion as day was breaking and Albert's chopper was coming in. Cracking the curtains in my room a tiny bit, I watched it land. I was expecting something gay and racy, with chrome trim and a bright stripe or two. But what landed on the lawn was dark, squat, and armor-plated, and carried two machine guns that I could see. I couldn't see any numbers nor any insignia. It looked like a flying pirate ship.

Two men in jumpsuits ran low under the swirling rotor and then walked toward the house. The one who was carrying the attaché case and gesturing with his free hand was Albert. He was still on the portly side, and had grown a little beard.

So fascinated was I with this new image of Albert that I opened the door and tiptoed out on the landing. I heard them come in the front door, heard footsteps below, a sliding sound, a thump, and then a soft clang. Then Albert said, "This should take care of everything. Please count it if you like."

Some small noises, then a gravelly voice that said, "It seems to be all here. We'll see you at 0800 hours on the nineteenth then."

"You can expect up to ten horses."

"Ten horses or ten cannons, it's all the same to us."

"Very good," said Albert. "Never heard of you."

"Never heard of you," said the other man. I heard his boots going to the front door as I tiptoed back to my room, where I watched him run back under the rotor. The chopper lifted off, banking swiftly over the trees at the edge of the lawn.

Quickly I hung up my clothes and slid under the covers. That seemed the safest place to be. All I had to do was close my eyes, and I would be the image of the innocent guest who had been behaving as he should all night. At first I lay there trying to think, but my mind would not engage. Aside from the hour I had spent out cold in the Rolls-Royce, and some catnaps in Jenna's arms, I'd had no sleep in close to twenty-four hours. It had been a very full day, and I was really starting to feel it. I would get a little shut-eye, and then make some excuse to be on my way, maybe after a friendly bit of brunch and some light banter about old school pranks.

An affair with someone's girlfriend was dicey enough and almost sure to lead to trouble and hard feelings. But now the arrival of that corsair helicopter had got me to thinking that the situation here, whatever it was, was very much out of my line, and the quicker I was out of there, the better.

I closed my eyes, relaxed my body, and as the images of the previous day were all just beginning to mingle together into gold-plated chauffeurs and bare-assed helicopters, there was a knock on the door. Cranking one eye open, I saw by the clock on the bedstand that I had actually been out for a couple of hours, not a couple of minutes as it had seemed. But I did not feel rested, and I was not happy to be awakened.

In the past when I had visited the estate, it was customary

for the servants to bring in morning tea and open the curtains. Apparently the custom continued, for it was Maxine, Émile's daughter, who opened the door and brought in the tea service. I struggled to look chipper and rested.

"Good morning," said Maxine with a smile. I could not detect any reproach in her face or voice. One usually assumes that the servants in a household like that know everything that goes on; fortunately it is very much in their best interest to keep it to themselves.

"Good morning, Maxine," I said, trying to smile back.

"Mr. Keane has come home," she said, "and wants to know if you will meet him in the den for breakfast."

I said I'd be delighted to, and she opened the curtains and left. Could I steal a little more sleep? Probably not. So, with a sigh and a curse, I took my tea into the bathroom.

On my way to the den I felt pretty good. A hot shower cures many ills. I had drawn a screen in my mind around most of the events of the previous day. I felt ready to renew my acquaintance with Albert and then get the hell out of there.

Albert stood up as I walked in, and came right over to shake my hand warmly in both of his. "Jack," he said, "what a joy it is to see you again."

One of the great mysteries of life is how people can change so dramatically and yet remain unmistakably the same. This man had much more force and focus in the way he presented himself. And with most of the baby fat leeched out of his face, and the well-trimmed and kingly beard he was now sporting, Albert had become quite a handsome man.

Yet in the eyes, so very light blue that you were drawn to look directly at the pupil rather than the iris, it was the same innocent and loving boy I had known at school. Perhaps the odd effect of his light eyes had something to do with it, but there seemed to be no shield, no barrier, no subterfuge in Albert. He seemed now, as he had always seemed before, completely sincere and open; and it made me just as nervous to feel all that undiluted and undisguised warmth pouring out of him as it had in the past. It was too much. It was too naked. But mostly it made me uncomfortable because I never felt able to return it in kind. It made me feel guarded and held back, which I am to some extent, but who isn't? Until you run into an oddball like Albert who doesn't seem to be that way, it seems perfectly normal and necessary.

When I first knew him I used to tell myself that it was because his family was so rich; that he had never been exposed to any trouble. Over time, I realized that the idea was a lot of crap; that Albert's defenselessness was his gift; very courageous really, very commendable, and very annoying at times.

"Nice to see you again, Albert. You're looking very well."

He beamed and even blushed a little at the compliment. He was full of light, and it would light him up over anything at all. "Come and have some breakfast, Jack. You still love sausages, don't you? Hélène is making sausages now which would win prizes all over the world."

"Thanks, Albert, don't mind if I do."

We sat down and began to help ourselves. The sausages were very delicious. Everything about the breakfast was fit for a king. I ate a few mouthfuls and then I said, "What's going on, Albert?"

"Why, Jack," he said with a broad smile, "you, of all people, don't have to ask *me* what's going on."

"Is that so?" I thought about it for a few moments, but I didn't get the joke. "You've been keeping tabs on me. Why?"

"Oh here now, I haven't been keeping *tabs* on you. Why do you say it that way? You make it sound so vulgar."

41

That was something else which apparently hadn't changed about Albert. Vulgarity, whatever that was or whatever he thought that was, was still something he couldn't tolerate.

"Well, I don't want to hurt your feelings, but I think sending some private eye to take photos of me is a little vulgar, wouldn't you say?"

In truth, I had never been sure what the word vulgar was supposed to mean in Albert's lexicon. I was just pushing his buttons. I hadn't talked with Albert in ever so long, and I wanted to know what he was like.

"Perhaps so, but I didn't *send* anyone to do any such thing."

"If you didn't *send* anyone, then how did it occur that someone was there?" It was difficult to talk to Albert without picking up his emphatic manner of speech. Conversation, communication, the life of the mind, these were all terribly important to him, and he chose his words the way a chemist would choose the ingredients in an experiment. "And how do you happen to know every little thing about me, right down to my shoe size, if you haven't sent some vulgar private eye to find it all out for you, hmm?" I thought I had him there.

"Because, my dear Jack, I never *sent* anyone to find out those things. And you needn't give me that fishy look, because it's true. I just happened to mention one evening at a party many years ago that I was curious what had become of a certain old friend. A few days later I was surprised to receive a complete report on you along with a bill, naturally, and since I paid the bill, I've continued to receive regular reports ever since."

"And continued to pay the bills."

"Yes. After that first report I was quite concerned about you, and though I knew better than to interfere, I preferred to stay informed."

We ate in silence for a while. The idea that Albert had been checking up on me all those years was infuriating. That he had been doing it out of concern was even more infuriating. Who the hell did he think he was?

On the other hand, I couldn't help but wonder if I was just being touchy about wasting so many years, or if I was feeling guilty about Jenna and just wanted to pick a fight to cover it up.

"These sausages are really something, Albert," I said, trying to find some neutral ground for my thoughts.

"Hélène will be very pleased to hear that you said so."

"Where is your lady friend this morning?"

"I think she's still in bed. She says she has trouble sleeping sometimes when I'm not here."

What was it that she said? *Albert doesn't want to know, so no one is going to tell him.* Well, it certainly wasn't going to be me. Images of our lovemaking had been drifting in my mind all morning, and I wanted very much to be with her again and again and again.

"She told me you went riding together. Was that fun?"

"Uh . . . yes, it was a lot of fun, thanks." More images of naked Jenna crowded into my mind. We already had a whole intimate relationship that Albert knew nothing about.

"I thought you would enjoy Pollux. Do you ride much anymore?"

"No, not much anymore, Albert. If I get the opportunity I do, but I never bothered to make enough money to be a horse person."

"Do you still ride well?"

"Fairly well. I didn't fall off even once."

"Do you still fence?"

"No."

"Never?"

I had to laugh at that. "I'm a little stiff and creaky for those long lunges."

"You still know how, though?"

"Of course I still know how, but I doubt I'd be very good at it. You have to practice if you want to keep up a skill."

"This is disappointing. You used to be a real champion."

"I used to be a lot of things. Why is it disappointing that I don't fence anymore?"

Albert didn't answer. He was thinking about something. I sat watching him while I stuffed in the last bits of sausage that my stomach would hold. "Why did you invite me here?"

"Uhm?" he said, still lost in thought. I made some circles in the air with my palm to attract his attention.

"I'm sorry, what did you say?"

"Why did you invite me here?"

"Well, that's not such an easy question, but I'll get to that, I promise you. Can't we just talk for a few minutes? It's been such a long time, Jack. When was the last time we saw each other?"

"It was the year they fixed the presidential election and nearly got caught."

"Yes, and you developed the notion that I had something to do with it."

"You were behaving very queerly, Albert. When I asked you a point-blank question about it, you almost dropped your teeth into the Béarnaise sauce."

"Well, I didn't have anything to do with it."

"Okay, Albert, I believe you. What difference does it make now?"

"But I did know that it was going to happen."

"So I really wasn't so far off base after all."

"No, you weren't."

"How did you know?"

"Because I wanted to know. And because I'm willing to pay people to find out what I want to know. Channels of communication tend to stay open between people who share a common interest."

"Between zillionaires, you mean."

Albert nodded. "That's one of the reasons we have country clubs. It's a pleasant and private place where we can gather and gossip about things that concern us."

"So why did you have me packed and crated and delivered up here?"

"Jack, I'm so sorry! Rudy told me what happened, and I meant to say something to you about it earlier, but I was so happy to see you, it totally slipped my mind!"

"Don't worry about it, Albert. I can take a joke. But if you don't tell me right now what this is all about, I'm going to come over and shake it out of you."

"Good morning, Albert dear. Good morning, Jack. I trust I'm not interrupting anything."

That was Jenna, making her appearance, freshly groomed in slacks and a silk blouse. She went right to Albert and kissed him sweetly. He looked up at her with his light blue eyes filled with affection, and I knew in that moment how dangerously infatuated I'd already become.

"Sit down, my dear," said Albert, "and help us finish this delicious breakfast. Jack asked me why I invited him here, and I'm afraid I've been beating about the bush."

Jenna held out a cup to Albert, and while he was pouring her coffee, she flashed me a look of such tender yearning and complicity that I saw I would have every possible opportunity for two-timing my host under his own roof.

"You haven't told him yet?" said Jenna to Albert.

"Perhaps he won't even believe it," said Albert.

"Perhaps not," said Jenna. Then she turned to me with a dazzling smile. "Jack, Albert has created a little country of his own. It's a monarchy, and he's the king."

"It didn't happen in a day, Jack," said Albert. "Actually, it's over fifteen years since we brought in the first people, mostly farming families that had lost their farms to banks and conglomerates but yearned to continue their old way of life."

"Of course there are tradesmen, too," said Jenna. "Blacksmiths and millers and weavers . . ."

"Wheelwrights and masons and fletchers," said Albert. "What do you think, my dear? I'm not so sure he believes us."

Jenna smiled at me. "You look a little confused, Jack."

"No, I'm sorry, but I don't get it. You made yourself a king, you say? How can you do that?"

"I gave people land to farm. I gave them seeds to plant. I gave them cows and goats and sheep and pigs and chickens and geese. In return I ask them to respect my sovreignty and to obey my rules."

For awhile I just sat there staring. He wasn't joking, as far as I could tell, but what he was saying didn't make any sense. "And what happens to people who don't obey your rules?"

"I throw them into the dungeon until they're ready to behave themselves."

"It's an awful dungeon, Jack," said Jenna. "No one who's been in it once ever wants to go back in again."

"Albert," I laughed, "you're making this up. How could you get away with such a thing?"

"It works very well. I don't keep a person in the dungeon

any longer than I think will do him good. He comes out filthy and stinking and rat-nipped, and everyone has a good laugh at his expense. Then he goes home and gets cleaned up and goes back to his farming or his trade with a more compliant attitude. Life goes on."

They both *looked* like they were telling the truth, but that didn't make it possible. "Albert, give me a break, will you? You can't have a kingdom in the United States."

"Oh, Jack, don't be so naïve. The U.S. is full of private roads with gates and guards, and you'd be very surprised at the queer sorts of things you'd find at the ends of those roads. This is a huge country, and there's plenty of room for any kind of a secret you can afford to keep."

Jenna was growing restless. "Albert, dear, just tell him about *our* kingdom. Jack, it isn't even *in* the United States. It's far north of the border."

"It's in Canada?"

"Well, technically yes," said Albert. "I had to put a great deal of money into some Canadian pockets for my ninety-nine year lease. I'm joking about the lease, you understand, but it's not really anywhere at all. You'll see what I mean. It's hundreds of miles from anything bigger than an Indian village, up there where everything is fresh and new."

My mind was still telling me that this was probably just a big put-on, and that any second they would burst out laughing. But from my toes to my scalp, my body was tingling with a new and strange kind of energy, very pleasant and exciting.

"Well, okay Albert, I sort of believe you. But what's it for?"

"What's it for? It's my life's work. You know I inherited hugely when my parents died. Their plane crash was so very unexpected, it almost killed me with confusion to have so much money dumped on me at such a young age. I hadn't any idea what to do with so much money, none at all." Albert paused, and I could almost see his memories come flooding back.

"And there were scads of people suddenly rushing at me from all sides with advice and schemes, not to mention the most vulgar propositions of every kind. Émile and Hélène really saved me from losing my mind, I think, by arranging a situation of deep and secret seclusion for me where I had the time and the privacy to adjust to my situation."

I could see in his eyes something of what he must have gone through. Jenna came around behind his chair and gave him a little hug.

"Well, that was ages ago, or so it seems anyway," he went on. "I wanted to do something special with that money. I wanted to do something unique. I knew that none of those schemers and sycophants had anything to offer me in the way of ideas. I knew I had to come up with a plan all by myself. And then very late one night I had a vision of a land that was free from pollution, free from corruption and greed and graft; free from the callous materialism that is tearing our beautiful world to shreds. In other words, a new land where people could live in peace and nurture their true, natural spirit within, free from . . ."

"Vulgarity," I said. It wasn't very nice of me to shoot him down out of the stratosphere of his vision, but he was pissing me off. I suppose that was because I myself at one time had a vision of a little theater that was free from a lot of those same things and it was all ashes now. Jenna shot me a disapproving look, but Albert just turned toward me and said, "Yes, exactly."

"And so how did you do? Did you succeed?"

"No. Not like that. I had a lot to learn about people, Jack, about humanity, about the human predicament. I had a lot to learn about myself, God knows. No, I didn't succeed in creating anything like my vision. But I did succeed in creating something very different from anything you've ever seen in your whole life. Am I right, my dear?"

"Yes, Albert," Jenna said softly, "quite right. There is nothing on this planet right now like your beautiful kingdom."

Neither of them were looking at me now. They were both seeing something in the mind's eye. I don't know quite how to describe it, except that it was as if their eyes had both turned the same shade of gray. There was an aura around them, a completeness, a kind of grandeur. Maybe it was right at that moment when the door of my fate closed softly behind me.

"Okay, Albert," I said. "Against my better judgment I feel like maybe I believe you. But with all the water that has gone under the dam since I last saw you, I can't believe that you had me kidnapped just to tell me about your dreams. So for the tenth time, what am I doing here?"

Well, they both looked at me, and then they looked at each other; and if I hadn't been soft-headed with curiosity, I would have recognized that look right away. We've all seen it a million times and what it said was, "We better not tell him too much!" But like a chump, I let it pass right by.

"It's lonely at the top, Jack," Albert said finally. "I need a real friend now, a man like yourself. I need someone who can beat me at chess occasionally and who'll tell me I'm an ass if that's what I need to hear. I need someone I can trust the way I trust you; someone who can see through the shadows into the true meaning of things. I need someone to make my kingdom a beacon in the darkness! But I'm not being entirely selfish either, you know. Given what I know about your present situation, I'd be very disappointed in you if you let an opportunity like this go by. Unless, of course, you're satisfied with your little cottage in Marysville."

"I have some debts I need to settle, Albert."

"Yes, I know. I hope you will forgive me, but it was such a piddling sum that I paid them off for you."

Floored, I didn't know what to say. I felt excited and energized, and I was already looking forward to something unusual and challenging. "Give me a minute, will you?" I left the table and headed out onto the terrace; a few minutes later Jenna joined me.

"It sounds like you really like it there," I said.

"Oh, yes," she replied, "I love it there. Each time I come back to the modern world, the life here seems a little more absurd, a little more intolerable. I'm not the least bit comfortable here any longer."

"Will you be going back this time with Albert?"

"Yes. My coronation takes place at the end of this month."

Her answer snapped my head around. "You're going to be queen?"

"Yes, Jack. I'm going to be queen."

"It's really a kingdom, this thing Albert cooked up? It's not just some kind of a commune or a co-op?"

"It's a real kingdom right out of a storybook."

"Swords and horses?"

"Yes."

"Wizards and dragons?"

"There's only one way to find out."

"Suppose it just isn't my cup of tea?"

She paused and seemed uncertain what to say. I was just beginning to wonder if there was a catch, when she said, "No one will try to keep you there against your will."

"Well, I guess it's a deal then."

She took my hand and squeezed it. "I'm glad, Jack. I'm so very glad. I'm going to tell Albert," she said, and she left me to my fantasies.

Chapter Three

In the afternoon on the nineteenth of that month, the transport helicopter set down in a field between two mountains, and we unloaded the horses and baggage.

It had been a long, noisy flight; it seemed like hours since we had seen so much as the smoke from a lonesome cabin. I had no idea how many hundreds of miles of wilderness had passed below us.

I was very glad to be on the ground, glad to pull the earplugs out. The horses were restless and stomping and Maxine's little girl, Mimi, was whining; but as soon as the helicopter with its crew of stonefaced young soldiers was gone, and the throbbing of the rotors faded away in the distance, the silence of those mountains descended around us like a healing benediction.

Everyone was affected by the silence. When you live around cities, you grow accustomed to thinking of the world as a crowded place where mankind and his works can hardly find room. But in that wild vastness, our little group of eight people seemed like a few grains of dust.

The horses were settling down. The little girl was quiet now, holding her mother's hand. Everyone was listening to the sound of the wind as it swayed the grasses, and the occasional bird, but mostly we were listening to the echoing of the silence.

"Begin," said Albert. To my surprise, everyone started

walking off in different directions. I didn't know what to do, so I just stood there with Albert.

"What's going on?" I asked him, but he tapped his lips for silence.

They were gathering wood. The women brought back twigs and sticks. The men dragged back dead boughs and broke them up. Pretty soon there was a neat pile big enough for a good size bonfire. They seemed to know when they had enough, but Émile looked to Albert for confirmation.

Albert nodded. There was a feeling of expectation, a sense of ritual. Something was going to happen, something pleasant. Whatever it was, they were looking forward to it. Even Rudy Strapp, who revealed little of what he was thinking or feeling, seemed caught up in the general anticipation.

Émile prepared the fire while everyone watched, and when it was crackling away, Albert nodded again. The women collected some of the luggage, and disappeared into a nearby grove of trees. The men started to undress, throwing their clothes into a common pile. Émile was unpacking clothes from the other bags and handing them around. He handed me a folded stack and I shook them out. I had worn clothes like these before, but only on the stage: tights and a tunic, boots and a cloak, a leather belt with a wallet and dagger, a hat with a feather, even a codpiece.

I started to pull on the tights, but Émile wagged a finger at me, pointing to my white cotton briefs. Onto the discard pile they went. Then I pulled on the tights and tied the codpiece on top. I'd never worn one before. It was made of molded leather and rather stiff, though roomy inside. It would offer a fair bit of protection from a blow or a kick.

Albert's clothes were very nice indeed, with gold thread in the tunic and fur on the collar of his cloak. After we were all dressed, we fed the fire and waited for the women in silence.

53

Finally they came back from the grove, wearing their new garments and dumping the old ones in the pile with ours. They were all wearing medieval riding costumes, with pantaloons tucked into soft boots and long jackets under their cloaks. The servants all wore the same colors, some kind of livery perhaps to identify them with Albert. Rudy and I were dressed similarly, with the right sides of our tunics padded with leather.

Whoever had designed all these clothes had done a good job. We were a very authentic-looking group. The men's tights were hand-loomed; the daggers had come from an armorer's forge, not a factory. Everything, even our hand-stitched leather baggage, had the unmistakable texture of handicraft. Everything, that is, except the pile of modern clothing that lay near the bonfire.

Albert picked up something from the pile, a blouse of Jenna's, and dropped it on the fire. It was made of a very light fabric and the fire consumed it in seconds. Then Jenna chose Émile's cashmere sweater and soon that was ashes. We all took turns as the pile grew smaller and smaller. It gave me a very odd feeling, as though we ourselves were getting smaller and smaller, and as if the Earth, the globe on which we were standing, was getting bigger and bigger.

The last article was a checkered scarf. Albert picked it up with two fingers and looked around the circle of faces. Everyone seemed to be holding their breath, and I remember wanting to take the scarf away from Albert and hide it somewhere safe. I didn't want to see it burn.

Albert said softly, "Goodbye," and the scarf fluttered down into the flames. When it was gone, when the last shred had changed into unrecognizable ash, I started to feel very queer. The sunshine seemed unnaturally bright, and the colors around me were very stark. I looked around at the others, but they were all focused on Albert, who seemed unusually radiant. They all seemed so happy and relaxed, but I felt very agitated. I wanted to run, to get away. But from what, and to where?

Jenna said, "He's looking a little pale, Sire."

"Yes, I noticed," said Albert. "Well, that can happen, as all of us know." He spread his hands in a paternal gesture and looked around the group. There was a ripple of laughter. "Listen, Jack," Albert said, "we all know how you're feeling. You're a thousand miles and a thousand years from everything you've been accustomed to all your life. It's all gone. We just burned it all."

I was feeling very queasy. I looked into his face. Was he crazy? Were they all crazy? No, it was the same kindly face, the same riveting blue eyes. I felt like crying. What was wrong with me? I looked into the faces of the others, and the warmth and sympathy I saw there reassured me. Why was I acting like such a baby?

"Let's have something to eat, Émile. That's the best medicine."

"Yes, Sire."

"Now, Jack, you might be feeling quite disoriented for a few days or so, or you might snap out of this in five minutes. We just went back in time. We did! It doesn't require magic, or a time machine. It's very simple and we just did it. If you feel strange for a while, that's normal. All you can do now is breathe deeply, and let go. Just let go, Jack. Let go of all those useless things we never needed for our health and happiness and comfort and safety. Let go of the whole silly pointless poisonous modern era." With a wave of his hand, he dismissed it all. "And when you do let go, you'll be in for a very pleasant surprise, believe me!"

Émile set down two big baskets full of bread and meat and wines and cheeses and fruit. Then he passed around some square wooden plates and brass goblets, and we all fell to.

"Thanks, Albert," I said. "Sorry I . . ." But I had to stop because Jenna and Hélène were both clucking their tongues at me.

"Very bad manners to call his majesty by his first name, Jack," said Émile. "You must say my king or my liege or sire or your majesty. Any of those titles will do."

Hélène patted my shoulder. "You'll catch on. You can call all of us by our first names just like before, except for her ladyship," she said, indicating Jenna, who nodded and smiled. "You must call her my lady or your ladyship until her coronation. After that it's your majesty or my queen."

Down one side of my body I thought it was the most insane thing I'd ever heard. I was supposed to call Albert *your majesty*? I was supposed to call Jenna, the bare-assed horsewoman, *my queen?* Down the other side I just wanted to get it right. I wanted to know how to behave. I didn't want to sound stupid or foolish. In between the one side and the other there was a very uncomfortable place of confusion, reminiscent of the way I felt after my theater was burned; I wanted that feeling to go away. I wanted both feet on the ground again, and I didn't much care which side of a thousand years of history they came down on. So I gave them my best courtly bow and said, "Thank you, my friends. A thousand pardons, my liege."

Jenna laughed. "Well done, Jack. You're a natural."

"Thank you, my lady," I replied in grave tones of deepest respect, meanwhile thinking about how her ladyship looked in the buff. "Your servant, as always."

"Look," said Albert. "We have company."

A child stood staring at us from the edge of the clearing; when we turned to look, he ran off into the woods.

"Boy!" Albert cried. "Come here, boy!"

The little face peeped out from behind a tree.

"Come out now. Don't be frightened."

The boy came out of the woods, walked slowly towards us, and stopped at a very respectful distance. He must have been seven or eight years old, barefoot, and wore only a crude pair of shorts belted with a twist of rope. His eyes were very wide as he stared at us, and at Albert in particular.

"That's a good boy," said Albert. "Now, your name is Warren, is it not?"

"Aaron, your majesty," said the boy, his eyes even wider now.

"Of course," said Albert. "I meant to say Aaron. Your father is Walter the smith."

"Yes, your majesty."

"I know your father, Aaron. He's a good man. Now tell me what you want to be when you grow up."

The boy seemed puzzled at the question. "A smith, your majesty, just like my dad."

"Of course you do. Are you helping your father in his forge?"

"Oh yes, your majesty, almost every day."

"That's a good boy. Now what do you have in your hand?"

"A sling, your majesty," he said, holding out a supple strip of leather that was widest in the middle and tapered at the ends.

"Thank you," said Albert, "but I meant in the other hand."

The boy's hand came slowly from behind his back. "Partridge, your majesty," he said, holding up the bird. The head lolled back and forth.

"Did you kill the bird with your sling?"

"Yes, your majesty."

"Hit it right in the head, did you?"

"No, your majesty. I broke its wing. Then I wrung its neck."

"Are you allowed to hunt birds?"

Again the boy seemed puzzled. "Yes, your majesty."

"Then why did you hide it behind you?"

"Um . . . I . . ."

"Did you think we would take it away from you?"

"Oh no, your majesty, for you have so much!" He was looking at the food we had spread out on our picnic blanket.

"That's a clever boy. Of course we won't. Here's some bread and cheese for you. Now I want you to remember something, my boy. Never hide anything from your king. Do you think you can remember that?"

"Yes, your majesty." I could see that he wanted to start eating the bread and cheese right away, but he hesitated, eyeing Albert.

"Very good, my boy. Now run along and tell your father that the king sends his best wishes." And run he did, eating as he ran.

"That boy," Albert said to me, "was born here. He has never been out of the kingdom, or seen anything except what there is here."

I didn't know what to say. How amazing it was! That barefoot boy had been hunting birds with a sling. Now he would tell people he had seen the king, and that the king had given him bread and cheese. For some reason that amazed and delighted me, and made me forget all about being anxious and disoriented.

After we finished eating, we put saddles on the horses, very beautifully made saddles of an ancient design with a high pommel and cantel.

"Where did these saddles come from, Sire?" It felt odd giving Albert that title, but he was the king, wasn't he?

What made a man a king? He had to have a kingdom and some subjects. Was that all there was to it? No, he had to have the power and the authority of a king. Did Albert really have a dungeon to soften people up when they forgot who the boss was? He would have to have something like that. If the alternative to obeying the law wasn't sufficiently unpleasant, people would just do as they pleased.

If he did throw people into his dungeon, it was a cinch he didn't do the throwing himself. So he had to have guards, knights, or an army, something to back him up. Well, I would get the chance to see it all, and in the meantime it certainly couldn't do me any harm to give him his title.

"These saddles were made right here in the kingdom by the leather craftsman who works with my armorer. He also designed your tunic."

I took another look at my tunic. It was warm and strong; slightly heavy because of the leather, but comfortable all the same. "Why is the padding all on one side?"

"It's to protect your sword arm and the right side of your body."

Now that he had told me, I wondered why I hadn't thought of it myself. When I used to fence, I wore a canvas jacket that did exactly the same thing. I had been asking myself about the nature of power and authority in Albert's kingdom. Was my sword arm, as he called it, supposed to be part of that power? Okay, the padding protected the right side of my body, but from what, and from whom?

Albert nodded to Émile, and Émile undid the straps on one of the bags and took out a sword in a scabbard with a belt and a harness to sling it. I could see immediately by

59

the distinctive hilt that it was a rapier, and that surprised me because the rapier had not made its appearance in history until the Renaissance. Émile approached me and in his usual graceful way held out the harness so I could slip an arm into it. It was the same way he might have helped a guest with his coat. I put my arm through the leather strap and fastened the belt around my waist. I had always enjoyed wearing swords on the stage because it had made me feel more complete, and I had that same feeling now. I felt more substantial, more masculine, my feet planted more firmly on the earth.

Now Émile brought Rudy a sword and helped him slip it on. He wore it well, which is to say that he let the sword wear him. A sword is such a powerful symbol that it can never be completely manipulated or controlled. One has to have a partnership with a sword, a mutual respect. You wear it, and it wears you. This is also one of the secrets of fine fencing.

Then Émile brought Albert a sword in an ornate scabbard, and after Albert had buckled up the belt, he drew the sword. It was also a rapier, a heavy and broad-bladed early version, to be sure, but a rapier all the same.

It is said that an Italian swordsmith named Agrippa was the first to create a sword designed to make a small hole through the body. The popular broadsword that came before it, eons old, was a chopping and cutting weapon, and well suited to its work, but people had become very clever at sewing up and healing the wounds it made. A deep gash might take some time to heal, be sore and troublesome, and even crippling. But a little hole through the middle of the body, with internal bleeding and a guaranteed infection, was almost always fatal.

"Kneel, Jack Darcey," said Albert in fine, round tones. I saw what was coming, and I had no objection. Down on one knee I went. I felt the sword touch me on both shoulders and on the top of my head.

"Rise, Sir Jack, knight and protector of the realm."

I rose to my feet. To say that I was amazed does not quite cover it. There are things one dreams of becoming, but never expects to be.

I felt a soft hand on my shoulder and turned. Jenna went up on her toes to kiss me on the cheek, a little too near the mouth; but when I glanced over at Albert, he was putting up his sword, blissfully unaware that he had a snake in his parlor.

"Congratulations, Sir Jack," she said, and her eyes were full of sweet promises. I noticed Rudy Strapp watching me, and the way he was standing gave me a flash of intuition.

"Not Sir Rudy, by any chance?"

"Even so," he said, and bowed very slightly in a courteous way.

I nodded appreciatively. "What am I supposed to call you?"

"You can call me Rudy when we're alone because we're equals. But in front of the common people, we always use our titles."

"I see."

"Why are you smiling?"

"I just became a knight. Didn't that make you smile?"

What I had really been smiling about was Rudy's remark about the common people. Rudy, unless I missed my guess, was a commoner born in the kingdom of Detroit, or maybe Cleveland. Well, that had been in the past, or the future, depending on how you looked at it. We had all slipped through a doorway in time, and now our reality was different. It would be wise, I thought to myself, to keep these little ironic notions to myself, to follow along and see what there was to see. I had no great nostalgia for the civilization I had left behind. Nor had my prospects there been very good. If fortune or fate was willing to deal me a whole new hand of cards, then I would play them and see what turned up.

Now we mounted up and rode on our way: one king, his lady, two knights, and a livery of servants. There was no track or trail by which we rode, but our direction was easterly by the sun toward a pass between the mountains.

Soon we had more company: all boys at first, hunters like Aaron, wearing homespun clothes and carrying slings and sticks. Word of our arrival had spread quickly. Then there were girls in woolen dresses down to the ground, who pointed shyly and whispered to each other as they walked along beside us.

By the time we topped the rise between the mountains, we had two dozen children in our procession. It surprised me that they didn't shout or even talk, though they seemed excited and happy for the novelty and whispered together quite a lot. One little boy cried out, "Ho, King Albert!" in his excitement, and got himself a rap on the head from one of the older boys. Very polite they were, these commoner boys and girls.

As we crested the pass, an old woman in a shapeless robe and cowl was waiting for us with a little bouquet of flowers which she held up for Jenna. "Good day, my lady," she said. "Good day, your majesty." There was no telling how old she was, but she seemed solid on her feet and her voice was deep and husky.

"Good day, old mother," said Albert, leaning down to take up the flowers. He passed them to Jenna, who smiled and looked pleased. "And how is your health?"

"Good, your majesty, though I'm about as old as a person can get."

"And how does my kingdom?"

"Good enough, your majesty, now that you're home."

Albert looked thoughtfully at the old woman, then dismounted and took her aside. They spoke quietly and earnestly, though I couldn't hear what they were saying.

It was late in the afternoon; the sun was sinking behind me and the valley before me was slipping into the shadow of the mountain. It was a large valley, long and wide, with two rivers I could see in the last rays of the sun. Here and there, so tiny I could easily have missed them, were wisps of smoke above the trees. And as the daylight faded away, here and there I could see specks of light.

It was then that I truly believed in Albert's kingdom. Costumes and swords hadn't convinced me. Even that flock of children hadn't really done it. Wisps of smoke and specks of light had brought me to the truth of it: hundreds of miles from anywhere, tucked away between northern mountains, there really was a kingdom where Albert was king.

Jenna rode up beside me, and we sat there wrapped in our cloaks, knee to knee, gazing down into the valley where the tiny lights flickered. Sometimes there were none at all, and the valley looked dark and dead. Sometimes as many as three or four little specks could be seen at once, and then the valley seemed alive with people.

"How many live here?" I asked her.

"I don't have any idea. Albert could tell you roughly how many holdings there are. With all the little babies, there must be several thousand at least."

"Does anybody count them from time to time?"

"What for? There's a tithe to be collected, but tithing is done by the holding, not by the head. I suppose I shall have to know more about this when I am queen."

That made me look at her more closely, for she said it so sadly. After a few moments she turned to me. "Oh, Jack," she whispered, "I hope it won't be too boring! Albert is always

63

very busy when he's here, and now that we're staying forever . . . Promise me I can count on you for some diversion now and then." ·

"Of course you can count on me, Jenna." I didn't know what else to say. I felt like I could see her nude body right through her riding habit, cloak and all. But I couldn't be sure what she was asking, or what I was promising either. I had never had an affair with a queen in a medieval kingdom before. And yet I wanted her. I yearned for her.

"I think we're ready to go," said Jenna, reaching under my cloak to give my hand a squeeze. Albert was mounting up. I could not see his face in the lingering twilight. The old woman was nowhere to be seen. Only two or three children still remained. I was wondering how the eight of us, including Maxine's little daughter, were going to ride down the other side of the pass in the dark, when I heard distant hoofbeats and saw lights approaching from below.

Five mounted men, two with torches, were coming up the draw. Even from a distance they had the look of soldiers, sitting on their horses very straight, and riding in a rhythm that connected them all as a unit. As they drew near, I saw that they were wearing leather armor with iron trim. They had very light saddles that resembled leather cushions with stirrups. Four of them wore long daggers and carried iron-trimmed staffs. The fifth man wore a rapier, and was every inch an officer. His hair and beard were dark and curly, and he had alert eyes that looked black in the torchlight. He must have been around forty, and was in excellent shape, wiry, close-knit, centered.

"Hail, King Albert!" he cried as they all reined in. Each of them thumped his chest with his fist in a robust salute. They all looked happy to see Albert.

"Hail, Sir Leo, well met," said Albert. "How did you know we were here?"

"Good news travels swiftly, my liege. The hare told the deer and the deer told the bird. Is this the fencing master?"

"Leo, this is Sir Jack, the last but not the least. Jack, this is Sir Leo, marshal of the garrison."

"Well met, Sir Jack," said Leo, smiling and extending his hand. When I reached out he grasped me by the forearm, so I gripped his in return, and that was the way we shook our greeting. It seemed quite natural and I rather liked it. He had a slight eastern European accent and I liked that too. In fact, I took an instant liking to him and I hoped we would be friends.

"Well met, Sir Leo," I replied. "Were you expecting me?"

"I've been looking forward to meeting you. The king says you have a way with a sword."

"I'm a bit out of practice."

"No matter," he said, indicating the valley below with a wave of his hand. "Here we have plenty of time to practice."

"It's late, Leo, and this girl is shivering," said Albert, pointing to Mimi. Leo quickly organized the march, and soon we were riding down into the valley by the flickering glare of the torches.

It had been a long day and a long journey. It had begun with our loading of the bags and horses into a huge iron bird that growled like thunder as it flew. That had been at least a thousand years ago, or maybe it was a thousand years in the future. I didn't care anymore. My brain had gone to sleep. By the time we reached our shelter for the night, I hardly glanced at it though I saw there was a fire inside. Someone put a bowl of soup in my hands, but I could barely eat for yawning.

"Put him to bed, Leo," said Albert. "He's as sleepy as this girl."

Gentle laughter rose from the crowd, but I didn't mind. Candlelight led me to warm blankets on a pallet bed, and I could barely tuck them up around me before I was fast asleep.

Chapter Four

"Sir Jack."

Who was Sir Jack?

"Sir Jack."

A hand was shaking me gently by the shoulder. I opened my eyes. I was in a strange, new place and there was something else too . . . Oh, yes! I was in a strange new time, cut off from the past which was also the future. How peculiar it felt to remember that! I had woken up in many strange places in my travels, but I had never woken up with quite the same feelings that I experienced that morning. I felt like a boy waking up in a new world that was full of mysterious and exciting possibilities.

It was Maxine, Émile's daughter, who had wakened me. She pressed a warm, wet towel into my hand, and said, "Breakfast is on the table when you're ready, Sir Jack." I applied the warm towel gratefully to my face and neck; there is nothing nicer in those first moments of the day. Then I looked around to see where I was.

I was in a long, narrow fieldstone building with a firepit in the middle and a low thatched roof. Around the perimeter of the room were shelves made of undressed planks on supports set in the stones; several of the shelves held clothing, blankets, and personal effects, neatly folded with an arrangement that suggested military order. Beneath each shelf was a thin mattress like mine, but under the empty shelves the mattresses were rolled up and secured by thongs. I had the impression that only five or six people lived in this barrack, though it was set up to accomodate quite a few more.

There were two windows with shutters open to the fresh air and the savory smell of cooking. Still in my tunic and tights, I stuck my feet into my boots, threw on my cloak, scratched myself, and ran my fingers through my hair. Wrapping my cloak around me against the chill, I went outside.

Seated at a long wooden table were Sir Leo and a few of the other soldiers. They were flirting with Maxine, who was waiting on them; she seemed to enjoy the attention. There was something of the flavor of an old country inn about the scene, but when I appeared, the banter subsided and they all turned to look at me.

"Welcome!" said Sir Leo. The word seemed pregnant with meaning. Welcome to our home. Welcome to our era. Welcome to our life. It also seemed to say: How are you? And who are you? And how do you feel waking up this morning in a place you can barely imagine?

No one else spoke. They went quietly back to eating, giving me plenty of space to look around and make myself comfortable. The remains of a large breakfast were spread across the table and there was plenty left over for me.

The stone barrack was situated at the bottom of the pass we had come down the night before. The dirt road ran across some meadowland, east by the sun, into the woods. It was a brilliantly clear day and in every direction the countryside appeared clean and fresh, the way it does when you backpack several days into unspoiled wilderness. Yet with camping you take with you as much of the accouterment of civilization as you care to carry: lightweight, compact, synthetic, state-of-the-art civilization all wrapped up in nylon and aluminum. This was an entirely different experience, and so far that was all I knew for sure.

Maxine gave me a square wooden plate, a two-tined iron fork, and a wooden spoon, and I began to help myself. In imitation of the others I used my own dagger to cut the meat.

"Where is everybody?" I said between bites.

"The king left at first light," said Sir Leo. "He's a very busy man, especially when he's just come home. Everyone else went to the monastery to hear Mass. Gordon here can show you the way after we have our fencing lesson." One of the soldiers nodded. He had thick, curly blond hair and a marvelous, oversize mustache.

"All right, Sir Leo," I said. "I'll be happy to help you any way I can. What time is it, anyway?"

They glanced at each other, and there was an odd silence.

"Did I say something foolish?"

"No, no, Sir Jack," said Maxine. "Never mind about thinking you're doing anything wrong. Just give yourself time to get used to the way things are. But, you see, no one can tell you what time it is because we don't have any clocks."

"There are no clocks?"

Sir Leo shook his head. "There are no clocks anywhere here, Sir Jack. They don't exist."

"Not one?"

"Not even one."

"There's a sundial in the monastery courtyard," said Maxine.

"Oh yes," said Sir Leo, laughing, "but the only person who can read it is the abbot who made it. It doesn't tell the hours but just marks the time for prayers."

The oddest thing about this discovery was that it didn't seem to matter. If there weren't any clocks, then there weren't any clocks. So what? Who needed clocks?

"Well, how much time," I said, "roughly speaking of course, would you say I have to catch up with them at the monastery?"

Leo laughed. "I don't know. But if you miss them at the monastery, you'll catch up with them at the castle."

"There's no risk of losing anyone because there's nowhere to go," said Maxine. "Keeping up with the king is another story, but that's because he has so much to look after, God bless him."

"Then let's have our fencing lesson, Sir Leo, and I'll be on my way."

"Very good, very good," said Leo, jumping up. "I've been looking forward to this."

"My sword's in the barrack. I'll . . ."

"Gordon, get the gentleman his weapon," said Leo.

"What did the king tell you about me?"

"He said you were a champion. He said you were an inspired swordsman."

"I was a competitive fencer in college, Sir Leo. I took some trophies at regional competitions. I taught stage dueling in the theater. I collected swords until my lifestyle got too drifty for that sort of thing. But just to let you know, Sir Leo, I haven't had a sword in my hand for a good many years. Will you give me time to warm up?"

He answered me with a polite bow. Time meant nothing here. There weren't even any clocks. I suddenly realized I was very happy about that. No clocks at all. All right!

I undid the clasp of my cloak and draped it over the bench. Gordon helped me into my harness. Then I walked out into the meadow to make sure I had lots of space as well as lots of time. The sword swung gently in its scabbard, and I let the rhythm of its swaying enter my body. I let it walk me around in circles to the left, then to the right, squares and triangles, stopping and starting, until I felt the physical familiarity that I had been anticipating. We weren't jarring against one another. We weren't pushing each other around. We were part of the same whole, that sword and I, and yet I had never held it in my hand.

When the right moment came, I felt it. A feeling is hard to describe, but let's just say I felt permission from the spirit of the sword. Dropping my arm down across my body, feeling my arm moving through space, pushing away the air as it fell, I enclosed the contours of the hilt with the sensitive skin and bones and muscles and nerves of my hand, my thumb and two fingers feeling for the junction between the blade and the crosspiece, taking hold with gentle friction, feeling the haft against my palm.

Now the blade freed itself from the scabbard, sliding out smoothly as though it moved by itself on the tiny ribs of a snake. It spun out on the end of my arm and began to cut the air.

Ah, how this sword wanted to cut something! How frustrated it must have been, lying in a dark scabbard with no chance to do what it was made to do. The weight of the blade pulled me round in a circle and I spun with the sword while it cut the air.

Now the meadow was only a blur around me, the outer edge of a vortex of energy. I clung to the hilt with just the tips of my fingers, just enough to keep it from flying away. Finally I brought the spinning under control and planted my feet, though the meadow still wanted to keep spinning around me. The sword continued to spin at the end of my arm, rotating on the axis of my wrist in circles, elipses, and figures-of-eight. I watched it closely as it wove patterns in the air like a bird drunk with the joy of flight.

71

The sword was full of energy now. I brought my elbow in against my side and began to control that energy by making the circles smaller and smaller, pushing the energy forward and focusing it into the point. With my thumb and two fingers at the fulcrum just ahead of the crosspiece, I swung the tip of the sword back and forth, back and forth, now a little circle, now a half circle and back the other way, focusing on the tip, for the true genius, the real daemon in a rapier is in the point—evasive, cunning, and devious.

Now I began to weave my defenses into the spirit of the blade while the energy was hot and new. The parries, which deflect your opponent's steel harmlessly past your body, are all along the sides of the blade. A good parry is very subtle, changing the direction of a cut or a lunge just enough that it misses its target. There are seven parries for the rapier, and I began to drill them over and over to lock them into the memory of my arm, hand, and blade, honing them down to the absolute minimal movement, because any excess energy in the defense is lost from the energy of the attack.

Then I began to put it all together: extend the arm to align the point, lunge over the bent knee, recover the balance, parry, disengage to the opposite side of the attacking blade, and disengage again and again with little half circles. Which side am I on? Are you sure? Are you sure? Extend, lunge, recover, cut to the cheek, cut to the knee, extend, lunge, recover, parry, disengage, disengage . . .

Advance and retreat with quick little steps, knees bent, thighs flexed, the soles of the feet gripping the earth, advance, advance, retreat, advance. Now the battle is on, and may the best man win!

The blood sang in my ears. Back and forth across the meadow I fought to the death with an imaginary opponent who was wily, vicious, and incomparably fast. Back and forth we pressed each other to the limits of our endurance until finally I broke him on my wheel and ran him through the heart.

Sinking to my knees, I felt very good. For one thing I had gotten some exercise and the blood was now rushing around inside my body. That will always cheer you up. Also I really liked my sword. If I was going to be a knight and carry a sword, I couldn't have chosen a better one.

My intuition was that the sword had been designed and made from start to finish by the same person, someone who continued working on it until he was completely satisfied with its integrity as both a weapon and a work of art. It was truly a piece of practical sculpture. The way the curved bars of the hilt flowed into the crosspiece and into the knuckleguard was like the flow of running water, natural and organic. It was like the way the sword felt when it danced in my hand, vital and unobstructed.

As to its size and weight, I thought it was a very successful compromise, for it was fast enough to keep up with a light blade, and strong enough not to be intimidated by a heavy one.

Most of all I liked its personality. It was beautiful, but it didn't flaunt its beauty. It was deadly, but it didn't brag about that either. It had self-esteem and it also had humility. It was a hero's sword.

When my heart stopped pounding, I walked slowly back to the table. I had taken a chance allowing myself to become so transported in front of people who might easily misunderstand. But Sir Leo gave me a low bow of appreciation.

"Sir Jack," he said, "my father was a soldier, and he taught me what he knew, which was discipline and daily drill. But I see that you are a true artist, and I am honored to be your student."

"Thank you, Sir Leo," I said. "I feel as rusty as the

Tin Woodman of Oz. But I'm sure we'll have a good time practicing together."

It was an enjoyable lesson. Leo's style was formal and stiff, not suited to a rapier, but he was motivated and a quick learner.

"That's enough for today, Sir Leo," I said finally, taking him aside. "The most important thing you have to learn is to quit treating your sword like an inanimate object. It has spirit, intelligence, and a style of its own. You need to make that discovery. Are you willing?"

"Yes sir, I am."

"Good. Three times this week I want you to take your sword out in the woods and just play with it. Forget discipline and drill and just let whatever happens happen. If it starts to talk to you, listen to what it has to say. Don't plan anything ahead of time. At the end of the week you can tell me what you learned. All right?"

"I will be happy to do as you say."

"Good job, Sir Leo. Now I want to start catching up to my friends."

Sir Leo was the kind of man who didn't have to be told twice. Before I knew it, I was riding down the road with the blond-haired, mustachioed soldier as my guide. It occured to me that I probably should have stayed with Sir Leo and picked his brains about exactly what a knight represented in this kingdom, and what we did with our time. There was no time here, of course, not in the way I was accustomed to thinking about time, but I assumed there would be something expected of me sooner or later.

I tried to remember what Albert had said. I was to beat him at chess occasionally. I was to tell him when I thought he was being an ass, but surely not in front of the common folk. I was to look past the shadows into the true meaning of things.

And I was to help him make his kingdom a beacon in the darkness. That was all I knew so far, and that didn't exactly amount to a job description.

"So what do you do exactly, Gordon?"

"I'm a soldier, sir. I follow orders. Right now my orders are to take you to the monastery. You could easily find it by yourself, but if you took the wrong turn at the covered bridge, you'd wind up at Earl Griswold's manor house instead of at the monastery."

"When you say Earl Griswold, do you mean that he's an earl, like a titled gentleman?"

"Yes sir," was Gordon's simple reply. What a place this was! I felt like a curious child who didn't know what question to ask first.

"What other things do soldiers do, Gordon? Help me out. I'm so new, the whole kingdom is a mystery to me."

"Well, sir, we keep order on market days. People can get very stirred up on market day about one thing or another because they often have a nip or two or three. So we're always there to settle disputes and break up fights if we have to. Also we will go around with the collectors who collect the tithe because that can get touchy too. We take turns standing guard at the castle. That's pretty dull duty most of the time, but of course it has to be done. We work with everyone else at harvest time. We round up stray cattle, look for lost children—a little bit of everything. Being a soldiers is mostly just being around and being ready in case you're needed."

Then all of a sudden he cried, "Ho! Shoo! Shoo! Git!" With practiced ease, he swung his iron-bound staff over his head and charged into the trees. Just as abruptly he stopped, backed his horse out, and fell in beside me again. He looked a little put out.

"What was that all about?"

He shook his head. "Just a Pict, sir. I don't care for them."

"A what?"

"A Pict, sir. Didn't anyone tell you about the Picts?"

"The Picts?" Was he joking? The Picts were one of the ancient peoples of Great Britain, driven into Scotland by the Britons and the Romans. "Was he painted blue?"

"No, sir, our Picts don't paint themselves blue, but if they took it up, it wouldn't surprise me."

"I didn't see anyone. What do they look like?"

"Oh, you'll see plenty of them in time. They're all over the place."

"But what do they look like?"

"Well, they . . . You see, they're . . . Oh, I don't know how to describe them," he said with some exasperation. "They're animals, you could say, except that they're not, of course. And they look like trees or rocks but not exactly. Anyway, I don't care for the Picts, and I think the king is far too soft with them. I'd run them all out of here if it was up to me, but I suppose the king is entitled to his own opinion."

Gordon laughed at his own joke, and then fell silent. He seemed to have retreated into his thoughts, and I wasn't too sure what to say to a man with a big iron-tipped stick who saw things in the bushes that he couldn't describe.

The trouble was that now I was on the lookout for Picts. It crossed my mind that maybe Gordon was playing a joke on the newcomer, but I had already taken the bait. My curiosity was aroused, and I wanted to see one for myself. What exactly was I looking for? Anything beyond the ordinary sights of forest and meadow. But didn't he say they looked like rocks or trees? I was certainly playing the fool.

Then I began to feel like I was being watched, and how

can one be sure about a thing like that? We all have obscure senses outside the ordinary five; and those extra senses can register subtle perceptions. But we can also imagine things, and I wasn't sure which this was.

A twig snapped and I spun my head around, but there was nothing to be seen. Slowly I scanned the woods, looking for any movement as we rode along.

Now I began to hear something very faint, like someone crying. When I focused my attention, the sound stopped. Then I thought I heard it again.

"Looking for Picts?" Gordon was smiling. "You'll see more of them than you want to as time goes by."

"I thought I heard someone crying. Did you hear it?"

"No," he said, but the smile vanished. Now Gordon was listening carefully too.

Then I heard a scream. It was muffled and cut off short, but it was surely a scream. Clapping my heels into Pollux's ribs, I bounded into the woods and made for the direction of the sound.

In a little clearing there were two teenage boys with fancy cloaks, booted and spurred, and they had a farm girl held down with her dress pulled over her head. One of them held the hem of her dress in one hand as though it was the mouth of a sack, and the other boy was kneeling between the pale, kicking legs. They both turned as I came crashing into the clearing, and the one on his knees gave me an insolent smile. It pleased me to see the expression change when I scrambled off my horse and kicked him in the face. The other let go of the girl's dress and tried to scuttle out of reach, but he wasn't quick enough to dodge a kick that doubled him up and took his breath away.

The first boy picked his sword off the ground as he jumped to his feet. "I'll kill you!" he screamed as he stumbled backwards, hauling up his tights.

"Come and do it then, you little coward." Given the way he was waving that sword, I didn't think I had much to fear.

The girl had untangled herself and sat cowering against a tree. The dress was torn and she had to hold it together to cover herself. She might have been fifteen years old. Her face was very pale.

The boy raised the sword over his head and rushed at me. I took two quick steps under his guard, grabbed him by the wrist, and with a snap, shook the sword out of his grasp. Then I gave him two short pops in the face with my fist that bloodied his nose and split his lip.

"Stop, Sir Jack!" Gordon shouted, as his horse crashed into the clearing. "That is the prince!"

The front of his tunic was still balled up in my fist. Albert's son! I pulled his face a few inches closer to mine. Yes, there was a resemblance, all right.

"What the hell did you think you were doing, young man?" He twisted in my grasp, and that made me yank him in closer. "Answer me, Prince!"

"Who are you? Mind your own business!" he blurted out. "How dare you touch me so?"

Looking at him through a red haze, my fist went back to stretch him out on the ground.

"Easy, Sir Jack," Gordon said, "for I'm bound to protect him from harm."

I was already too angry to think straight, but Gordon was behind me with his iron-mounted knocker, and I couldn't very well ignore him. I turned, pulling the boy around between us. "What should I do with these two, Gordon?"

He looked uncomfortable. "You could tell the reeve that this happened." What was a reeve? Gordon looked as if he had no better idea than I did what to do.

"I'll talk to Alb . . ." I began to say. "I'll talk to the king as soon as I see him."

"Impertinent!" said Albert's son. "You'll be sitting in the dungeon when my father hears about this!"

"You've got ten seconds to get out of my sight," I told him, and he lost no time retrieving his sword and disappearing into the woods.

"Who's this other boy?" He was still lying on the ground, panting.

"He's Lord Bennett's eldest."

I took hold of his ear and stood him on his feet. "You're hurting me," he whimpered.

"Try that ever again, and I'll tie your ears in a knot." I gave him a rattling kick in the backside and off he ran. Soon I heard the sound of horses pounding away through the brush.

"It's all right, honey," I said, turning to the girl. "You're safe now. What's your name?"

"Please, sir," she began pleading, "don't let my father find out. Please, sir, I'll be more careful, I promise I will."

Gordon said, "The knight asked you what your name is, girl."

She rose quickly to her feet, still holding her torn dress together, and dropped me an awkward curtsy. "I'm Anna, sir."

"Why are you worried that your father will find out?"

"He'll beat me, sir. He'll say I should have been more careful."

"Surely he wouldn't do that, Anna."

She was crying now. "Oh, he will, sir. Please don't tell anyone about this, sir."

Now I was really stumped. We all stood there looking at

one another until Gordon said, "Run home now, Anna, and be more careful in the woods."

"Oh, I will, sir," she said, beginning to run. "Thank you, sir," she called to me over her shoulder, and then she was gone.

I got back on my horse and we rode out of the woods and continued up the road. We came to a bridge made of heavy planks. "This is the road that goes to Griswold's manor house?"

"There are trails here which will take you to the earl's manor. But the market road is at the next bridge."

"Why did that girl think her father would beat her?"

Gordon shrugged. "I suppose she knows her own father."

"You're looking at me very strangely, Gordon. Is something wrong?"

"Sir Jack, if you don't mind my saying so, it's going to take more than a day or two for you to understand the way things work around here."

"Are you telling me I should have let them rape that girl?"

"No, no, I would have broken that up myself. But I might not have bloodied the face of the heir to the throne. Calm yourself, Sir Jack, I'm not trying to tell you what to do. I'm not saying you did anything wrong. If a brawl breaks out on market day, I may knock a few heads together without being quite sure they're the right heads. We have to settle for whatever we do in the moment, I suppose. All I can tell you is that ever since Anna started budding, she's been acting wild and flouncing around, and I'm just not all that surprised, that's all."

"You know her?"

"Of course I know her. I know everybody. Everybody knows everybody."

I thought it over as we rode along. Here was a little kingdom in a river valley, split up into different estates, with several thousand peasants and a sprinkling of nobility. However unlikely the whole idea may have sounded to me two days ago, it was now perfectly real, and the more I saw of it, the more complicated it appeared.

Well, I would have a talk with Albert about it the first chance I got. I didn't think that farm girls getting raped by his nobles' sons was something he would be casual about. Much too vulgar for his taste, surely.

I wondered what he would say when he found out I had smacked the prince around. I wondered why he hadn't mentioned that he had a son, or about the the the Picts either—that is, if they existed. I wondered what other big surprises I was in for.

But my thoughts were distracted now that we were coming into the farmlands. West of the bridge I had noticed cart tracks every so often heading into the trees, and I assumed the presence of farms, though I couldn't see them from the road. East of the bridge the cultivated fields began, first on one side of the road, then on both sides, until I could see them stretching far toward the south. Dwellings and barns and pens were visible now, and everywhere there was activity.

Here a man was plowing; here a woman was sowing; here a man split logs with a mallet and wedge; here a woman stirred a great pot with a long stick; here some boys were slaughtering a pig; here some girls carried wash to the river. Traffic increased on the market road until it was full of carts and flocks and people coming and going. Some waved or spoke greetings to Gordon, and everyone peered at me with curiosity. I smiled and nodded and said "Good day," and they bobbed their heads and said "Good day, sir," and the men took off their hats in a friendly way. The women also seemed open and friendly, and the younger ones giggled if I took off my hat to them. In the main all these people seemed busy and happy and prosperous.

Their clothing was all hand-made, heavy and practical. The men dressed mostly in leggings with long shirts in a variety of styles, belted at the waist, and each man had his wallet and his knife. The women wore dresses down to the ground, and many had brightly colored jackets and shawls. There was a definite similarity and medieval flavor in the cut and style of these simple clothes, as though the same designer who had conceived my clothes and Gordon's also had an influence on the clothing of the farmers.

At the crossroads by the second bridge, I had a moment of vertigo similar to the one I had experienced when we all burned our modern clothing. At the bonfire, though, I had been fearful of losing touch with what had been familiar; now I was fearful of losing what was still new and strange. I felt handsome and dashing with my horse and my sword and my feathered hat. I felt excited to have a place in this well designed kingdom as a knight, a fencing master, a friend to the king. For a moment I had a dizzy feeling of loss. I was afraid of waking up and realizing this was all a dream.

"How long have you been here, Gordon?"

"Years and years. So many now that the life I knew before seems as faded as the photos of my grandparents when they were children."

That was exactly what I wanted to hear: that the dream would continue and become my new home and my new life.

"You speak very well. You have a talent for it. What did you do before you came here?"

He smiled shyly. "I thought of myself as a poet, but I made my living as a merchant seaman. When we were at sea, I had plenty of time to read and write to my heart's content. I wasn't published very often, but it opened my heart and mind."

"How did you like that line of work?"

"In the beginning I liked it. I was making money and seeing a bit of the world. Then there came a point when it began to annoy me that we had to burn a million gallons of fuel to bring some chopsticks over from China. I started to have a very bad attitude, but that turned out to be a good thing for me in the end."

"How was that?"

"I knew another seaman who was starting to feel the same way I was. We were both in the same boat, you might say. He said he was going to take some kind of an employment test and he invited me to go along. Six months later we arrived here."

"What kind of test was it?"

"It was one of those tests where you're not supposed to know what you're being tested for. It was a long test. There were several parts to it. I was a hasty man in those days, and I almost walked out on it. Thank God I didn't!"

"You're happy here?"

"I never knew what it meant to be alive before I came here. Everything I did, and everything everybody else did, was for the sake of some nameless butterball somewhere with twenty buttons on his telephone."

"And now?"

He thought for a moment. "I can't explain it. Of course we don't make a way of life out of pointless and wasteful activity, because that wouldn't get us through the winter. But it's much more than that. It's something that you feel. You feel it in your body as well as in your mind. It has to do with what a human being really is. Perhaps you'll see what I mean."

"I'll take your word for it, Gordon. Is your seaman friend

here also?"

He grimaced. "I think he's still here, but we're not friends anymore."

"Why not?"

"Because he became a Pict." Gordon slowed his horse and pointed. "Look, there's the monastery."

Chapter Five

The monastery graced the top of its own little hill north of the market road, and I sensed once again the presence of that unseen designer who seemed to have a hand in everything here. Harmonious and balanced, as though it had grown organically among the trees that sheltered it, the abbey with its wooden church and outbuildings radiated an aura of peace and serenity.

"Is that a Catholic monastery?"

"No, I don't think so. Not exactly. I guess it is for those who want it to be. For the rest of us, it's just the monastery."

We tied our horses at a long hitching rail, and hung up our weapons in a sort of lean-to which had shelves and pegs for that purpose. "You can bring the cut-meat inside," said Gordon, indicating the dagger on my belt, "in case we stay for supper."

Jenna's horse was tied at the rail along with the horses of the French servants. Albert's horse was not there, nor was Émile's. There were a number of things I wanted to talk to Albert about, and yet I was glad he wasn't there. I wanted a chance to be near Jenna when he wasn't around, and this cloister was as good a place as any. It made me excited just to see her horse.

The first person Gordon and I came across was an elderly man dressed in a brown robe. He was standing by the sanctuary door as though he had been expecting us.

"Hello, Gordon," he said in a kindly voice. "I haven't seen you in quite a while. Who's this you've brought with you?"

"Abbot, this is Sir Jack, our new fencing master."

"Very pleased to make your acquaintance, Sir Jack," said the abbot. "Are you here to hone our dueling skills?"

"No, Father," I said. "I'm here to inspect the kitchen and the wine cellar."

He smiled at that. "What I meant to ask, in a more general way, is what brings you to this kingdom of the apocalypse?"

"Well, that's a good question, Father. Actually I was shanghaied by my old friend, King Albert."

After a pause, he said, "Gordon, would you mind going over to the bakery for me and asking Brother Robert to put on two more plates for supper?"

Once Gordon was gone, the abbot took a couple of deep breaths. "Please forgive me for anything I may have inadvertently done to put you off."

"Oh, that's okay, Father. I . . ."

"No, no," he held up his hand. "I try to put people at ease, but often I seem to make them uncomfortable instead. And I've been looking forward to meeting you."

"You have?"

"Do you know that you're the first new arrival in over a year? The kingdom was finished. That was the general understanding. The roster was complete. The king had some final arrangements to make down south, and then he was going to burn the bridge, once and for all. Now one more person arrives: a new knight and a skilled swordsman, of all things. That's interesting, isn't it?"

"Keep talking, Father, I'm all ears."

"Did you take a test before you came here?"

"No, I didn't take that test."

"And what kind of a briefing did you have, if I may ask?"

"I'm not sure what you mean."

"What did King Albert tell you about the situation here?"

"Not that much. I've been trying very hard to get my bearings ever since I arrived yesterday."

"And what do you think so far?"

"I'm very impressed. It's quite an amazing place. I've never seen anything like it in my life." The abbot seemed to be waiting for me to go on, but I didn't know what else to say.

"But this is incredible," he said finally. "You really don't have any idea what's going on here, do you?"

"That's what I just got finished saying, Father."

"But that's so hard to believe. Why did the king say he wanted you to come?"

"He said it was lonely at the top."

"Well, so it is. But that doesn't answer the question. Aren't you wondering why he brought you here?"

"I had my doubts that the kingdom even existed until I saw it with my own eyes."

"And now that you've seen it with your own eyes, where do you think you fit in? Farmers till the soil, millers grind the grain, monks keep school and visit the sick. What is Sir Jack here to do?"

"The king said he needed some help."

"With what?"

"He didn't say."

"And you didn't ask?"

"I didn't have anything better to do, Abbot," I said, exasperated by all these questions I couldn't answer. "I was at loose ends. My prospects were uncertain. This opportunity popped up, and here I am."

"Opportunity to do what? This isn't a spa. This is a lonesome candle on the edge of the world. One good puff would blow it out. Now tell me, did you not make any kind of an agreement with the king?"

"It didn't seem necessary."

"But you've already been knighted, isn't that so?"

I had, of course, been knighted, but what did that mean? In my confusion I said, "I was told that if I didn't like it, nobody would try to keep me here."

The abbot looked puzzled, and gave me a long, serious look. "And what did you think that meant, Sir Jack?"

"Well, obviously that I . . . uh . . ."

"It is certainly true that you're free to go," said the abbot quietly. "So are we all. That was the agreement that we all made. If you don't like it, then go. If life is too difficult here, then go. No one will try to stop you. Go, but God be with you, because the kingdom is surrounded by thousands of square miles of trackless wilderness, and the compass hasn't been invented yet!"

"Oh, Jack!" It was Jenna's voice, and I turned toward the sound like a flower turns toward sunshine. "I was wondering what was keeping you."

She had changed into a long-waisted dress with a decorative belt, and she must have known how becoming it was because she spun around to show it off.

My smile must have cracked, because she stopped and peered into my face. "You look strange, Jack. What has Abbot Frederick been saying to you?" That was quite an intuitive leap, I thought, and it made me appreciate her all the more. "Abbot," she said, tapping her foot on the wooden porch, "you have been upsetting our new knight. Why is that?"

"My ladyship . . ." began the abbot, smiling and spreading his palms.

"I am going to ask the king to make Sir Jack into a bishop instead of a knight, and then you will have to kiss his ring."

"It will be my duty and my pleasure to obey you both, my lady," said the abbot. It sounded quite genuine, and my impression was that he liked her.

"Sir Jack," Jenna continued, "if you will be so kind as to come along with me, I have something to show you." When I offered her my arm, she took it and led me off. I did manage one glance at the abbot, by which I meant to convey that the subject of our conversation was still open, and he nodded in return. Jenna did not regard him again. He had been dismissed.

"That priest is very nosy," Jenna said as she led me through the cloister, "and he adores asking questions which are difficult to answer. What was he saying to you?"

"I don't remember," I said, and that was mostly true. She had lied about my ability to leave, hadn't she? But it had been out of her love, hadn't it? That was all right, wasn't it? What difference did it make whether I could leave? There was nowhere else I wanted to go. "You look very lovely in that dress, my lady."

Her eyes sparkled. "You may call me Jenna when we are alone, but you must be very careful otherwise, especially when I become queen."

"Are you really going to have Albert turn me into a bishop?"

"No! I think you would make a very pretentious bishop, strolling around in a robe with your hands clasped on your belly. I like you with a sword swinging from your hip. But truly, Jack, what did you think about what I said to him?"

"I thought it was very charming."

"You see, I am practicing to be queen. But I don't know if I've got it right."

"My advice to you, Jenna, is just to be yourself, and you'll make a wonderful queen."

"What, shall I throw away my clothes, and ride bare-ass down the road in my crown? There was a woman who actually did that long ago. Her name was Lady Godiva."

"I've heard of her."

"Do you think she really did that?"

"I don't know, Jenna. I think history is mostly stuff that people make up."

"Every woman wants to be queen, I suppose. But now it seems so . . ." She shuddered. "I think I'm too crazy, Jack. I don't know how long I can play that role."

"You mustn't try to play a role. You'll only make yourself unhappy. You have to be yourself, and if you're crazy sometimes, then you're crazy. What's wrong with that?"

"Crazy Queen Jenna!"

"Before you ever considered being queen, did you care what people thought?"

"Hell, no, I didn't."

"Well, there's no reason to change now."

"Screw 'em if they can't take a joke."

"Spoken like a true queen."

"You comfort me, Jack."

"I love you, Jenna, just the way you are."

She looked up at me with soft, brown eyes. "I love you too, Jack. But promise me you won't become possessive, dear. Promise you won't be jealous of Albert. And that you'll never try to own me. No one is ever going to own me, Jack. Not Albert, not you, not anyone."

"Can't I be a little jealous of Albert sometimes? It's just the way it is with us knights, Jenna. We're very sentimental."

"And, Jack, don't ever feel guilty about what we're doing, because I've already told Albert that I may take lovers. He's quite forgotten I ever said so, I'm sure, but I did tell him more than once. So you see there's nothing illicit in what we're doing."

In my mind was an image of a scaffold and a chopping block. "I can't tell you what a feeling of security that gives me, Jenna."

"On the other hand, it's very important that we keep up appearances around the common people. I don't think they understand these things the way we do. You're looking at me strangely, dear. What I mean is that the common people love Albert and look up to him, and it just wouldn't be possible to explain to them why it's quite proper for his queen to have a lover."

"But in this valley where everybody knows everybody, there will be rumors and gossip."

"As long as what goes on between us is only a rumor to them and not an obvious fact, then Albert's charisma will not be affected. That's why we have to be careful."

"I will be guided by you, my lady."

"Thank you, Jack. You're so understanding." She sank gently to her knees, and kissed me on the codpiece. "Take this off."

"Jenna . . ."

"No one will see."

We were some distance from the cloister now, in the meadow just to the north, where a footpath ran through waist-high grasses and flowers.

"Jenna, be sensible," I said, but sensibility wasn't what I wanted from her.

"I don't want to be sensible, dear. Only careful. Now help me." She was tugging on one of the thongs that held the codpiece. I undid the knot, and as she caressed me, my knees turned to butter; I slid helplessly down among the fragrant grasses and wildflowers.

"Is there any grass on my dress?" she asked me later.

I felt happy and satisfied lying there in the peaceful meadow and didn't want to move a muscle; but I managed to struggle up on one elbow. "Yes, a little," I said, brushing her off. "Turn around. That's got it."

"Well, that was fun, Jack. I wonder if we couldn't get away with it inside the cloister."

"Now you're just being wicked."

She smiled. "Well, let's continue our walk. There really is something I want to show you."

The path ended in a grove of trees with some wooden benches in a semicircle. She took my hand and led me through the bushes just beyond. "Watch your step. It's steep here. Now, look!"

Not so far away, just on the near side of another river, was the loveliest castle anyone could have wanted to live happily ever after in. It was just a castle, not a palace; there was nothing ostentatious about it, and it was all of stone except for the drawbridge. Yet there the hand of that invisible designer had placed his signature. The castle was clearly the kingdom's centerpiece, its masterful work of art. And what the castle seemed to proclaim with every line and in every detail was that in this kingdom, this was where power and intelligence and beauty had finally come together to form a perfect bond.

It beckoned me. It invited me to come live there. I felt from the moment I saw it that my happiness on earth could never be quite complete until it could be my own castle. And the feeling was so strong, I was appalled by it. Not content with making love to Albert's queen, now I wanted his castle too.

"Jenna, who designed that castle?" When she didn't answer, I turned to look at her, and her eyes were moist with tears.

"He died of the flu three years ago. What a wonderful man he was!"

I felt a little jealous. Would she be crying for me if I had died of the flu three years ago? "Did he design the monastery too?"

"Oh, yes. He was a great genius."

"What was his name?"

"Joel. Joel Mason."

Joel Mason! One of America's most celebrated architects, his name practically a household word, he had vanished without a trace, leaving a scathing letter behind criticizing western civilization up one leg and down the other. A score of rumors had circulated around his disappearance, but the mystery had never been solved.

"He died here in the kingdom?"

"It was a great loss to us."

I couldn't ignore my sense that Joel had also been her lover. "He was an old man, wasn't he?"

"Oh, no! He was very mature, but he wasn't old. Not at all."

The drumming of hoofbeats on the road behind us was not entirely a welcome sound. Just since morning, I'd punched out the prince and made love to the queen; it occurred to me now that I'd never bothered to find out what the penalty was for high treason.

"That's Albert," Jenna said without any hint of anxiety. We looked each other over one last time for telltale grasses, and walked back toward the cloister.

Albert met us halfway. I was relieved to see him looking radiant and congenial. "Well, I suppose this means you've seen the castle, Jack. What a lovely view it is from the top of this hill! This is where I brought her ladyship to see it for the first time, isn't it, my dear? I'm sorry I missed the look on your face, Jack, but one can't be everywhere at once. So what do you think, Jack? Is there really a kingdom here, or was I making it all up?"

"Your majesty, I don't know what to say. It is a profound achievement, and I salute you." I gave him a deep bow.

Happiness bubbled out of him. Tears came to his eyes. "Thank you, Jack. A great deal of thought and planning and work went into it, and every time I come home, I'm amazed and delighted by it all over again. *This* time I'm home for good, thank God!"

"Dearest, I'm a little itchy from walking in the field," said Jenna, touching him lightly on the arm, "so I'm going to have a bath and get ready for dinner. I'm sure you and Sir Jack will have a thousand things to discuss." Off she went with perfect poise, smiling back at us as she turned the corner; she knew we wouldn't take our eyes off her until she was out of sight.

"Well, Jack, I saw Sir Leo and I must say he is very impressed with you. That's quite an accolade coming from Leo. I'd say you're doing pretty well for someone who's been here slightly more than twenty-four hours."

"Thank you, your majesty," I said, feeling somewhat relieved. "I like Sir Leo a great deal, and he's going to be a fine fencer when I get him loosened up."

"And then you rode over with Gordon, eh? What do you think of him?"

"I like him too. He's very deep. But I have to ask, what is this test that everybody took before they came here?"

"Not everybody took the test. Only the common people. The nobility didn't have to take it. I may have made a big mistake there. But it was very hard to find people for the nobility. That sounds funny, doesn't it, but it's true. They were all required to make quite a large financial investment, you see, and the test . . . well, it didn't seem appropriate at the time."

"What was the test about?"

"The test was developed to measure how deeply an individual was addicted to the modern world. I didn't want people here who would miss what the modern age had to offer and try to recreate it. I wanted people who yearned for the life that is available here."

"Okay, I get it. And who are the Picts?"

"Did you run into some Picts?"

"Gordon went charging into the woods after something he called a Pict. Whatever it was, I didn't see it. I wasn't sure if he was daffy or what."

"Oh, they're real enough!"

"What are they?"

"That's a very good question, Jack. What are they, indeed! They're one very good example of how easy it is to outsmart yourself."

"Gordon couldn't tell me much about them. He got himself all twisted around, and then gave up."

"I'm not sure I can do much better. All I can say is that they passed my test with flying colors. I transported them out of the modern era into the past, and when they got here they kept on going. But where it is they went to, I can't really say."

"So they're people who've turned wild?"

95

"Apparently I overdid it a little when I had that test developed. A percentage of the people who came here weren't interested in civilization at all, modern or otherwise."

"They took one look at the woods and off they went?"

"Not quite. It started with one man. A very unusual, very gifted man. A meditation master. He arrived at the invitation of the abbot. He was the first to go, and since then many others have joined him."

"How many?"

"I'm not sure. Maybe a hundred and fifty. Maybe not quite so many. How many of them are still alive, I have no idea."

"Women too?"

"Oh, yes! Whole families."

"Gordon seemed very pissed off at them."

"Some people want me to wipe them out or chase them away, as if I could really do either. They steal things sometimes, or so people say. Stealing is a very serious crime here, and if people kill Picts and say they caught them stealing, there isn't much I can say about that. But I'm not so sure it's the stealing. I think it just makes it that much harder to raise children and look after the womenfolk when the woods are full of wild men. Do you know what I mean?"

"The farmers fear them, so they want them dead?"

"Some do. Some are indifferent to them. Some are in awe of them."

"What about you, Sire?"

"I'm not going to tell you anything more. Here is an assignment for you. Once you have an experience with them—and you will—come and tell me what *you* think."

"Beg pardon, your majesty." A monk waving a wooden spoon was calling to us across the meadow. "If you're having supper with us this evening, we are about to sit down."

"We're coming, Brother Joseph! Well, Jack, are you hungry?"

I was very hungry, not having eaten since breakfast, and I was hoping as we walked in from the field that the monastery fare wouldn't be too abstemious. I was happy to discover that the monks liked to eat as much as they liked to cook.

Jenna and Albert and the abbot and I and several monks ate dinner in the monastery refectory. We had chicken in a delicious sauce, fresh potatoes and carrots and peas, bread right out of the oven, fruit wine, and custard pie. Leaning back in my chair with a full belly, I felt very glad to be living in Albert's kingdom. I felt peaceful and satisfied in a way that was so new to me that I couldn't help wondering what exactly to attribute it to.

"What did you put in this food, Brother Robert?" I said to the cook. "It's made me high as a kite."

People looked at one another and smiled in a mischievous way that made me wonder if I'd set myself up for something.

"It's a very well-kept secret, Jack," Jenna teased me.

"You have to attain a very high level of sanctity before it can be revealed," said Albert. He looked pretty high himself, and I knew it couldn't be the wine, which was tasty but not potent.

"But since you're a friend of the king," said the abbot, "we'll make an exception."

"We don't put anything in it," said Brother Robert. There was an expectant pause. They were playing some kind of game with me. "But that's not the secret." There was another pause. They wanted me to say something or take a guess, but I couldn't think what to say.

"I give up," I said.

"The secret is what *doesn't* go into the food."

"Pesticides," I guessed.

They all looked at one another in a very stylized way that was obviously part of the game. "Pesti-what?" said Brother Joseph.

"Pesticides," I repeated.

"What a strange word," said Émile.

"The man's raving," said Albert. "Get the straightjacket."

"Straight-what?" said the abbot.

Something seemed to dawn on Albert, and he squirmed a bit. "Oh, come now!"

"Straight-what?" said the abbot. Everyone was smiling except Albert. I could tell he had lost some points, but I didn't quite get the rules of the game yet.

"Referees!" said the abbot.

"The abbot's correct," said Émile.

"I'm afraid so, dear," said Jenna.

"But surely there have always been straightjackets," said Albert, but he didn't seem convinced. He was just swimming against the tide.

"Madmen, yes; straightjackets, no," said the abbot. "The straightjacket was invented in the late eighteenth century, and was originally called a straight waistcoat."

"Oh, very well, I concede!" said Albert, pushing his sleeve up and extending his bare forearm to the abbot, who licked his first two fingers and gave Albert a stinging slap on the arm.

"Ouch!" said Albert, and everybody laughed.

"Pesti-what?" Brother Joseph said to me.

I understood now: modern words were forbidden. "I don't know what you mean," I side-stepped. "All I said was Bless the Child." And I tented my fingers together very piously.

"Nice try," said Brother Joseph, licking two fingers.

"Oh, very well, I concede!" I said, mimicking Albert's intonation perfectly, and that got a very good laugh. It was apparently all right to make fun of the king in that situation. God was the king in the monastery, and that gave Albert a little break.

I pulled back my sleeve and got my sting on the arm, and it made me feel merry and happy. It was part of my initiation. I was less of an outsider than I'd been when supper began.

The conversation moved on to local matters, local people, and local animals. I sat and listened, soaking up names and bits of lore. While I was listening, I wandered through that incredible kingdom with my imagination. People were having supper, putting the children to bed, generally wrapping it up for the day because it was getting too dark to work.

In another part of the world, people were flipping on the electric lights and getting set for the swing shift. Here, darkness was filling the valley with an inevitability that was quite thrilling. We weren't in some national park a few miles off the highway. We couldn't drive into town to see a movie, or go home to the suburbs where the television and the washing machine and the dishwasher were all ready and willing to work all night if we wanted them to.

No, the planet that contained the whole modern experience might just as well have been in some other solar system, it seemed that far away. And it seemed a queer place, like a funny old legend, not quite real anymore. A dreamy mist was already developing around my memories there. Even the pathos was gone from the story. It was just an ancient and rather obvious parable about how not to live.

Our life here borrowed nothing from that civilization, not a yard of synthetic cloth, not a tool or a trick, not one paper match. Yet nothing was missing. That in itself was a tremendous revelation, but it was only the beginning. Something that had very definitely been missing from my life was beginning to stir inside me.

How can I describe it? My skin felt like it was all one continuous cover and I could feel my body inside it. It wasn't as if I had one hand over there and one leg over there and my head somewhere up on a shelf, the way I was accustomed to feeling. I never used to be aware of my body unless something called my attention to it. Now I was aware of my whole body and the skin around it. It wasn't just an abstract skin. It was my living skin.

What was making such a profound difference in the way I felt? It was everything around me. The chair that I was sitting on, the clothes we were all wearing, every plank and peg in that whole monastery, every single thing in that entire river valley without exception had been handmade out of whatever was available from the valley itself by the people who lived here. There was nothing around me that came out of a chemical vat or was cranked out by machines and disaffected people who punched time cards and then drove home to watch TV.

I got up and walked slowly around the room; everything I touched seemed to touch me back and speak to me in some very personal way about the person who had made it. That was the genius of Albert's time machine, and somehow that was making me feel the way I felt.

Someone touched me on my shoulder and when I turned, there was Albert. "Yes, your majesty?"

"Nicely done, old boy," said Albert. "I knew you were a natural." And somehow I knew exactly what he was talking about.

"Does it show?" I said, amazed.

"I told you that you'd be in for a very pleasant surprise."

"But did you . . . I mean when you were planning all this,

you couldn't possibly have known . . ."

"No, it was something we all discovered together over a period of time. In the very early days we still had a few artifacts from the modern age. We thought that would be all right because frankly we couldn't imagine how we would get along without them."

"Like clocks."

"Exactly! And when we finally realized that their presence was spoiling something very marvelous and powerful, something none of us had ever experienced before—well, into the big bonfire they went. From that point on, nothing was ever imported again."

"My skin feels different."

Albert laughed. "Oh yes, I know the feeling. Go take a walk out under the stars and see what that's like."

So I went back out into the meadow with my cloak wrapped tightly around me, and stood under the huge bowl of the night, all stippled with hundreds of thousands of little dots of light that were all huge, flaming suns a zillion miles away. The feeling swelled up inside me until I could hardly breathe except with great, gasping breaths. Then it subsided, percolating away with little bubbles of joy and power.

I didn't feel insignificant standing between dark mountains under the infinity of space. Rather I felt like it all belonged to me. I was part of it and it was part of me, the wind and the sky and the cold and the darkness. What was it that Gordon had said? *It has to do with what a human being really is.*

Just at that moment one of the brightest shooting stars I'd ever seen hurtled across the sky; as I turned to follow its path, I felt the breeze of something that whipped right past my face. Without thinking, I dropped down and ran crouching across the lawn until I reached the shelter of the arched doorway.

What the hell was that? Had someone taken a shot at me? It must have been a night bird or a hunting bat. Still, I had a funny feeling that wouldn't go away.

I thought about those two boys whose butts I'd kicked in the forest that afternoon. They had no good reason to like me much after that incident. I recalled that Albert's son had attacked me with a sword in a hot-headed way, and had said he would kill me. But my intuition told me I had little to fear from those boys

Who else then? No one came to mind, and once again I told myself that it must have been some flying creature, nothing more; still, I decided I'd better go back inside. I passed Rudy Strapp in the hallway, and he paused to take a long look at me. "Something happen to you?"

"No, I don't think so. Something flew by my face in the dark. Probably a bat. It startled me."

He continued to watch me. "Let me give you a little tip. Don't take too many chances until you know this place better."

"Meaning what exactly?"

"Use your head. Don't be foolish. You're in a strange place. Doesn't that sound like good advice?" He continued down the hall, but I had a strong feeling there was more he could have told me. I put a smile on my face and went back to join the crowd.

"Sir Jack," said Albert, "we're all going to the chapel for a meditation before we turn in. Won't you join us?"

"I don't know how to meditate."

There was a ripple of laughter, but it was such a friendly-sounding laughter that I had to join in.

"That's no problem," said Albert. "We don't know how to do it either!" Everyone laughed even harder. "But it's something we're all trying very hard to learn." Several heads nodded agreement. "What is meditation anyway?" Albert went on. "You sit still and you try to put aside your restless thoughts. The intention is to have some kind of communion with the Divine. Is it easy? No, not so easy particularly in the beginning because all our restless habits oppose it. But what it can do for us is profound. It can make a continuous subtle improvement in every aspect of your life; and that's why we do it. Would you like to try?"

We filed into a small chapel with two windows looking out onto the darkness. I chose a seat far from both windows. The abbot gave a short prayer evoking the divine Presence and asking for assistance in our efforts. Then there was silence.

Much as I didn't want to disturb the others, I couldn't seem to get comfortable however I tried sitting, and I developed little itches everywhere that demanded attention. After about ten minutes of that torture, Albert said softly, "Jack, can you feel your heart beating in your chest?"

"Yes, I can."

"Can you feel the pulse in your hands?"

"Yes," I said after a few moments.

"Try taking a little tour all over your body and see how many places you can feel that pulse. At the same time, try to be aware as your breath goes in and as it goes out. In and out, in and out, feeling the pulse at the same time. Try that."

Silence ensued, and I found that by following his instructions, I was more comfortable. Soon, the itching subsided and I began to feel a sense of peacefulness augmented by the peaceful night. Even the monotonous night noises of crickets and tree frogs seemed to blend together with the pulse of my heart.

How long I was sitting there I haven't any idea, but finally Albert tapped me on the shoulder and we let ourselves quietly out of the chapel, leaving the monks and the abbot sitting in the candlelight.

"That wasn't so unpleasant, was it?"

"No, I liked it."

"I don't think you can really appreciate what this kingdom has to offer, or what life has to offer, for that matter, unless you make a habit of meditation."

"If you say so, my liege," I yawned, and suddenly I felt like I couldn't keep my eyes open any longer. He showed me to a cell with a bed that was on the hard side but comfortable enough. I fell asleep quickly, but not before I made sure the shutters were bolted and my sword lay close by.

Chapter Six

In the forenoon of the following day Sir Leo arrived with a small escort of soldiers, and we all rode in procession to the castle. This was Albert's final homecoming after many absences over the last fifteen years, and the kingdom was celebrating as though it was a holiday.

The soldiers rode with banners on their staffs that featured a white dragon on a blue field, and Albert and Jenna wore cloaks with the same device. Rudy and I rode behind them and I felt merry and fine. My outlook had been altered in a certain way by what had happened in the dark outside the monastery and also by Rudy Strapp's enigmatic advice about watching my step, and part of my mind was on the alert, scanning the crowds gathered to watch Albert ride in. But I had also decided that morning that if I was going to live fearfully as a knight in Albert's kingdom, then I might as well get a bag of food and start back through the woods toward the life I had left behind. On the contrary, I was determined to enjoy myself and to rediscover the feeling of connectedness I had experienced the night before.

Looking around, I saw no signs of danger or antagonism, but only happy and eager faces. Our procession was as good as a parade and everyone came to watch us. Albert was the center of attention, and it was clear that he was beloved by his people. Many greeted him and smiled at him; Albert smiled at everyone, and greeted people here and there by name, and sometimes inquired after a person's family or their particular enterprise.

Jenna was also very popular and many of the young girls gave her little bouquets. The servants carried baskets for the flowers, and after Jenna had acknowledged the gift of a bouquet, it was passed back to them. I could see in the adoring eyes of the girls that they dreamed of growing up just like Jenna, so beautiful, so poised, and betrothed to a king. Truly Albert and Jenna were a living fairy tale to these people.

I also drew my share of attention as the mysterious new arrival. Many scrutinized me, and I saw their eyes flick back and forth between my face and my sword. No doubt there were a good many rumors flying around about who I was and why I had come. It made me smile to think about it. Who was I? What was I doing here? Good questions!

As we approached the castle I was struck once again by the same feelings I had experienced when I had seen it from a distance. The castle beckoned to me; it made me want to own it and live there. But owning a castle had never been one of my dreams. I knew nothing about castles and had no particular interest in them. So why should I covet this one? It made me wonder whether the designer, Joel Mason, had conceived it with that effect in mind, weaving something irresistible right into the architecture.

Our procession poured over the drawbridge and under the portcullis into a great courtyard where even more people were waiting for us. A cheer rang out from the crowd that startled birds into flight from every battlement. Albert turned in his saddle to acknowledge the cheering, and it made me feel sad about my drifty life. I knew no crowd anywhere would ever welcome me that way.

On the steps of the castle was a small group of nobles who also looked glad to see Albert. As we were dismounting, one of the noblemen held up a hand to me in greeting; it took me only a few seconds to recognize him as another acquaintance from my prep school days. We had never been particularly close, nor did I remember him being close to anyone else; back then, he seemed to find everyone and everything equally ludicrous. But he had been a good person to hang out with when I was taking life too seriously, and I was glad to see him now.

"So *you're* the Earl of Griswold. This is too funny," I said, looking him up and down. "Harvey, you don't look like you've changed a bit."

"I'm getting a lot more pussy," he said.

That made me laugh, and the laughter felt good. "Well, that's an improvement," I said, for his remark had bridged the gap all the way back to the days of our mid-teens.

"Yes," he said, his eyes twinkling, "that *is* an improvement. How about yourself?"

"Nah, I just go to a lot of movies."

"Moo . . . What was that now?"

"All right, you got me there, Harvey," I said, pushing back my sleeve. After I had received my punishment, we shared a moment of mutual appreciation for just how crazy life can be.

"Are you ready for your next surprise?" he said.

"No, I'm not, so just forget it."

"Glad to hear it. I'd like to present the Earl and Lady Dugdale."

The person he was indicating was another man our age, slim, blonde, and aristocratic. He put out a diffident hand. "Nice to see you again, Darcey." I took the hand, which was just a shade limp in the grip, and stared. "Alton Dugdale?" I asked. He nodded as though he was pretty sure that was his name, but not positive. It was the name of yet another boy from our class, but my memory contained no face to go along with it. If this was the same person, then I had sneaked into his dormitory room one night and filled it with the contents of two feather pillows. While he slept, I had scattered feathers in his closet, stuffed them in his drawers, and even sprinkled them on his bed. I couldn't remember why I had picked him out for that prank. I couldn't remember anything at all about him except for his name.

"I'd like you to meet my wife, Lady Dugdale. My dear, this is Sir Jack Darcey."

"Lady Dugdale," I said, making her a slight bow.

"Oh, please call me Charlsey. We're very informal here. That's probably the understatement of the year, unfortunately, but there it is. We do the best we can, don't we, Alton? I'm *so* pleased to meet *you*, Sir Jack. I heard that someone new was arriving, but I didn't realize until Alton told me just now that you were an old school friend of his. Imagine! Another person from his old school, that's quite something, isn't it, Alton? We don't see very many new faces here. Actually we *never* see a new face from one year to the next, do we? But yours is a new face, and I certainly hope—in fact, I insist— I mean you really must come visit us soon. Anyone can show you the way, anyone at all, just ask for the Dugdale manse, the market road goes right past our door, you can't miss it."

She had put out her hand to me, palm down, and I had taken her fingertips in mine, and was holding her hand while she talked. She had short, curly brown hair and a rosebud mouth, and she must have been a knockout when she was a co-ed. She was still very pretty, but there was an air of desperation about her, as though she couldn't understand where the years had flown or why. It also seemed like she would never stop talking unless someone did something to break her rhythm, so

I doffed my hat and leaned over to kiss her hand.

"Your servant, my lady," I said.

"Oh, thank you!" she said, delighted. "Alton, did you see what he did? It would certainly be nice if *you* did that once in a while. Do you think you could?"

"Of course I could, Charlsey, if that would make you happy."

She put out her hand and he took it very gently and kissed it as though it was fragile and priceless. It was clear that he cherished her, and I wondered how much she was inclined to take advantage of him. Their eyes met over her hand, and for just a moment in both their faces, there was such a naked look of pain and bewilderment that it shocked me right out of being cynical about their relationship, and made my heart go out to both of them.

Had Harvey Griswold seen what I had seen? No, he was busy smirking away at the world, something he had been doing since I first met him on the playing fields of Chesham. "That was a nice surprise, Harvey. Got anything else up your sleeve?"

"Oh, yes," he said with a grin, "but first a pop quiz." He licked two fingers. "Is a mere landless knight allowed to call an earl by his first name, especially in front of the townies?"

"Town-what?" said I. It was pretty thin but I thought I would give it a try. We preppies used that word to refer to the people who lived in the little town near our school, especially the girls. It was mildly derogatory. Harvey had used the word to evoke our old school days, and we had been modern boys. So didn't that make it a modern word? I licked two fingers.

"I think not," said Harvey.

"Referees!" I called out.

"Dugdale," said Harvey. "Can Darcey lick me up for

saying townies?"

"As in town girls?"

"Yes, Duckie."

"Well, no, I don't think so."

"Towns haven't been invented yet," I pointed out.

"Good try but not quite," said Harvey.

"Kindly show me the way to the nearest town," I said to Dugdale.

"There isn't one."

"See?"

"No way. Dugdale is the referee and he says no."

"If this earl votes in your favor, my lord earl, I'm going over his head to the king."

Dugdale looked uncomfortable. "I still say no," he said, pulling his shoulders back. "One more word and you get an extra one for being a poor sport, Darcey."

"Double and quits or I go to the king."

"We don't play double and quits," Harvey said. "Anyway, the king's busy."

I looked around the crowd at the castle steps for Albert and spotted him talking very earnestly with a trio of men.

"Pray prithee and pardon me, your majesty," I said, walking up to him, "but what sayst thou? Have towns been invented yet or not?"

Albert turned to look at me, but it was a few moments before he could sort out his thoughts. Finally he said, "What's come over you, Jack? You look positively giddy."

"Those two earls aren't playing fair and I need some help."

Albert gave his head an exasperated little shake. "What is it about? I'm quite busy right now, Jack."

"Just tell Griswold I can lick him up or go double and quits."

"I can't stop for games now," Albert said impatiently. "Come see me another time."

His impatience made me stubborn. "Oh, come on, my liege. Bring your friends and we can all play."

Albert leaned over and looked me straight in the eye. "Kindly leave us immediately unless you want to go sit in the dungeon."

There were a number of people watching us now and that made me even more obstinate. Who did this guy think he was, anyway?

"Lighten up, Albert," I said.

There was a dead pause in the air around us, a kind of silent gasp from the people who were watching. I realized right away that I had done something foolhardy. A look came into Albert's face that made me wish I could retrieve the moment and make a different choice.

Albert turned in the direction of the castle and called out in a voice that was surprisingly deep and resonant, "Guards!" In no time at all I was gripped by several strong and heavy hands. Albert didn't even have to speak to them. He just gave his head a little jerk.

The guards took me down a flight of stone steps below ground level. One carried a torch, which was the only source of light down there; two others held me by the arms. They weren't mean or pushy, and because I knew I had been really stupid, I went along quietly without a fuss.

The dungeon door was made of wood and iron, and it was so short that I had to stoop down to go through it. The guards slammed it shut and threw a couple of bolts on the outside, and there I was in the pitch dark. I pulled my cloak tightly around me, and just stood there feeling numb inside.

111

I knew that my experience in the dark underground wasn't going to be pleasant, but I also knew that the time would pass. Albert would let me out of there sooner or later, and next time I would obey him when he told me to get lost. In the meantime there was not much I could do to improve my situation, or to make it worse for that matter, so I just stood there wrapped in my cloak and waited.

How had I ever gotten myself into this mess? I'd been farting around with Griswold and Dugdale like we were teenagers again, and I had taken a leave of my senses. I had forgotten where I was. Given the changes I had experienced over the past three days, I wasn't doing that badly, was I? How could anybody be expected to keep track of all his marbles after a journey of a thousand years into the past?

Off to my left I heard a scurrying sound and I hoped that there weren't very many of them. *Filthy and stinking and rat-nipped*: that had been Albert's description of how people came out of his dungeon. Yes, it was certainly redolent of all kinds of human by-products, along with rotten straw, mildew, and rat stink. I could already tell why people avoided a second visit.

I don't keep a person in there any longer than I think will do him good. How long would Albert think it would do me good to stay in here? A few hours? Overnight? It was amazing to me that my friend actually had the power to stick me in here in the first place.

Standing there in the darkness with the rats and the stink, I recalled some of the questions that the abbot had asked me the previous day. Unhappy with my prospects and thoroughly smitten by a lovely woman, I had decided to come to Albert's kingdom without asking a single important question about what I was getting myself into. Becoming a knight, dressing in fancy clothes, and riding alongside the king had all been

112

good fun, but being slammed suddenly up in an honest-to-God dungeon at a nod of Albert's head was giving me second thoughts. Did the kingdom have a bill of rights? Were there any real laws at all, or were all decisions simply made according to Albert's whimsy? Suppose he got really pissed off at me for slapping his boy around, or worse, for screwing around with Jenna. Could he just put my head on a block and order someone to chop it off?

I decided to go exploring. I wanted to know how big the cell was, and whether there was something to sit or lie down on. By inching forward with my arms outstretched, I found one wall, and then I began to work my way around the perimeter.

I shuffled through some straw which was damp to the touch. Something climbed up on my boot, and I hurled it away with as much force as possible, though I doubt I did it much harm. I found a wide bench that hung from the wall by two chains and a rickety three-legged stool. After I had been around all four walls, I went around a second time to pace it off. The dungeon was roughly twelve feet on a side, which was bigger than I had expected. Finally I crisscrossed the cell several times, but I didn't find anything else. No bread, no water, no table, no candle. It was about as basic a dungeon as one could imagine.

I found the bench on the wall again and clambered up on it, making sure my cloak wasn't trailing on the floor. Could the rats get up there with me? Very soon I discovered they could. One fat horror dropped down right on my belly, and caused a scramble in the dark that left me breathless and shaken.

The guards had taken my sword and dagger, so I wrapped my belt several times around my hand with the intention of using the heavy buckle as a club. It did not work well. In the dark I was just as likely to hit myself as anything else, and after I had knocked myself a good one on the knee, I gave up. The rats were not really attacking me; I didn't need to fight them off. The problem was that they wouldn't leave me alone for very long, and it prevented me from ever relaxing.

After what seemed like many hours, I managed to achieve a kind of tense balance between sleeping and waking which was less like resting than it was like being in hell. I did my best to ignore the rats, but when one of them bit me, I had to flounder around and shake it off. Finally the guards came to take me to Albert, and I knew by their faces that the smell of the dungeon had seeped right into my clothes.

The throne room was a hexagonal hall with sconces on the walls. Albert sat comfortably on his throne with his chin in his hand and gazed at me for a short while before dismissing the guards.

"You look awful," he said. "And you smell. I'll have someone show you where you can bathe and have a nap. Your clothes will be washed and they'll be ready for you when you wake up."

"Thank you, my liege."

"Then I want you to take a few days and just ride around. See the kingdom. Follow your nose. Talk to people. When you get back, I want you to tell me your thoughts, and we'll discuss what it means to be a knight in this kingdom."

"All right, Sire."

"You don't need to be embarrassed about your time in the dungeon. Quite a few people have had to learn their lesson in there. Griswold has been in the dungeon twice, and so far that's the record. Like you, he has a childish inclination to thumb his nose at authority."

"How long was I in there?"

"You went in sometime yesterday afternoon. It's

mid-afternoon now. That was a bad thing you did, Jack, back talking me in front of those people. A little seed like that could grow a lot of evil."

"I apologize."

"All the rules in this kingdom are as clear and simple as I can make them. Their purpose is the survival and prosperity of the whole community. There are no lawyers, no loopholes, no appeals, and no plea bargaining. Our kind of justice is far from perfect, but it is fairly consistent, and most of the time fairly efficient. We don't allow people to flout authority here because chaos in the commonwealth means starvation and death. I don't allow people to back talk me because I frankly don't have the time or the patience for it, and because I myself take responsibility for everything that goes on in this whole kingdom."

Albert's eyes were flashing now; I had never seen him like this. And though I was dead on my feet and just wanted to lie down someplace where I wouldn't be disturbed, I couldn't help feeling very proud of him.

"Now go get a bath and rest. Talk to Sir Leo before you leave on your quest. He'll see that you have everything you need. Rescue some fair damsels. Get some cats down out of trees. Let your guide be your own high sense of ethics. Any questions?"

Something in what he said made me wonder whether he had already heard about the incident with the girl in the woods. I still needed to talk to him about that, and I promised myself I'd catch him in the morning before I left. "Not right now, your majesty."

He rang a little bell and a young maid came in. She seemed to know what to do without having to be told. "Will you please come with me, sir?" she said, and I followed her out of the hall. She was very efficient in a polite and friendly way and didn't wrinkle up her nose or ask me any questions, but just steered me into a tub of hot water and made off with my clothes. I lay in the tub and soaked and snoozed. When the girl came back, she washed my hair with some pleasant-smelling soap, helped me into a robe, and led me to a little room with a pallet bed. As I slipped under the blankets, she said, "You poor thing, you got quite a many bites. I'll find the mage and tell her where you are. She'll come look in on you."

"Thank you, dear," I said. I was already falling asleep, and didn't think to ask her who or what the mage was.

When I woke up I felt warm and clean and rested. The room glowed with the gentle light of a candle, and outside it was dark. Looking over my shoulder to see where the candlelight was coming from, I discovered I was not alone. A woman, wearing a light brown robe with the cowl hanging down her back, was sitting cross-legged on the floor with her back to me. I could see by the way she was sitting, with her back very straight and her hands lying palms-up on her knees, that she was meditating. For some reason I felt very warm and friendly toward this woman. I felt as though I had known her for years, and that we had spent many a peaceful night like this together by candlelight. Whoever she was, I was glad she was here.

I must have dozed off again, for when I opened my eyes, the woman was sitting quite close and gazing down on me. Her cowl was up and the candle was behind her, so I couldn't see her face. But I still had the same strong impression of familiarity, even of kinship, with her. It made me think that she must have a very kind and loving soul to make me feel so comfortable in her presence.

"You, I take it," I said softly, feeling extremely relaxed and somewhat disembodied, "must be the mage."

She nodded and that was all. In the silence that followed, I was aware of the night sounds of crickets and frogs. Then she said, "You got that right, bubberoo."

The look of astonishment on my face must have been classic, for her shoulders shook with silent laughter. Then with a slow gesture that carried all the significance of a ritual, she put up a hand and pushed the cowl back until it fell from her face.

When we had been lovers, eons ago in our college days, she had leading roles in the local Gilbert and Sullivan Society's productions and had a sideline in belly dancing because she liked to see the college boys go mad with lust for her. Among all my friends and acquaintances, she was far and away the nuttiest with her astrology and her numerology, her runes and her Tarot cards. Other people I knew bandied about arcane ideas and dropped names, but when Marya Randall spoke about the unseen web of meaning which held together all the coincidences of life, it was with the complete assurance that came from making all that lore truly her own. As mysterious and elusive as those ideas might be, they were still as real to her as knives, forks, and spoons, and just as much a part of her daily life.

It was a long time before I broke the silence. In our intimacy we had often shared long periods of unspoken communion, and I was grateful to realize that we could still do that after so many years. I knew she was thinking that fate had brought us back together for its own transcendent reasons, and I was wondering what had caused two tiny needles to find each other again in the huge haystack of the world. We gazed at each other, and our eyes held a conversation which was all the more complex and profound for not using words.

Finally she said, "One of the maids told me you had been in the dungeon and got some bites."

"They're not bad. They're mostly on my hands and

117

arms."

"Mind if I have a look?" She helped me to my feet, and eased off my robe. Then she brought over the candlestick, and examined me all over. I noticed that she had a touch of gray in her hair now, but it seemed like only yesterday that we had been alone together by candlelight. I had the impulse to reach out to her, to stroke her hair. We had had a very wild relationship. We had tried to stretch the boundaries of experience to the limit and beyond. We had had no secrets. I felt like it would be very natural to make love to her now, almost the polite thing to do, like shaking hands or saying hello.

She took a little box of salve from a satchel full of oddments, and dabbed at the bites. Then she helped me with my robe.

"I can't help thinking how nice it would be to make love to you, Marya."

"Yes," she said, "I'm sure it would be very nice. It would be easy for us to do that, Jack. The trouble is that it would complicate things. Are you sure that's what you want?"

I understood what she meant. The friendship was there. It felt stable and strong and comfortable. But making love would be the first step toward another kind of relationship. It wouldn't be possible for us to make love without setting up expectations about tomorrow and the next day.

"You were always wiser about these things than I was, Marya."

"I'm flattered that you still want me, Jack," she said. "And I'm glad to see that you're just as horny as ever," she added with a smile. "But let's wait a little, okay?"

"All right, Marya. How do the bites look?"

"Oh, our Northwoods rat is a pretty clean little guy. If you saw him in the light, you might just let him snuggle up to get warm."

I shuddered, and she reached out and touched me gently. "I know it must be an awful experience to be in Albert's dungeon, but I don't know anyone who's gotten sick in there. I made him take me down once. He keeps it pretty clean, for all that it stinks."

"Why would you want to go down there?"

"Because I'm the mage, and the state of the dungeon is a health matter." She sat down on a cushion and adjusted the folds of her robe. I lay down on my pallet, the candlestick between us.

"What exactly is a mage?"

"Oh, that's just a word I got from a novel I read somewhere. Some little girls were asking me one day if I was a witch. I could tell they wanted to like me, but they weren't so sure it was a good idea to like a witch. So without even thinking about it, I said, 'Oh, no, I'm a mage!' That was just what they wanted to hear, and they spread it all around, so now that's what people call me."

"Is that what you do up here? That's like your job?"

"Yup. I'm the local mage. I give people practical advice about staying healthy, and dose them with herbs and love them up when they're sick. I tell fortunes and make love potions. I have a good time, and I get paid in eggs and vegetables or pieces of cloth—whatever people have to give."

"What about doctors? Are there any regular doctors here?"

"The only doctor Albert could find who was willing to go back in time was a retired general practitioner whose grandfather was a country doctor who made house calls with a horse and buggy. He was here for nine or ten years before he died. The monks and I worked with him closely, and I will say truthfully that we finally wore him out. Yet he was a very happy man, much fulfilled, very serene. I miss Dr. Knox."

"So now it's you and the monks?"

"It's me and the monks and the king and the Goddess and every housewife with her herb garden and everybody who lends his neighbor a hand or helps someone with his burden. I've been here a long time, Jack, and I can't remember the modern world that well anymore. Isn't that funny? But what I remember seems like an endless junkyard where each person went his lonesome way in a toxic fog. It's very different here. We work together and we help each other. We spend most of our time outdoors in the fresh air and sunshine. We eat the organic food that we grow and we live alongside all the animals and plants in the natural rhythms of nature, so we're generally very healthy. We have accidents and disease and death, but we don't use disease to get rich and we don't set aside any particular space for it."

"It sounds like a good life for you."

"It is. And of course I do all the things that everybody does together, like getting the harvest in and getting ready for the festivals. It's a terrific life we have up here, Jack. You're going to love it."

"How did you get here in the first place?"

"I had a little herb market in Manhattan. It was just a little hole in the wall, you know? I did health counseling and card readings and whatever else I could. Our old friend Albert just appeared one day, and said he was looking for a healer for a picturesque and unpolluted kingdom he was organizing. Well, I must have been ready for a change, because it didn't take me five minutes to decide to pick him up on *that* offer, let me tell you!"

"Well, so far I'm glad to be here, Marya. I have a good feeling about Albert's kingdom. Do you know what I mean?

It's a *feeling*. There are no clocks here, no electricity or doctors. There's nothing here that we used to have, and yet nothing seems to be missing, nothing at all. And the big thing that was missing in the modern world, the inside thing, the thing that makes you feel connected to people and the sun and the moon and all the little stars in the sky—that's starting to come back to me. And it's a feeling, just this tremendous, amazing feeling."

"Yes, I know what you're talking about, Jack. I think just about everybody had a little dose of that when they first arrived. I certainly felt it, but it's not a feeling that lasts."

"No?"

"I mean that it's something you have to cultivate if you want it to last. With the silence and the freshness and the vastness of the territory that surrounds us, you can't help but feel differently at first. But when all this becomes normal . . . well, it doesn't get you high anymore. So if you want the feeling to continue, then you have to cultivate it."

"How?"

"By meditating. By becoming more aware of the divine Presence in yourself and all around you."

"I meditated for a little while with Albert and the monks at the monastery. It felt pretty good. He said if I wanted to appreciate this kingdom, I would have to make a habit of it."

"You know something, Jack? Time passes no matter what you do, so the smart thing is to use it wisely and to put a little effort into your spiritual growth every day. Then the little bits add up and as the years go by, you see that you made some progress. How do you feel right now?"

"Well, I feel sad that the feeling doesn't last. I think that's the thing I like best of all about Albert's kingdom."

"Pull your legs under you."

"Like this?"

"Yes, but straighten your spine. That's better. Keeping a straight spine is important. Now close your eyes and see if you can feel the beating of your heart."

"Albert taught me that trick at the monastery."

"Okay. That's a good technique for bringing your mind back into the present moment very quickly. Now for the next step."

So I sat there with my legs crossed and let her coach me, and I was surprised to find that once again it was as though the night and the night sounds and the breeze through the casement came together like a peaceful balm and that my body and my mind could embrace that peace.

"Well, that feels pretty nice all right," I said finally. "I never felt anything like that before I came here."

"You can cultivate that feeling just the same in the modern world, but it's more difficult because the distractions are so intense and continuous. Listen, Jack, I have to tell you something. Albert's kingdom, when you get to know it, is just another loony bin like anyplace else in the world. People here are growing and changing and making mistakes just like anywhere else. The real question is whether this place suits you or not; whether it's your kind of loony bin. Albert went to a lot of trouble to find people who would be attracted to this life. I'm hoping that you like it too, that's all."

"So far so good. I was a little shocked to find out that the only way out of here is a hard chance through the deep woods. Albert never mentioned that."

"What *did* Albert tell you?"

"You know, the abbot at the monastery asked me the same question. Albert really didn't tell me anything. He gave me a windy line that doesn't mean anything when I think about it. Maybe I would have been more suspicious except that I already had a hell of a case on Jenna Yumans."

"Oh, no! Did she seduce you?"

"Well, I suppose you could put it that way. What do *you* know about all this?"

Marya was gazing into the candle and gave no indication of what was going on in her mind. Finally she said, "It was my idea to bring you here, Jack."

"You?"

She turned to me. "Actually the idea came from the Tarot cards."

Well, there it was. You either try to plan your life, or you drift. And if you drift, then you have to be pleased with whatever you get. "All right," I said, as a huge yawn began to pry my jaws apart. "I give up. I'm through trying to figure things out. Let it be the Tarot then. I don't care. My brain is tired, Marya."

"Well, I'm glad that you're taking it like a good sport, bubber," she said. There was something in her voice that I should have paid more attention to, except that I was already beginning to drift away. She went on, "Maybe that's enough for now. There's something else I need to tell you, but it'll keep until morning. Turn over and I'll rub your back."

Massage had always been one of her talents, and she gave me the full treatment, as though she were rolling me up in a bank of clouds; with the relaxation came that wonderful feeling again.

"Thank you, Marya," I managed to say though my tongue was lolling. "That is much better."

"Go to sleep, sweetie," she said as she pressed her thumb firmly into the soft spot at the base of my skull. It was like a little fireworks display of pure pleasure, and when it was over, I was asleep.

Chapter Seven

I woke the next morning eager to venture out into my new and unexplored kingdom and play at being a knight. Marya was gone, but I remembered that she had something more to tell me. So I donned my boots and sword and cloak, ran my fingers through my hair, and went to look for Marya.

The first person I ran into was the young maid who had seen to my needs when I came out of the dungeon. "Mage has gone to a birthing, sir."

"Oh? And where might that be?"

"Thinking of going and helping out yourself?" she asked, and I was surprised by the sarcasm in her voice because the day before she had been very demure.

"I don't think I'd be much help," I admitted. "But I do have a few questions I want to ask her."

"Plenty of time for questions when she returns, sir," she said as though she were talking to me through a barred gate. I changed the direction of my inquiry to finding myself some breakfast.

Now she was eager to assist me and led me through the corridors to the kitchen. "Of course, we all had breakfast hours ago," she said, teasing me, "but if you ask her nicely, I'm sure cook will put something up for you." Dropping me a curtsy, she went on her way.

The cook clasped me to her ample bosom and clucked her tongue about my time in the dungeon. I wasn't sure whether

Hélène was annoyed at me for making trouble for Albert or with Albert for punishing me. It didn't matter. To Hélène we were both just boys home from school, and she wanted us to play nicely and stay out of mischief. She gave me a whopping breakfast, and when I told her I was going on quest, she made a series of emphatic and incomprehensible French gestures and put me up a sack of food that would easily last me four or five days. Then she gave me another hug and sent me off to play.

Sir Leo was glad to see me and shook my hand warmly. I had caught up with him in the field outside the walls where he was practicing with a bow and arrow. "Do you shoot?" he asked me.

"I haven't since I was a boy."

He handed me his bow and quiver and watched me put two arrows in the target and scatter five or six others in the grass beyond it.

"That was not too good," he said, holding out his hand for the bow. In one fluid motion he nocked and drew and loosed and that arrow sprang into the bullseye like it couldn't wait to do anything he wanted it to.

"That's fantastic, Leo," I said, and he grinned with pleasure. "How did you learn to do that?"

"Well, I taught myself. Or you could say I learned it from the birds. Have you ever wished you could fly?"

"Who hasn't?"

"I made myself miserable with envy watching the birds when I was a boy. But when I discovered archery, I realized there was more than one way to ride the wind. If my body couldn't do it, my spirit could. Here, take this arrow and throw it at the target."

When I tried, the arrow twisted in the air and landed a few yards away pointing back at me. "Keep trying," he said, but no matter what I did, the result was pathetic.

"It's like trying to make a dead bird fly," I said.

"*Now* try the bow."

When I took up the bow this time, I had a different attitude toward it. It was a pleasure to nock my arrow, and to draw the feather back to my cheek. And when I loosed at the target, my heart leapt forward with the arrow as it hummed over the field. When it thumped into the target, I felt an entirely different sense of satisfaction than archery had ever given me before.

"That was better," said Sir Leo. "Now let my explain something about your feet."

Well, for the next hour or so I had one of the most exhilerating lessons of my life. Leo was a real genius when it came to archery and his enthusiasm was contagious. By the end of the lesson, I was determined to learn everything the man could teach me.

"I think we have a lot to learn from each other," he said.

"A pleasure, Sir Leo," I said. "Thanks ever so much."

He reached out with his hand and we clasped forearms in the ancient way, his dark blue eyes smiling into mine. What was happening to me? I had never in my life had the slightest notion of ever becoming a soldier. But standing there beneath the outer walls of Albert's castle with this comrade-at-arms, I felt as though I was being challenged to focus all my intelligence and intuition, and even my warmth and love, into my new profession as one of Albert's knights. *Rescue some fair damsels. Get some cats down out of trees. Let your guide be your own high sense of ethics.*

"I'm going on quest, Leo."

"Oh, that's wonderful!" he said. "The first time I went out on quest . . . Well, you'll see for yourself. I don't have to tell you. There's nothing like a quest. When are you going?"

"As soon as you can get me ready."

The armory had many things in common with a blacksmithy, but it was neater, not as sooty, and very interesting to me because I had an eye for the aesthetics of old weaponry. The armorer was a short man with a potbelly who looked me up and down when we walked in. "Oh, so you're the fencing master," he said, as though he'd seen better.

"How did you know?"

"For one thing, I've never seen your face before. Also, you're wearing the sword the king had me make for you. What do you think of it?"

"It likes me well. It's a superlative weapon that was fashioned by a consummate artist."

"Well, if you know that much," he said, smiling with one side of his mouth, "maybe you do know something. What can I do for you lads today?"

"Sir Jack is going on quest, Don. He needs a bit of this and that."

"I think we can fix him up," said the armorer with pleasure, rubbing his hands together. "This will be your very own bow, and here's your quiver."

The bow had a reflex curve like Leo's and the quiver was divided into compartments for different kinds of arrows. "These arrows are for small game," Leo explained. "These are for big game. And these," he said, holding up an arrow which had a long thin iron head, "are armor-piercing."

I thought he was joking, but he gave me a deadly serious look that made me wonder if I was missing the point. Now Don was showing me a two-foot, hickory-handled clobberer with one triangular spike on the side of its iron head, and I recognized it right away from my weapon-collecting days. It was called a war hammer, and it too was meant for piercing armor.

"This is from a Spanish design," he said, offering it to me handle-first.

"Uh, hold on a second here, Don," I said. "Are the rabbits and the bluebirds out there really as dangerous as all that?"

"Oh, no," he replied good-naturedly, "but Lord Hawke's soldiers are very heavily armed now, as I'm sure you've heard, and so we really have to—"

"Lord who in the hell did you just say?" I suddenly felt like the sky had come down very low and heavy, ready to drop right on my head.

Leo and the armorer exchanged a very amazed look. "Lord Hawke has the fourth fief," said Leo, and he and the armorer exchanged another look. "Is it possible that you haven't heard about him?"

Guy Hawke? I opened my mouth but no words came out. Still holding the war hammer, I walked slowly over to the door of the armory and stared out at the edge of the thousands of miles of deep woods that held me virtually a prisoner in that kingdom. There was no longer any mystery about the situation. All the answers to all the puzzles came crashing together in the same horrible instant.

Yes, I had certainly earned my prize as the most gullible of chumps back to the beginning of chump time, but I understood it all now. Everything all the way back to Rudy Strapp's rather unconventional way of making sure I took Albert up on his invitation to a little study break at the old homestead.

I laid the war hammer nonchalantly across my shoulder like a giant in a fairy tale, and turned back to the room. Whatever look was on my face at that moment must have been a scary sight because both men took a defensive step backwards.

"So what else hast thou, O Don, for my protection and self-preservation?" I asked.

We all understood that there was more to be said, but they gave me the time I needed to get ready. "Well," said the armorer, "there is an extra something that I made up special. Slip off your tunic and try this on for size."

It was an undervest of chain mail, heavy but not excessively so. It must have taken great patience to fit those tiny rings together. "Thanks, Don," I said, smiling through the heavy fog of my thoughts. I was touched by his skill and his thoroughness, his concern for someone he had only just met. And as the truth of my situation was sinking in, I also felt grateful for anything that would make me feel safer.

"The next thing on the list," continued the armorer, "is your battle axe. You'll see quite a few of those out there. They are very handy for getting in the firewood." A short, double-edged version of the ancient weapon, it was economical in size, but sharp and heavy enough to chop a man in half. There was a small round shield of leather and steel, and heavy leather gloves with steel strips in strategic places. To top it off, there was a light helm just low enough on the sides to cover the ears. It had a nose guard but no visor. "That's all for now," he said. "Your saddle has slings for your gear, so it will all be conveniently at hand."

I felt very strange indeed. Reality had not caught up with me, and I could only experience myself as a character in a story or in a dream. "Gentlemen," I began haltingly, "you may have noticed that I was surprised to hear about this Lord Hawke. Would that by any chance be Guy Hawke, who went to school with the king?"

"I'm not sure of the first name," said Leo. "But, yes, I think that might be it. What do you say, Don?"

The armorer looked uncertain. "Yes," he said finally, "I believe that's right. And it's for sure he went to high school with the king, just like Lord Griswold and Lord Dugdale."

I had been hoping and praying that it wasn't so, but now the truth resounded in my mind like the slamming of a heavy iron door.

"And this Lord Hawke—I'm just guessing now, gentlemen—this Lord Hawke is causing some problem, shall we say, in the kingdom. Am I on the right track?"

"I'm shocked that nobody has told you about this," said Leo.

"Inexcusable," echoed the armorer.

"Yes, well, okay, but this is the big question now, gentlemen. Did someone have the crazy notion that somehow I was going to do something about whatever problem Lord Hawke is creating?"

"The mage saw it in her cards," said the armorer. There was no irony in his tone or expression; it was obvious that he had nothing but respect for Marya and her prescience.

"Well, I suppose that's enough of a surprise for right now," I said, meaning that I felt like any minute my brain was going to start bleeding. "I think you said there was some way to put all this stuff on my horse. Could you show me how to do that, please?"

While we were saddling my horse and Sir Leo was showing me how to sling my armaments so as to make them most comfortable and accessible, I was trying to pay attention; but it was difficult because my thoughts were in such a turmoil. *Do you still ride well? Do you still fence? You used to be a real champion.*

"Are you still going on quest?" Leo asked me.

You really don't have any idea what's going on here, do you? "Yes, I suppose so. I need to do some thinking alone. I don't want to see the king right now."

"I cannot tell you . . ." Leo began.

"Yes, yes," I said, putting up my hand. "Let it be. What's done is done." I wasn't feeling stoic or forgiving. I just didn't want to talk about it.

"Well, mount up then," said Leo. "There's one more thing I need to show you. Ha, ha! It's a little harder getting aboard when you're wearing all that iron, isn't it? Never mind, you can do it. Up you go! Now pay attention. Pollux is a real war-horse. He's had some very special training. Get a good grip on him now. Make sure you're set." Leo dropped his voice to a rough whisper. "Now yell: Albert!"

"Albert!" I yelled, and Pollux sprang forward so suddenly that it took everything I had to keep from going backwards over his tail. By the time I had regained my seat, he was running at a full gallop. Some Pollux! He was so possessed that it was difficult to turn him. We galloped in a wide circle and came back to where Leo was standing. I waggled my head in appreciation, and Leo laughed. "I guess that's what you call a charger," I said.

"Exactly right. He's a real charger. Have a good quest, Sir Jack! Here's a little bag of gold, though you probably won't need it. Everyone likes Albert's knights and everyone will be glad to see you coming. But keep your wits about you if you cross into Lord Hawke's fief. You have every right to be there, but sometimes his soldiers don't act that way. Don't let them intimidate you. Remember that you ride for the high king."

I jiggled the little bag of gold in my hand. "And Leo, what about the Picts? Can you tell me . . . Oh, never mind," I said, as this look of total perplexity spread over his face. "Sorry I asked. I'll just have a look for myself. Good-bye, thanks for everything. See you in a few days."

"Good-bye, my friend," he waved. "May God go with you!"

As I rode away the absurdity of my whole situation broke

131

upon me like a wave. I began to giggle and chuckle insanely, and my laughter made my armor jingle in counterpoint to the rhythm of my horse. You may have noticed that people who are sure of themselves and focused on what they are doing have little sense of humor; a little now and again, but not much. I think a real sense of humor is the main safety valve for people who lead erratic or desperate lives. It protects them from insanity and despair.

I was riding slowly and aimlessly, and I hadn't gone far before I came across Marya Mage. She was out of breath, and she had been looking for me.

"There's something I need to tell you before you ride out on quest."

"I already heard."

"Are you angry?"

"I just heard about it. I don't know what I feel. Whatever possessed that fathead king of yours to let Guy Hawke into his kingdom?" No, what I said wasn't true. I felt angry as hell.

Marya put a finger to her lips—I was not to express disrespect for the king. Then she beckoned me off my horse. "All right," I said. "What's the story?"

Marya led me into the privacy of a nearby grove. "It's an old story, Jack. It takes a lot of money to set up a kingdom like this, and Guy Hawke had a lot of money to kick in. That's why he's a duke instead of a marquess like Bennett, or an earl like Griswold. It's just the history of the world repeating itself."

"But . . ."

"Listen, I'll tell you how it was. Duke Hawke didn't do so badly in the beginning. In fact, you could say we owe him a great deal. That's what makes it complicated. You see, in the early days of the kingdom, when Albert was trying to put the pieces of this puzzle together—well, they didn't fit together very well. There was something missing, and you know what it was? Albert really didn't know how to be a king. He didn't know how to command. He was too nice, too obliging. He wanted people to do what he told them to because they understood and agreed with him. So there was too much delay when decisions had to be made, and it started to get chaotic here. Little factions formed among the farmers, and there was hostility and even a few violent encounters between them. The whole project was about to come unglued."

"He was always too sweet for his own good. I'm amazed by the change in him."

"According to Albert, it was Guy Hawke who pulled it all together during that crisis. He knew how to act, and he knew what to do. He *is* a medieval man, Jack. You'll see that when you meet him. He might never have lived in the modern age at all, so little of it shows in his personality. Anyway, he kicked some butts, and he cracked some heads; he had the dungeon dug under the castle, and he taught Albert how to be a king."

"So what's the problem?"

"The problem is that now we have the social order and the kingdom functioning smoothly and the people are about as happy as people are likely to be. So Lord Hawke doesn't have any butts to kick. The problem is, Jack, that underneath his good qualities he's really an unhappy and rather brutal man, and he's the one person in this kingdom Albert has no control over."

"Why doesn't Albert stick him in the dungeon? That's the cure-all around here, isn't it?"

"Jack, maybe he should have but he hasn't. I don't want to say he doesn't dare, but you'll understand it better when you meet Lord Hawke."

"So you went to your oracle and the Tarot told you to import Jack, the bully-buster. Is that the story in a nutshell?"

"More or less."

"And Albert didn't bother to tell me about any of this because if he had, I never would have come here in the first place."

"That's part of it."

"And because once I was here, I was trapped here anyway."

"No," she told me. And suddenly I saw, for the first time I guess, the real Mage Marya that wasn't a college co-ed anymore—no, not by a long shot! Her eyes had turned into steel ball bearings, and I was taking an involuntary step backwards when she reached out and took me by the collar and yanked me in close.

"No, you're wrong about that. We didn't tell you until now because we wanted you to have a chance to fall in love with this kingdom, which happens to be the nicest kingdom that ever was."

She had me pulled in very tight, but I wasn't trying to get away because I was too busy admiring what a lot of raw power she had developed.

"And here's the bottom line, Jack. We've got a desperate problem here, and my oracle, my Goddess, thinks you can help us somehow. But if you're not up for this—if you haven't got the sand—then I will take you to the king and I will move heaven and earth, Jack, to get you back out through those woods and get you a nice limousine ride back to your crappy little cottage in Marysville!"

She let me go then; and if you don't think I felt totally crazy, you have to remember that I was dressed from head to foot as a medieval warrior, and with what I had on my horse thrown in, I was carrying about two hundred pounds of armor and weapons and standing in the middle of some impossible kingdom on the farthest edge of reality. I wasn't in any state to make a rational decision about anything, but in my gut I knew that going back to Marysville wasn't an option, whether or not that could be accomplished anyway. The life I had left behind didn't seem attractive or even real anymore. It was more like a half-remembered dream. The only solid ground I had in the world was right under my feet. I couldn't say that I was actually in love with Albert's kingdom, but I was certainly intrigued and amazed by what I had already seen, and I had been anxious to begin my quest because I wanted to see more. So I knew in my gut that my course was set, dangerous as it obviously now appeared to be.

"So what exactly has Duke Bully-boy been up to that no one seems to know what to do about?"

"He's doing what he likes best, I guess, and that's making people afraid of him. There's a shadow over his fief, an apprehensiveness, as though his peasants are worried that they might accidentally do something wrong and have to pay dearly for it. I'm not saying every single person feels that way, but it's like a disease, this fear, and if it keeps spreading, God help us all."

"What does he do that makes people afraid?"

"He does it just by looking at them. He's very good at that. He threatens people with his eyes. But that's not all, of course. He has a mean bailiff who follows his example, and a spineless reeve who—"

"A which and a what?"

"A bailiff is an overseer. The reeve is a peasant chosen by the peasants to represent them in councils. But the Duke's reeve is too cowed to speak up. The worst of it is the way he recruits his soldiers. Each of the fiefs has different soldiery, and this reflects the lord's personality. Albert's soldiers are the best. They're the most helpful and the most responsible because that's what Albert wants and expects of them."

"I know one of them. His name is Gordon. He's a pip."

"Isn't he? I love Gordon. Well, the duke's soldiers are all little buckoes because that's what he promotes in them."

"And Albert says nothing?"

"Albert does not say nothing, but Lord Hawke is not good at listening. He is quick to recall that his own strict methods held the kingdom together at one time; then he will turn around and attack Albert for being soft on the Picts."

"What says Duke Hawke about the Picts?"

"That they should be driven away. Killed if necessary. It's horrible!"

"Tell me more about these soldiers. What do they do exactly, Guy Hawke's buckoes?"

"They are up in people's faces when they have no reason to be. They stop peasants on the market road without cause, search their wagons, help themselves to a snack. Sometimes they say things to the women, even paw them."

"What, in front of the men?"

"Sometimes. It's getting worse every season."

"And what do the men do?"

"They have to put up with it. The duke's soldiers are heavily armed and they always travel in pairs. And there's no excuse for it, Jack. They don't have to be so heavily armed. No one is going to bother them. In fact, there's no trouble or danger in the whole kingdom compared to those soldiers themselves. Last year two of the peasants mixed it up with them. I'm not sure exactly how it got started, but there was a ruckus and the soldiers killed one of the peasants and crippled the other. He walks with a limp now, and of course it's his word against theirs. Albert spoke to Lord Hawke about it, but as usual Lord Hawke was not very receptive. He said he would keep an eye on the two soldiers concerned; but what he did was make them his personal guard, so it was actually a promotion. After that, his other soldiers began to behave even worse."

While she was talking I could feel my jaw tighten, and I knew my temper was coming up. I have never gone out of my way to look for trouble, but at the same time I have always had a hard place in my heart for bullies. I guess each of us has something that he especially dislikes, something that seems impossible to tolerate. Heavily armed bullies that traveled in pairs . . .

"Well, Marya," I said, "I got up this morning to go on quest, and that's what I'm going to do."

She walked me to my horse and I clambered aboard in my warlike duds. "Be careful, Jack."

"What a funny thing to say!" I nudged Pollux into a trot.

At first I was feeling very grim as I rode along, headed nowhere with no idea which way I ought to go. But it was a beautiful day and everything I saw was new and interesting. The people that I passed on the road waved and spoke greetings and regarded me with a curiosity that I now understood. I was the one who had been chosen by the mage's Tarot cards. I was a celebrity although I had done nothing to deserve it, and that gave me a funny feeling that is difficult to describe, as if I had turned into a character in a story. It was an exciting and expansive feeling; but there was, of course, a catch.

Where was I going? It didn't really matter. If I turned around, I could ride past the monastery, turn south on the market road at the bridge, and head for Griswold Manor. But I was not in the mood for Griswold. It occurred to me then to pay a visit to the Earl and Lady Dugdale. I was curious to see how the nobility lived and I could pick up some more information about the situation in the kingdom.

Soon I came upon a man who was digging dirt out of the

road and putting it into his ox-cart, and didn't he give me a funny look when I asked him where to find Dugdale's manor. "Why, you're the king's new knight, aren't you?" he said, laughing. "It'll be something to tell the missus that someone asked me the way to Lord Dugdale's today. She'll never believe me."

He chuckled away about that, and I waited patiently for him to have his joke. "Well, where is it then?"

He pointed in the direction I was going. "You're almost there," he said.

"Thank you, my good man," I said. "Why are you digging up the road?"

"I need this clay for my mill."

"That's quite a hole you're making. Don't you think that's dangerous?" It was right at the bend of the road, and a man or a horse could have easily stumbled into it.

He looked at the hole and made a helpless gesture. "But where else will I find such good clay?"

"I don't know, but you'd better get that hole filled up before you leave."

He began to squirm, as though it was an impossible amount of trouble I wanted him to go to. "All right, all right, I will," he grumbled finally.

I didn't really believe he would, but I had done about all I could, so I tapped Pollux with my heel and continued down the road. Presently I came to a pretty little bridge, the most ornate of all the bridges I'd yet seen in that valley of many rivers, and on the other side of the bridge hung a carved wooden escutcheon about four feet high with a coat of arms and DUGDALE carved across the top.

Dugdale's fief looked different; it had a different flavor. As soon as I crossed the bridge I noticed it; it didn't seem to me that the landscape was perfectly natural. Especially around the bridge it looked more like a park than a woods, and as I continued north on the other side of the river I had the same impression that some serious landscaping had been attempted in certain spots. It would be something to make conversation about, and maybe to tease Charlsey with, for who else but she would have wanted to refine the woods that way.

Their manor house, made of fieldstone and timbers with a wall all around, also had a stylish look for a fortified building, and a great deal of care had gone into the flower gardens. Then I got a rather bad twinge of time-vertigo, for there was Charlsey kneeling among her flowers wearing a straw hat and gloves with a little trowel in one hand. The long skirt she wore barely maintained the medieval integrity that I was beginning to cherish and I felt annoyed at her for looking so modern. My impulse was to turn my horse quietly and slip away unnoticed, but I didn't make up my mind quickly enough.

"Sir Jack!" cried Charlsey, jumping to her feet and coming to greet me. "I'm so glad you came. Alton, guess who is here!" she shouted into the house. All the shutters seemed to open at once and several unfamiliar faces poked out to see the novelty. Before I knew it I was having tea and cakes with Charlsey and Dugdale in the garden, my sword with its scabbard and harness leaning against the hedge.

"This is such a pleasure," said Charlsey. "You can't imagine how tedious it can get without any society. Don't you think so, Alton? Actually, Alton has quite a lot to keep up with running the earldom, so I don't think he gets quite as lonesome as I do. It's better in the winter when there's less to do and people go visiting more. But at this time of year it's all work, work, work, and no one seems to consider their social obligations."

"You looked busy in your garden when I rode up," I said.

Charlsey had been going on a mile a minute since I arrived, and it was making me a little tense. She wanted a lot of attention and she made you feel obliged to give it to her. Also, try as you might to change her train of thought, it always came back to this: however much she might sugarcoat it with her pretty smile and her stylized vivaciousness, Charlsey was sorry she had come.

"Well, I do love my gardens, that's true. My mother was a fine gardener, and *her* mother was a gardener—a flower gardener, you understand—and they both took prizes in shows."

"You've won several prizes at the fair, my dear," said Dugdale proudly.

"Thank you, Alton. I am trying to carry on the tradition. One of the reasons I agreed to come all the way out here, Sir Jack, was that my family lacked land. Mother was always saying she could do with a bit more land. We had quite a substantial lot for Cambridge, but it was still only a couple of acres, and mother felt limited. So when we were considering becoming part of the peerage here, the promise of unlimited land quite made me lose my reason."

"How much land have you got?" I asked Dugdale.

"I don't know," said Dugdale. "We share a border with Lord Hawke and another with the royal domain. But our land to the northwest keeps going right up into the mountains, if you want to look at it that way. The amount of land you have up here really has no significance. What matters are the people you have to work it."

"My lady," said a servant, "will you pick out a chicken?"

"Cook can do that, Betty."

"Cook sent me to ask if your ladyship would be pleased to pick which one you like."

"Well, I suppose the red hen," said Charlsey.

140

"There are three red hens, your ladyship."

"Not that I recall," said Charlsey after a pause.

"If your ladyship would be pleased . . ."

"Oh, I'll come! Alton, why don't you give Sir Jack a tour while I see to this."

Charlsey went off with the servant and Dugdale showed me the stables and the falconry and the buttery and the wine cellar and the central hall and something he called the solar, which was a big bedroom and den above the hall.

"Albert really didn't let you smuggle in a thing, did he?"

"No. He was very strict. Everything you see was made right here in this valley. And yet we have some beautiful things, do we not?"

"Was this manor designed by Joel Mason?"

"Oh yes, of course. He designed the whole kingdom. Anything made since his death naturally follows his style since his are the only models to copy. His signature will be on the kingdom as long as it lasts."

"It seems built to last forever."

"The Middle Ages didn't last forever. It was a transition period between the fall of Rome and the rise of other empires."

"Do you miss the modern world?"

"Do I miss it? No, I can't truthfully say I do. This is our busiest season right now, and I'm feeling harried looking after everything, but mostly I'm content. Charlsey, on the other hand . . . Well, sometimes I feel like I've taken her away from everything she really loves: fashion and art and society."

"Had to be dragged here kicking and screaming, did she?"

Dugdale gave me an odd look. "Oh goodness, no," he said. "I would never ask Charlsey to do anything she wouldn't like to do. She was actually more enthusiastic about coming here than I was. I think the opportunity to be a titled lady was the attraction for her in the beginning, along with the amount of land. We were to be neighbors to a king! But I don't think she understood how much she'd be leaving behind."

Dugdale and I walked back to the garden without speaking. He seemed lost in his own thoughts, as was I.

Charlsey had changed into a different gown for lunch. Dugdale was wearing a long robe, belted with an elaborate dagger, and a short jacket with puff sleeves. It felt to me like we were all in costume, and it was the first time I had felt that way since I'd arrived in Albert's kingdom. Perhaps it was the way the garden was arranged, but it didn't feel far from Cambridge; and I was already wishing that our visit was over so I could get back on my horse and soak myself in those new, heavy-textured feelings that my new life evoked in me.

"You would think," said Charlsey with some asperity, "that they could pick out a chicken without having to pester me. You would think they could prepare a simple wine sauce without my having to tell them how for the fiftieth time, but they can't. You'll notice soon enough how complacent the servants are in this kingdom, Sir Jack. You can send them back to the fields and pick someone else, but it does no good for they are all the same. They would rather wait for you to tell them what to do than to just do what needs to be done."

"Alton, tell me what you think," I said. "I passed a man digging clay out of the road not far from here. He said he wanted the clay for his mill."

"Oh, that man!" said Charlsey.

"A fat fellow? Clean shaven with black, spiky hair?"

"That's him," I said.

"Thank you for telling me. The king said that if he leaves

another hole in the road, he's going into the dungeon, and it's about time."

"There is simply no reasoning with some of these peasants," said Charlsey. "I would like to see that man dig up the road in Lord Hawke's fief."

"What would happen if he did that?" I asked.

"The duke would have him beaten black and blue," said Charlsey. "We've been much too lenient with that miller, Alton."

"Would Lord Hawke be within his rights to beat up that man?" I asked.

After a moment or two Dugdale said, "Lord Hawke is rather more strict that we are."

"But would he be within his rights?"

"The man will probably not get the beating because he will know better than to ask for it."

"But indulge me for a minute, Alton, if you would. I'm new here and I don't even know what the laws are."

"Well, you don't have much to learn there, because there aren't any laws."

I was amazed. "No laws?"

"There are rules," said Dugdale, "but there is no legal system as such with written statutes and all the rest of it. If something out of the ordinary comes up, we talk it over among the nobility and make a decision. Otherwise, everyone knows what the rules are. No cows in the corn. No diverting of streams. No fighting in the church. Simple, common-sense rules. They don't need to be written down."

We ate in silence. "But there must be disputes," I said finally.

Dugdale smiled wanly. "There are. All the time."

"What happens then?"

He shrugged. "That depends."

"All right. Here's an example. A man has bought and paid for a cow. The previous owner is delivering it and the cow drops dead in the road. Does the new owner get his money back?"

"Of course. Isn't it obvious that he should?"

"Okay. The cow drops dead in the new owner's barn the morning after she's delivered. Does he get his money back?"

"Probably not."

"What does probably mean? What's the rule?"

"How could you make such a rule? Let's you and I make up a rule right now: a cow is considered to be sold in fair exchange if the animal lives for two hours and forty-five minutes after the tether rope passes from hand to hand. Don't you see how absurd that is?"

"So how would a dispute get settled?"

"If people absolutely cannot come to terms, the matter can be brought before the manor court. The court meets four times a year."

"And how do decisions get made?"

"According to what his lord thinks is just and fair."

"But . . ."

"Look, Jack—may I call you Jack? It's just the three of us. Suppose a cow dies in the course of the trading that goes on between peasants all the time. It wouldn't go to the manor court. Whoever got the worst of the deal would try to do better the next time, that's all. But suppose someone passes off a sick cow on an old widow woman, a woman whose eyesight is known to be poor. If she complained to my court about that, then she would get her money back and also collect a fine from the man to teach him to be kinder to old women. That's the way

I would look at it. My responsibility would be to do the best I could for the old woman, and at the same time to discourage the man from taking advantage of people. Now if there were two men who kept coming to my court with disputes about cows, I would fine them both for wasting everyone's time, and I would give some of their cows to someone who needed them more than they did. Do you begin to see?"

I wasn't sure what to think. "It's like parents deciding which child gets to play with the toy."

Dugdale laughed. "I think that's a reasonable comparison. Yes, it's the family approach to government, if you like, and it's the only way to run a kingdom like this. We can't afford a class of lawyers and lobbyists and legislators and a lot of *quid pro quo*. We have to get the harvest in. We have to keep food on the table."

Images passed through my mind of the active, happy-looking people I'd passed along the road when I rode in with Gordon, and the ringing cheers that had greeted Albert when he arrived at his castle. "Well," I said finally, "I haven't been here for long, and so far I'm impressed with what I've seen. It feels funny to think that there are no laws here, though."

"Oh, I know. We all went through the same thing when we first came up here. But just sit down and try to write some laws yourself and you'll discover that that kind of litigiousness just doesn't make any sense in this situation. We're in a little valley on the edge of nowhere, and we'd be crazy to wait around for the innocent to be proven guilty beyond a reasonable doubt and all the rest of if before we could give someone who needs it a kick in the pants."

"Like that miller who was digging in the road."

Dugdale nodded. "People have had quite enough of falling into his holes."

"So if Lord Hawke caught the miller and beat the piss out of him, that would just be the way things are around here."

Dugdale and Charlsey looked at one another, and I read confusion in their faces.

"I don't know quite what to say, Jack. Each fief is a bit different. Griswold tends to be ironic about his responsibilities and he likes to see people hash things out for themselves. I also tend to hold back and try not to be too patriarchal. Bennett, as you may have heard, is a bit of a lush, and it's hard to know how he's going to behave. But his wife is a serious woman and she can be quite severe. The king himself has probably got the best mix. His peasants know just where they stand, and they like him enormously."

I waited for him to go on, but he didn't. "You forgot somebody."

"Well, Lord Hawke is certainly a man of parts," said Dugdale. "There was a time when we couldn't possibly have done without him. Overall though, one could say that he tends to use the club where the switch would do just as well. Wouldn't you say so, my dear?"

"His peasants are very well-behaved," said Charlsey.

"That's true," said Dugdale, "but they are also too much in the shadow."

I felt chilly, though the sun was shining in the garden, and a shiver ran through my body. "Come on, Dugdale, quit being so diffident and lay it on me, would you please?"

Charlsey raised an eyebrow, but Dugdale continued. "There was an ugly incident last year during tithe collection. A soldier or two always accompanies the collector. It's a lonely job at best. Well, there was some kind of a misunderstanding, and one of the peasants was killed and another crippled. As soon as the king heard about it, he went to see what was what, and the duke told the king to mind his own business."

146

"I was stuffed in the dungeon for less than that," I said.

Dugdale nodded. "Yes, it's very much against the rules to get cheeky with the king. But Albert had only a small escort and the duke was surrounded by his own soldiers on his own land."

"Albert backed down?"

"Albert was very angry. He went back to his castle, and he was gathering his soldiers when a messenger came from the duke. He said he would make restitution to the peasant's family and reprimand the soldiers, but that he would regard any armed incursion by the king as an act of war."

"Did Albert let him get away with that?"

"The king replied that if the duke kept faith by making restitution to the peasants, then he, Albert, would make no reprisals as long as it never happened again."

"So Albert chickened out."

"Well, maybe it sounds like an obvious mistake to you, but that was a difficult year in many ways. The harvest was poor. Tempers were frayed. Relations between the fiefs were tense at best. No one wanted to see a war break out between the duke and the king."

"What happened then?"

"That was all there was to that. The duke made the family a gift of money and took responsibility for the mistake. There was also the implied promise that he would keep his soldiers in line, and that was very important, for this was just the worst of a long string of complaints about the way his soldiers behaved."

"But from what I hear, his soldiers are still out of control."

Dugdale sighed. "Yes, I'm afraid so."

"Worse than ever?"

He nodded.

Again I felt that chilly, tingling feeling all through my body: a kind of raw excitement, a mustering of dark energies deep within my bones. *Do you still ride well? Do you still fence?* Yes, Albert, I do, and I still can't stand bullies. All of a sudden I had a longing to strap my sword back on and to feel the strange, embracing heft of my armor. Was I losing the little bit of good sense that I had? Was I looking forward to the trouble that I now distinctly felt was right around the bend?

"Enough about all that, Alton," said Charlsey. "I'm sure Sir Jack doesn't want to talk about politics all day." She looked at me for confirmation and I replied with a shrug. It was her teapot.

Dugdale was watching her with a peculiar expression. He seemed happy that she was getting a chance to be social and hold forth, but at the same time he looked concerned. She seemed like a child who was too tired to play, but having too much fun to go down for a nap.

"I noticed when I came over that bridge that you were doing some landscaping. Maybe we could ride by after lunch and take another look at it." My sly intention, of course, was to make some excuse once I was mounted, and get out of there as fast as I could.

"Thank you for noticing," said Charlsey, but a dark look passed across her face. Something in the way Dugdale shifted in his chair, also gave me the impression I'd said the wrong thing.

"I tried," Charlsey went on, "I *tried*, but our peasants didn't want to cooperate, you see. What is the use of all this land, I would say to them, if it's just left to the confusion of nature? Overgrown woods with everything every which way and no aesthetic arrangement. But I could never win their enthusiasm—never! If I asked them to transplant a tree, they

148

did it grudgingly, and it took them forever! You can't imagine how I had to keep after them to accomplish even the little bit that I did." Her hands were opening and closing into fists in her frustration, and Dugdale was looking even more concerned. "Then King Albert asked me to forego my projects, saying that it wasn't *appropriate* to try to enroll our peasants in that kind of work. They had actually gone and complained about me to the king—*complained* about me for trying to create a little beauty amongst all this fecundity! The king said it wasn't part of their responsibility to the fief to help me develop my walks and parks. Well, what could I say to the king? And so I stopped, and they can all go to the devil before I will ever lift another finger—"

"Now, darling," said Dugdale, who had gone behind her chair and was stroking her shoulders with his long, white hands, "Sir Jack admires what you were trying to do, and I certainly appreciate all the beauty you bring into our lives. Why, look at these lovely flower gardens, and think of all the prizes you've won at the fairs."

Charlsey was looking confused now, and one of her hands went to her forehead. Then she clutched her head with both hands and let out a little scream, short and sharp. "Oh, no," she mumbled. "Oh, no."

Dugdale called one of his servants out of the house and they helped her out of her chair. "I'm *so* sorry," said Charlsey.

"Never mind, darling, let's get you into the house. These things happen. It's nobody's fault."

"Is there anything I can do?" I said, but Dugdale shook his head.

I picked at my salad and waited. It wasn't long before Dugdale came back, but it was just to say goodbye. "I hope you don't mind," he said, "but when this happens I need to stay with her. Please come see us again soon, won't you? It's very good for Charlsey to have company. What happened today was unusual. You won't be put off by it, will you?"

"It's okay, Alton," I said. "I hope she feels better."

Pretty soon I was jingling down the road in full armor, heading nowhere in particular, and feeling uncomfortable and disoriented. My time-sense was totally confused, and I couldn't seem to get settled down in the past or the present or wherever I was. My time with Dugdale had brought up feelings and images from my boyhood, and Charlsey had done her best to conjure up the sophisticated world that she missed so much. All that in medieval costumes with modern table manners was too much of a hotchpotch for my poor brain to handle, so I just rode along feeling insane.

I passed the bridge with the Dugdales' escutcheon, but instead of crossing the river I continued in a southerly direction down the road on the west side of the river. After a while, the weight of my armor and the rhythm of my horse began to make me feel more grounded. I was one of Albert's knights in the New Middle Ages. I was out on quest in a beautiful valley where life was so simple that no one bothered to write down the rules. Sword, horse, road, rock, trees, sky, wind: that was all there was.

The many smells of the world began to surround me; my armor tugged down on my shoulders, making me feel heavy and solid and real. Birds sang to me. My state of mind continued to improve.

Now I began to feel a little sleepy, and I was just nodding off, my chin in my chest, when Pollux stopped dead in his tracks and then took a couple of steps backwards. Glancing up from my reverie, I let out a gasp of amazement. I had wondered about them, and asked people about them to no avail. Well, there they were, right in front of me.

Chapter Eight

They stood there in their masks, without moving a muscle, radiating a presence unlike anything I had ever encountered in my life. It was no longer a mystery why people grew tongue-tied in their attempts to describe the Picts!

The largest one was a brown bear; standing on his hind legs, he looked about seven feet tall. I could see little of the human inside, only the mask, which was made out of everything in the forest: vines, bark, grass, furs, mud, stones, leaves, and flowers.

Very majestic he was, this bear, a real king of the forest. There was a challenge in his manner, but it wasn't menacing, for he was a very artistic and marvelous bear. What a lot of patience and creativity it must have taken to make a bear mask out of twigs and leaves and wildflowers! I stared into the bear's eyes, but they were only polished stones.

The mouse was tiny, about four feet high. Only a child or a midget could have inhabited that mask. The body was motionless but the little nose seemed to be twitching, the whiskers sensitive to every current of air. I thought, *Oh, mouse, what are you trying to tell me?* For something was definitely coming across, something they were all projecting.

The wolf sat on his haunches, keen ears pricked to the wind. Someone's eyes were watching me from the back of that open mouth full of sharp, white teeth. What did this wolf of wildflowers want with me?

There were two other creatures, very much alike, but I had no idea what they were supposed to represent. They might have been extraterrestrials, or forest spirits, or abstract art, but they had been just as painstakingly created. This pair was standing together at the center of the grouping, flanked by bear, mouse, and wolf a few yards to either side; they were all radiating the same mysterious, unspoken message. All my senses and my intuition told me so, and the little hairs on the back of my neck stood up like antennae trying to pick up whatever these Picts were broadcasting.

I nudged Pollux forward. "What is it? What do you want?" I called softly. I felt like I was trying to talk to the forest itself. What do you say to the forest? What would the forest be trying to say to me?

Then I began to hear music. It was just a few notes, such as might have come from a wooden flute. Now there was a bit of melody, very crude, like a small child playing on the piano with one finger.

The Picts began to move now, but I know no words to describe their movements. They weren't swaying, and they weren't stretching, and they certainly weren't dancing. It was very subtle, as if they were responding to currents of energy or emotion within their bodies stirred up by the music, the way water does to wind by rising in waves.

The music continued in primitive, unresolved phrases, and now the Picts were moving toward me, ever so slowly, and in a meandering way. I wasn't worried. I didn't feel like I was being stalked, or tricked. I simply felt amazed and intrigued by that dreamlike spectacle.

Soon the music stopped. The Picts were quite close to me now, surrounding me on three sides. If I leaned out of my saddle, I could have touched the bear.

From the forest stepped a figure, unmasked and scarcely

152

dressed at all except for a garment of leaves and flowers, hardly more then a sash that draped across one shoulder. The figure was barefoot and graceful with long gray hair and piercing green eyes in a face that was lean and lined. One hand held those simple pipes we associate with antiquity and the forest god. In my dreamy state I felt neither afraid nor skeptical. Rather, I felt willing for any kind of encounter, whether with man or god.

Holding the pipes lightly to one side, he danced. Without tempo or style, it was like a tree being blown around in a gusty wind. Across the strip of meadow he danced toward me, forward and back, side to side, closer and closer. The leafy sash began to fall away. As he turned, it unwrapped itself until the last loop dropped away, and the god danced naked.

Or goddess? For the god had a woman's breasts, creased and pendulous, that swayed as she moved. But my perception of her continued to shift back and forth, because now I saw that she also had a man's genitals flipping around between his legs as he went stepping and swaying past me. He was heading for the trees on the opposite side of the meadow from which he'd appeared. I gave a tug on the reins and turned Pollux in a half circle; I could not take my eyes off this apparition.

Suddenly he stopped, his fists on his hips, and stared at me, his bright green eyes blazing into mine with energy and merriment and clarity. He looked me up and down, horse and all, and shook his head; and then he looked me up and down again, as though I was a most astonishing and peculiar sight indeed. Now he looked into my eyes once more. It was a very warm and friendly look. And then he let out a shriek of laughter and ran as fast as he could across the meadow, still laughing, until he disappeared into the trees.

I sat in the saddle, stunned and witless. After a time, I turned to look over one shoulder, and then the other; and then

I turned Pollux around in a full circle looking for the Picts who were no longer there. I was all alone in the middle of that empty meadow. Lying on the earth was the sash of leaves and flowers that had been worn by the god.

Dismounting in a daze, I picked up the sash, made a coil of it, and struggled back into the saddle. My armor and weapons seemed to weigh more than ever. When I had secured the sash to one of the saddle straps, I nudged Pollux to a walk.

Why I wanted the god's apparel, or whether I wanted it or not, I had no idea. My mind was quite blank. I was one of Albert's knights riding out on quest, carrying all these weapons because that was what knights did. But beyond those simple facts there was a void. All the things I had been wondering about and worrying over had been erased from my mind. I was content just to sit on Pollux's back as he walked up the road.

The sky was blue, the air was fresh, the leaves trembled in the breeze. My name was Jack. Why was I carrying all these weapons around? Why was I wearing an iron undershirt? If I made a mask out of leaves and flowers, what would it be?

A fox. I had a cherished memory of a real fox that had run in the open back door of my house, glanced once at me, and run out again. That was the whole experience, but it made a permanent impression on me because I had never seen anything so light on its feet and so impossibly fast. Any dog would have slid halfway across that slippery floor, windmilling and falling down in a heap before it got itself turned around. But this fox never touched the floor, I'm certain of that. It was riding a lightning bolt; time and space meant nothing.

Yes, I would be a fox, eat mice, snatch chickens, and be one of the moon's minions. At moonrise I would don my garb of wildflowers and cruise the night world on feet that never touched the ground.

It was pleasant to be out of touch with reality on such a beautiful day. I was just a man on a horse headed up a road that could have led anywhere at all. Then a delightful perfume began to insinuate itself on my awareness, but where was it coming from? Back in the days when I was first discovering that girls had different smells of their own, I went with a girl who smelled so beautifully between her legs; and that same smell was in her hair and on her breath, and all over her body. The scent that was in the air reminded me of her.

My head was tilted back and I was trying to catch a good whiff of it, when I felt a little tug on my stirrup strap. When I glanced down, startled, there was a girl walking alongside my horse, and she was tugging on my stirrup leather to get my attention. Looking down at her from my horse, I could see down the front of her loose-fitting homespun dress to her round ripe breasts, pink nipples and all. She was looking up at me with friendly green eyes, unaware of the spectacle she was making of her lovely young bubs, and she said, "Hello."

"Hello," I said, quite surprised. I leaned over in my saddle to get a better whiff of her, and also to get the best possible view down the front of her dress. Her fragrance rose up to me like a whole field of roses and lilacs mixed with something more personal that made me feel quite wild.

She was small and young and barefoot, and her wavy blond hair fell to the middle of her back. I was in love with her already; but there was a problem, of course, because she couldn't possibly have been twenty years old yet, and I was very much older. I shouldn't even have been taking advantage of her inexperience by gazing down the front of her dress like that, but I couldn't tear my eyes away. And more than that, I was enveloped by the fragrance that was rising up from her body. In my own way, I was very ripe and innocent at that moment myself, and when she said, "Won't you stop?"—I did.

"Let me guess," I said, pretending to myself that I wanted to keep it light. "Your cat's up a tree and can't get down."

"Oh, no," she said with a pleasant smile. "We had a cat, but we had to eat it last winter."

I wasn't sure what to say. "How was it?"

"Not so bad," she said. Then she made a little face and tugged on my stirrup strap again.

I was enjoying the view I had from my saddle, but she seemed to know what she wanted, and I wanted to be polite. When I slid off my horse, she was right up against me, a little over five feet tall and smiling brightly, the tips of her breasts almost touching my tunic. The perfume from her body was seeping into my brain like some intoxicating incense, and my high sense of ethics was like a little ship tossed on a raging sea of lust.

Her hand came up and rested gently on my chest. I sensed the softness of it right through the chain mail. "Aren't you hot in that armor?"

She's just a child. My dazed conscience was trying to rally support, but it was no use. "Yes, actually, I *am* a trifle warm."

"Here's some shade," she said, taking my hand and leading me to an intimate grassy glade. She had to help me tie up my horse because I couldn't manage a knot. "You're the new knight everyone is talking about."

"Well, not exactly new," I began. "I've been here almost a week."

That made her laugh, and she went right to work helping me off with my sword belt. When she was finished she sat down in front of me in such a way that I could look down the front of her dress again.

"Nice, eh?" she said. I think she was referring to the glade.

"Very nice indeed." I knew I wasn't doing the right thing, but I couldn't help it. She was gazing at me in such an open and defenseless way, and I was staring at her like a hungry bum at a bakery window.

"It's all right," she said. "No one will bother us here."

That was all I needed to hear. I kissed her and undressed her and admired her and took my time petting her. And when she was very ready for me, I was a very naughty knight-errant. That I was!

She was quite passive, but that seemed to be a lack of experience, for she was certainly very responsive. She made all kinds of wonderful noises, which are always flattering to a man, and when we were done she rewarded me with that look of awed appreciation a girl will give you when you've shown her the way to a new kind of pleasure. She could have been a virgin except for one curious thing: her breasts were full of milk.

When I first noticed it, I was too busy ravishing her to pay much attention. The appearance of this sweet-smelling girl had been like a magical climax to my encounter with the Picts. Reality had taken a holiday and good riddance to it. But when I awoke from my happy and satisfied snooze in her arms, reality had returned, unbidden and unwelcome, along with that awful compulsion to rationalize everything.

What was the story with this girl-woman who had stopped me in the road and given herself to me without even telling me her name? There was nothing to do but ask her. But she was still sleeping on her back with her legs slightly spread, so exposed, so innocent, making no attempt to conceal or protect herself.

After a while she stirred, opened her eyes, and smiled at me. I helped her sit up, and held her close to me with one arm while I played with her breasts. When I squeezed them in a certain way, they dribbled, and I found it quite fascinating. She sat very still and watched me while I experimented.

"Will it squirt?" I asked.

"Sure."

"Make it squirt."

She took hold of her breast, said "Open your mouth," and gave it a tug. It certainly did squirt, but she missed the target, and now my face was dripping with milk. That set us both to laughing.

"Let's try the other one. Open wide now." She took aim and squirted a long jet of milk all over my face again, and we laughed until she got the hiccups. I liked her a lot. She was a pleasant, passionate lay, she smelled like the dream heaven of the hashish-eaters, and she knew how to have fun and get a laugh out of life.

The distant sound of a horn in the woods had some significance to the girl, for her manner changed when she heard it. Getting to her feet, she held out her hand. "Come," she said, and helped me up. She slipped her dress over her head, and that was all the difference there was between being naked and dressed. "It's time I went home and fed my baby. Will you come with me? I'll give you a nice hot lunch."

There was certainly nothing else I needed to do, and I was curious about her. She seemed a little too good to be true, giving me all her favors and a hot lunch to top it off. And what better way to find out more about Albert's kingdom than to go along with her? That was the purpose of my quest, wasn't it?

"All right," I said, pulling on clothes. Untying Pollux, I mounted and gave her a hand and a stirrup to climb up behind me. "That way," she said, pointing, and off we went down the market road. Her arms around my waist felt warm and soft.

We crossed a bridge and continued downstream on the other side. Pretty soon my nose told me we were coming into another settlement. There were a lot of things to smell in Albert's kingdom, and what I was noticing now was a mixture of cow dung and cooking smoke. Sure enough there were cultivated fields around the next bend in the river; and when we came to the first cart track leading away from the market road, the girl said, "Here we are."

It was a nice farm with a river view, but it seemed a bit run-down. The gate had two leather hinges, but the lower one was rotted away so that you had to lift the gate to pass through. Part of the walk had been cobbled with stones, but there were patches where they had sunk into the mud and hadn't been replaced.

"Don't mind the way the place looks," she said, as if she knew what I was thinking. "We've had kind of a hard time of it, now that it's just Mom and me."

Again I heard the sound of the horn, not quite so far away as before; when the girl heard it, she paused and seemed to be weighing something in her mind. I had assumed it was a signal from her people, but it came from farther down the road.

"I'm home, Mother," she said as we entered the house. It was pretty dark inside even with the shutters open, for the windows were small, and it smelled of wood smoke, animals, and vegetables. "How are you feeling?"

"Fine, fine," said a voice that sounded anything but fine. All I could see was a dark shape wrapped in a blanket sitting hunched in front of the hearth. The girl went over to her.

"It's chilly in here, Mother," the girl said softly. "I'll make up the fire for you. How's my baby?"

"Fine, fine," said the weak old voice.

"Come here, sweetie," said the girl, lifting her baby out of a cradle that hung suspended from the roof beam. "Oh, my, you're all wet, and you didn't even cry, you sweet thing! You're so good!"

"She cried," said the old woman without much interest. "I tried to . . ." But the voice trailed away.

I stood in the shadows looking around while the girl changed the baby, made up the fire, and hung a pot over it. She seemed very practiced and efficient, moving gracefully around in the room.

Now the horn sounded very close. I was about to step out the door to satisfy my curiosity when I felt her hand on my shoulder.

"That's Lord Hawke, and I need to pay my respects," she said, a hint of anxiety in her voice. Lord Hawke! The rush of adrenaline was a painful twinge. "Could you just wait for me here? I won't be long." She had tied her hair back and put on a scarf. As I understood it, she was asking me not to show myself.

"Okay," I said. "I'll just make myself at home." Out the door she went with her baby.

Lord Hawke! No, I didn't want him to see me yet, but I badly wanted to have a look at him. One of the windows faced the road, and there was a nice, big crack beside the half open shutter. There he was. Ah, Guy, I never would have recognized you.

It was not far to the market road where Hawke had reined in his charger, and I could see him clearly. His beard was similar to Albert's except that it was black. I had to admit that it became him. Marya was right: he looked every inch a medieval nobleman, one of the proud and cruel variety. The pride was evident in the way he sat his horse, the way he held his reins, and particularly in the way he held his head. Seated on his charger, he had taken a pose that said: *I am so much better than everyone else that it isn't even funny!*

The cruelty was reflected in his two bodyguards. They were dressed more or less like I was, and carried the same weapons—but these boys hadn't been recruited to rescue cats or damsels. They looked more like fierce dogs trained to run cats up trees, and people too. They sat low and hunched in their saddles like living reminders of what you could expect from Lord Hawke if you crossed him.

It made me angry to look at the three of them, all that pride wrapped up in the threat of violence. It made me feel like growling, as if I were a dog bred to snap back at dogs like that. As for Guy Hawke with that snotty look on his face, I wanted to sink my teeth in his butt and chase him down the road so people could see what he was really made of behind that mask of superiority.

The girl went down the path carrying the baby, stopped at the edge of the road, and dropped him a curtsy. But Hawke didn't respond with so much as a nod. His horse was facing straight up the road, and his head and eyes were turned barely enough to look down his nose at her.

She must have been saying something to him, though her back was turned to me. Then she held up the baby, as if for his inspection; but he continued to look down his nose, giving her no reaction of any kind. She lowered the baby, and rocked it in her arms.

They made quite a picture of medieval social order: she, small and barefoot and dressed in one layer of homespun cloth; he, tall and grand astride his charger, his face framed by a helm with a hawk for a device, its wings sweeping back over his ears. He wore a long surcoat, and the sword at his side looked to me like it might be a true broadsword. Even his charger had a horse-helm with a spike on its brow.

He produced a few coins, tossed them into the dirt in front of the girl, and nudged his charger to a walk. His two bodyguards followed immediately in his wake, but not without leering at the girl as they passed in a predatory way that made me want to charge out of the house on all fours.

The girl dropped another curtsy as the coins fell, bent to pick them up, and returned up the path. As far as I could understand it, she had hurried home at the sound of the horn to get a primitive welfare payment from the government which was making its rounds. Apparently that was why she didn't want me to be seen. I watched her face as she walked back to the house, and she didn't seem angry or upset to have coins tossed in the dirt by supercilious Guy Hawke and his leering henchmen. She seemed pleased to have them, and even had a sort of dreamy look as if she was thinking about what they could buy.

She smiled as she came in, gave the soup a stir, and sat down on a bench to nurse her baby. The coins had already disappeared into some secret cache, and I never saw them again.

"We had another chair when Dad was alive, but it's broken now. Would you like to sit here with me?" She had left room on the bench.

I had never had the opportunity to watch someone nurse a baby, and I was just about to cuddle up with her, when her mother spoke up. It took me by surprise because I had completely forgotten she was there.

"Mora," she said in a voice that seemed evenly balanced between this world and the next. "Who is that man?"

I suppose that is what a mother has to say to her young daughter. My heart went out to her because it seemed to take a lot of her energy just to ask the question.

"He's one of King Albert's men, Mom," said the girl. "He brought me home."

A silence followed, and there was so little energy coming from the spot where her mother was sitting, I wondered if she hadn't gone back to sleep. I went and sat down next to the girl, our hips touching on the little bench, and watched her feed her baby. They radiated an aura of peace and love so profound that it seemed to make its own light in the dark cottage. The longer I sat there, the more peaceful I felt; the whole universe seemed to be wrapped gently around the three of us.

"A soldier," said her mother. How long had it been since she spoke last? I had no idea. Time had stopped; and what is time anyway, that we pay so much attention to it?

"Not a soldier, Momma. He's a knight. One of King Albert's knights."

"A knight," said her mother. "Well, that's a fine thing." She tried to laugh a little ghost of a laugh, and that started her coughing; in between the coughs she was gasping in a way that was frightening to hear. Too much air was going out, and not enough was going back in.

"Oh, Momma," said the girl, putting the baby into its cradle, where it immediately set up a howl. She put her arms around her mother and held her tightly.

I didn't know what to do. Death with his scythe was standing in the doorway, and if he decided to go away, he would likely be back soon, the way it sounded to me. The old woman gradually began to fill her racked and starving lungs, and the crisis passed.

"You need to lie down now, Mother," said the girl. "Can you help?" she said to me, and together we got the woman out of her chair and into a bed which was like a big box full of straw with a bedspread over it. In moving her, I was surprised to discover that she was no older that I was, just very sick and very weak.

"She's a good girl," said the woman to me.

"Momma, *please* don't talk," said the girl. The woman gave in with a sigh, and then she fell asleep.

The woman was dying; that seemed pretty clear. There

was no place to take her to, so she would die in her own home. There was no one to care for her except her own daughter, so her daughter would care for her as best she could. It seemed like a lot to be placed on the shoulders of such a young person. But as I continued to watch the girl, who had already gone to poke up the fire and stir the pot and take up her baby to nurse again, I didn't feel sorry for her. On the contrary, she was living in the richness of her youth, with her new baby and her dying mother, and there was nothing tragic about it. Life and death were working hand in hand in a cycle that supported everything there was.

When the baby had finished nursing, we sat together on the little bench to eat our dinner of potato and vegetable soup. It was tasty, but not very filling, so I went out to my horse and brought in the cheese and cooked meat that Hélène had put up for me. The girl cut the meat into chunks, and we heated it in the fire on sticks like marshmallows and ate it with our fingers.

"Your name's Mora."

"Yes," she smiled, "I'm Mora."

"I'm Jack," I said, and she smiled again.

I wasn't sure what to say to her now because I wasn't sure what I could do for her. Once again, I'd let myself drift, making love to her just because she smelled so good, and going home with her because I was curious. Now it was beginning to dawn on me that this girl had more than her share of problems and needed help.

"What happened to your dad?"

"He died last fall."

"What of?"

"We think it was something he ate. He woke up in a lot of pain the day after Harvest Home, and by nightfall he was dead."

Dead of some undiagnosed something or other, just like her mother was dying now. I glanced over toward the bed, and the girl seemed to know what I was thinking.

"I don't think she wants to go on living without Dad. But I think it's mean of her to leave me and the baby. She knows we need her." Two tears ran down her cheeks, and she brushed them away. "I can't run this farm all by myself. Would you be interested?"

"Me?"

"Well, you've got to have a farm. All the knights have farms. You need a home, don't you? You can't just stay at court."

"Wait a second now."

"I know you have other things to do for King Albert, but you wouldn't have to spend all your time farming. It's really cheap to get help when you need it, because lots of families want hard cash for wintertime, and I could see to that. I know everybody, and I know who's worth hiring, and who's not."

"Mora . . ."

"You'd love it here. This is one of the nicest farms in the whole valley. We don't have to haul water in barrels. We can irrigate right off the river. And when it's hot, and you want a swim, there it is. We're only two miles from market, and it's only four or five miles to the castle, which is ever so much closer than—"

I held up my hands. "Mora, slow down a little, will you? I haven't even been here a week, you know? And I hardly know you."

"Well, that's not true," she said, visibly hurt.

"Look, I'll do anything I can to help you, but I don't think we . . . I mean I'm way too old for you."

Nothing I said was coming out quite right. If I was so

much older, I should have had the sense not to take advantage of her. But somehow that wasn't the point either. Ever since I had come to Albert's kingdom, the sands had been shifting under my feet; I was still too new to know how to act.

"Don't you like me?"

"Yes, I do, Mora. I like you a lot."

"Really?"

"Yes, really. I think you're very sweet and pretty, and you smell like all the flowers in the Garden of Eden."

"Well?"

That made me laugh. Some kingdom! It didn't matter how old I was. To a near-orphan with a baby and a farm on her hands, it didn't matter. To this girl who had made a meal of her cat to get through the winter, it didn't matter. In a land where Death could take you off with a stomachache after a holiday dinner, it didn't matter in the least. And there, suddenly, was that wonderful feeling swelling up inside me, like a big reward just for being alive.

"Mora, wouldn't you rather find yourself a young man, somebody with his whole life in front of him?"

"A few boys have been coming around. They all have their eye on the farm, and that's okay, I guess. That's natural. They're nice boys, but they're just boys, and . . ." She paused, and there was a darkness in her face that I hadn't seen before. Going over to the hearth, she adjusted the fire and put another log on. Then she went over to the cradle and stood looking at the baby. "This is a sweet little girl," she said finally. "And I want someone who can protect us."

Slowly the whole picture began to come together. I remembered what Marya had been saying about Lord Hawke's bucko soldiers and the situation in general in Lord Hawke's fife. An image flashed before my eyes of his two bodyguards leering at Mora as they rode away. Mora was also remembering something, for she looked suddenly quite shaken and afraid. Now there were tears in her eyes. She started to say something, but then she stopped and began to cry. Not knowing what to say, I took her on my lap; and she cried and cried as the sun was going down.

While she was crying I felt so angry that I decided I could never ask her who had done that to her. The kingdom was too small, and when I ran into whoever it was, I would never be able to control myself. I was also beginning to understand what I was doing there in that kingdom, and I needed very badly to have a talk with Albert.

Suddenly I had another image of Mora standing barefoot in front of Hawke's charger, holding up her baby as if for his inspection, the coins falling at her feet. My teeth came together with a snap. Of course it didn't prove anything, but even the thought that it could have been Guy Hawke himself was enough to send me howling into the woods like a werewolf after his blood.

"What's the matter?" said the girl. She was looking closely into my face.

"I feel angry about what happened to you, Mora."

She put her cheek against mine and stroked my hair; she didn't want me to feel badly on her account. Slowly my anger subsided under the touch of her kindness.

Later we sat outside and watched the moon come up. It was a clear night and the stars all looked brand new. First one star to make a wish on, and I wished she would have better luck this year than last. Then, before you knew it, the whole sky filled up with more stars than anyone could count in a lifetime. Finally the moon rose, just a delicate sliver of silver light.

Mora had practically no memories of the modern world. "There was a box that showed pictures of people fighting, and when Dad was watching it, he didn't want to talk or play." She could not remember the farm they had lost. Her earliest memories were uneasy and fearful. Her dad came home from the factory resentful and abusive, and the family stayed out of his way. "Then we moved to this valley and everything changed. There was so much to love, and so much we could do together."

Soon Mora fell asleep with her head on my arm, and I helped her into bed with her mother. Full of strange feelings, I lay myself down next to them and let the deep, silent night close over my head.

Chapter Nine

Mora was up and going about her business before the sun rose, and I had to roll out at the same time or else lie in bed with her mother. As the morning light through the small windows began to illuminate the cottage, I felt eager to continue my quest. For the moment there was nothing I could do for her unless I decided to move in and be her man, and I was not ready to do that. After we had some breakfast together, I went out to my horse and brought in my little bag of gold.

"Listen, Mora, I really like you a lot and I will do anything I can to help you. But I've only been here a few days and I'm on an assignment for the king. So for the time being you're just going to have to let me be your friend."

She was looking right into my eyes, but I couldn't tell what she was thinking. "All right."

"I'd like you to accept a gift of some money so you can get some help for your mother and get this farm fixed up right. Will you do that?"

"Sure."

"Whatever the future may bring, from now on you are under my protection. If anybody bothers you, you get word to me and I will chase 'em up the tallest tree in this kingdom."

"Thank you, Jack. I hope you'll come back real soon."

I shook some coins out. They were square gold slugs with no pictures or writing. Holding out my hand to her, I said, "I don't even know what these are worth. Take what you need."

She picked five of the coins off my palm. "This will be enough."

"Take another one anyway."

She took one more and slipped the coins into a fold in her clothing. Then she walked me to my horse and stood by while I tightened the saddle girth and put my gear in order. She pointed to the leafy sash that the god had left behind. "What's that?"

The flowers were wilted, but the leaves were still green. It seemed as if that encounter had taken place a long time ago. In my memory it was more like a legend or a fairy tale than something that had really happened the day before.

I didn't know what to call it. "Pict stuff," I said.

"I thought so! Where did you get it?" She sounded very excited.

"I met Picts on the road. A man with breasts and long gray hair was wearing it."

"Jo Mama! And he gave you that?"

"You could say so. Why, is it special?"

"It's very good luck," she said with such credence that it made me smile.

"Would you like to have it?"

"Oh, I couldn't."

"Here, I want you to have it."

She accepted it with awestruck appreciation, much more impressed with this gift than with the gold. I hoped it would bring her luck and lots of it.

Donning my sword belt and helm, I boarded my charger. He stamped and shook his bridle, and I felt like he might gallop off on his own accord if I didn't keep him under a tight rein. Mora stood by the side of the road in her simple dress and bare feet and the breeze blew me her lovely scent. I held up my palm and so did she. When I turned back for a last look, before the trees hid Mora from view, she was still watching me, her hand raised in a gesture like a benediction.

As I rode away, I felt relieved to be free once again to enjoy the open road and the adventure of my quest, but I was also weighed down by my thoughts. Okay, I understood in a more personal and visceral way the trouble in Albert's kingdom, but how my presence in the kingdom was going to change the situation, I had no idea. If anything my experience had taught me to leave people alone to their own crazy ways. If you could change yourself, you were doing a good enough job. Trying to change other people was just naturally a big waste of time.

My thoughts were going around and around in circles to no purpose. I felt like a good gallop would clear my head, but I didn't know what might be up ahead, and I didn't want to gallop over a child or run smack into a wagon. In the mood I sensed Pollux was in, he might be hard to stop, or even turn, if I gave him his head.

Lost in thought, I continued to drift into Lord Hawke's domain. I had been headed in that direction when I met Mora, and now I was mindlessly headed the same way. I was just thinking about turning around when two riders broke cover from the forest and blocked the road in front of me with crossbows in their hands. I recognized them at once as the men who had been riding behind Guy Hawke; by themselves, they looked even more malicious.

They were both smiling, but their smiles were belligerent and cruel. They were enjoying menacing me with their crossbows. There was no doubt in my mind that a crossbow bolt could tear right through my armor; but it would have to hit me first. And if they had known how their leering at Mora had made me feel, and how deeply angry I was about something that had been done to her, maybe they would have had second thoughts about crossing me.

"Halt!" said one of them, waving his crossbow at me, not really aiming, just showing off his power. I continued to ride toward them, and I noticed a nervous glance flicker between them. Gauging the distance between us with regard to their bows, I reined in.

"You are under arrest," said the same one. When I made no response and just sat my horse calmly, the men looked uncertain.

"Armed strangers are not allowed in this fief. We will collect your weapons, and you will come with us."

I shrugged. "I can ride wherever I please."

"This is Lord Hawke's fief, and he commands here."

"This is Albert's kingdom, and I ride for King Albert."

His laugh was snarly and cold. "Albert, the Pict-lover, has no power here. You will come with us."

"That is treason, and you had both better get out of my way."

They looked at each other, conferring what to do next. For myself, I thought I knew what I needed to know, for they were talking too freely. I was not supposed to return to Albert's court. I was supposed to have a fatal accident, or maybe just disappear. All my intuition told me that if I surrendered to these two, I was pig meat.

"Throw down your weapons!" The crossbows shifted in their hands, beginning to take aim.

"Albert!" I screamed, and as Pollux catapulted straight at them, my sword leapt into my hand. I felt the wind from one of the crossbow bolts as it hissed past my cheek, but they had been startled and shot too quickly and that had saved me.

Pollux crashed into the nearest rider and nearly upset him,

horse and all, but the rider managed to keep his seat and draw his sword. I made one slashing feint to his right side, and as his parry came out to block it, I whipped my blade over to the opposite side, and cut him through the side of his neck. He looked surprised as he fell slowly out of his saddle.

Something hard and heavy hit me in the chest, and now I was also falling. Was I dead? Apparently not, for I was madly dodging the hooves of both horses and trying to get to my feet. Above me the other rider was slashing down at me, and cursing because Pollux was in his way and spoiling his aim. I was trying to jab up at him and keep myself from being trampled at the same time. It was all chaos and confusion. Then it occurred to me to cut his saddle girth; that brought him crashing down.

He jumped to his feet, waving his sword, but I just stood there, trying to catch my breath. The horses had moved off to the side, and now there was plenty of room. There was time and space for me to realize I had just killed a man.

Then he attacked me, but I went on the defensive and continued to rest myself while the same image of that first soldier falling slowly from his saddle with his throat cut played over and over again in my mind's eye. I had never killed anybody, never even seriously considered killing anybody even when my temper was up. I fully intended to go through my whole life without killing anybody. Now I had done it, as simply as using that old feint and cut that used to get me points in college matches. Over and over in my mind, the dead man fell from his saddle. At the same time with another part of my mind I was weaving a simple defense against the second soldier's blows.

I had gotten my breath back, and I was not in any immediate danger from this soldier who must have learned his fencing from a fly-fisherman or a rug beater; but I wanted space to think about what I had done, and I wanted him to get away from me.

"You're the worst fencer I've ever seen," I told him. "Be sensible. You don't have a chance against me."

Then he charged me, and that was the end of him. I don't know what he thought he was doing, rushing at me with all his weight like that. I gave his blade a little tap to one side, and let him run right onto my point. And he kept coming at me, not realizing what had happened, not realizing that he had a sword through his heart. I had to retreat a couple of steps so he wouldn't ram into me. His face was still contorted with rage when he finally fell down, with my sword sticking through him and out his back. He kicked awkwardly a few times, like a dog having its belly scratched. Then he shuddered and lay still.

I dropped to my knees. In front of me lay the two men I had killed. The three horses were standing quietly, and one of them began to graze. All around me the forest was calm and still.

What now? The idea popped into my head that I ought to find a phone and call the police. That crazy notion almost made me laugh, but my chest hurt too much.

What had hit me? Wincing with pain, I managed to pull up my chain mail undershirt far enough to see the straight row of peculiar cuts where the iron links had been mashed right into my skin. It was five or six inches long. An axe blade? Sure enough, there was the battle-axe, much like the one hanging from my saddle, lying on the ground. Aimed a foot higher, it would have hit me right in the face. I never would have felt a thing. That crossbow bolt had barely missed me too. All around, it had been very, very close.

And now I was a killer. But what else could I have done? I could have told Albert to forget it when he invited me to his crazy kingdom in the first place. I could have made a plan for my life and followed it, instead of drifting like a chip in a river. I could have made something of myself. Now I was a killer.

I felt dizzy now, and when I put my hand to my head, it came away bloody. Exploring with my fingers, I found a gash in my scalp over my ear. When had that happened? It must have been during that scuffle between the horses. I looked myself over for other wounds, but except for my chest and my head, everything seemed to be okay.

What was I supposed to do now? My chest hurt too much for me to think about it clearly. I needed to go back to the castle and tell Albert what had happened. It was his kingdom. He would have to decide what to do about it. It had been self-defense, hadn't it? They had tried to take my weapons; tried to force me to go with them. They had threatened me with their crossbows. There were two of them, and I was alone. I had the right to defend myself, didn't I?

I got to my feet and looked Pollux over while he stood there calmly, unconcerned with the dead men in the grass and with the violence that had erupted a short time ago. Embedded deep in the wood of my saddle, I found the second crossbow bolt. That was good—it would support my story. I was still thinking about investigations, and evidence, and criminal courts, as though I still lived in the twenty-first century. But that wasn't true anymore. I was a knight living in the Middle Ages now. Well, then, would any of the knights of the olden days, like Lancelot or Gawain or Gareth, have worried about killing a couple of scruffy villains who jumped them on the highroad? No, they would have drunk some mead out of a horn cup and put their weapons in order for whatever life sent them next.

My own sword was still sticking in that dead body. I

grasped the hilt and tried to pull it out but it was stuck fast. I had to put my boot on his chest and yank hard. The sword had been holding him propped up on one side, but now he settled onto his back. A trickle of blood was drying on the side of his mouth.

I tried to wipe my blade on the grass, but it didn't come very clean, so I finished the job with my cloak. I was quite dizzy now, and my body hurt all over, especially my chest. It took me ever so long to climb aboard Pollux, and then I pointed his nose toward home. He took about ten steps before darkness began to swallow me. I tried to push it away, but there was nothing I could do. I knew I was falling off my horse, though I never seemed to hit the ground. Falling, falling, I fell through the darkness.

When I woke up, I was lying on a straw bed, looking up at a straw roof. "What a lot of straw!" I thought. Then I was out again.

The second time I woke up, I recognized Mora, who was nursing her baby. Something important had happened, but I couldn't remember what it was. She came over, still holding the baby to her breast, and looked deeply into my eyes. Taking the cloth from my forehead, she rinsed it in a bowl and laid it back in place. "You had a nice sleep," she said.

The third time I woke up, Mora was sitting by the bed gazing at me. Hadn't I left her? What was I doing back here again? I was sure I had left on a horse, and ridden down the road. Then the memory came flooding back, and I groaned with the horror of it.

"I wanted to watch you, so I climbed the hill. I saw you fight Mike and Mitch. When you fell off your horse, I came after you."

"You brought me here?"

"Yes. You kept falling off your horse. Don't you remember?"

"Nothing. . ."

"I think you got kicked."

"It was brave of you to bring me here."

Mora started to say something, but then she gave a little shrug. "Nobody liked Mike and Mitch."

"Have those bodies been found?"

She nodded. "Soldiers have been galloping up and down the road. No one's come here yet."

"Where's my horse?"

"I hid it in the woods."

"Show me where."

"Can you ride? I think you should stay here. They'll catch you on the road."

"I don't want you mixed up in this. Is there some way through the woods back to the castle?"

"You could ride along the river as far as the bridge. Once you cross the river you'll be in the royal domain."

"Let's give it a try."

Pretty soon I was leading Pollux through a tangle of brush while Mora led the way. When we came to the bank of the river, the other side was only about fifteen yards away, but there was a steep bank and the water was deep and swift. As heavily laden as Pollux was, it would be a hard chance to swim it.

"Just before you get to the bridge, the river is wide and shallow. You could cross easily there."

"I won't forget this, Mora." I owed my life to this sweet-smelling girl, but I didn't want to lead her on by kissing her like a lover. I took her hand and kissed it instead. She smiled, and dropped me a curtsy.

Mounting up, I set off upstream along the river. The path was barely wide enough for a horse, and sometimes I had to dismount and lead him by the bridle. Getting on and off the horse was agony to my chest, but at least my head was clear.

It seemed a long time before I came in sight of the bridge, but sure enough, the river broadened, and it was so shallow that the rocky bottom was visible. I was halfway across when I heard the sound of hoofbeats approaching the bridge. I had been trying to make the crossing as quietly as possible, but now I urged Pollux forward over the slippery river rocks as quickly as I dared. Although I was close to the opposite bank when the riders burst into view, I was not close enough.

"There he is!" came the shout as they clattered across the bridge; within moments I was cut off, with four riders in front of me and the river all around me. None of them carried bows that I could see, and they did not seem inclined to enter the river; still, the open road to Albert's castle was blocked. Looking at their horses, which were as heavily laden with arms and armor as Pollux, I was willing to bet Pollux could outrun them. All I had to do was break through to the other side, but in order to do that I had to get out of the river.

One spot looked as bad as another. There was nowhere to get a running start, and although the bank was not very steep, it was sure to go badly if they attacked me when I was halfway up. Now I could hear more riders coming from the same direction. I had to do something fast, but what?

Suddenly I remembered my bow, snatched it from its scabbard, nocked an arrow, and shot almost without aiming into that clump of riders. With such a big target, my arrow had to hit something, and it took one of the riders in the thigh. He let out a cry and set his horse backing; it reared and threw him. I sent another arrow into their midst, and now there was confusion, and they were all in each other's way, giving me the chance I needed to climb the bank and gain the road. Behind me I could hear the other riders coming hard. I had no time for a third arrow. Stuffing the bow into its quiver, I drew my sword and charged, screaming Albert's name.

Several blows were aimed at me, but none landed. The open road was in front of me, and I galloped toward the castle. Looking over my shoulder I saw the new riders cross the bridge with Lord Hawke in the lead. How far to the castle? Three miles? I was very afraid I'd never make it at that hard gallop that seemed to be cracking my chest wide open.

"Darcey!" It was a voice I hadn't heard in a long, long time; the voice of someone that it galled me to be running from. Looking over my shoulder, I could see that his troop of soldiers had stopped. It was only Guy Hawke coming on at a comfortable lope, as though he was sure that I would stop.

And I did. But not before I had put a considerable distance between myself and his soldiers. Hawke slowed to a trot, and then to a walk, reining in just out of striking distance. I had to admit that he sat his horse well, and looked very natural in his armor and surcoat. He was a striking figure of a man: strong, erect, alive. And there was something else that a man like me, who is just a puzzle all patched together out of disparate ideas and yearnings and experiences, might be inclined to envy: Guy Hawke was carved out of one chunk. He had no doubts at all about who he was.

"What are you doing here, Darcey?" He had a good voice, deep and rich and full of ambiguous overtones that made the question difficult to understand, as if it were a bunch of different questions all rolled into one. "You don't belong here. We stopped adding new people a long time ago, Albert and I, and he had no business bringing you here. He also had no right to make a knight of you on a whim. That is an honor a man ought to earn and deserve."

"As far as that goes," I replied, "you bought your title with your money, so don't give me that crap, Guy Hawke."

"Do you dare to call me that?" he flared up. "In this kingdom I am a duke, and it is Lord Hawke to you, outlander!"

"May it be as you wish, my lord. But the king of this kingdom made me a knight. And I am known as Sir Jack."

He looked disdainfully away into the woods, and sat with his lips pursed, as though some offensive odor had passed beneath his nostrils. How I wanted to push him off his horse!

"No," he said quietly. "You could never be a knight. What you are is a mercenary, Albert's hired sword. Do you think I don't know what goes on around here? That gypsy witch looked into her crystal ball, and now here you are," he said with scathing contempt. "Here you are to solve Albert's problems, of which I am the worst. I, who stitched this kingdom back together when it was ripping to pieces at every seam!"

"Did you do that for Albert? Did you do that to serve your king?"

"You have no right to question me!"

"Then good day to you, Lord Hawke. I'm sure we'll meet again." I began to turn my horse around.

"Darcey," he said, and against my better judgment I faced him again. "I am not through with you yet. You murdered two of my men, in case it may have slipped your mind, and now you have to answer for that."

"I will tell Albert what happened. He will decide what to do about it. He is the king."

"Albert and I will decide what to do about it together. In the meantime, you are coming with me."

"I am going to Albert's castle. Detain me at your peril."

He gave a little nod, but it was not to me; and I understood immediately that he had been distracting me in order to bring someone around behind me. He turned his horse and tried to move away from me, and on a hunch I moved with him, not daring to take the time to look behind. Then he tried to move away again. Now I was sure that he was trying to get out of the line of fire, and once again I stayed with him.

"Shoot him, you fools!" he shouted, trying to dart away. But this time I was determined to get behind him, to put his body between myself and his bowmen. "Shoot!" he screamed. But I had the fraction of a second I needed, and now I was behind him. Whipping out my sword, I laid the edge against his neck

"If you want to live, tell them to throw their bows into the woods. You have three seconds. One . . . two . . ."

"Do as he says, idiots!" he screamed at the bowmen, angrier at them than he was scared of me.

What now? A quick thrust through the soft tissue behind the ear into his brain. Could I do it? He had strained every nerve trying to get his men to shoot me in the back. Wasn't that enough of a reason? I was a thorn in his side. I stood in the way of his ambitions. He was bound to try again.

What was I waiting for? Behind me I could hear a commotion of voices and a rattle of gear back at the bridge. His men could easily see that I was holding their lord at swordpoint, and all hell could break loose in seconds. Why was I stalling?

I had already killed two people that very same day, and the fact of it was still huge and heavy and unassimilated. I needed a chance to gather some thoughts around it and make a place for it in my psyche where it wouldn't chew away at my spirit. I just wasn't ready to kill anyone else; certainly not in cold blood and from behind. That was the decision I made; and in the light of everything that followed, it was a very bad decision, one of the worst I ever made. All I can say is that the right choice would have been the wrong one too. That's my excuse.

Behind me I heard a shout and a clatter of hoof beats, and I knew the duke's men had made up their minds. "You owe me one, m'lord," I said as I sheathed my sword. Then I dug my heels into Pollux's flanks and we went pounding away up the road. The first time I looked back, I could see they weren't pursuing me. The duke's men had formed up around him, and he was beating those three bowmen with something I couldn't make out at that distance.

I slowed down to a more comfortable lope, one that would get me home almost as quickly, but which wasn't so excruciatingly painful to my wounded chest. I was very tired and sore, and I felt like I didn't understand anything anymore.

Chapter Ten

Sir Leo was the first person I saw when I reached the castle. He was practicing with his bow, but as soon as I was close enough for him to get a good look at me, he dropped everything and ran to help me off my horse. "Never mind, my friend," he said when I tried to tell him the story. "Let's get you inside." Then I collapsed.

When I woke up it was dark outside, and I was all bandaged up and lying in bed. Albert was there, and Jenna, and Marya, and Sir Leo, and Sir Rudy Strapp, and a couple of men who I had never seen before who were apparently knights by the leather trim on their clothes.

"He's awake, Sire," said Marya.

Albert came over and sat down in a chair by the bed. "Can you hear me, Jack?"

"Yes, your majesty." I had to say it twice, because the first time it came out as a croak.

"How are you feeling?"

My chest was still sore under the tight wrapping of bandages, but nothing like it had been before. "I feel a lot better, Sire," I said. "But I think I'm going to have to skip jousting practice tomorrow."

That seemed to clear the tension in the air. I could see that they had all been very worried about me.

"If you feel up to it, we'd like to know what happened."

So I told them about the fight with Mike and Mitch, and

about my confrontation with Lord Hawke. I told them that a peasant girl had taken care of me while I was unconscious and that she had shown me the river trail to the bridge; but other than that I didn't tell them anything about my relationship with Mora. When I had finished, I felt tired and sore all over again.

"I think he ought to rest now, Sire," said Marya.

"Yes, I'm sure you're right, Mage," said Albert. "All right, lads, we'll reconvene in the hall." The men filed out, with friendly nods and smiles in my direction as though I'd broken my leg catching a touchdown pass. I found that rather confusing, but I tried to smile back.

"I'm going to let these women look after you, Jack," said Albert. "You won't mind that, will you? We'll talk more in the morning."

"I hope I haven't screwed things up."

"Just rest now. I'm the king. You can leave the fretting to me."

"I never killed anyone before, Albert."

"Oh yes, I understand, Jack. Believe me, I understand very well." He paused in the doorway, and I imagined that a whole review of his experiences as king was passing through his memory. "The life here takes some getting used to," he said finally. "This isn't Connecticut." Then he went out.

"Mage," said Jenna with just a touch of queenly hauteur, "would you leave me alone with Sir Jack for a moment? I promise not to tire him." I wondered what she wanted. I didn't want to be left alone with Jenna. I wanted to go back to sleep.

But Marya dropped a dainty curtsy that was just as pretty as a play, said, "Yes, m'lady," and left, closing the door behind her.

Jenna waited until the silence had settled in the room. Then she said, "Good for you, Jack."

I waited for more, but that was it. "Good for me what?"

"Good for you for killing that trash."

Did she think I wanted to be congratulated for that? "Thanks, Jenna, but I never wanted to kill anybody, and it makes me feel sick to think about it."

"I know you're a sensitive man, Jack. That is to your credit, I'm sure. But whatever you may think about it, you did a great service to the kingdom today. A great many people, commoners and nobles too, will be drinking to your health tonight. You're a hero, Jack. Did you see the way those knights looked at you?"

The cogwheels of my mind were turning reluctantly. "I'm a hero because . . ."

"Because two of Lord Hawke's worst bullies went up against one of Albert's knights, and got what they so richly deserved."

"Death."

"Yes, death! Why do you look at me like that? Is that such an awful thing to say? If it takes a few deaths to keep this beautiful kingdom secure against the machinations of a man like Lord Hawke, then let's hear it for death!"

Although I was very tired now and my chest had begun to throb, it was quite thrilling to see Jenna, the neurotic, bare-assed rider, shining with light and power the way she was at that moment. "Why, Jenna," I said, "that was spoken like a true queen."

"Well, thank you," she said; and now she looked self-conscious and a little embarrassed, but nonetheless pleased. "Thank you, Sir Jack. I really *am* going to be the queen."

"Oh yes, my lady, I can see that you are."

"I promised not to tire you. I suppose you'd like to rest now." I think she had startled herself a little, and now she wanted to be alone and go over it in her mind.

"Yes, m'lady, I would."

"Well, good night then, Sir Jack," she said, taking my hand in both of hers and kissing it. "And thank you for everything." Then she was gone.

In the middle of the night I felt a finger stroking my cheek, and when I opened my eyes there was Marya with a candlestick. "I want to change your poultice."

I sat up and rubbed my eyes. She unwrapped the rags around my chest and then wrapped me up again with some others that were a pretty green color and made my chest feel warm. "What's on the poultice?"

"Wintergreen, turpentine, a few other things. How's the chest?"

"It feels a lot better, Marya," I said, yawning. "I thought maybe something was broken in there, but it doesn't feel like that now."

"And how's your spirit?"

"I have a lot of mixed feelings about killing those two yahoodies."

Marya nodded and for a time she was silent. "Killing people is something to be taken very seriously," she said finally. "But I think you did okay, Jack. You weren't out there looking for trouble. Something happened and you handled it the best you could. As far as Mike and Mitch are concerned, they've been asking for it, and asking for it, and they finally got it. If you were chosen to be the agent of their fate, then the thing for you to do is to accept what happened with a little detachment and not beat yourself up about it. You're not here

186

by accident, Jack. If you have some tough decisions to make in the days to come, then you just do the best you can and let the Goddess take care of the rest. Hear me?"

"Thanks, Marya. I appreciate your saying that. I value your opinion a lot."

"You're welcome. Are you sorry you came?"

"No, I'm not. This was a scary day, but I'm still glad I came. There isn't any question in my mind about that."

"Good. We're very glad you're here. Now roll over on your tum. I'm going to give you a massage."

The next thing I knew, someone was shaking my shoulder and the sun was coming up. "Rise and shine, Sir Jack," said Sir Leo. "It's time to make history."

"There must be some mistake, Leo. Didn't you see the DO NOT DISTURB sign on the doorknob?"

"Ha, ha, very good, my friend. But something is happening you won't want to miss, and what's more, we need you. Come on now, into your clothes."

It was with a good deal of reluctance and some un-knightly grumbling that I managed to get myself dressed. Down I went to the hall, and there a tremendous breakfast was being served to a dozen knights and at least two dozen soldiers, all joking and laughing and eating in very high spirits. As I walked in the talking stopped, and they all rose and gave me a cheer.

"Hail, Sir Jack!" echoed King Albert. He proceeded to introduce me to a number of the men, and they all seemed honored to make my acquaintance. Then he called over his son, who I hadn't seen since the incident in the woods. The boy gave me an apprehensive look, as though he was wondering what I might say.

"This is my son, Renny. Renny, this is Sir Jack, a very old

friend from when I was a boy your age."

Renny bridled ever so slightly, as if he felt insulted to be called a boy. At his age, I reminded myself, I had been selfish, self-absorbed, and confident that I knew everything. I also remembered that with all the new hormones smoking in my socks, I had really been nothing more than a predatory little animal as far as girls were concerned.

"Nice to meet you, Renny."

"I'm pleased to make your acquaintance, sir," said Renny, and he sounded quite sincere. He seemed to want me to like him, and I decided I would try.

There were dozens of people to meet. All around me the hall was rocking with a kind of masculine energy that reminded me of a pre-game locker room. The talk was all of weapons and horses, and Lord Hawke's name popped up regularly as the butt of some caustic reference or joke. Now I was given a seat next to Albert and a heaping plate of food; and while I ate I was looking around and listening to the conversations with growing dread, because I was beginning to understand what all this was leading up to.

Albert jumped to his feet and lifted his cup high in the air. "Well, lads, are we ready to give Lord Hawke a little surprise today?" The response was a joyful roar, and all the cups went up in a manly salute to the cause. My own cup went up as well, of course, because there was no sneaking out of what was happening today.

"To horse then, lads! Let's not keep him waiting!" cried Albert, and breakfast was over. Out we marched into the great courtyard where the horses were saddled and ready, including Pollux, who was hung about with all my warlike gear. The king himself handed me my helm, and there was another cheer when I set it on my head.

I was not looking forward to riding a horse in my

condition, and I was certainly not looking forward to going to war. But more than just a participant, I was clearly a symbol that morning for all those men. When we took our places in the cavalcade, I was ushered up to Albert's right side, and when the drawbridge thundered down on its massive chains, out we rode in procession.

We headed north on the river road, and I rode side-by-side with Albert. I had seen dozens of war movies in my time, and read books and articles about many different wars. It always puzzled me why anyone with a working brain and open eyes would ever consent to go.

Now I knew. You went because everyone else was going and there was nothing else you could do. There was no excuse for not going. There was nowhere to hide. And today I was an important part of the party Albert and his knights and soldiers were planning to throw for Lord Hawke.

I also learned that what you do in such a situation, to take the sting out of the fear, is to say to yourself that nothing bad will happen to you. People might get hurt, and people may get killed, but not you. Saying it over and over to yourself, you begin to believe it after awhile; and then you can even start to enjoy the high energy, the anticipation, the excitement, the jokes and bantering, and the camaraderie, which is always heightened by danger. Pretty soon you might begin to wonder how you ever considered staying behind.

I had not reached that stage yet. A few days in bed with lots of good meals and some nice visits from Jenna once my chest wasn't so tender, would have suited me better. At the same time it was so amazing to find myself riding beside a king at the head of a column of armed men, that I was content to put off my holiday for a little while, since nothing bad was going to happen to *me*.

Soon we passed a man who I took to be some kind of

woodsman because he was carrying an axe over his shoulder along with a bow and a quiver full of arrows. He fell into step beside one of the soldiers, who greeted him with a laugh and a clap on the shoulder.

A little further up the road, two more men and a boy came out of the woods. One man was carrying a scythe and the other was carrying a knobby club. Both men carried bows and arrows, and the boy was carrying a sling and a pouch of stones. "We want to come with you, your majesty," announced the man with the scythe, "and my boy is coming too!"

"Welcome, Howard!" cried Albert. "Now tell me your boy's name. You have so many I get them all mixed up."

"This is Paul, my oldest," said Howard, his hand on the boy's shoulder. "There are four boys now, for Mandy gave me another this spring."

"Give her my best when you see her, Howard, and congratulations to you both. Now Paul, can you hit what you are aiming at with that sling?"

"Yes, your majesty," said the boy, awed to be addressed directly by the king. "Mostly always, your majesty."

"Good for you, my boy," said Albert. "And welcome."

By the time we reached Dugdale's manor house, we had picked up more than fifty men and a dozen boys. Some spoke to Albert and got their royal greeting. Some joined with friends. Others just fell silently into step. Some looked grim and businesslike; others seemed happy and joyful. All of them carried weapons: bows, knives, clubs, axes, and sharp tools tied to staffs. All the boys carried slings and pouches of rocks.

Dugdale was out in front of his manor house with his soldiers and another large group of peasants. I found it a little comical to see Dugdale in his armor. It was as if the wrong actor had gotten into the costume by mistake. Charlsey was standing next to him with his helm, carrying it in both her arms like a big flower pot. She was smiling in a tight and frightened way and chattering away at Dugdale, who was nodding dutifully and trying to coax his helm away from her.

"Good morning, Dugdale," said Albert. "Lady Dugdale, your garden is breathtaking as usual. I should be honored if you would walk me through it when we get back." Charlsey opened her mouth to say something, but Albert didn't give her a chance. "Dugdale, your helm. You there, young man. Bring that horse and give your lord a hand up smartly now!"

In no time at all, with a few crisp commands, Albert had the column headed back the way we had come. Charlsey waved from the gate.

Albert shook his head. "Poor Charlsey," he sighed. "Let's pick up the pace a little." We began to trot, and immediately the jingling of the arms and armor set up a rhythm, almost like music, that was refreshing and inspiring. I felt a wave of admiration for this man who could feel concern for a frightened woman and look after an army all in the same moment. I knew I could follow him anywhere.

"Hello, Darcey," said Dugdale. "Heard you had a bit of a scrape. Everything all right?"

"Yes, thanks," I said. "Just sore." That was something of an understatement, but I was determined to tough it out.

"We heard those men stopped you on the road with crossbows. Is that true?"

"That was the way of it."

"I'm positive we all agreed," said Dugdale, "that there were to be no crossbows at all. Isn't that right, Sire?"

"That is correct," said Albert.

"The crossbow is not a sporting weapon," said Sir Leo, who was riding on Albert's left, "and they are prone to going off accidentally."

"I was shocked when I heard Lord Hawke's men had crossbows," said Dugdale. "Charlsey was very upset too. She didn't want me to come today, but I could hardly stay home when half my peasants are here. You don't think this is going to turn into a brawl, do you?" Dugdale asked me.

"I don't know," I said. "They woke me up this morning and put me on a horse. Ask your commander-in-chief."

Albert looked over at me. Then he put up a hand to stop the cavalcade, and turned his horse around to face us.

"Be so kind, Sir Rudy, as to give the standard to Sir Jack." Rudy Strapp untied a long staff from his saddle and handed it to me. There was a flag rolled up at one end.

"Go ahead, Jack," said Albert. "Show it to the people."

Twisting the staff, I let the flag unfurl; and there was a nicely crafted representation of a big hornet in front of a swarming hornets' nest.

"Ride down the line with it," said Albert.

It was a very exciting standard. Someone with a fine graphic talent had laid it out, for it was simple and clear, and yet it evoked a lot of motion and energy. As I started down the line of men and boys, I could see their eyes shine with excitement as soon as they saw it.

"Here it is, my doughty lads," I cried, and I'll bet my eyes were shining too. "Are we going to swarm all over Lord Hawke today? What do you say?"

"Yes!" they cried. "Yes, we will! We're with you, Sir Jack!"

"He'll be running for the river when he sees us coming, my friends," I cried over the din. "Get your stingers ready!"

"Yes, yes!" they cried. "We'll sting him today!"

Such a shouting and carrying on I never heard before. And a few minutes later, when Griswold and his army appeared, coming west along the market road to join us, I galloped over and led them back under the standard, and we all yelled and stamped and rattled our weapons. I confess it was intoxicating to be treated as someone that important for the first time in my life; and by the time I was back at Albert's side, I was very high indeed and my chest had completely stopped hurting.

"Thank you, your majesty," I said, somewhat breathless. "That did me a lot of good."

"You're welcome, and the same to you," said Albert. "You've done us all a lot of good, just as Mage Marya said you would."

"I'm still not sure exactly what I did, except to fight my way out of a jam."

"Well, what you did was break the spell of fear and inaction that we had all fallen under. Perhaps it wasn't what you meant to do. Perhaps you didn't even know it needed to be done. But you did it anyway, so you might as well take some credit for it, don't you think?"

"All right, Sire, since you put it that way."

"You've always had greatness of heart, Jack. Now it's time for you to take your place in the world."

"If I have a world to take my place in, I owe that to you, Sire."

For the next few miles the jubilant spirit prevailed, and we were joined along the way by perhaps another hundred and fifty peasants with their weapons. But as we neared Lord Hawke's boundaries, the army began to quiet down; and when we came in sight of the bridge, even the talking stopped altogether. The rhythm of the horses' hooves and the clinking of our arms was all the noise we made as we marched across that bridge.

If the Dugdales' fief had a stylish and manicured look to it, Lord Hawke's fief looked gloomy and forbidding. I cannot account for this in any way. Maybe it was only my imagination; maybe it was because gray clouds were beginning to gather and the weather was turning chilly. Whatever it was, I'm sure I wasn't the only one to notice the change of atmosphere as we crossed into Lord Hawke's domain.

"Now that the invasion has begun, Sire," I said, "I'd like very much to have both hands free. Who do you think I ought to give this standard to?"

Albert was peering down the road ahead and scanning the trees on both sides of the road. He shrugged impatiently. "Pick someone," he said.

I looked around, and my eyes fell on Rudy Strapp. But he shook his head; he didn't want it. He had already slipped his buckler over his arm and was checking his weapons.

Gordon was riding with the soldiers. He was the dutiful type. He probably would not object. On the other hand, if we were attacked, I wanted him busting heads with that iron-tipped staff, not waving the flag. Somewhere in this crowd was the perfect person, someone who would appreciate the glory of it. Someone who . . .

"Renny," I shouted. Renny spurred his mount forward, and when he came abreast I thrust the staff out to him. "I'm making you bannerman. Whatever you do, don't drop it. That's important." I tried to make my voice rumble with authority, for I didn't want any argument from him. But he was flattered and grasped the staff happily. He fell in behind us with the flag held high and billowing out in the cold wind that was beginning to pick up.

"That's a dangerous job you've given him," Albert said to me. "I could never have chosen him to do that. But the king carries the standard for the whole kingdom, and if he's going to be king after me . . . Your instinct is good, Jack."

"Do you think we're going to be in a fight?"

"I don't know. I'm very pleased with the turnout from the peasants. I think Lord Hawke would be foolish to provoke us."

"Can he muster support among his own peasants?"

"Yes, I think he could, but not spontaneously like this. He would have to go out and round them up. It would take a lot of time. We have several hundred people on this march, do you realize that?" he said with a gratified smile. "And every one of them came gladly of his own volition except possibly you." He gave me a smile to show that it was just a joke despite the truth in it.

"Did you ask for volunteers?"

"No, not exactly. I made it known that my knights and I would be paying Lord Hawke a royal visit. I made it known that my friends would be welcome. It's hard to explain. In a way, I didn't do anything. A bird flew out of my window, and that bird turned into a thousand birds. You have to live here awhile before you can understand how certain things happen."

"But you invited Dugdale and Griswold."

"Yes, they have an obligation to support the throne—as does Lord Hawke, for that matter. Dugdale is loyal to me because it's the proper thing to be. Griswold is too ironical for real loyalty, but he suffers from boredom, as ironical people do, and he would never miss anything like this. Dugdale and Griswold go around together quite a bit. They complement each other."

"What about Bennett?"

"Hoho! You've been doing your homework. That's good. For your information, Lord Bennett goes to bed sozzled every night, and is no good for anything before midday. One reason we're up so early is so that Lord Hawke can't muster any support from Bennett."

"Would he support Lord Hawke at a more convenient time of day?"

"Possibly so. He and Lord Hawke went to the same college, and Bennett looks up to him. But at this hour, no. I don't think Bennett will figure into this at all."

"Yet four hundred people jumped up at the crack of dawn to support you today. You must be doing something right."

"Yes, and because the whole valley talked of nothing else yesterday except the warrior knight who sent Mike and Mitch to hell. Oh, I'm not saying my people don't love me. I'm not saying they don't approve of the way I rule. But it was a certain extra something—a catalyst, a spirit, a legend in the making—that had them tying their sickles onto poles this morning and changing their bowstrings. Tomorrow or the next day or the day after that . . . who knows how long that spirit could be counted on."

"So you had to ride this morning."

"Everyone at the council thought so."

Since we crossed the bridge, I hadn't seen a single person. The river road was empty of carts and flocks and people. After we passed Mora's, there were an increasing number of farms that could be seen from the road, but no one was about.

"Everyone's gone to the moon," I said, wrapping my cloak around me against the chilly wind.

"No, no," said Albert. "They wouldn't miss this. Gordon!"

Gordon caught up with us. "Yes, Sire?"

"You have the sharp eyes, Gordon. Since we crossed the bridge, have you seen anyone in the woods?"

Gordon laughed. "Yes, Sire. There are as many children watching us from the woods this morning as there are trees."

"Did you see any soldiers or bowmen?"

"No, Sire."

"Picts?"

"None."

"Take two men and ride up ahead."

"Yes, Sire."

Soon we came out of the woods into open farmland that stretched as far west from the river as I could see. Across the fields we could see scattered groups of people, five or ten in a clump, watching us from a distance.

"Are these fields farmed commonly, Sire?"

"It's rather complicated how the land is apportioned year by year. I'll explain it to you when we have more time."

"And there are individual farms also?"

"Yes. Those families still owe service to their lord's domain, and they still have to tithe toward food storage for winter rationing, but they organize their holding as they see fit."

"I met a young woman who has a farm of her own. Her father is dead now, and her mother is sick."

"Is that the young woman who helped you?"

"Yes, Sire."

"I know her. Blonde and sweet-smelling, is she not?"

"Yes, that's her."

"And what interest have you in Mora the Rose?" he said, with a penetrating look.

"Well, for one thing, she was raped. She feels afraid for herself and also for her child."

"Fear and violence in this fief have gone unchecked far too long, and I am very much at fault, Jack. The situation has to be changed. That's why we're here today. That's why *you're* here. Well, Leo," he said, turning to Sir Leo, "we've come this far. What are we going to do now?"

"That depends on our objective, Sire."

"Our objective is to confront Lord Hawke and force him to change his ways."

"Then I would say it depends on how aggressively the manor is defended. If the way is blocked by soldiers, we will have to cut our way through. If we can achieve the manor house without a fight, then I think we should surround it. We have plenty of people to do that, and it will make a good demonstration of our power."

"And then?"

"Then we call for a parley or send in an ultimatum."

"And if it's rejected?"

"Then we have no choice but to cut our way in. We will have to capture Lord Hawke."

"There is a chance here for a lot of killing."

"Yes, Sire."

"Couldn't we lay siege to the manor?"

"Yes, we could, but we would lose our momentum. We can't stop now and wait. We have to see this through to its conclusion, whatever that may be."

"Yes, you're right. Thank you, Sir Leo. You're quite right."

"Your servant, Sire, as always."

"Kindly take charge of surrounding the manor."

"Yes, Sire."

"Well, at least now we know what we're going to do, eh? Here comes Gordon. Well, what does it look like up there?"

"Everything is very quiet around the manor, Sire," said Gordon. "I didn't see any guards or soldiers. No one seems to be about at all."

"A trap, perhaps?"

"It seems very suspicious, Sire. I don't understand it."

"Well, let's have a look. Are we ready, Leo? Forward then! Quick march!"

We rounded the bend at a brisk trot, and just as Gordon had said, there was no defending force, no soldiers, no guards, no obstruction. There was the manor house, much like Dugdale's without all the flower gardens, and the front gate was standing open. It was very quiet, for the wind had died down; quiet and unnatural, as if everyone had gone away on a cold day that was threatening rain, and left the door open.

Albert brought the column to a halt about fifty yards from the gate. He looked perplexed. "What do you think?" he asked me.

"I don't know. Don't ask *me*!" I felt very agitated. Several hundred people had gotten up early to make a show of force. Now that energy was backed up behind us. Had we led all these people to an empty manor house, and were we just going to turn around now and go home? The situation gave me a bad feeling. It was worse, I think, than if we had come upon a thorny barricade with fifty bowmen behind it.

"There's a light in the hall, Sire," said Gordon.

"Sir Leo," said Albert, "we will still surround the manor as quickly as can be done without confusion. In the event of a trap, you must do as you think best until we are in control of the situation."

"Thank you, Sire," said Sir Leo. "You can leave it to me."

"Ready now?" said Albert, and up went his arm. "Forward!"

It took no time at all to make our show of securing the manor. I was watching the upper windows as we circled, but the shutters remained closed. Sir Leo deployed the knights and the rest of the army quickly and efficiently, and for such a haphazard plan, everything seemed to be falling into place.

Albert, Sir Leo, Gordon and I rode in through the gate. The grounds seemed deserted. The cold wind was picking up again, and it blew our cloaks around and made them snap. Dismounting, we approached the great door on foot. At a nod from Albert, Gordon raised the heavy knocker and let it fall. The echo boomed hollowly inside.

Gordon was just reaching for the knocker again when Albert said, "Try the door."

Gordon swung the door out on its huge hinges and we entered the hall together. It was very quiet in the hall, but there was no feeling of peace in the stillness. I felt like putting my fingers in my ears, as if someone was screaming.

There, at the opposite end of the hall, was Lord Hawke. He stood behind a massive wooden chair, quite a masterpiece of woodcarving even at a distance. With his hands gripping the knobs on the upper corners of the chair back, he presented a strange image, like a captain at the wheel of his ship. That image was duplicated in the huge shadow cast by the fire in the hearth. All the way across the room, I could see his eyes glittering like broken glass.

We approached within half a dozen yards and then stopped. Though there were several of us and we had come with an army at our back, and though he was alone with only that massive chair for a prop, he didn't appear at much of a disadvantage. I had the feeling that he was deciding what to do with us, rather than the other way around, and that made me think again of traps or an ambush. Although he was wearing neither armor nor weapons, he looked very dangerous.

Finally he approached us. "Welcome, my liege," he said with an unpleasant smile. "What a pleasant surprise!"

"Where are your soldiers?" said Albert. "Where are your servants?"

"When I heard that you were leading an army here to tear me to pieces, I sent them all on holiday."

"Spare me the sarcasm," said the king. "Your plan is to give me nothing to attack. That is clever. Quite brilliant in fact. But suppose I simply take you and throw you into the dungeon?"

"That would be very ungrateful, seeing that you would hardly have a kingdom at all if not for me."

"What you say is true, but that is all very much in the past. At the present time you are wounding my kingdom daily for your pleasure in making people afraid of you. That must change and it must change now. If your lack of resistance today means that you are willing to alter your behavior considerably, it will spare me from a task which will be much more unpleasant for you than it will be for me."

"I'm sure that we can come to terms," said the duke in a nonchalant manner. "But I also have a word or two to say. For one thing, I do not welcome this false knight in my house. The others are welcome, but I would prefer that he be sent away, if not from the kingdom, then at least from my hall."

"I am sorry if his presence discomforts you, but he is my own true knight and I prefer to have him by my side. Is there anything else?"

"Yes. I am wondering why you choose to lead an army of peasants with scythes and pitchforks against your own nobility. Is part of your program of change to institute a democracy and to run for office?"

"I appreciate your sense of humor at a time like this."

"But I am not joking," said the duke, and the look in his eyes made me shiver. "It was a monarchy that you and I and the other nobles strove to create, was it not? How much more

201

inconsistent can you possibly be than to lead a peasant army against me? It is even worse than your policy of giving them license to run naked in the woods instead of tending the land. If you would prefer to be some new kind of president, or an Indian chief, or just to be supremely popular, perhaps you should say so and stop calling yourself a king."

"On the contrary," said Albert, drawing himself up. "If I am disposed toward benevolence rather than tyranny, I am the better monarch. As for the Picts, they are a phenomenon which I wish to understand more clearly, and for the time being we will let them be. You are the one who has been forgetting who is king, and we are all here to remind you for the last time. This is that armed incursion which you once had the colossal nerve to forbid me to make. We have had more than enough of your threats and your posturing, and we are calling your bluff. Will you call your men in, and shall we have war? Would you like a few hours to prepare? I think the meadow by Half Moon Lake would be ideally suited if you have the stomach for it. Well, what say you?"

"My liege, I have no intention of hurling my few worthy servitors against your barefoot hordes."

"Gordon, call the guard," said Albert, and Gordon hurried out. The duke planted his feet, crossed his arms, and drew his chin to his chest. It was hard not to be impressed with his audacity. When Gordon returned with a half dozen men-at-arms, the king said, "Escort the duke to the gate."

"Don't touch me!" snapped the duke as one of the soldiers reached out to grasp his arm. The man pulled his hand back as if he'd been scorched. Ignoring the soldiers, the duke began to walk so briskly that his escort had to run to catch up to him.

A cry went up from the army when we came through the door, and then the chanting began: Albert! Albert! Albert! The duke planted himself in the center of the gate and shouted to Albert over the sound of the chanting. "Sire, I have done nothing to deserve this treatment, and I say to you in all seriousness that if you put me into that dungeon, we can never be friends again."

Albert held up his hand and the chanting subsided. "Choose for yourself, my lord duke," said Albert, raising his voice for all to hear. "There are a few things I'd like you to do for me, and the first is to disarm your soldiers. From now on they will dress in leather and carry a staff and a dirk as mine do. Do you concur or would you prefer to visit the dungeon?"

"Throw him in the dungeon! Into the dungeon with him!" came a chorus of voices from the army, and Albert had to raise his hand again for quiet.

After a moment, the duke said, "Very well, I concur."

"Secondly," said the king, "there will be no more crossbows in my kingdom. Destroy the ones you have and make no more. Is this clear?"

"Very well, your majesty," said the duke, but he seemed distracted, as if he was thinking about something else entirely.

"Third, your soldiers must change their attitude completely. No one is to be unreasonably detained by them. No one is to be annoyed by them without an extremely good cause. Those who cannot change their ways immediately will immediately cease to be soldiers. Do you agree?"

"Yes, my liege," said the duke, and that brought a great roar of approval from the army.

Albert drew his sword and held it up by the blade in his gloved fist like a cross in front of the duke. "Swear on your holy oath," said the king.

"My king," said the duke, making the sign of the cross on his breast and touching his fingers to his lips, "I swear on my holy oath to uphold your edicts and to honor your sovereignty

203

as long as you live." Then he turned to the army, and with a wave of his hand, he cried out, "Long live the king!"

"Long live the king!" cried the whole army.

"Long live the king!" cried Leo, and the great shout echoed between the mountains. The people were shouting and whistling and stamping and throwing their hats in the air. The duke, without asking permission, turned on his heel, strode back through the gate, up the path, into his house, and slammed the door. While the cheering and stamping continued outside, Lord Hawke's manor seemed wrapped in its own brooding silence.

Chapter Eleven

"And that was the end of it," I said to Jenna. We were both still naked after making love on the shore of a small secluded lake. "We gathered up the army and marched away." Days had passed since our bloodless victory over Guy Hawke, but this was the first time I had managed to get some time alone with Jenna.

"Albert said he made a speech."

"Yes, he did. As soon as we came to a field big enough to gather his army around him, he made a speech from his horse. It was the airiest speech I ever heard. It was worse than the ones the presidents in the U.S. used to make."

"Used to make?"

"I almost forgot that the U.S. still exists. It's easy to forget, isn't it?"

"I'm only teasing you, Jack. I know exactly what you mean. As far as we're concerned it simply doesn't matter whether it ever existed or not. What did he say in his speech?"

"He thanked everyone for their loyalty and courage. He promised them peace and prosperity. He invited them all to your coronation. It had nothing to do with Lord Hawke."

"Yet everyone felt that the confrontation was a great success."

"That's true. Everyone was glad they came. That's the most important thing in case Albert has to turn them all out again. And the people who weren't there seemed to know all the details of what had gone on by the time we got back to the castle. The stablemen, and the kitchen help, and everybody else was talking about it when we arrived."

"Yes, the river valley grapevine is quite uncanny."

"I suppose everyone knows all about us, then."

She turned to look at me with just the hint of a pout, and I was sorry I'd mentioned it. "No, dear," she said. "No one knows a thing."

We began to get dressed. "I'm wondering whether Albert missed an opportunity," Jenna said.

"When was that?"

"When you were inside the duke's hall, did you by any chance see a hideous carved chair like a coffin with armrests?"

"Yes, I saw that. What about it?"

"Well, it wasn't made here, you see, and it's strictly against the rules to bring in anything from the outside. But the duke had it smuggled in somehow and there it sits in his hall. When Charlsey Dugdale heard about it she had a fit! The duke refused to part with it despite the scandal it created. It's like a symbol of his unwillingness to truly acknowledge Albert."

"That chair wasn't part of the terms."

"Well, it should have been. I'm very sorry Albert didn't think of it. The duke was compliant enough about all the other decrees. He destroyed the crossbows publicly. He disarmed his soldiers right away. He seems to be changing his whole attitude, although I suppose it's too early to say that. All in all, I think it's going to make for a very joyful coronation day."

Back in the stables, I helped Jenna down from her horse. In public, I was always very attentive to her in a friendly, brotherly way to blur other people's suspicions; with Albert it seemed to work fine. He often expressed his gratitude that I paid attention to her, since he was often busy and worried she was lonely.

His trust made me feel all the more guilty, of course. I had known Albert a long time and we had many shared experiences. In some ways I loved Albert more than I loved Jenna. But Jenna was a drug to me. She made the universe seem ineffably sweet and exciting, and I could not resist her. That I would some day have to pay for my treachery, I was certain. But it made no difference in how I behaved in the present. As for Jenna herself, she was loyal to Albert in her way, attentive to his moods and his needs. They seemed to be a happy couple and suited to one another.

"Thank you, Sir Jack," said Jenna. "That was a delightful outing. I'm going to bathe now; perhaps you will join us for dinner?"

"I would be very happy to, my lady." I watched her out of sight, and when I turned, there was Sir Rudy Strapp standing behind me.

"Hello, Rudy. I didn't see you come up." I had made it a personal policy to be more careful about what was going on behind me; obviously I wasn't being careful enough.

He gave me a hint of a smile, about as friendly as he ever got. "People never see me unless I want them to."

I thought immediately of a certain secluded lake, but I suppose it was just my guilt. "What's on your mind?"

"We need to talk about the coronation."

"What about it?"

"It's going to be very noisy and crowded. It's a perfect time for him to make a try for the king."

For a few moments I stared at him blankly until it dawned on me what he was talking about. "You think Hawke is going to try to hurt Albert?"

"Sure, don't you?"

"Well, I hadn't really thought about it."

"Well, maybe you oughta think about it."

The last few days since Albert had settled with Guy Hawke had been the most idyllic of my life. My chest had been sore again when we came home from the confrontation, so I spent the first day lying around in my robe, eating often and enjoying my popularity. The second day I went hawking with Albert and Jenna and some of the knights, and though we didn't catch anything we had a delightful time singing rounds and passing the wineskin. There seemed to be nothing to worry about under the sun, no excuse for not being perfectly happy. The little bag of gold I had been given would easily last forever, and everyone I met wanted to give me something to eat or drink, or pay me a compliment.

I wanted to believe that the problem with the duke had been laid to rest, at least for the time being, and I wanted a vacation. But as soon as I decided to think about it, it was easy to see that the duke's compliance had been nothing more than a mask. It was easy enough to remember the look in his eyes, the tone of his voice, and the ambiguity of his words.

"Maybe you oughta think about what's gonna happen to you without King Albert. Have you thought about that?"

"But do you honestly think he would try to murder the king?"

"Okay, listen. The king used to go away from time to time, right? Sometimes he was gone a month or even more. If anything serious came up, the duke was always in charge. He was like acting king. And even when Albert was here, he always did what he wanted to do. If he wanted to make crossbows, he made crossbows. Now Albert is going to stay home for good, and he's trying to take over the power he used to share with the duke. He wants the duke to be like Dugdale or Griswold now."

"And you don't think he's going to back down that far."

"Put it this way: he's not going to back down at all."

"Let's go talk to Sir Leo."

We found Sir Leo at the first place we looked, which was the archery butt. He was just beginning an archery lesson for some of the knights and soldiers, so Rudy and I took the class along with them. Afterwards we told him what we were thinking about the coronation, and he caught on right away.

"I have been very blind about this," he said. "Of course I didn't think it was the end of the story with the duke. But I thought—or I wanted to think—that we were going to have a rest from that problem for awhile. I am not suspicious enough by nature for the responsibility I have here."

"Maybe the next person we need to talk to is King Albert."

"Nenny," said Rudy.

Leo shook his head.

"Why not?"

"Let's go get ourselves something to eat, and we can talk it over," said Leo.

Pretty soon we were sitting around the table by the hearth in the empty dining room, eating a meal that Hélène had put up for us. "I don't see any possibility of an attack in force," said Leo. "Everyone would rally to the king, and the attack would fail. The duke would be dead or in the dungeon, and he would never get a second chance."

"That's my opinion too, for what it's worth," I said. "If the attack comes at all, it will have to be some kind of treachery like a fatal accident, or poison, or an arrow out of nowhere. Maybe a stabbing. I don't know what we can do except stick to the king like glue."

"That's not going to be easy," said Rudy. "The king likes to mingle. He has his private business. If he excuses himself to go off with somebody, all you can do is excuse him."

"I think we need to talk to him about this," I said.

"He's not gonna listen," said Rudy.

"I'm afraid that's true," said Leo. "We've all talked to him about security at one time or another. Beyond a very minimal amount, he finds it oppressive."

"But if he holds the monarchy together, it is irresponsible of him to take chances," I said. "I will talk to him."

"Good luck," said Rudy.

"The king is philosophical about that," said Leo. "He will tell you that too many precautions invite the trouble they are meant to forestall. And having lived in the U.S., who is to say that he is wrong about that? You can talk to him if you like, but I think it will actually be harder for us to look after him if he knows what we're doing."

"We need a dozen men to watch him without him noticing it," said Rudy. "We can pass him from team to team so he won't catch on. Even if he excuses himself, we can police the vicinity."

"I am inclined toward that plan," said Leo.

"What about poison?" I said.

We all exchanged glances. Leo laughed. "Who wants to be the taster?"

"Poison control requires a certain amount of cooperation from the person you don't want poisoned," I said.

"How would you want him to cooperate?"

"How about only eating what Hélène prepares? That would be pretty foolproof."

"He'd never agree to that," said Rudy. "The coronation is going to be a huge party. People are going to be bringing all kinds of stuff to eat and drink, and the king loves to eat."

"Most of the wedding gifts are going to be flowers and food," said Leo. "What else do people have to give? It would be an insult if the king didn't eat it."

"Poison is a hard way to make work right," said Rudy, "especially in a crowd. I'm thinking more about a knifing, or possibly an arrow."

"But if the knifer gets caught, it leads right back to the source," I said.

"Right," said Rudy. "There has to be a good opportunity to do it and get away. Or else it won't be tried. So we have to make sure the opportunity isn't there."

"All right," said Leo, "let's pick our teams and start practicing."

"I want to talk to the mage about this before we get started," I said. "I've known her a long time, and she doesn't miss much."

"By all means," said Leo. "It was certainly very good advice to bring you here."

"Thank you, Leo. I hope so, I really do."

It didn't take me long to find Marya, since she was looking for me. "Jack," she said, "I'm worried. The last few days, while everybody has been celebrating, I've had this very uncomfortable feeling. I can't sit still, I'm not sleeping well, and I have this impulse all the time to glance over my shoulder as if someone was stalking me."

"What's it all about?"

"I wish I knew for sure. That's the trouble with being what people call psychic. You're always trying to sort out what might be real from what you might be making up."

"Okay, I get that, but if something is coming in on the old teletype, I'm very interested, Marya."

"Tele-what? No, don't look at me like that. Those words from the future don't belong here, and that's why we have this game. Now roll it up."

"Ouch! You're too good at that."

"I remember you telling me that when you walked into the duke's hall, you felt like sticking your fingers in your ears, even though it was quiet. That's what it feels like in my body, like someone screaming with rage. I don't think we ought to be underestimating Hawke right now, or what he might be capable of."

When I told her about our plan to guard Albert, she began to shake so violently that we had to look for a place to sit down. "I'm okay," she said. "I'm actually very relieved. This is exactly what I wanted to hear. Thank God you're here, Jack. Take care of the king. He needs you more than ever now."

That very day we began shadowing Albert. We picked Gordon and eight others and filled them in on the game, which was to stay in close proximity to Albert all the time. If possible, one or more of us would keep him company, and since Albert was a convivial and social person, that was often easy. If he seemed to need some space, we would drift a short distance and form a protective ring around him.

Gordon was very creative in thinking up ways for us to communicate with each other through the whistling of certain tunes, and knocking codes on wood and on steel, special laughs and coughs and key words that made up a message system which worked up close and also at a distance. We could tell each other where Albert was going or what he was doing or what we were planning to do. In a week's time we had a network that was working well, and we continued to polish it. We shadowed Albert's visitors, coming and going. We monitored his food from wherever it came from to wherever he ate it. When he retired to bed, we left him alone, but other than that we held him in a tight circle of surveillance.

"I'm very pleased," said Leo to me. "This is a fine, committed team. We have a good system and we know how to improvise too. Of course some of our tricks are not going to work at a noisy party, but I think we can handle any situation."

"Well, let's keep our fingers crossed; but I agree with you, Leo. I think we've got it pretty well whipped."

That week, people by the hundreds came from all over the valley to bring something for the coronation, or to help with the preparations. Émile and Hélène lived in the eye of the hurricane, supervising the cleaning and decorating of the castle and the preparation of a feast for thousands of people. The livestock pens were bursting and the pantry and the larder overflowed into the halls. "It's not so difficult if you have the help," said Hélène serenely, though she was directing traffic with both hands. "The same thing happens every Christmas and Easter."

Sometimes Jenna tried to pitch in, but she was nervous and so full of her feelings that she misdirected people and botched things up. Hélène was like a mother to her, treating her with patience and understanding even though she was mostly in the way. "I was the same way just before I got married," she told me.

Time passed quickly, and before I knew it, coronation day dawned bright and clear. It seemed like a good sign, because the weather had been gusty and uncertain all week. Now the mid-morning sky was a brilliant blue, graced with a few fleecy clouds, and people were arriving in streams. They came by foot and in all manner of carts, merry and eager to enjoy the holiday.

How Albert's staff kept any order among so many guests was beyond me, but as Hélène said, they were used to it. The flowers all went to the special gallery that had been erected for the coronation ceremony. Foodstuff, depending on what it was, either was put aside for the banquet, or went right out on the tables for people to snack on. The carts were directed to the big meadow south of the castle as soon as they were unloaded.

I had seen bigger crowds in my time, but never one so merry and so talented at entertaining itself. Instruments appeared everywhere, all sorts of flutes and drums and homemade stringed instruments of all sizes and shapes, and everywhere were small circles of people who played and sang and danced. Amateur performers also gathered their crowds with juggling, acrobatics, and magic tricks. Barefoot children ran in and out of the crowds.

Albert, shining with his inner light and as full of joy as anyone there, went from one little group to the next, staying long enough to sing a little and dance a little, before moving on. Never losing his dignity or his humanity either, he touched everyone with his love, and blushed with all the love he received.

Dugdale and Charlsey arrived in an open coach with several servants in livery, followed by a wagonload of flowers and presents. Charlsey looked very pretty in what looked to be a new gown, and happier than I had ever seen her previously. At an event like this she would never have to stop twirling and talking, and she seemed ready to make the most of it. Dugdale, immaculately dressed and barbered, tagged along, happy as a hound to see his lady enjoying herself so much.

Griswold rode in about the same time, all by himself. He looked a little uncomfortable, as though it was hard for him to keep up his ironic front in the face of such universal gaiety. He rode slowly, glancing around like a new arrival, as though he was wondering what all those people could possibly be doing. When he saw me, he walked his horse over to where I was standing and dismounted, giving me his usual smirk for a greeting.

"Hello, Darcey. See any girls you like?" It was typical for him to talk as though everyone's instincts were always base. Griswold was very pure in his philosophy; he believed humans had begun wearing clothes by accident, and that civilization had always been more than we could handle.

"Give me a chance, Harvey. I'm just getting my feet on the ground around here."

"Sure you are." It was also typical for him to behave as if everything anyone said was a cover-up. "How about walking me over to the stables?"

"Sure," I said, signaling to Leo that I was going off with Griswold. Leo returned a slight nod: he would take over. Griswold surprised me by reading our silent communication like a book.

"Are you guys tightening up the security around the king?"

I nodded, seeing no reason to lie about it.

"Did Albert tell you to do that?"

"No, this is our own idea, and you need to keep it to yourself."

"Don't worry," he shrugged, as though it was a pointless thing to say to him. "That Albert! He's such a baby! Going around pretending he knows everybody's name. Actually, it's a good thing you came along when you did, Darcey. Hawke had Albert outmaneuvered every which way, and Albert just wasn't about to stand up to him."

"I thought he did a pretty good job of it the other day."

"Yes, but he had to, don't you see? You set him up for it, and there was nothing else he could do."

"We won't argue about it," I said, feeling annoyed with him. "I know you have your own way of looking at things, Harvey, but I see one hell of a good king in Albert."

He gave me an appraising look. "You sound very loyal."

"I am. To begin with this kingdom is his dream-child, and I like it here better than anywhere I've ever lived in my life."

"Okay, I don't blame you for liking it here. And I think Albert is doing a pretty good half-assed job of being a king."

"Oh? And what kind of a job are you doing as an earl?"

"Who cares about being an earl? I'm interested in coitus. Look, Darcey, I like it here too, just the way it is. And as a matter of fact, I was going to suggest that we keep a closer eye on Albert, but I see you guys are way ahead of me. By the way, what do you think of this castle?"

"What do I think of the castle?"

"Do you like it? Do you think it's beautiful?"

"Yes, I do." Why was he smiling at me that way?

"Have you ever thought to yourself how nice it would be if it was *your* castle, instead of Albert's?"

A lump came up in my throat and I didn't want to swallow, because that seemed like a dead giveaway to certain feelings I was hiding even from myself. But it was such a troublesome lump, I had no choice but to swallow it, and Griswold pointed his finger at me and laughed.

"You can't hide anything from me, Darcey. Old Harvey, the Earl of Quim, knows all and sees all. And do you want to know how I know?"

"How do you know?"

"Because everybody feels the same way. Because Albert got down on his hands and knees and begged Joel Mason to design him the most seductive and alluring little castle there ever was. Can you guess why?"

". . . Because of Jenna."

"Of course. She wasn't exactly sure how she felt about Albert. She had other lives to lead, other prospects. She was having trouble making up her mind."

Something on my face must have tickled him, for he pointed at me again and laughed. "Isn't it a stitch? If we had a little less castle, we might have a lot less trouble. You and I can look at that lovely pile of stones, float a little daydream by, and then go about our business. But when our friend Guy Hawke looks at it, it's a whole different story!"

I tended to take anything Harvey told me with a grain of salt, but it all seemed pretty close to the mark. I myself was all tangled up with irresistible Jenna, in a situation that could only end in a lot of trouble. And Albert wasn't the first person to try to buy someone's love. Little mistakes in the beginning; big mistakes in the end.

"Anyway, what I'm getting at," Griswold went on, "is that what happened the other day over at Hawke Manor was a big setback in the duke's campaign to trade places with Albert that has been going on for years. And I can tell you with complete certainty that the duke is not the least bit mellow about it. So it's well worth thinking about what he's going to do next."

At that moment a family of five rode in on horseback: a man, a woman, and three young men, one of whom had been involved in the incident with the girl in the woods. This would have to be the marquess, Terry Bennett, and his family. He was the only nobleman I hadn't yet met.

Bennett rode like a horseman, but there was a slackness about the man inside the holiday clothes, and his face was fiery from alcohol poisoning. His eyes were glazed and fearful, like many drunks I had met who live in perpetual fear of themselves.

The woman was clearly the leader of the group. I could

see right away that it was her pride and her discipline that held them together. The eldest boy, the one who had been with Albert's son, tried to show himself off by side-stepping his horse, a dangerous trick in that crowd; but she spoke sharply to him, and he obeyed her without hesitation. She was a strong and quite a beautiful woman with dark hair and a full mouth, a serious face, and clear intelligent eyes.

Her eyes fell on me as the group rode by, and they lingered just long enough to make an identification. "Oh, yes," she seemed to be saying to herself, "that must be Darcey, the new one, the fencing master." If she had any notions about me, good or bad, they didn't show.

The oldest boy had a wild look, as though he sought to take after his father. But like his mother, he turned away once he'd picked me out of the crowd and kept his thoughts to himself. The second son seemed complacent, relaxed, and a little aloof, as if life to him was an enjoyable game. The youngest rode closest to his mother, and was still looking around at everything as though life was new and fresh.

"Handsome woman," I said to Griswold.

"Marsha Bennett. She's the only one who can tell her husband that he's had enough."

"What about Bennett? Is he any danger to Albert?"

"No, he loves drinking and sport. He can't see straight enough to be a danger to anybody except himself and his horse."

"What's his relationship with Hawke? I hear they went to college together."

"He looks up to the duke, and the duke likes being looked up to, so he tolerates Bennett and strings him along."

"Why does he look up to the duke?"

"Because the duke is a real man, and Bennett is a sick juicehead."

218

"Is that all there is between them?"

"As far as I can see."

Not far behind the Bennett family came Lord Hawke with twenty of his men, a grim-looking bunch who were dressed in leather and carried staffs and daggers, just as Albert had insisted. I thought it was aggressive of the duke to come riding in with so many men; but everyone in the valley was invited to the coronation and they had every right to be there. As soon as they entered the great courtyard, his men dismounted and hitched up to the long rail, stacked their staffs in bunches near the gate, and dispersed into the crowd in twos and threes, heading toward the tables where the food and the ale were. They seemed benign enough. We were already keeping a close watch on the situation, and that was all we could do.

Hawke peered around until he spied Albert, and rode carefully through the crowd to where the king was standing. Dismounting, he gave his reins to the stable boy who came running up. Then he surprised everyone who was near enough to see it by going down on one knee in front of Albert and saluting with his fist against his chest. It brought a startled gasp from the crowd; and then everyone who had seen it happen had to tell everyone who hadn't.

"My dear duke, pray do not kneel," said Albert.

The duke rose, bowed to Albert, and said, "Your majesty, please accept my best wishes and the allegiance of my house on this momentous day."

"I am truly touched," said Albert, "and I accept with all my heart."

Albert seemed willing to believe him, and as I looked about, there were many people in the crowd as touched as Albert, and as willing to believe that some kindly Providence had shown the duke the error of his arrogant ways; that now he was trying to reform himself, trying to change.

I was chilled. That Hawke was willing to make a gesture so false and out of character as kneeling and bowing to Albert, made me realize how imminent the danger was. No ring of protection could be too secure, no precautions too strict, for what now seemed surely to be coming. How it was coming or from where, under what guise or pretense, there was no telling. But clearly we hadn't begun to get ready a moment too soon.

"What do you make of that?" I said to Griswold.

"I think I'd better help you keep an eye on the duke today."

"Very good, Harvey, thanks a lot. Talk to Sir Leo if you can't find me. We want to know every move he makes, can you do that?"

"Sure I can," said Griswold, and he moved away into the crowd.

I found Sir Leo conferring with Gordon and Rudy and two others from our team. "Ah, Jack," he said, "did you see that? We all agree that this is a very bad sign."

"I think so too. Look, we've been very discreet with our security measures, giving the king lots of space and all that. Let's forget about that tactic for the time being and close right in on him. Sir Leo, with your permission, I'd like six people right around him as close as they can reasonably get, and the other six close by. If he gets completely suffocated, we can spread out a little, but as much as possible I'd like him completely surrounded all the time. What do you say?"

"I'm in favor of that," said Leo, "but what about six in close, and three nearby, and three out roving to see whatever else there might be to see?"

"Even better. Lord Griswold just signed on to help. He's going to watch the duke and report anything he sees."

"It's settled then," said Leo. "You five get right on him.

I'll tell the others."

When we caught up with Albert, he was still making his rounds of all the little parties and gatherings, and I will say again that it was the liveliest and most talented crowd of people I had ever experienced. Everyone wanted to do something nice for Albert since it was his wedding day, and probably also because Albert was like everybody's dad, one that had time to stop and pay attention; and so we were treated to every kind of recital, particularly musical pieces, songs, and dances. Some of the smaller children took a little coaxing because they were in awe of the king; but everyone else seemed eager for their turn to perform, or to offer him something they had cooked, or to tell a funny story. It was all done so unaffectedly and simply that after awhile I was in a sort of trance from all that loving spirit.

"Gordon," I said, reaching out to touch his sleeve, "this is too beautiful. How do these people come to be so free and open?"

"Well, if you ask me, it has a lot to do with the children. These little ones have been here all their lives. They haven't been bombarded with images of sex and violence day and night the way modern children are; and they've never felt the paranoia of a big city. They can see a dragon in a bug; a fairy princess in a stick and a bit of rag. And their purity, if that's what you like to call it, sets the example for all of us as the years go by. You have to have sane children to keep the adults sane, that's what I think."

"When I hear you talk, Gordon, I think sometimes there's a better place for you in this kingdom than to be a cop on market day."

"I don't want a promotion, Sir Jack. I'm the luckiest man on earth. I earn my bread roving around with a horse and a stick, and most of the time I'm free just to listen to the voices

221

of the angels. And speaking of angels, I think we're going to have a song from Mora the Rose."

She was sitting with some other people with her baby on her lap when we came walking up, and she gave me such a friendly, clear-eyed, and happy look when she saw me coming, that my heart went right out to her. She was wearing a skirt and a blouse and an embroidered vest, which must have been her party clothes, and she had sandals on her pretty feet. Her wavy blond hair hung loose around her shoulders.

Everyone stood up when the king approached and all the women curtsied. "Will your majesty be pleased to have a drink with us?" asked one of the men.

"Yes, Fred, I will," said the king, "but just a teeny tiny one, for I'm getting married very shortly and I don't want to be fuzzy-headed. And after my drink, I'd like to hear Mora sing."

Mora smiled, but she didn't giggle or fidget or make any modest protestations. She flashed me one brief glance that was a little self-conscious and that was all. Maybe she was hoping I would like her singing.

Albert had his drink, which was only a pretend drink, just a sip, because he would have been three sheets to the wind a long time ago if he had had a real drink with everyone who asked him. Then he took the stool someone offered him.

Mora stood up, put the baby on her hip, and began to sing a merry little song about some forest animals that went on a picnic together, and about what each one brought for them all to eat, like the rabbit brought carrots, and so on, until they all enjoyed a delicious stew together. She had a clear, youthful voice which radiated joy in a way that brought tears to my eyes. When she finished her song, she let out a deep breath and grinned at the king.

Someone else was singing now. I could hear it faintly,

so faintly I had to listen closely to make sure it wasn't my imagination. Sure enough, a procession of chanting monks led by Father Frederick, the abbot, was approaching the castle carrying crosses and censers. The church procession marked the beginning of the coronation.

Albert rose from his stool and took Mora's hands in his. "Thank you, my child," he said. "It always makes me so happy to hear you sing."

Mora curtsied. "You're very welcome, your majesty."

"And now," said Albert, "if you will all kindly excuse me, I have an appointment even a king can't be late for."

"Well, did you like it?" Mora asked me.

"Yes, Mora, I certainly did. It was pure delight, like everything else about you."

Well, that lit the light in her eyes. "If we go now," she said, "we can get a good seat down front to watch the ceremony."

My first impulse was to give her my arm and go right along with her. While she was singing, I was certainly in love with her. But then it occurred to me that it wouldn't do at all for me to be Mora's date in the front row at the wedding. That would be much too symbolic, and much too public; and what would that do to her chances of finding a nice, young husband her own age? *What, you're thinking of courting Mora the Rose? Didn't you know she was sitting with Sir Jack himself at the coronation?*

I was also thinking about Jenna and what she might think if she saw Mora and me together. It would be obvious to her that there was something going on between us. Of course there was the possibility she might just be amused by the situation, but I saw no reason to count on that. Actually, I didn't know much about what Jenna thought. Thinking had very little to do with our relationship. I was inclined to believe she felt somehow obliged to cheat on Albert, though I couldn't say why. We all

223

have our loose screws, and that was one of hers. One of mine was that I couldn't resist taking what women offered me, no matter how much trouble it was likely to cause.

"I have to stay close to the king today, Mora. I'm on guard duty."

"Can't you get someone else to do it?"

"I can't. Not today." Why was I hedging? Because I could smell her, that's why. Because she looked so healthy and young and sweet. I knew what I was supposed to do, but I wasn't going to do it.

"Look, Mora," I tried, "I've already got gray in my hair. In a couple of years all my teeth are going to start falling out."

She smiled at that. "They are not."

"Yes, they are. This one's loose already, see?" I reached up and pretended to wiggle one of them, but she just continued to smile at my antics. It was no use. I was just playing with her, and I wasn't going to play it straight. My age didn't matter to her; I knew that already. Maybe it even attracted her. So what kind of a game was I running anyway?

Sir Leo had come back for me. "The ceremony is about to begin. You and I and Gordon are going to take seats right up front. Ask the young lady to join you if you want, but let's go now."

When he turned to lead the way I followed, and Mora came right along with me as though I had asked her to. My brain was racing. For a number of good reasons I had decided that this wasn't a good idea, and here it was happening anyway.

"Look, Mora," I said, stopping. "We have to take care of business. It's a long story, but we're worried that something might happen to the king today. If I pay attention to you, I'm not going to be able to do my job."

She looked puzzled. "What could happen to the king today?"

"We're worried about the duke. Did you ever think he'd rather be king than duke?"

"Oh, yes."

"Well, we think he's cooking something up."

"What's he cooking up?"

"Sir Jack, we must go," said Leo.

"I'm coming, Sir Leo," I said over my shoulder. "We think he might try to kill the king."

She seemed amazed at that. "The people would tear him into little pieces," she said. "And I'd help."

How could I explain it to her? "There are a lot of ways it could be done. We've got to be prepared for anything. I can't stay and talk. I have to go now."

"Sir Jack!" said Leo.

"I have to go. I'll talk to you after the ceremony." I turned and ran to catch up with Leo, hoping she wouldn't follow me. Clever Sir Jack! I was actually hoping I could see her later on. I just didn't want Jenna to see us together. The duke was right to wonder, I thought to myself, how I had ever become a knight!

In front of the castle was a gallery of flowers that people had brought from all over the kingdom, and in the center of the gallery was an altar. Plank benches made about twenty rows with standing room behind on the side of a low hill so everyone had a chance to see everything.

The seats were beginning to fill up, but Gordon had saved three for us in the front row. I sat down between Gordon and Sir Leo; and now that I had effectively prevented her from sitting down next to me, I turned around to see where Mora was. She was taking a seat about a dozen rows back with some of her friends. As though she felt my eyes on her, she looked up at me and smiled. I smiled back and turned around to the front. Everything seemed to have fallen into place for the moment anyway.

As it turned out, Jenna never so much as glanced my way during the entire ceremony, and I doubt she even remembered that I existed, for the coronation was as perfect and as beautiful as a fairy tale, complete with Albert's designer castle in the background. Jenna was as lovely and demure in her elaborate, handmade robes as ever a woman could be, and Albert was as handsome and noble as any king out of the legends. Forgetting even to be jealous, I sat spellbound in a happy stupor.

I was not the only one. Everyone else was as mesmerized as I was. No one fidgeted. No one talked. Everyone was absorbed in the ceremony as if they were watching something both magical and holy.

Finally the moment arrived when Jenna actually became the queen. She waited with acute anticipation shining in her face, and we all waited with her as the abbot slowly lowered the crown. The moment the gold circle touched her brow, we all gave a little gasp, as if we could feel her mystic transformation.

The sun was setting slowly into a notch between two mountains, and the sky was full of shifting colors of every hue. The priests were lighting candles for the final procession, and the chanting, so deep and mysterious, had begun again. Happiness and a feeling of completion at the end of a mythic day, seemed to fill the valley like a sacred vessel.

Three Picts came out of the strip of woods that bordered the river and stood motionless at the edge of the meadow about fifty yards from the altar. In their leafy masks, they looked like a part of the forest that had disengaged itself from the whole in order to honor the coronation.

If there were mixed feelings in the kingdom about the Picts, the mood at that moment was one of reconciliation.

I could feel it in the air. Somehow these Picts ought to be included in this salubrious and epic occasion.

But how was it to be accomplished? How could that crowd of thousands accommodate three forest creatures standing so silently at the edge of their endless domain? It was up to Albert, the king of the civilized world, to make the gesture; and we all watched as he rose from the throne, lifted a silver platter of bread from the altar, and moved across the meadow with the tray held in both hands. We waited almost breathlessly, as quiet and motionless as the Picts.

There was some slight commotion behind me that broke the perfect stillness. Someone seemed to be trying to push closer down through the tightly-packed crowd. It irked me that someone would show so little appreciation of what was happening. Why couldn't they just relax and keep still?

I felt a tug on my sleeve and turned sharply. Mora was looking down at me, and she said, "Those aren't Picts."

My sword was in my hand, and I was running toward the king screaming a warning, but it was too late. He had already walked right up to them and was holding out the tray. Now he took a step backwards and the tray tumbled to the ground.

Gordon was running too and swept past me, bounding across the field toward Albert, his iron-tipped staff twirling in the air over his head. The Picts turned and disappeared into the woods, and they had hardly left the meadow before Gordon went crashing into the trees after them.

I continued to run toward the king, who was just standing there looking toward the woods where the Picts had disappeared. He seemed perfectly all right. We had scared them off in time, but it had been close. Much too close. He turned toward me as I came running up, looking puzzled and annoyed; now I suddenly had second thoughts. Could Mora have been wrong? Had Gordon and I just spoiled everything?

I stopped in front of him, gasping for breath. "I can explain everything, my liege," though I wasn't sure I could.

But Albert wasn't listening. He looked pale. "Jack," he said in a strange voice. "Oh, Jack, I think I've been stabbed."

The earth seemed to tilt under my feet. "Where, Albert?"

He reached under his right armpit. "As I held out the tray, I thought one of them struck me. But now I feel . . . Am I bleeding?"

My fear was making everything blurry. Going down on one knee, I lifted his arm and looked for blood.

"Stay back, please." It was Leo's voice. "Please stand back. Everything is all right. Stand back now."

I couldn't see anything wrong, but the king was wearing a lot of clothes. Was that a tear in the cloth, there under his arm? Then I saw the stain of his blood and I knew that we had failed.

Chapter Twelve

Albert made it walking as far as the castle before he keeled over. We carried him upstairs on my cloak, put him to bed, and treated him for shock. That was all we knew how to do. The mage, who had not been seen at the coronation, was sought for. It was thought that she was away caring for a sick woman in Bennett's fief. In the meantime I waited in an agony of self-reproach.

Upstairs in the king's chambers were the queen and her new step-son Renny, Leo and myself, and Émile and Hélène. The other members of our security team had scattered to look for the mage. I don't think Renny understood the danger Albert was in. Nor perhaps did Jenna, for she seemed more put out than anything else. Albert had been hurt, and what might have been a perfect coronation had been spoiled. She hadn't come to consider what Leo and I knew—that Albert's chances were slim at best; that throughout history, a dirty hole through the body wall was usually fatal.

Émile and Hélène were family to Albert, or maybe even more loyal than family, and they were clearly suffering. They were well aware, I'm sure, of his danger, but they also believed in a God who could do whatever he felt like. They didn't make any show of it, but I believe they prayed constantly.

"Where's Gordon?" We had been too busy to count noses, and it had just occurred to me that I hadn't seen him since he'd charged into the woods.

"I'll go," said Leo, and he slipped out of the room that now contained a new wife who might soon be a widow, a son who might soon be an orphan, a fine and dedicated king who might soon be nothing more than a memory, two family servitors who might soon have no one to serve, and one jackass who had let himself be lulled into uselessness on guard duty with the fate of thousands hanging in the balance. One little slip. One little hole; and now there were a few million germs running out of control in the warm and wet. That was all it would take to unmake our world.

It was through the open window of Albert's chamber that I watched Guy Hawke taking charge. Minutes after Albert fell, rumors were circulating that some Picts had torched a farmhouse in Dugdale's fife; that a sheperd had been beaten and sheep stolen on Bennett's lands, also by Picts. Many peasants left to go home, and those who stayed were as angry and volatile now as they had been happy and peaceful fifteen minutes before, so the duke's men joined with the palace guard to direct traffic and keep order.

The duke gave orders now as he had when Albert was away, and his orders were obeyed as they had been in the past. Sir Leo normally commanded the king's soldiers, answering directly to Albert. But in these special circumstances Lord Hawke's authority superseded Sir Leo's. At the moment Lord Hawke controlled the kingdom; and if Albert died, who was there to oppose his power?

As I numbly watched this change in the power structure, I was far too full of fear and guilt to think systematically about any of it. Suffering and suspended, I waited for the mage to arrive. Albert was pale, his breathing was labored, and his pulse was racing; and though I was no medic, I knew that these were not good signs.

When Marya finally arrived, throwing off her dusty cloak

and kicking off her boots, she made us undress the king and wrap quilts around him while she examined him from head to foot by candle and torchlight. Finding no other wounds, she had me support his arm while she stared long and hard at the wound high in his side.

"Did you see it happen?"

"I was looking right at him, but I didn't see exactly how it was done."

"How was he standing?"

"With his arms stretched out in front. Marya, I want you to tell me he's going to pull through. He is, isn't he?"

"Move the torch in closer."

I did as she told me. "What can we do?"

"There isn't anything to do," she said. Her voice seemed to come from far away. It was difficult to hear her.

"A hot compress," I suggested, "with some herbs to draw the . . ." I had no idea what I was trying to say. I just couldn't believe there was no solution. There had to be a solution.

"I'm sorry, Jack," she said softly.

"Listen, I've got an idea. It's the germs that are the problem, right? And penicillin is nothing but bread mold, right? It could make all the difference. There must be some moldy bread around here. We could feed the mold to Albert and the penicillin . . ."

Her eyes were brimming with tears. "Jack," she said, her voice catching in her throat, "if you want to look for some moldy bread, you can. If it will make you feel better."

"But wouldn't it . . ."

She shook her head and the tears splashed out of her eyes. She tried to say something but her voice wouldn't work, so she reached up and grabbed me by the neck of my tunic to pull me down. Pointing to Albert's side with a trembling finger, she

231

began to trace an outline on his side. At first it made no sense. But as I looked more closely, I saw that below the wound and underneath Albert's pale skin, there was a darker patch, a stain that was visible right through the skin. The stain came most of the way down his side; and what could it be but his blood running into places where it didn't belong. Even as I watched the outline seemed to grow larger. It was too late to rediscover penicillin. It was just plain too late.

"Mage?" Renny was standing by the bed now, looking down at Albert. "Why is my dad so pale?"

Marya rose to her feet and laid a gentle hand on his shoulder. Looking into his eyes, she said, "Renny, I'm afraid your dad is dying."

"Dying? But why?"

It was a question for all the ages of man and the whole creation too. It was the question God heard more than any other. Why, why, why? Why did a man like Albert get killed at his own wedding surrounded by thousands of people who loved him? It least that was an unusual question, a novel question. But why children had to lose their parents was such a continual and incessant question, it must have God stuffing his fingers in his ears all the time.

"He's bleeding inside his body, Renny," Marya said, tears brimming in her eyes as she spoke to him.

"Make it stop."

"I can't, Renny. I would if I could."

"Make it stop!" Good try, kid. Shout at the world loudly enough and maybe it will change. We've all tried it; now it's your turn. Shout and stamp and turn blue in the face. Maybe the greedy people will open their hearts and their hands. Maybe the warmongers will get mellow and open florist shops. Maybe the good dead will come back to life and all the sons-of-bitches will take their places in the graves. Maybe,

maybe, but not tonight. Tonight the oblivious earth is just going to continue circling into the morning without changing anything at all.

Jenna had been standing by the window chewing on her knuckle as she looked out over the dark terrain. Now she turned from the window and came over to the bed. She still looked annoyed. "Albert," she said, "wake up."

And to my surprise, he did. He looked blinkingly up at Jenna, and smiled wanly. "Excuse me, my dear, I must have dozed off." Maybe it was the sound of his own voice that reminded him, or maybe it was pain, or merely the memory itself, but his face became grave. "I was having such a beautiful dream. There was . . . it seemed . . . no, I can't think how it goes. So difficult to remember dreams, especially that sort of dream, where everything falls into place and makes such perfect sense."

He was silent for a time, gazing off into space. Then he glanced over toward his side. "I'm wounded, aren't I? I feel very weak and strange. I don't feel like I'm quite all there. Or should I say all here? Mage, am I going to be all right?"

Émile and Hélène had also come over to the bed, and Albert looked up into all our faces one by one; but no one spoke.

"Well, that seems unanimous. Yes, that would be my guess too. I'm leaking badly, that's what I feel like. The sands of time are running right out."

"Dad, you're going to be all right!" Renny said vehemently.

Albert looked up at him, and his eyes were full of love. "Thank you, my boy. Everything is going to be all right. That's what it said in my dream, you see? Everything's going to be all right because . . . well, because that's all there is—the all right part—and the rest is just a dream." And he laughed several silent huffs of laughter which cost him quite a bit in the way of energy, it seemed, because he stopped right away and composed himself. "It's not really a laughing matter," he said, "but it's still all right. I'm afraid that sounds confusing but it's a good thing to know, especially if you're dying."

Then he seemed to recall something and that something made him cry. He cried effortlessly, without panting and screwing up his face. His mouth opened, that was all, and the tears came rolling out of his eyes. I had never seen anyone cry like that, for he didn't seem to be in a whole lot of pain, but the tears were just a flood, running over his cheeks and down his neck. It started everyone else crying too, though I'm sure Émile and Hélène had a good start already on the rest of us.

Finally he blinked out the last rush of tears. Putting up a weak hand, he brushed his fingers over his eyelids, and looked around at all of us again. We waited for him to speak, for a person about to depart on the journey of death always has the floor.

"I really love my little kingdom," he said. "It seems as if I just finally got it set up and now I have to go away. Renny, my son, and you, my dear, you know I made it for everyone but especially for you. Both of you were always on my mind, and I'm so sorry I can't stay to enjoy it with you. Damn it, it seems very unfair," he said, and then he began to cry again, and this time it seemed more painful for him, though it was mostly just that amazing flood of tears.

The door opened behind me, and as I turned to look over my shoulder my hand slipped down over the hilt of my sword. I was relieved to see Father Frederick, though his presence was a reminder that events outside were not standing still as Albert lay dying. Where was Leo? Where was Gordon? It gave me a sinking feeling of dread.

We made room for the abbot, who knelt down by the bed

and gently took hold of the king's wrist. "How is your majesty feeling?"

"My legs are getting cold," said the king. "I feel like I'm . . . made out of paper."

The priest nodded gravely, gazing into the king's eyes and continuing to hold him by the wrist. I believe he was taking his pulse. "Your majesty, if there is anything that needs to be said, it would be best not to waste any time."

Albert gave him an odd look. "You're not trying to confess me, are you, Frederick? I've never done that in my life and I frankly don't know how."

The priest smiled at that, and shook his head. "I'm afraid I'm just as heretical as I was when we first met, if not more so; and as far as I am concerned, confessing is entirely optional. If there is something you want to confess, it does no harm as long as you remember that the real essence of salvation is forgiveness, not repentance."

"Ah yes, forgiveness," sighed the king. "This is difficult. I feel very angry at those Picts, Frederick. They did kill me, after all, and I don't know what I did to deserve this from them."

My mouth opened, but then I closed it again. It was of no importance at the moment whether those men were Picts or not, and there was certainly no time to discuss it. Albert was very pale now. Paper was a good description. Pale, slightly greenish paper.

"Forgive them as best you can," said the priest.

"Yes, that will have to do." The king shut his eyes, and it seemed a long time before he opened them again. He was so still and his skin was so opaque that I wondered whether he was already gone.

"Oh, that felt very good," said the king, opening his eyes. "This dying is quite an experience. Everything becomes very clear and simple."

"Your majesty should announce the heir to the throne," said the priest.

Albert cocked his head. "Why Renny, of course. Everybody knows that."

"Your majesty should take this time to make that especially clear in front of as many witnesses as possible."

"Yes, I see what you mean. Are these people sufficient?"

"Perhaps. But many more would be better."

The door opened again and my heart sank, for there was Lord Hawke with a bunch of his buckoes. His soldiers had changed from their regulation leather armor into outfits sporting a good deal more steel, and though they still retained their iron-tipped staffs, they were armed with maces and short swords.

Hawke came forward and knelt before Albert. "My liege, this is a day that will live in the annals of infamy forever."

In that moment I decided to kill him. Only one long leap separated us. I was guaging the distance when Albert reached out consolingly to pat the duke on the knee. "Carry me to the hall."

"You men!" cried the duke, and my chance was gone, for the room was instantly full of soldiers between me and my prey. Had I really made up my mind to spring on him? Yes, in my heart I had decided to kill him, and anyway I was already a killer. My innocence was gone. But I had also hesitated just long enough for the opportunity to slip away. I was still a little green, and that made me ineffective. I had a lot to learn.

"Not like that, you idiots," snapped the duke as his men reached for Albert to lift him out of bed. "Take up that couch and put it here. Ease him onto it. You there, take up that bedding." I was so overwhelmed with guilt for having let the king down that I could barely make my legs move to follow behind them.

When the soldiers set Albert's couch near the upper end of the hall, it created a kind of magic circle of respect into which the common people would not go. But outside that circle the hall was filling quickly, for by now everyone knew the king was dying. The room could only hold so many people, but its capacity was being stretched and people were still trying to squeeze in. Every window ledge was full and every doorway contained a dozen heads peering in from every angle.

Within the magic circle there was plenty of room for Renny, and Queen Jenna, and Émile and Hélène, the abbot, Marya and myself to attend the dying king. Lord Hawke, flanked by a few of his soldiers, was standing just inside the circle, his arms folded across his chest and his broadsword with its wide crossguard hanging down in front of his body. His manner proclaimed that he had already taken charge, and that any loose ends that were still dangling would soon be taken into his hands.

Finally the hall stopped filling since every conceivable place was taken, and now there was a deep silence. Albert was sitting up on his couch-bed, propped up by pillows with a quilt across his legs. He was still luminous, like sunlight filtered through a wet fog, but it was a chilly light for there was so little blood to warm it. Death, with his scythe and bony face, was as substantial a presence in that room as Albert himself.

"My friends," said Albert, "I want to welcome you all, and to thank you for coming to see me at this time. Unfortunately my body is becoming so heavy and my spirit is so light that I hardly think the two will stay together much longer, so I will be brief. Something happened to me today that I don't understand. In fact I don't even have time enough left to try to understand it. And so, as I wish to be forgiven for anything wrong that I may have done during my life, I wish merely to forgive what was done to me today. And it is my fervent hope, and also my command as your still-living king, that no reprisals will be taken against innocent people because of today's mysterious attack. If the guilty party can be apprehended, let him be judged and punished in accordance with our way of life. But let no one make this an excuse to multiply the evils of the world in the name of justice or goodness. Remember my words."

Albert paused to rest. Deep silence abided in the hall. It was not until that moment that I truly realized that the uncool and defenseless boy who had befriended me so long ago had gone about as far as a person could go in the course of a human life. Since my first day in his kingdom I had watched him with increasing respect and wonder, but it was not until this moment that I recognized his saintliness—that pure loving innocence that sets the human race an example it can never manage to live up to. In the face of all the temptations of a very wealthy man, he had chosen to cultivate his soul. And he had bypassed the entire hypnotic delusion of the modern world to create a haven in which the simple and sustaining grandeur of life could be rediscovered.

"Finally, I wish to announce my will," the king continued with an effort, "that the kingship pass into the hands of my only son, Renfrew, and that he assume the reins of government on his eighteenth birthday. Queen Jenna will retain the scepter and preside in the hall of justice until then. To aid her in every capacity and to facilitate her decrees, I name as first minister my loyal friend and brave servitor, Sir Jack Darcey, now Lord Darcey, prime minister of the realm. I have spoken."

There was an instant reaction, like the buzzing of a thousand bees, as Albert's decree spread to the crowd outside. Then silence fell as quickly as it had been broken.

"I have one more thing to say." Albert's voice was turning to paper also. "And that is that I have loved you all deeply, each and every one of you, and I only regret that I cannot stay with you longer. There has never been a king who had such loyal and wonderful subjects. Be faithful now to the queen. Farewell, and God bless you all."

Somewhere in the crowd someone began to sob quietly. Then there was another and another and another. Those of us in Albert's circle instinctively drew close around him now, for Death was reaching out his bony arm.

"Albert, you can't do this to me," said Jenna. "I absolutely forbid you to die." Her voice was so soft, it was difficult to tell whether she was teasing or quite serious.

"My dear," said Albert, his voice now more like ashes than paper, "it was not my intention. Please forgive me." Then he turned his eyes to me. "Jack, I'm counting on you. Support the queen. Take care of my son. Nurture my kingdom. Be persevering. There is nothing more I can do. There is nothing more . . ."

And he was gone.

Chapter Thirteen

In the very same moment that Albert died, everything changed. I could almost hear the change, like a massive door slamming shut on what had been before but wasn't anymore. I could certainly feel the change, and it felt like fear. Albert had supported a certain kind of reality based on his principles, his spirit, his warm heart, his nuttiness, and everything that made him what he was. The moment he died, that reality collapsed into dust and blew away.

There was still a kingdom. There were rivers and forests and meadows and farmlands, a castle and a monastery, all different kinds of people and animals and homes; everything a kingdom had to have. But it wasn't Albert's kingdom anymore. It was a kingdom up for grabs.

True, Albert had named an heir. But the teenage king had no power. The queen looked lovely in the part, but she had little interest or aptitude for government. And then there was me: dilettante, drifter, failure. I was to stand alongside the queen and facilitate her decrees. In other words, I was supposed to makes things work. Hell's bells, how about saving my own skin? If I had hair all over my body it would have been sticking straight up like a cat who'd been dropped into a kennel full of hungry mastiffs.

Out of the corner of one eye I was counting Lord Hawke's men. He had ridden in with twenty, but there were a good deal more than that now. Out of the corner of my other eye I was watching Lord Hawke, and wishing I was far away from there. In the silence of that hall, broken only by the sound of mourning, I had an eerie sensation akin to the one I had had in the duke's manor house. It was as though someone was laughing—harsh, high-pitched, shrill laughter—laughing at Albert's last words, laughing at the new government, and especially at me.

"Do something," said Jenna. She said it quietly, hardly moving her lips.

I covered my mouth with my hand, pretending to scratch my lip. "What would you like me to do, your majesty?"

"I'm sure I don't know. But we can't just stand here, can we?"

She had a point. Many of the people in that room were oblivious to everything but their sorrow; the rest were watching us. We were the brand-new rulers, and people wanted to see what we were going to do.

"Those weren't really Picts, were they?"

"No, I don't think they were."

"Kill him," she whispered.

"I like the idea," I whispered back, and that was true, "but how am I supposed to do it?"

"How should I know? You're the killer. Just do it. Is it so hard to kill a man?" She was looking at what was left of Albert.

I cast a covert glance at the duke and figured the odds on a sudden rush with sword and dagger. It would be a very hard chance. There was no surprise factor with the duke and all his men looking our way. How could I possibly cut my way through so many to get to the one I wanted? It couldn't be done single-handedly.

Where was Leo? He should have been back long before now. Where was Gordon? None of the men from our guard team had returned from their search for the mage. What had happened to them? There was the palace guard, of course, but they looked like a pretty tame bunch compared to Lord Hawke's warriors, and they weren't used to taking orders from me. How would they respond if I suddenly announced that we were going to jump the duke and his boys and kill as many as we could? Yeah, sure, Lord Jack!

"Well, then?" whispered Jenna.

"I'll do it as soon as I can," I replied, and oddly enough I meant it. Provided the duke didn't get me first, I was going to kill him the second he let his guard down.

"Émile, please help me," said Jenna. "What should we do with the king?"

Émile moved closer to Jenna, wiping his eyes. He looked pale and gaunt and I could feel how much he was suffering. "He ought to lie in state for a time, your majesty, so that people can make their farewells. Hélène and Marya Mage can attend the body, and I will arrange for a suitable bier here in the hall."

"Where do you want the body taken, Émile?" I asked him.

"The king's chamber, I would think, my lord," he said, glancing at Hélène, who nodded. Good old Émile. He never missed a beat. Lord is what Albert had made me, and so lord was what I already was to him. But I felt more like a fat rabbit in a barnyard full of hungry cats.

I called to a group of men in Albert's livery. "You men carry the king upstairs to his chamber."

"Nay," said the duke, and his voice carried to the far ends of the hall. "Who are you to command those men?"

I didn't know how to respond except by repeating, "Carry the king upstairs to his chamber!" I said it rather sharply this time, praying I could override the duke; for if I couldn't, the game was his, check and mate.

"Obey him not!" shouted the duke, and the men, who had started for Albert's couch, stopped in their tracks. I could see them trying to decide which course would get them into the least trouble; clearly, their fear of the duke carried more force than their loyalty to the dead king's wishes. Glancing around, I noticed that the duke's men were spreading out through the hall, taking up strategic positions everywhere and elbowing Albert's poorly armed palace guard out of their way.

"You men!" shouted Jenna, stamping her foot. "Have you gone deaf? Carry the king to his chamber!"

"Do as the Queen commands," echoed the duke, and the men scurried forward to take up the couch.

"Gently there, you knaves," snapped the duke. "What do you think you are carrying?"

Visibly rattled and afraid of being scolded again, the men now made an elaborate pantomime of carrying the couch with respect.

Fear was spreading through the castle. The hands that carried Albert's couch were trembling, and so were mine. The duke was so far ahead of the game, there seemed to be no way even to slow him down. Within minutes of Albert's death he had pushed me out of his way as successfully as his warriors had supplanted Albert's palace guards. Every moment that the duke remained unchallenged, his power grew and mine declined.

But what could I do or say while Albert's body was being slowly carried up the stairs? Even the mourners were hushed as the king's body departed. Now the death couch turned the corner and disappeared from our sight, and there was a kind of gasp or shudder that ran throughout the hall. I felt it too. Everything Albert represented was merely memory now unless some champion could reestablish it. Between dark mountains, amid the trackless forests, cut off from the rest of the world and even from time itself, the fate of the kingdom hung suspended; and in the torch-lit arena of the hall, Lord Hawke seemed to have no opponents.

Suddenly a voice broke the appalling silence, a voice that I had never heard before. There was a little gallery at one side of the hall. Musicians might have used it during a dance; or perhaps the royal family occupied it during feasts. It was slightly raised and surrounded by a railing; and it was there that our nobility had gathered to witness Albert's death.

"Lord Hawke," said Marsha Bennett, "is it your intention to overturn the king's decrees before his flesh is even cold?"

The duke was clearly angry to be confronted, but he made an effort to speak suavely. "Lady Bennett," he said, clasping his hands on his breast in an angelic gesture that was perfectly chilling, "it is my duty, now that the king is dead, to stabilize the situation for the good of all."

"Yet you are precipitous," said Lady Bennett. "What, I ask you, is so unstable in this situation that it cannot wait until the king is decently buried, and until those of us who remain have had a chance to confer?"

Lord Bennett looked embarrassed. "I'm sure the duke knows what he's doing, Marsha," he said, and he tried to take her hand.

Lady Bennett smiled at him, but she withdrew her hand. "Thank you, Terry. I am certain Lord Hawke knows exactly what he's doing. But I do not know what he's doing because he hasn't bothered to tell anybody, and now I wish to know." She turned back to the duke with a patient and inquiring look on her face that said she was prepared to keep after him all night until he gave her a straight answer.

"Lady Bennett, I believe that King Albert has made a

grave mistake in his dying dispensation."

She laughed at that. "Yes, I think that is obvious from your behavior. Kindly tell us more."

It was impossible for me to tell whether I had some support against the duke from Lady Bennett, or whether she was just being catty and urbane about his manners and his lack of protocol. Still I was impressed by her fearlessness and I knew that my first impression of her as a remarkable person had been correct.

"To be more precise, my lady," said the duke with a ghastly smile, "I cannot permit this interloper who arrived a week ago to assume power to which he has no right."

She nodded. "This is better, Lord Hawke. I'm sure we're all pleased to be sharing your confidence." Then she turned and smiled at Harvey Griswold who smiled back and nodded.

Did Lady Bennett and Earl Harvey find all this amusing? My anger came up in a rush, and I made no attempt to suppress it because it was such a relief from the depression and helplessness into which I had been sinking. What the hell was the matter with Harvey, sitting there with his legs crossed and that complacent smirk on his face at a time like this? Was he so cynical that he could take all this for his amusement?

Now I looked out into the faces of the common people, those I could see by the light of the torches. Some still wept, but the others, in the main, looked dazed and depressed, and worst of all, resigned. Like the men who had carried Albert away, they were waiting in their fear to do whatever would threaten them the least.

Perhaps I might have done the same, but I knew I was already targeted as an obstacle to be eliminated. For me there was no place of safety to retire to. Mostly though, I think it was the game of footsie those nobles were playing around the death of my friend that suddenly drove me mad.

245

I was surprised to find my sword in my hand. Reaching for it is not in my recollection. Already I was advancing across the flagstones, my weapon whipping the air in front of me and glittering in the torchlight. Surprise was very much in my favor, for startled soldiers and commoners too were scrambling to get out of my way, and through their stumbling, chaotic retreat, a path was opening straight to the duke.

He drew his broadsword, and that made me grin, for it was much too heavy and too slow to serve him against the light and nimble blade that was dancing in my hand. Up went the broadsword over his head, and now his weight came forward, aiming one cleaving blow to chop me in half. There was a scream in the air, but whether it came from my mouth or his or many mouths at once, I never knew.

Something hit me behind the knee and I fell. Pain exploded in my elbow, searing my arm from my shoulder to my fingertips. And my sword! Where was my sword? Then a blow to the side of my head made me forget what I was looking for. There had simply been too many of them.

Now I knew that Death was coming for me too, and it wasn't all right and it didn't make sense and it sure as hell didn't make me want to forgive anybody. Twisting on the floor, lashing out in all directions with my boots and my bare hands, I fought to ward it off for just one more second if I could. I barely heard the voice that seemed to come from so far away that said, "Stop! Don't kill him. Bring him to me."

Hands were grabbing me roughly and hauling me to my feet. I managed to twist my body and jab one of the men in the stomach with my elbow. He went right to his knees, and then I was flailing and kicking at all his buddies who jumped on top of me and beat me into a worse mess than I was before.

"I said bring him here!" roared the duke, and now a half-dozen of his men carried me bodily across the floor and forced me to my knees in front of him.

"Look at me, Darcey," he said, and one of his men grabbed me by the hair and yanked my head back. I had to cough up some blood and spit out a couple of teeth. My clothes were torn and spattered, I was injured inside and out, and I knew there was no limit to the bad things that could happen to me now.

"I'm not going to have you killed," the duke said softly, just between him and me and soldiers who were holding me, "because that would be too easy."

"Let him go!" said Queen Jenna. I couldn't turn my head to look at her, but I could hear her voice shaking.

"Forgive me, your majesty," said the duke, "but this madman just tried to kill me." No one made a move to let me go.

"That is my prime minister, and I wish him here with me!" Dear Jenna! She was doing her best, but her power was just as imaginary as mine.

"The prime minister?" said the duke in mock surprise. "But your majesty, this isn't the prime minister."

"Let him go, I command it!" cried Jenna, and she stamped her foot. God love her, I would never forget it.

"Your majesty, I assure you there has been some mistake. This is merely the court fool dressed in someone else's clothes. Where did you get these clothes, churl?" he said to me, leaning down to bring his face closer to mine. His eyes were dancing with his triumph, and I guess he wanted me to appreciate it. "Well, it's no matter where you got the clothes. A fool's a fool. Strip him down. You there! Fetch me the mummer's trunk, and be quick about it!"

Before I knew it, they were stuffing me into a different suit of clothes that smelled as though it had been in that trunk for many months. This suit was all different colors and had a hat to match with little bells on it. Finally they thrust a stick into my hand topped with a padded jester's head that was wearing a little hat just like mine, bells and all. Why the soldiers thought it was so comical, I don't know. But by the time they were done changing me, they were all chuckling over what they had done, and now they pushed me out into the middle of the hall.

I wandered around in a circle wondering what to do, and the bells on my clothes jingled whenever I moved. One of the soldiers laughed, and when I turned to stare at him, that made someone else laugh. What was so funny? Looking around, I noticed that Lady Bennett had her hand up to her mouth as if she was trying *not* to laugh. The duke was laughing silently, his arms folded across his chest. The soldiers were nudging each other, and even some of the peasants were starting to laugh.

Finally, guided by my intuition, I reached behind, and I realized what the joke was. My jester clothes had a flap in the back like kids' pajamas. The flap was undone and I was exhibiting my white moons to the audience. I guess that was kind of funny, especially since I didn't realize it. A laugh is a good thing, and it was just what everybody needed. The sweetest king that ever lived had just been murdered, but now they had my bare ass to laugh at, so everything was all right again. In one little corner of my poor, tired brain I felt very discouraged with the human race. What was the use of trying to do anything for people anyway?

It took a few seconds to button myself up behind, and the laughter subsided, but they were all still staring at me. What I wanted was a magic mirror to show them all how *they* looked to *me* at that moment, but all I had was that jester's head. So I threw off my hat, yanked the fancy collar of my costume with all its pleats and bells up over my head, and drew my head down between my shoulders. Now the only head they could see was the one on that stick, and it must have been eerie-looking in the light of the torches, for suddenly it was very quiet in that hall. Peeping out with one eye through the neck-slit of my costume, and stepping silently around the perimeter of the open space that was my little stage, I turned the stick this way and that and took my time while the head on the stick looked them over slowly and carefully one by one. It was very gratifying to see people shrinking into themselves when the eyes of that floating head came to rest on them.

The hat with the bells had fallen off that stuffed head, and suddenly I noticed that the face looked more than a little like Albert. It had the same nose and the same brow; even the chin was similar. I grinned maliciously to myself, and in a voice that had long been familiar to me, and which was easy enough to imitate, I said to them all, "Oh, don't be so vulgar!"

Several people screamed and children started to cry. I believe everyone in that hall was as wiped out emotionally from the events of the day as I was myself. "Do you think that the dead can't see?" I put the question to them in Albert's voice, turning the head this way and that, taking them all in, and adding a little nodding gesture that was characteristic of Albert when he was being persuasive. "Do you think the dead can't talk? I can!"

I didn't have a clear objective in this miming. I felt so groggy and light-headed, I even had the fanciful notion that it was Albert himself speaking through that head on a stick.

"Do you think I don't know who killed me?" said Albert's head, floating in the smoke of the torches. "In life I was fooled, but the dead see clearly, Lord Hawke!"

The head turned suddenly to stare at the duke, who grimaced and turned pale. "It was a clever trick to dress your men as Picts, murderer," said Albert's head, "but now

249

I *know*!"

"Guards!" cried the duke, his face blanched white.

"And I am going to come and sit on your chest every night for the rest of your miserable and guilty life!"

"Guards!" screamed the duke, and I went down beneath them for the last time.

Chapter Fourteen

I became aware that I was back in the dungeon when I realized rats were crawling on me. It was all I could do to get to my feet and shake them off because my whole body felt broken and I was stiff with cold.

The last time I had been in the dungeon I had been healthy and warmly dressed in leather with a lined cloak and good boots. I had done nothing worse than talk back to Albert, and I knew he would be letting me out soon enough. From minute to minute I had been sure of that. But with all that in my favor, it had still been a very bad experience, like a kind of true hell.

This time I was dressed in one layer of patchwork with no cloak and no boots. I was a mess from the beatings I had received, and now my body was cold, as cold and damp as the stones I had been lying on.

My jaw hurt horribly where I had lost the teeth, and the pain made my whole head ache and throb. My right hand was swollen to twice its normal size, and so laced with pain I didn't dare move a finger. My body was screaming for help, but my brain knew that things were only going to get worse. If I couldn't get warm, I was going to get sick. If I didn't care for my injuries, I was going to be crippled. And if the whole situation didn't improve in a lot of ways, and pretty soon too—well, I would probably die. That was where the fear began, fear as I had never experienced it before: that the unendurable could continue without reprieve.

My mind searched madly for solutions. Maybe time would run backwards to that critical moment when I had sealed my fate. I would have a chance to reconsider, and I would know better than to attack the duke against all odds. Biding my time, I would get the opportunity I needed to slip a knife between his ribs.

Of course I knew second chances didn't exist; not in that way. What I needed was a miracle if I was going to survive. At this very moment Sir Leo might have the duke in his sights, a long, cross-courtyard shot taking a light breeze into consideration, the arrow entering at the back of the duke's neck and coming out his Adam's apple. Or Gordon might be splashing his brains across the hall with an awesome, skull-splattering blow with his iron-tipped stick. Perhaps Marya was slipping a quick-acting poison into his goblet. Or Jenna, having seduced him onto the battlements, was pointing to the moon to distract him before giving him a shove over the edge. This very second he was screaming with his last breath as the stones of the courtyard rushed up toward him to snuff out his life.

Someone would do something. I could never be left at the mercy of the rats and the cold and the pain. Surely in an hour, I assured myself, something will improve. My jaw will hurt less. Someone will bring me a blanket. For an hour I can endure all this suffering, and by then something will change, and it won't be quite as bad.

Of course I had no way to tell an hour. But after what seemed vaguely like an hour had passed, I began again to tell myself that in an hour, something would improve. It was a con game that I played against fear and despair.

The only change that occurred was the shifting of my attention. The cold would begin to plague me, and that would tie up my concentration for a time. I tried burrowing in the straw. I tried walking a measured number of steps in the pitch dark, turning, and walking back, to try to get my blood moving. But nothing I did made any difference. I was always cold, with a dangerous, unhealthy, fearful cold.

Then the pain would take over, especially the pain from my jaw. Periodically there would be a crescendo of pain that began in my mouth and then savaged my skull until there was nothing left in the world but that pain. I went down on my knees, wrapped my arms around my head, and hung on for dear life until the pain peaked and subsided, leaving me exhausted and shaken.

Sometimes I worried about my hand. Either it was numb or it ached, and there were sharp pains if I tried to flex my fingers. The quicker I could start taking care of it, the better chance it would have to heal properly. But there was nothing I could do for it now except to worry, and worrying about it was a kind of torture all by itself.

Where were my friends? Gordon had disappeared into the woods; Leo had gone searching for him and hadn't returned. I had not seen Rudy Strapp since the coronation, and there were eight other members of our security squad who I hadn't seen since they'd left to look for Marya. Was it possible that all twelve of us had been targeted in the duke's plot? Could they all now be prisoners or dead men? The answer was that anything was possible; and all I really knew was that I didn't know anything.

Marya could be counted on to do what she could. But what could she do? She was not very high on the duke's list. She had no power to sway him. How could she help me? And what about the Queen? The duke obviously didn't take her seriously.

I suspected that the rest of the nobles would do what most people mostly did: try to hang on to what they had. The easiest way to do that was to go right along with the duke and reject me as an interloper and a false knight, a pet of Albert's who had neither paid for his place in the pecking order with gold nor done anything else to earn it. The terrifying truth was that no one had any real power except the duke himself. Rudy Strapp had put it plainly enough: *What's gonna happen to you without King Albert?*

What mercy could I expect from the duke? Would it bother him that I might be crippled or die? Of course not. Clearly I was less of a threat without a sword hand, and if I was dead—well, then I was no threat at all. There seemed to be no good reason to expect to come out of this predicament healthy or even alive.

Oddly enough the rats were no problem. When I was in the dungeon before they had annoyed me and bitten me and kept me feeling tense, and they were always on my mind. This time I just shooed them away, and their presense was nothing compared to the cold and the pain in my jaw and my injured hand and the overwhelming fear that had my mind whirling in hopeless circles.

Stop it! I said to my mind. I was sure that if I didn't get control of it soon, I would go mad.

Stop, I mean it! My mind was a terrified child. It wanted answers. It wanted comfort.

I am not going to die, I said firmly. *I am in a bad spot, but I am not going to die, and I am not going to be crippled!*

The cycle of pain in my jaw began, and I went to my knees and held my head in my arms while the universe filled up with red fire and burned until it burned itself out. *I am going to be all right. I am not in a good place, but I am going to make it through this.*

Just then it occurred to me to stuff my clothes with straw. I could pack it tightly to make a defense against the cold. At last I had a plan and something to do.

It was the work of many hours; and while I was working, I could measure time against the various tasks: so long to find the driest straw and to gather it around my bench; so long to stuff the right side of my body; so long to unstuff it after I realized I would never be able to bend over enough to stuff the legs if I stuffed the upper body first. Maybe it sounds easy to stuff your clothes with straw, but only one of my hands was fit to work with. By trial and error, by doing and undoing and starting over, I learned to do what I needed to do.

I was comparatively happy while I was working because it stopped my mind from swirling and focused my thoughts on improving the situation. There was an unexpected dividend too: what padded me against the cold also protected me from the rats. I was grateful that the costume was very baggy; otherwise the idea would never have worked.

What next? I sat on the plank and tried to think of another project, but nothing came to mind. There was nothing in the dungeon but straw and dirt and rats and darkness. What came to mind instead were the questions that had plagued me before. What had happened to my friends? What would happen to my hand? Was I ever going to get out of there alive? How could I have been so stupid, so blind? Around and around went those maddening thoughts.

My time sense was also collapsing again, and instead of time to use, I had time to fear. Without water I would last several days, a week at most. If I found a water source, even moisture oozing through the rocks, I could last longer. Naturally I would do everything I could to stay alive as long as I could, even if life was painful and pointless and hope was reduced to shreds. That was the human way.

I had read once about a prisoner in solitary confinement, literally for years, who was able to transport himself mentally out of his prison in flights of totally lifelike fantasy. He did it by walking and turning, walking back the other way and turning again, over and over, until the motion and the rhythm became hypnotic.

I tried to imitate his method without success. The movement unsettled the straw and it rustled and itched and scratched until eventually it began to fall out. Repairing my insulation gave me something to do, but soon I was back where I had started. If anything, the failure of the experiment made me more afraid.

"God," I said, "I am very, very afraid, and if you don't help me, I don't think I can get through this." And just like that, I had an idea. Marya Mage had given me a meditation technique that consisted of counting my breaths up to ten. *One . . . Two . . . Three . . .* I could feel right away that it was better than nothing. The fear, though still close, still hungry, was held just at bay. *Nine . . . Ten . . .* Begin again.

How long did it take to count ten breaths? How many cycles in an hour? In a day? Best not to think about that. One breath at a time. *Six . . . Seven . . . Eight . . .* Keep the fear and the desperation at bay. I would have to settle for that. *One . . . Two . . .* Rats pestered me. Pain came and went. Lashings of fear burst my concentration. How long I could endure, I didn't know, but for the moment I was managing.

There was a scraping sound, and the door opened wide enough to show me the gleam of a torch before slamming shut. Something had been set inside. Making my way over in the darkness, I found a wooden pot filled with some kind of soup, still warm. My fingers continued to search until they felt a wooden spoon lying on top of a folded blanket. No child at Christmas was ever so happy and excited as I was to find all that bounty. I took my treasure back to my plank, draped the blanket around my shoulders, and began to eat.

One reads about prisons that serve all kinds of nauseating fare, but there was nothing wrong with that soup. It tasted like boiled grain with potatoes and salt and herbs, and it raised my spirits considerably. Eating food gave me something to do and it also made me feel less doomed.

When I had eaten everything I could with the spoon, I tipped the pot up and drank what was left. I would have licked the inside if I had been able to get my face into it. Instead, I ran my fingers around the edges and licked them until the pot was dry. Afterwards, I sucked on the spoon, reluctant to let go of the experience.

What to do with the pot and spoon? Some ancient, ancestral memory shared by all prisoners told me that I had better put it by the door, so that was what I did. Then I wrapped myself in my blanket, and enjoyed having something new to think about.

Hélène had cooked that soup. Who else? There was no prison kitchen because there were usually no prisoners. The dungeon had been designed so people would want to spend as little time there as possible. All right, let's say Hélène did cook that soup. Knowing Hélène, she would have preferred to send me a leg of lamb, carrots and potatoes with gravy, mint jelly, and a first class bottle of wine. But she hadn't, and that meant she was following orders: warm gruel, period! Maybe she had taken a chance by adding the potatoes.

Then I had a thought that made the darkness and the fear close in suddenly. Albert hadn't bothered to feed me because I was only in for twenty-four hours. Did the fact that I was getting fed now mean that I was in for a real stretch? He couldn't be thinking about keeping me in there for a week, could he? *I'm not going to have you killed, because that would be too easy.* Sure, he could.

What about a month? I had to draw back from that idea

very quickly. Whether or not it was a possibility, I had to stuff it way down where the most alarming thoughts were, the ones I couldn't begin to face. No way, I said to myself, could he possibly leave me in here for a month.

Another day passed. I say another day, but what I mean is that after an interminable time, during which I endured my suffering and somehow managed to keep from going insane, I was fed again. The door scraped open and banged shut, and my pot had disappeared when I went to investigate, though I found the spoon on the ground. After a long interval the door opened and closed and there again was my pot with my portion of boiled grain and potatoes.

This time when I sat to eat I was still grateful for the food and for having something to do, but it lacked the holiday happiness of the previous meal. It had been a very difficult day or night, whichever you like. Physically I was leaner, I believe, because there was a little more room to stuff straw inside my clothes. Mentally I was also leaner, as if another day in the dungeon had taken something from me that I was not capable of replacing. There were needs that were not being fulfilled, like the need for light and activity and freedom. Being shut up underground was starving me and draining me on a whole lot of levels.

By repeating assurances to myself and by counting my breaths, I could keep myself from bashing my head against the stones, but I was weaker and more fragile, and that's what I was thinking about as I ate my soup. In order to let every bit of nourishment soak into my system, I ate very slowly; but I knew there were many things I needed that I could never get from soup.

Another day passed between feedings. There were periods of something that was a little bit like sleep, but I was sleeping with one eye open, so to speak, for the rats. That, combined with my physical discomfort, prevented me from ever escaping completely into sleep, and that was also draining me. The acuteness of my physical pain seemed to have diminished slightly, but my whole body, it seemed, was stiffening up in a way that was almost as frightening as the pain. I felt like a man who had been made rather carelessly out of bits of wood.

Sometime during the next interval, which I called a day because it lasted so long it couldn't have been any less than a day, I experienced a storm of hate that was incredibly intense and virulent. I had killed Guy Hawke already many times in my imagination, but now I went after the rest and no one escaped: Jenna, the Dugdales, all the rest of the nobility including Renny and the Bennett boys, Marsha Bennett: everyone. Then the rest of the valley went down: Marya, Gordon, Émile and Hélène, Mora and all the rest of the peasants. My plague of hate wiped them all out. When it was over I was standing in my imagination on a mountain peak overlooking the ruined, burned and obliterated valley where there were no survivors, human or otherwise. It was all gone. The animals, the birds; everything was dead.

Horrible as it was, there was some aspect of recreation about the experience. It was something to do. It finally passed the way a storm in nature passes, gradually clearing up and then disappearing altogether. And when it was over it left me still weaker and more frightened than ever, because I seemed to be finally losing control of my mind.

I slept for a long time after that storm. At least it seemed like a long time. It was a very deep sleep without dreams, without any awareness of rats or cold or pain. When I awoke I felt depressed and hopeless, but not so acutely afraid. Something had snapped. Something had given way. There was a blank, empty space in my mind that seemed well suited to just enduring. It was a half-alive, uncaring lack of feeling that was closer to death, but which was pleasant in a way for being less painful.

When my meal was delivered, I didn't go immediately to get it. I wasn't particularly hungry, and moving my body to the other side of the cell seemed like a lot of trouble. It was not until I heard the rats scrambling in it that I jerked myself up, yelling hoarsely at them, and clunked across the floor, stiff-legged in my straw padding, to fight them for what was mine.

I'm not in very good shape, I said to myself as I ate mechanically, putting the food safely away in my belly. *A person could die in this state just from not being interested enough to stay alive.*

Yes, I know, I replied, *but I am past caring. If I live, I live; if I don't, I don't. I am tired of worrying about it. What difference does it make?*

Not much difference in here, I replied in turn, *but there may be something outside that is worth holding on for.*

I am holding on. Some of my circuits are unplugged, that's all. It will not kill me. Leave me alone.

Very well, but I am going to count my breaths for awhile. I think that is better than giving in totally to this death-ness.

Do what you want. What difference does it make?

So I counted my breaths as much as I could, and that was an affirmation of life for me, and a counterbalance against the bargain with dying and death that another part of me had made.

Time fell apart. Intervals of so-called days lost their meaning. I suffered pain, but pain was not important either, and it held no more terror for me. I had already met death more than half way, and when you are more than half dead, going all the way doesn't seem like such a big deal. The part of me that wanted to stay alive ate the food that was left for me, kept the blanket secured around my shoulders, and shooed the rats away, but without energy or optimism. Life and death had merged and become almost the same thing.

Then the door opened, two soldiers marched in, grabbed me, and hustled me upstairs. I couldn't possibly have walked as fast as they wanted me to go, so they held me roughly between them and whisked me along, while my feet did their best to do some of the walking. "Whew, does he ever stink!" said one to the other.

The torchlight was bright enough to hurt my eyes, and when we reached the ground floor, with the daylight streaming through the casements, I had to shut my eyes tight. The soldiers marched me along level ground, around a few turns, and came to an abrupt halt. One of them released his grip but the other continued to hold on tight.

"He stinks like a hog pen," complained the soldier who was holding me.

"Enough of that!" snapped the voice of Lord Hawke, and the soldier froze. Squinting between my eyelids, I could just make out shapes, and the shape that looked like the duke was sitting behind a shape that looked like a big table. Cranking open my eyelids a little at a time against the smarting of the light, I finally made him out. There was a quill pen in his hand and an inkwell in front of him, and around the table top there were rolls of parchment. Finally I could see his eyes.

I had lost my blanket while the soldiers were dragging me upstairs, and I must have been quite a rare sight in my straw snowsuit, but the duke didn't look amused. Actually, my impression was that he looked tired and old and sick, though I was in no shape even to wonder why that was so. I remember that it surprised me in a vague way, just as everything at that time was vague, because mentally I was taking no chances.

My mind had found a refuge in a limbo of not caring,

261

where the unendurable could be endured. I wasn't going to give up that refuge just because two goons had dragged me upstairs to see the duke. In another two minutes I might be back in that black hole, so I didn't fantasize about being released into that sunlight, into the wide world that I had lost. It was all the same to me what happened; it didn't matter.

At the same time, on a saner level, I was open to clues as to how to behave so that I wouldn't have to go back into the darkness. Far from not caring, I was willing to do anything, no matter how self-abasing, to be allowed to go free. But so far no one had told me what they wanted.

The duke stared at me for a time, and the feather in his hand flicked back and forth like the tip of a cat's tail. Finally he looked away and dipped his quill in the inkwell. He wrote something on the parchment in front of him, and considered it for a few moments. Then he looked up as though he was mildly surprised to see me still standing there, and gave his head a little jerk.

Both soldiers grabbed me and whisked me away between them, my feet barely touching the ground, until we were outside the castle. Before I knew what was happening they had pushed me up against the flank of a horse.

"Get on, commoner," said one of them. They muscled me aboard, for I couldn't possibly have gotten up myself, there being no saddle or stirrup. Then they mounted up and rode away, leading my horse by a rope halter. Over the drawbridge and down the road we went. It was everything I could do to keep from falling off. With no strength in my legs and nothing to hold onto, I wound up leaning along the horse's neck and hanging onto the mane with my good hand.

Where were they taking me? There seemed to be only one answer: somewhere to get rid of me once and for all. And what was I supposed to do? Yank the halter free and make a dash for it on a horse I could hardly stay on? The horse was a skinny nag—it could never run fast enough anyway. It hit me with a terrible jolt in the pit of my stomach that if they meant to do away with me, I couldn't give them much trouble at all.

My eyes were more or less accustomed to the sunlight now, though it seemed extraordinarily bright, brighter than any sunshine I'd ever seen before. Such a lovely day it was too, with a riot of colors in the autumn leaves. It would be sad to have to die on such a beautiful day, sadder than if it was rainy and cold and miserable. Maybe Hawke had waited for the nicest possible weather to have me taken out to be hanged or stabbed or whatever they planned to do to me. Well, he had certainly gotten his licks in. I was sorry I'd tangled with him. I had been a fool, and now I was going to collect a fool's wages, paid in full.

We were moving along at a brisk trot, and I actually found myself hoping we would get to wherever we were going pretty soon; I was tired of hanging on. Where were they taking me anyway? Now I saw that we were going to go right past Mora's farm. It would be nice to say goodbye to her. It would be nice to go out among a group of friends, to have a chance to say goodbye to everybody. But how would you know what to say?

I envied Albert his peace of mind. I guess some people have it and some people don't. He said that dying made everything simple and clear; but nothing was simple and clear to me. I was sad and angry and afraid all at the same time.

Now they turned onto the cart track that led to Mora's cottage. No way! This was carrying it too far. If those bastards thought they were going to involve Mora in this, maybe I had some fight left in me yet!

But the soldier who had been leading me just turned his horse, reached out with his boot, and gave me a shove in the ribs. Down I went in front of the cottage and lay there with all the wind knocked out of me. They rode away without a word, taking the horse with them.

I could smell her before I saw her. Then I felt those small, strong hands tugging at me. "Come on," she said. "Let's get you into the house."

Chapter Fifteen

I sat in the sunshine on Mora's rickety bench and soaked my hand. It was swollen and stiff and the look of it worried me. I still could not flex my fingers without excruciating pain, but it didn't seem as if life could continue until I began to get that hand working, so I soaked it and stretched it day and night.

How can I explain what was going on in my mind? I was pleased to sit and enjoy being warm and dry and amply fed, looking at the trees and the clouds and listening to the birds. I could see with my eyes that I was not in the dungeon anymore, but the dungeon was still there in my mind, and the fear was still there. The part of me that had died in the dungeon hadn't come back to life yet. Sometimes I felt very empty in a peculiar way, as though I had no insides at all.

Mora was busy taking care of her farm with the help of two young men who came to work there during the day. She wasn't pressing me to do anything. We would smile at each other when she came by, going about her farm work in her cheerful way, singing to herself the little songs she made up. Sometimes I would help her by rocking the cradle when the baby was fussy, but beyond that I wasn't capable of much. My hand made me feel crippled and fragile, and I still had horrible flashes of pain in my jaw.

The third or fourth day, Mora took me to the blacksmithy and helped his two burly sons hold me down while the smith pulled out a tooth that had been broken in half. As soon as he had it out, I felt very relieved, as if a short circuit in my nervous system had been corrected. My whole body seemed to feel better for it. My jaw was still very sore, but such an improvement was more like pleasure than pain.

When I got back to the cottage I realized that I hadn't seen Mora's mother even once since the soldiers had dumped me off. "Where's your mother?" I asked her.

Mora pointed through the trees into a clearing. There were two graves there, an older one and a newer one where the earth formed a hump; the wooden marker was still green.

"When did that happen?"

"A week after the king was killed."

"I'm sorry, Mora. I'm sorry that I didn't even notice."

"That's all right. I know you're not yourself yet."

And just who was I when I was myself? Before Albert was killed I was a knight, but that was a fantasy, wasn't it? Albert had made me a knight because that was the easiest way to put me on the chessboard. I had to be called something to be in the game, and I couldn't be an earl or a duke because I didn't have the money to buy in. But was I ever really a knight?

Yes, I had had the clothes and the arms and the horse, and I had really been a knight because Albert had made me one. Now Albert was dead, and that wasn't true anymore.

Or was it? Albert had made me a lord on his death bed. By all rights I was prime minister of the kingdom, second only to Jenna in power, wasn't that true? Lord Hawke had used his power to turn me into a jester and then into a jailbird, but he didn't have the right to do that. I was really a lord.

Okay, but how many more trips to the dungeon did I have to make before I figured out how things worked in the New Middle Ages? Albert was dead and all his power belonged to the duke. That was all there was to it. At this moment I was a nobody, a guest on Mora's farm. I barely even qualified as a

266

commoner, because commoners knew where they fit in, and I didn't even know that.

"Are you all right?" Mora asked me.

"I'm okay, but I think I'll go lie down for awhile."

I tried to relax. There was no need to understand everything right away. Except, why had those soldiers brought me here?

"Hello, Mora, how are you this afternoon?" It was Marya's voice.

"Very well, thank you, Mage."

"And how's the little one?"

"Oh, she's just growing and growing!" And they laughed together with that special delight women have about babies.

"Is he here?"

"He's inside. He had a tooth pulled today."

I swung my legs over the side of the bed, embarrassed by my peasant's clothes, my missing teeth, my broken hand.

Marya gazed into my eyes and put her arms around me. "I'm very glad you made it, Jack," she said when she let me go. "How do you feel?"

"I don't know what to feel first, Marya. I've been in a daze. They pulled a tooth for me today and now I feel a little insane. More alive, but more insane. That girl is in love with me. She wants me to stay here and be her man."

"Yes, I know. Are you going to stay with her?"

"Marya, I don't even know what's going on. Two soldiers dragged me up to see the duke. He didn't say a word to me. Then they dumped me in Mora's front yard. Do you know what the scoop is?"

"I can only guess what's going on in the duke's mind right now, but I do know what everybody else knows. The duke hasn't had a night's sleep since the day he had Albert killed."

"What, his conscience is bothering him?"

267

"Something is bothering him. Maybe Albert is bothering him."

I just looked at her.

"Maybe Albert is coming to sit on his chest every night. You can't just murder someone and get away with it, you know. That isn't the way it works."

"So what does that mean? He let me out of the dungeon because he didn't want me sitting on his chest along with Albert?"

"I'm not sure why he let you out, Jack. May I see your hand?"

I held it out to her and she took it gently between both of hers and spent a long time examining it. Then she closed her eyes and seemed to be making some kind of communion. Finally she opened her eyes.

"You just keep soaking this," she said. "Soaking it and working it. You're going to need a lot of determination, bubber. You've got to keep working on it, no matter how much it hurts, and you can't even think of giving up."

"Will it heal?"

"Yes, because you're going to heal it."

"How long will it take?"

"I wish I could tell you, but I don't know. I've seen people heal injuries that were worse than this just because they set their mind to it. And I've seen people die from next to nothing at all because they were tired of living. It all depends on you."

"Isn't there anything you can do to help me?"

"I'll give you some salve to rub on it, and I'll come massage it every chance I get. But the truth is this is an inside job."

"Okay, Marya, I'm not going to give up as long as there's hope for it."

"I know you won't, Jack. Otherwise you never would have come out of that dungeon alive."

"I had a very bad time in there. I was so afraid, Marya. The only way I could keep the fear from swallowing me up was by counting my breaths."

Her eyes lit up. "Okay, let's keep going with that. We can put that to good use."

"I've tried meditating since I came out, but when I close my eyes it seems like I'm back in the dungeon again, and the fear comes back."

"Then keep your eyes halfway open and concentrate on the fact that you're *not* in the dungeon. Heal your thoughts and you will heal the fear."

"Okay, I'll try it."

"I'm going to give you a healing mantra. It's a thought to repeat when you meditate or any other time you can remember to do it."

"I'll do whatever you say."

"It will help you. I use mantras for healing all the time. It might surprise you how many people here meditate regularly."

"Yes, that does surprise me."

"This is our legacy from Jo Mama, the leader of the Picts. You met him, remember? He was in the theater before he went to Tibet, where he spent many years in a monastery. When he came back he wasn't interested in theater anymore, and he couldn't believe in conventional society anymore, either. He met the abbot, and the abbot invited him here. He taught a lot of people here how to meditate, and after he went off into the forest, the abbot and I have been teaching anybody willing to give it a try. Mora meditates. You better believe the Picts meditate. It's very important if you want to be happy and discover what life is all about."

"Albert said something like that, I remember."

"Sit down and let me give you your mantra."

I sat down, and Marya invoked the help of the Goddess. She gave me the mantra and rehearsed it with me until I had it down pat. I certainly wanted to believe that it would help.

"I've been like a zombie, Marya. I've hardly said five words since I came out of the dungeon, even to Mora. What's going on in this kingdom now, or would it be better not to ask?"

She took a deep breath. "The duke is living in the castle now. He's calling himself prime minister now as if Albert had bequeathed him the job. I'm sorry to have to tell you this, Jack, but he's also paying a lot of attention to Jenna."

The words refused to organize themselves in my mind. "He's . . . what did you say?"

"He's courting the queen."

Then I felt the pain. "And how is the duke doing with his courtship?"

"I think Jenna's doing her best to resist him, but the duke is charismatic when he chooses to be. And the queen is . . . well, I don't know how long . . ."

"You think she's going to tumble."

"Albert's death was a shock to her, Jack. Then suddenly you were gone too. I think she feels very lost right now."

It seemed like retribution, but for which of my sins? "Anything else I need to know?"

"Gordon and Sir Leo and the rest of Albert's knights never returned to court after Albert was killed. Since then, other soldiers and even some peasants have gone missing."

I found myself wishing I had died in the dungeon rather than face so much loss. "I swear I will kill that evil bastard if it's the last thing I do," I said, but I felt only the emptiness of my words, because I didn't truly believe I could do it even if it *was* the last thing I did.

"Jack, I didn't mean they were dead."

"What's happened to them if they're not dead?"

Hoofbeats drummed on the road. "Someone's coming," said Marya.

Sure enough, there was Lord Hawke with a couple of soldiers, blowing up the road like an ill wind. "Goddamn him," I said. "He'd better not be coming here." But again my words sounded empty and false, because most of what I was feeling was fear.

Marya slipped her cowl over her head and gave me a quick kiss on the cheek. "This isn't a good time for me to be seen with you, Jack. Watch your temper and trust in the light. The story isn't over yet." With that, she melted into the trees.

The horsemen were very near now, and they slowed to a trot. The duke made a little gesture to his soldiers and they stopped on the road while he alone rode up the path. It was no surprise to me that the soldiers were armed to the teeth.

Reining in, the duke sat staring down at me. He was dressed as he normally was in his surcoat and helm with the hawk device. I couldn't help noticing from the way my bowels were churning that I was very afraid of him now.

He sensed it easily enough, I'm sure. I wasn't challenging him with my body nor even holding my head up very straight. Though I didn't want to appear subservient, I wanted very much to avoid trouble, and that fearful uncertainty is something any bully can spot.

"Give you good day, farmer," said the duke, and his tone surprised me, for although it was aloof, it was not overtly insulting. He had cut me down to size and now he could afford to be almost friendly.

"Good day, my lord," I replied, surprised by the tone of my own voice. Where was hot-tempered, loose-tongued, irrepressible Jack?

The duke gazed off toward the woods and stroked his goatee. "That's good, Darcey," he said, as though he had just tasted something I'd served him. "That's good. I like that. Keep that up and you'll be all right. Mind your manners and work diligently. Remember that when winter comes you'll either be enjoying the fruits of your labors or going begging around to the neighbors. That's all you need to know." Then he tried to suppress a yawn.

Clearly he didn't want me to see him yawn, but I had caught just the hint of it. It gave me the same impression that I'd had when his guards first dragged me up from the dungeon. All I could see of him was the circle of his face that was exposed by his helm, and that face looked old and tired, with unhealthy-looking dark circles under his eyes.

"Any questions?" He was sitting up very straight on his horse, but his energy was low, like a man who had a case of the flu but had to go to work anyway.

Of course I wanted to know why he had dumped me in Mora's front yard, but I was too afraid. "No, my lord."

He was studying me carefully now, and the machinations of some decision he was making were reflected in his eyes, which were glittering like coals. He seemed to be fitting me up for some scheme of his; and if he decided that it didn't fit me, then I would die. I couldn't suppress the shiver that shook my body while I watched him decide my fate.

"So be it then," he said finally, and I had to hold my knees very stiff for fear they would buckle. "I hope you like farming, Darcey. Stay out of trouble and you can enjoy the land and the wench. Cross me again, and I'll snuff you out." He turned his horse back into the road and cantered away, followed by his men. In a few moments I was alone among the silent mountains that surrounded the valley.

For a long time I stood frozen to that spot. I was Guy Hawke's serf! I tried to tell myself there had to be some mistake, but whichever way my mind tried to dodge, it ran right up against the same facts. There was nowhere to run. It would be suicide to try to make the long trek out of this wilderness with my injured hand. I was stuck right where he had thrown me, and lucky to be alive at that.

Going into the cottage, I stirred up the fire and put water on to heat. Everything I saw, everything I touched, was in much sharper focus now that I knew this farm was going to be my home. The peasants I had seen were an attractive lot, healthy and hardy and happy as far as I could tell. Couldn't I manage just as well?

Mora and others could teach me the farm work. I caught on quickly to new things, and I was sure I could be good at it. The most important thing I could do for myself was to heal that hand of mine. When the water was hot, I gave it a good soak, and then tried to flex the fingers until sweat broke out on my forehead and I felt dizzy with the pain. Then I soaked it some more and tried again. First I would make my hand flex, bit by bit. Then I would make it do farm work. Finally, it would be ready to hold a sword again and then I would present my bill to Guy Hawke and make him pay on the spot!

Try as I might, I could not remember anything happening to my hand in those brawls with the soldiers. No, it had been deliberately smashed while I was unconscious to finish me as a swordsman. Well, I would nurse it and exercise it until it was ready to give someone the last surprise of his life. In fact, I thought to myself, it would be better to keep its healing a secret. That way nobody would get suspicious, and it would be ready to do its job when the time was right.

Mora came in with the baby on her hip and a sack of food for supper. I took the sack and emptied it out on the table near the hearth. She smiled at me in that friendly and appreciative manner that was as consistent as her lovely fragrance, and sat down to nurse the baby. This was the woman I was going to make a home with. Was I glad about that?

Yes, I was. It brightened my spirit to be around her; and that was because her own spirit was so bright that it was impossible not to be affected by it. She was like a fountain that life bubbled out of cheerfully and steadily. Right this moment it was bubbling out of her nipple into her baby's mouth, and mother and baby were surrounded by that aura of peace and silent joy that was always so apparent when she was nursing. The whole cottage was filled with it, but it was especially bright around the bench where she always sat to nurse, and I couldn't resist sitting down beside her to bask in it.

"I saw hoofprints in the yard," she said softly, looking over at me. I put a finger to my lips, not wanting to lose that feeling of contentment. But when Mora's baby had fallen asleep at the nipple and she had tucked it up in its cradle and began to make dinner, the old worries came crowding back.

"We had a visit from Lord Hawke," I said.

"Oh?" She glanced over at me, concerned.

"Why do you suppose he got me out of the dungeon and dumped me in your front yard?"

She looked at me over the vegetables she was chopping, and said, "I went to the duke and asked him to let you out."

"And so he did?"

She nodded. "I was so worried about you that something was happening to my milk. The mage went with me to see

274

the duke. She told him I had . . ." It took her a moment to remember the unfamiliar word. ". . . Anxiety."

"And that's why he let me out?"

She nodded again. "For the sake of the baby. Are you all right?"

"Yes, I'm okay, Mora, but my brains are swirling around in my head and it's making me dizzy."

"I've had that happen. Do you want to lie down?"

"No, I think I'll walk around a bit."

I headed down toward the river, found a rock to sit on, and tried to think it through. Of course I believed what Mora had told me, but it didn't make any sense. Marya had gone with her to see the duke, but Marya hadn't mentioned it. Marya didn't know why the duke let me go and I still didn't know either. All I could figure was that somehow I was more use to him alive than dead; he was saving me for a rainy day.

I started back toward the cottage, and who did I come upon but Jo Mama, his or her own self, reclining within the branches of a fallen tree as naturally and comfortably as a cat on a couch. The god was alone—or at least I didn't see anyone else around—but his presence cast such a spell on me that the trees and flowers seemed sentient, and the whole forest sparkled with magic.

He wasn't looking at me directly, and it wasn't long before I felt self-conscious, wondering whether I ought to do or say something. He looked so relaxed and so gracefully entwined in the branches of his tree-couch that I felt almost grotesque by comparison. Like a novice on the stage, I didn't know what foot to put my weight on or what to do with my hands. Though I was just standing there, I felt as if I was doing everything wrong.

Finally, he released a peaceful sigh and languidly stretched out one bare arm, pointing to the place where he wanted me to sit. I sat, and immediately felt more comfortable. The ground was mossy and there was a tree to rest my back against. Jo Mama waited until I had got myself settled, and then he looked at me for the first time.

It was nothing like a greeting. More than anything else he seemed curious, as though he had never seen anything quite like me. His examination was thorough. He looked at me and around me and through me; sometimes he looked away and seemed to lose interest. But then his attention would return with a clarity that was disturbing, because I was convinced that he was seeing right into me and I had no idea what he was seeing.

Finally he peered into my eyes, and though he didn't actually move at all, my impression was that he came closer and closer until we were nose-to–nose; he seemed to be gazing right into my brain. His voice, crackling as if from long disuse, took a long time to come up his throat. "Where's your iron hat?"

I didn't know what to say. Did he really expect me to answer him? The first time I had encountered Jo Mama, I had watched him from my horse, dressed in my armor and adorned with weapons. He had danced naked in the field and scampered away screaming with laughter. This time I was sitting on the ground in woolen homespun, weaponless, my wounded hand in my lap, and he seemed to be taking me seriously. But what was I supposed to say to him, if anything?

"I lost it." That seemed to cover it pretty well. Actually, it had been taken away from me, along with my horse and my sword and my knighthood and my bag of gold and my friend, King Albert and my darling Jenna. But somehow it seemed more truthful just to say I had lost it, just as I had lost all the other things I no longer had, by losing my temper, by being a fool.

He smiled and nodded as though my answer made sense to him. I felt gratified by that, though I couldn't have said why. Who was Jo Mama to me that I should crave his approval? But I did.

Once again that voice came creaking up the steep staircase of his throat. "Listen!" I heard him say, but had he really spoken?

"Listen!" There it was again, but I'm almost sure that his lips never moved. His face seemed to be made out of rocks and trees and leaves; or maybe the forest had changed into one great face. All that remained of Jo Mama were his eyes, and they were more like tunnels than eyes.

"I'm listening, Jo Mama." But it was so tiring looking into those tunnels. I felt as if I would lose my balance and tumble right into them. Now there was only one tunnel, and I was teetering on the brink of it.

"Listen!"

"I'm really listening, Jo Mama. I swear I'm listening with all my might."

"Stop living in the past!" The words echoed up and down the tunnel.

"Okay, I promise. No more living in the past. Good idea, Jo Mama." Was I really talking? Did I have a body, and if so, where was it?

"Stop living in the future!"

I felt delirious but I was trying hard to understand. How could I live in the future? How could I live in the past? Where was the past? Where was the future? "You're right, Jo Mama. I won't do it anymore, I promise."

"Just live now!" The words were like great bronze bells.

I opened my eyes. I was lying on my face on the moss. How long had I been there? The tree-couch was empty and the god was gone. Pulling my legs up to my chest and leaning on my good hand, I got up to my knees. At first I couldn't tell which direction led back to the cottage, but with the setting sun behind me I made my way to the meadow at the edge of the farm.

By the way Mora stared when I entered the cottage, I must have looked very odd. "What happened?" she asked me, her eyes wide.

Taking her by the hand, I led her to the bed. I put my arms around her and tumbled us both over onto the straw mattress. Then I snuggled up all over her and buried my nose in her hair, drinking up the lovely smell of her body, and letting it fill up my soul. She giggled, pleased and happy, and when I tugged at her dress she raised herself so I could slip it off. She helped me off with my tunic and leggings while I was nuzzling and sniffing and stroking her, and as the sun went down we panted and bundled and snuggled and made a warm and sweet little playland of love under the blankets.

Chapter Sixteen

Why is the clarity that comes to us once in a blue moon so fragile and evanescent? After my encounter with Jo Mama, I went to sleep in Mora's arms without a care in the world, conscious only of love and peace. But in the morning I was confused and resentful again. No way in hell was I going to be Guy Hawke's serf! But what was I going to do about it? My mind paced angrily around in a cage of impossible schemes.

"When does it start to get cold?" I asked Mora while we were cleaning up after breakfast.

"That's hard to say," she said. "If this mild weather holds for another few weeks, we'll have a fine harvest."

"What happens after the harvest?"

"We take a long holiday and celebrate, especially if the harvest is good. But this year many people will still be sad, remembering the king."

"Do the peasants think the Picts killed Albert?"

"There are a few who say so."

"And what do the others think?"

"We all know he was killed by Lord Hawke."

"Is anybody planning to do anything about it?"

The single wrinkle on her forehead told me she was struggling with the question. "Who do you mean?" she said.

"People. The people in this valley."

"The farmers?"

Why couldn't she understand me? "Mora, I'm sad that Albert is dead, but I'm also very angry. Do other people feel that way?"

"Yes, Jack."

"Well, don't they want to do anything about it?"

"Like what?"

"Like chopping the duke's head off and sticking it on a pole in the castle courtyard."

She looked at me strangely. "We have to get the harvest in."

So that was that. If I wanted his head on a pole, I would have to see to it myself. For the time being he was as safe as any man alive. Walking over to Mora's bench, I plunked myself down, but the bench swayed precariously and collapsed.

"Are you all right?" Mora hurried over, but I was more amused than hurt. There always seem to be messages in accidents like that, and this message seemed to be: *Just live now!*

"Well, I guess that gives me something to do," I said, gathering up the pieces and taking them outside.

Mora followed. "You don't have to worry about that. Matt and Ben will fix it." Those were the two young men she had hired to help her.

"No, it's about time I got busy around here. It'll help to heal my hand if I keep trying to work with it. And if I'm going to be a farmer all winter, I might as well start with this."

She showed me the shed where she kept her tools. The bench had been pegged together and the pegs had loosened from wear. My task was to make some bigger pegs, and I soon found what I needed: a hammer and a chisel and a hatchet.

For a couple of hours I struggled with Mora's bench. Using my right hand was painful and frustrating, but at the same time I knew that I was doing the best thing for it, and that the pain was part of the cure. By the time I got the bench together, I was ready for a hot soak and some lunch.

"There," I said, putting the bench back where it belonged, "I think that will hold together for a while." I had a nice feeling of accomplishment from my morning's work.

After lunch I went outside to find something else to do. Matt and Ben were cleaning the goat pen. I had met them before but that was days ago when I was fresh out of the dungeon and hardly even human yet. Since then I hadn't paid any attention to them, and they had stayed respectfully out of my way. They were young men in their twenties, open-faced and hard-working.

"Good day," I said as I came walking up to the pen.

"Good day, Sir Jack," they said almost in unison. That was a bit of a surprise; it had not been that many hours since I had begun to accept the latest developments in my life and felt willing to put my knighthood behind me for a try at some simple farming. They both seemed flattered that I was talking to them, as though I was still the big celebrity I had been for a couple of weeks between the march on Guy Hawke's manor house and Albert's death.

I reached for the wooden rake that was leaning against the fence, but I bobbled it with my bad hand and the rake tumbled to the ground. Matt bent to pick it up and held it out to me. "Pa said a cow once stepped on his hand and hurt him cruelly, but he cured it with hot soaks just like you."

"My mum says you ought to put some comfrey root in the hot water," said Ben. "She told me to say you can have all you need from our garden."

"I appreciate that, Ben. Why don't you bring some tomorrow."

"Oh, I have some with me, sir. I was going to give it to

you, but . . ." He stopped, embarrassed, and I realized that he had been too shy to approach me. I was touched that all these people were concerned about my hand. Being a wanderer and a city boy too, I wasn't used to people taking any trouble over me.

"What kind of goats are these?" I asked. They were attractive little black and white goats, and one of them was rubbing against my leg and *baa*-ing for attention.

"That's a billy goat and those are nanny goats," said Matt.

"I mean what kind of goats, like . . . isn't there a name for these particular kind of goats?"

"No," said Ben. "Just goats."

"Tell me everything I need to know about goats."

"Well, goats are easy to keep and the meat makes a good stew. The hide is soft when it's tanned right and makes a good shoe. What else, Ben?"

"Goats'll eat anything and stay fat, and they don't take sick much. Some people like goat's milk and goat cheese, but I don't care for it myself until at least February." They both laughed.

That got the conversation going, and we continued to talk as we worked. If they ran out of things to say, I asked another question, and so it went all afternoon. I was mostly in the way since I didn't know how to do anything and especially because of my hand. Still, I was determined to be a better farmer by the end of the day, and the boys were patient with me. They were big boys, tall and broad, who had worked hard all their young lives. Either one of them could lift more with one hand than I ever could have with two. At my age, time would make me weaker rather than stronger. It worried me to see how strenuous farm work was going to be.

Matt and Ben told me stories about local people and how they succeeded and failed. Some were venerated for their talent and their savvy and their consistent good results. Others were only average and had their share of good times and bad. A few were hopeless, even though they tried hard, and would have starved to death but for the helpfulness of their neighbors.

About mid-afternoon another peasant lad stopped briefly by to talk to Matt over the fence. "August the miller was beaten by our lord's soldiers," Matt told us. "They knocked out all his teeth."

"What, all of them?" said Ben.

"So it's said."

"Why?" I asked.

"For digging clay out of the road. Some people will never have any sense. But to lose all your teeth . . . That's very bad."

"Where was he digging?" Ben asked.

"In the royal domain," said Matt. "But that should be the queen's affair, not our lord's."

"But don't you know our lord's made himself king now?" said Ben.

"Hush, you! It isn't so."

"Then who is king, I wonder?"

"The king's son is the king, but the queen is looking after us until he's old enough."

"And who's looking after the queen?" said Ben.

Matt had no ready reply for that. "It's best not to talk about it," he said finally.

"Fine, but don't tell me our lord's not made himself king."

"Is that what you want, Ben?" I had the feeling the whole conversation was directed at me. Whether I wanted to think about it or not—whether I could do anything about it or not—I was still mixed up in the kingdom's politics.

"No, sir," said Ben firmly, "that is not what I want. But it's foolish to pretend it isn't so. Now the talk is that he wants to marry the queen, and that would settle it once and for all."

"What about Albert's son?"

"My dad says when the time comes, he'll just have an accident or be killed by the Picts like the king."

"This talk will just bring trouble on all of us," said Matt.

"And what kind of trouble are we in for already, with the duke getting crankier every day? First he deals out blows to his men, and then they deal them down to us. How will you like it when you lose all your teeth?"

"I'll do my best to stay out of their way."

"And where will you go to do that, I'd like to know?"

"I'll just do the best I can."

"Not me," said Ben. "After harvest I'm going to join the band."

"Well, if you are, then so am I."

"What band is this?" I asked. I had a picture in my mind of a band of musicians. What good would that do?

They both turned to look at me, and then looked at each other and back at me again. "There's only one," said Matt.

"Thanks, Matt, but you've still got the best of me on this one. What band is that?"

They were staring at me in disbelief. "Haven't you heard about the band, Sir Jack?"

"Forgive me, boys, I just got out of the slammer. Now what is it?"

Now they both tumbled over each other telling me what it was, and I could hardly take it in. Leo and the other knights and most of Albert's soldiers and a bunch of other people from all over the kingdom had moved into the forest and formed a band to overthrow the duke and avenge the king's death.

284

Leo alive? Gordon alive? All the boys from our guard service alive? That was what Marya had started to tell me. I was so relieved, I felt like crying. But what could a little band in the forest do against Lord Hawke?

And besides that, it was late in the year now. What could they do to survive in this wilderness once winter came? Who would leave a cozy cottage fireside to support them when snow was on the ground? When Albert went to march against Lord Hawke, hundreds had flocked to support him, but Albert had known that he had to take advantage of the high energy of the moment before it dissipated and the opportunity was lost. What kind of energy was there to draw on now, with Albert dead and the duke entrenched in his power?

"So, what will you do now that you know about the band?" Ben asked me.

"I don't know," I said, and I could sense their disappointment. Did they think I was going to rush off into the forest with my screwed-up hand and join an uprising? However I looked at it, I saw no reason for confidence or optimism. It seemed more like a terrific opportunity to die in the snow.

"Let me think it over, boys," I said, stalling. I continued to try to work, but my mind was full of confusion. What could I do with only one hand, and my left hand at that? I couldn't even hoe a row properly, let alone fight!

By sundown I was tired but I felt like I had learned a lot. After we put the tools away, Ben and Matt stopped at the cottage door for a few words with Mora and got a snack for the walk home through the woods. Here and there, off in the trees I saw a light or two as the valley farmers settled in to eat and trade stories of the day before they went to bed.

When I went inside, there was Mora with her apron on, looking like some young mountain mother out of a children's storybook. I gave her a big hug and kissed her while she stood there with a wooden spoon in one hand and the other tangled in my hair.

"Matt and Ben think you'll make a good farmer," she said as we were eating supper by the light of the hearth.

"Why is that?"

"They said they never heard anyone ask so many questions."

"If they came to live in Manhattan, the shoe would be on the other foot."

She smiled but she didn't get it. "What is Manhattan?"

"Just some place. It doesn't matter anymore. You know, Mora, it's not such early days for me to be learning a whole new line of work."

"Don't worry, Jack. We all do it together, and it's not so hard. All you have to do is keep trying, and the things that go right will make up for the things that go wrong. It's only really hard for the lazy ones and the grumblers. That's what my dad used to say."

"Do you miss your mom and dad a lot?"

"Yes, very much sometimes. But I have my baby and all my friends. I'm not lonely, especially now that you're here."

It was dark outside under the stars, and inside the cottage the amber light from the fire danced with the shadows. With the darkness came a different kind of stillness, very intimate, as if the whole outer world had become insubstantial and nothing existed outside our fire-lit cottage. Mora and I and the baby were the only people in the world until tomorrow morning, and the baby slept soundly with a tummy full of warm milk. I was just slipping my arm around Mora's waist when I heard a sharp "Pssst!" that was so totally unexpected that I must have jumped a yard in the air.

"What was that?" I said to Mora. I was reaching around with my useless hand for a weapon. The best thing I could find was the iron rod we used to poke up the fire, and I took it up with my left hand when I remembered that I couldn't grasp it with my right.

"Someone's outside," said Mora. She didn't seem worried, but a little perplexed, for it certainly wasn't the sound folks usually made when they came calling.

"Pssst! Sir Jack!"

"Who the hell is it?" I tried to sound firm and in control, but my voice quavered. My experience in the dungeon had wounded me in subtle ways, and I was still full of all the nameless fears that had seeped into my soul. The last thing I needed was to be startled by an unseen voice in the dark.

"Sir Jack! It's Leo!" said a coarse whisper, but I wasn't at all sure that I recognized his voice.

"Leo!" I called back. "Is that you?"

"Come out!" came the same hoarse whisper; though I listened carefully, I still wasn't sure it was really him.

"Come on in, Leo. Don't stand out there in the dark." I crept around with the poker so I would be behind the door when it opened. Urgently, I waved Mora out of the firelight and she slipped into the shadows. Then I raised the poker over my head with both hands as well as I could. It seemed quite a long time before the door finally opened.

Leo looked different. His hair and beard were longer and needed a trim. His clothes were wrinkled and dusty and there was a tear in his tunic. There was a new look in his eyes too, something wild and furtive. "Are you alone?" he asked, peering around.

"No, Mora is here."

She came out of the shadows and dropped him a curtsy.

287

"Good evening, Sir Leo," she said. "Can I give you a bowl of stew?"

"Yes, thank you," he said like a hungry man. While Mora was dishing it up, we stared at each other in the dim light. "You're thinner," he said.

"So are you." I was trying to smile but there was an awkwardness between us.

"I'm sorry we couldn't get you out of the dungeon. We would have if we could have. I hope you know that."

"It's okay, Leo."

"Those bogus Picts lay in ambush for Gordon. They left him for dead, and it was close at that."

"Is he all right?"

"Pretty much so. He's outside."

"Really? I want to see him."

"He's on guard." There was a strange tone in his voice and I knew what it meant. We had all been on guard when Albert was stabbed. We had failed him and the whole kingdom. We had failed ourselves.

"Okay, Leo, but have him come in."

Leo went to the door and made a woodland noise with his mouth, sort of a low warble. I felt very strange. Leo was alive and Gordon too, but instead of feeling joyous, I felt agitated.

"I've changed a little," said Gordon, pushing back his hood. A disfiguring scar ran diagonally across his face from hairline to jaw line.

"I'm very glad to see you again, Gordon," I said. "Come in and have some stew."

"Yes, I would like some," he said, and he too sounded hungry.

Mora served the two men and they dug right in. I had a cup of Mora's fern tea and watched them eat. I was not looking forward to what I knew this visit was bringing us.

"Thank you, Mora," said Leo when he finished eating. "That was a fine stew. We could certainly use your talent in the greenwood if you'd like to come along with Sir Jack."

Mora didn't reply, and her face was closed as she took the bowl from Sir Leo.

"We're fairly well set up now," Leo continued, "but it hasn't been easy. None of us knew quite what to do at first. We were all in shock from the king's death, and every one of us felt responsible. Sir Bradley and Sir Maynard were just coming back to court when I went out looking for Gordon. Between the three of us we got Gordon to safety and finally we managed to gather all the other knights together. Then we decided we would never go back to court until we were ready to avenge the king."

"So what's the plan?"

"Well, the plan in the beginning was to devise a way to get you out of the dungeon, and then to mobilize the same army that marched with Albert against the duke. But the plan didn't work because the duke's security was very tight and we couldn't find a way to get to you."

"Why didn't you storm the castle?"

"Yes, well and good," said Leo, laughing as though I'd made a joke. "But we needed you to lead the army as you did before."

"Albert led that army, not I."

"Yes, but don't you see? There never would have been any army without a champion to rally around. If the king hadn't needed your presence to muster that army, we would have let you stay in bed."

"You're the only champion this kingdom has ever had, Sir Jack," said Gordon. "Everybody loved King Albert, but he didn't think of himself as a fighting man and neither did anyone else. The duke walked all over him until you got here."

"And now you want me to be your champion again."

"Yes, that's exactly what we want," said Leo, a little impatiently, as though I was dragging my heels; and of course, that was exactly what I was doing.

"I still don't understand the plan. You know everybody is expecting the harvest to begin anytime now. If the weather holds, it'll be in a few weeks. But if the weather turns bad, the harvest has to happen right away. Isn't that true?" I said to Mora.

"Yes, Jack," she said.

"Well, then is anybody going to come out for a campaign right now, champion or no champion? Maybe we should wait until after the harvest."

"After the harvest the castle will be full of provisions," said Leo, "enough to last the duke all winter. If we have to lay siege to the castle, the time to do it is now."

"Maybe we should wait for spring," I said.

"In the spring, people will be concerned about getting some meat on their bones. There is no advantage in waiting until spring. We might just as well bow our heads and forget the whole thing!"

"How many people have you got in your band?"

"Counting men and women, there are about seventy-five of us living in the forest," said Leo, staring hard at me.

There was a silence and the cottage was full of tension. I didn't want to say what I was going to say, but I couldn't think of any other way to stall. There was simply no way in hell I was going off into the woods that night with scruffy-looking Sir Leo and scarred-up Gordon to spearhead a campaign against Lord Hawke. I just wasn't going to do it.

"I'm sorry, Leo, but I'm not ready for this."

"Sir Jack, I beg of you—"

"My hand is all screwed up, Leo," I interrupted. "I couldn't hold a weapon if I tried."

"I'm sure there's a way around that if—"

"Being in that dungeon was very bad for me, Leo. I need some time to find myself again, whoever I am."

Leo shook his hands in the air. "Then you need to come with us tonight! King Albert made you a lord and that's what you are. Tilling the soil for Lord Hawke is not the way to find yourself!"

"Sir Leo, I'd like to help you, but I can't right now. Do you want to hear me say it? I'm scared right down to my bones. I died in that dungeon, Leo. I was buried alive and I died down there. Now a part of me is alive again, but I'm not ready to be your warrior and lead your goddamn army of seventy-five people against the duke. I need some peace and a chance to get well."

"But you mistake yourself," said Leo, his body beginning to tremble. "Lord Hawke doesn't want peace. He is not a man of peace. With him in charge of the kingdom there will never—"

Gordon had laid his hand on Leo's shoulder. He shook his head slowly and glanced toward the door.

"But—"

Gordon shook his head.

Leo looked quite wild now, but he made an effort to pull himself together. "Very well," he said. "Mora, thank you for dinner. Sir Jack, I hope you are feeling better very soon because we need you desperately."

"Thanks, Leo. Don't be a stranger," I said, feeling

awkward and cowardly too.

Leo's hands shook as he put on his robe and cowl, and Gordon had to steer him a little on his way out the door.

"I think I understand your fear, Sir Jack," said Gordon, pausing in the doorway. "But Sir Leo is correct when he says the situation can only get worse. Did you hear about the miller who lost his teeth?"

"I did."

"He died."

"I'm sorry, Gordon."

"In the modern world, if a million people died, we shrugged our shoulders because those people didn't seem real to us, and we ourselves never felt truly real. But here in this kingdom a man's life has a lot of meaning. When a man dies here, it's the real death of a real man. That is part of King Albert's legacy."

"Thank you, Gordon."

"But that could change."

I couldn't answer right away. "Come back and keep me posted on how things are going," I said finally.

"I will," he said, and closed the door behind him.

Chapter Seventeen

When they were gone I filled a pot with hot water and worked my hand until the sweat poured down my face. I wanted to believe that I was justified in letting Sir Leo down because of my injury and my fear, but I had no feeling of peace and my thoughts went round and round without any resolution.

Mora was solicitous and rubbed my shoulders. When the fire had burned low and she had banked the coals, we went to bed and snuggled, but I could not make love to her. I slept fitfully and awoke several times to ordinary night sounds that shouldn't have disturbed me. Having given in to my fear, my fear had increased. But what was I to do? I still had no intention of going off into the woods with Leo's band. Yet I agreed with Leo that Lord Hawke would only become more of a menace because that was his nature. By trying to avoid trouble now, I was surely making greater trouble for myself in the future; there seemed to be no right course of action.

Restless and unrested, I worked with Ben and Matt, but I didn't have much to say and they became shy with me again and talked with each other almost in whispers. At one point I overheard Ben say something to Matt about a challenge that had been sent to the duke from the band in the forest. Of course I was curious, but I didn't ask about it, stubbornly refusing to get involved.

Sometime after midday we had a visitor. She rode right up the path and reined in her mare at the edge of the garden where we were working. Handsome, confident, and aloof, she waited without looking at us for someone to attend her. Taking my hoe along with me, and feeling very self-conscious in my peasant tunic and wooden shoes that had belonged to Mora's father, I walked over to see what she wanted

"Good afternoon, Lady Bennett," I said. "What can I do for you?" I had no idea how I ought to behave with her.

"Good afternoon, Sir Jack," she said in her well-shaped, upper-class tones. "Or is it Yeoman Jack today?"

"I think they call me Jester Jack or Jack the Fool, my lady, or Scarecrow Jack or maybe just plain Jack Straw."

Lady Bennett took her time before she spoke. I thought she would find my joke amusing, but she didn't even smile. She sat watching me from her horse, and there was no way to guess what was going through her mind.

"If you think people are calling you names like that, you're greatly mistaken. To the people of this valley you are still very much the warrior who sent Mike and Mitch to perdition."

"I'll take your word for it, my lady, but I'm not sure I know the difference between good news and bad news right now."

"You may call me Marsha if you wish. And I understand that you've been through the wringer. All I want is to talk to the real Jack Darcey, not to some mask you're wearing."

"Well, my name's Jack Darcey and that's about all I know for sure." Her horse kept backing up, a few steps at a time; I was sure she was doing it on purpose to draw me farther away from Ben and Matt. A few more yards and we would be separated from them by trees and brush. No matter, I saw no danger in following her.

"I heard you were a classmate of King Albert."

"We went to the same high school."

"And what school was that?"

"Chesham Prep in Birchfield, Connecticut."

She laughed at that, a short laugh like a bark. "Well, then I hardly think you need to be confused about who you are."

"Because I went to Chesham?"

"Did you graduate?"

"I did."

"There, you see? When I first saw you, you were dressed as one of the king's knights, and I thought that role suited you very naturally. You could just as easily be a lord as a knight, but a peasant? Never!"

"Marsha, what do you want?"

Again she laughed. "Can't we just talk? Are you so busy with your farming that you can't spare me a moment? I'm really not such a bad person, Sir Jack. You might be interested to know that I attended Finch."

That was an interesting coincidence all right. Chesham boys used to have a couple of dances every year with the girls from Finch. "Is that so?" I said. Was she being kittenish with me? It was hard to be sure, but I was certainly getting that impression.

"Yes, that's so," she said, dismounting and looping her reins over a low branch. "I suppose it really doesn't matter where we went to school. That was on a different star a long time ago. But who knows, we may have something in common."

Now I was certain she was flirting with me. "Dear lady," I said gallantly, "what can a lad with a diploma from Chesham do for you that you honor me with this visit?"

She gave me a smile of recognition, but then she turned away, adjusting her cape. She had put out the bait and I had taken a nibble. That, for the present, seemed to satisfy her. "First I want to say that I'm very sorry about Albert. His death was a tragedy."

That made me take a hard look at her. What was she up to now? "Yes," I said, "and that is an understatement."

"To call something a tragedy can hardly be an understatement," she corrected me. "In the modern world, yes. The media loved to call every car wreck a tragedy and so the word lost its meaning. But here in our little kingdom, words have regained their force, and Albert's death was indeed a tragedy in every sense of the word including the fact that anyone with open eyes could have seen it coming."

The flirtation having served its purpose, whatever that purpose was, she now seemed bent on proving she was a woman to be reckoned with. But that was something I had never doubted since the moment I first laid eyes on her riding up to Albert's castle at Jenna's coronation with her husband and sons in tow.

"Tell me more," I said.

"I don't say this to hurt your feelings. I know that you and he were close. I say this to you hoping that you are a man of understanding who will listen to what I have to say, because this kingdom is deep in crisis."

"Lady, I'm sure you're way ahead of me, and I'm very interested in what you have to say."

"Thank you. In the first place, you can get it out of your head that people are calling you Straw Jack or whatever it was you said. You're the only hero this kingdom has ever had, and I'm afraid you're stuck with that, whatever may happen. Yes, I can see you're rather at a low point, but what of that? All the great heroes had their share of hard knocks: Beowulf, Roland, Lancelot, all of them. It's a necessary part of any legend."

"Those were storybook characters."

She laughed. "So are you; or you will be as soon as we get around to writing storybooks. Maybe I'll write one myself about how you tried to cut your way through two dozen soldiers to kill the duke. I haven't forgotten that epic charge any more than anyone else has."

"If I had it to do over, I would have more sense."

"We can all say that about our whole lives, I'm sure, but it hardly matters. We do what we do; and you did what only a great hero would have done. Would you like to take a walk? I don't think the river is very far, and this might be one of the last lovely days before the weather turns."

There it was again: the hint of a kittenish smile, the subtle body language. I was intrigued by her and curious too.

"I guess Ben and Matt can get along without me," I said, and soon we were completely alone, ambling among the beautiful autumn trees. But if I suspected she was going to seduce me I was wrong, for she turned businesslike again.

"How's your hand?"

"Stiff as a board," I said, for that was what I wanted people to think. I tried to sound resigned and a little bitter, but she wasn't convinced.

"Can't we be friends? Why do you think you have to protect yourself against me? Besides," she said with her bark of a laugh, "the whole kingdom knows that you're nursing your hand, even how often you soak it. It's an important bit of news how our hero is getting along and that he might be able to use that famous sword again. Do you doubt it?"

"Marsha, I'll believe anything you tell me."

"Here's another bit of news, then, and if you haven't heard it, you're the last person to know. Albert's knights have organized a resistance against the duke, and they've just sent him an ultimatum. They're demanding that he vacate the castle and relinquish the reins of government."

"Relinquish them to who?"

"To whom? To the ones Albert named on his death bed.

To a spoiled boy heir, an ineffectual queen, and you, Albert's lord minister designate."

"Lord Hawke will tell them to get stuffed with poison ivy."

"Of course he will, but how long can he hold out?"

"If he can hold out until the harvest, he can hold out until spring. And if he can hold out until spring, he can hold out forever because Sir Leo and his band will be dead of cold and hunger and from then on everyone will swallow whatever the duke dishes out."

"Well, I see you're feeling discouraged and I suppose I can hardly blame you. But if you ask me, he won't be able to hold out long at all. He hasn't been able to sleep since the day he had the king murdered, and that will wear any man down very quickly."

I sat down on a fallen tree and put my chin in my hand. I had seen the duke with my own eyes, and it was true that he looked like a mess. Marya had mentioned it too, and it didn't seem far-fetched to her that maybe Albert himself was keeping the duke from sleeping. But what did that all mean for me?

"Lady Bennett," I said finally, "you came here to give me some advice, is that it?"

"Stop chopping clods and get involved here. Things can't stay as they are and there's no safety in holding back. Lord Hawke is going to start to crack, and when he does he's going to make mistakes. Get ready for him. Contact the band in the forest. Go secretly and talk to Dugdale and Griswold. Lay your plans and schemes. You're not a serf that belongs to the duke. You are Sir Jack, hero and rightful lord minister of this realm."

"Why did you come here to tell me this?"

She surprised me by going down on one knee in front of

the fallen tree I was sitting on and gazing earnestly into my face. "I see something in you," she said, laying a hand on my knee. "You have some integrity, some force. That teenage boy and Queen Jenna aren't capable of running a kingdom. The duke might have been a likely ruler in some ways, but he's lost his chance now, don't you see? He made a terrible mistake thinking he could get away with murdering Albert, but it's too late now, and it's going to break him up just like a ship on the rocks."

"Okay, Marsha, but I still don't know why you're here."

"Because I want to help you. Because I know how lonely it is at the top, and how easy it would be for you to make mistakes from lack of any practical experience here. Because you're going to need someone to turn to for counsel and advice, someone who has lived here as long as I have, someone who can help you develop your vision of how a kingdom ought to be ruled."

"Me?"

"Yes, you, damn it!" she said, jumping up and waving her hand in the air. "Who do you think we're talking about?"

How long I sat there with my mouth hanging open, I have no idea; but after awhile the idea finally squeezed its way into my brain. This woman wanted to fix me up to be the new king. And she was going to be the woman behind the throne.

"Is your husband in on this crazy idea?"

"Oh, poor Bennett," she said with more contempt than sympathy. "He hardly ever really knows what's going on anymore. He's permanently pickled his brain already, it's a terrible shame. He was a man of parts when I married him. But I don't think he's a factor in this at all." She finished up with a kittenish smile that made me very uncomfortable indeed.

"Lady Bennett, I hate to break this to you, but you're talking to the wrong man. I'm not interested in being a king.

I'm not that kind of person at all."

"I know this must be something of a shock, but you're not the first person to be called to greater responsibilities than you think you're capable of. Trust me, Sir Jack. Be strong and resolute."

"What I mean to say is that I don't want that job. I'm more the beachcomber type. You'd understand if you saw me in my cut-off jeans."

"Oh, stop clowning. It doesn't become you as much as you think. There aren't that many jobs to choose from here. Do you want to spend the rest of your life in wooden shoes?"

"If you're looking for someone to be king, maybe you should try Sir Leo. He's charismatic and he's got his head on straight. He's been here a long time. He knows the ropes."

"I think not. Sir Leo is an incomparable servitor; none better. But he's not ruling class."

"There's a soldier named Gordon who has as much class as anybody I've ever met. What about Gordon?"

"Gordon? I can't believe you're serious. He's never even been to school. I think he was in the Navy."

"Merchant marines."

"There, you see?"

"We need someone with some breeding, eh?" I was feeling a little detached now from this lady from Finch who was so concerned about where people went to school. "What about Griswold? He's read at least a few chapters of *Caesar's Commentaries* in Latin. I can personally vouch for it."

"Never! Griswold designates his responsibilities to his peasants and spends his time in rut. He is not so very far from being a socialist!"

"Dugdale then." I felt like I was looking at her through the wrong end of a telescope.

"Dugdale has become more manly since he came up here; but

300

what he wants most is to please Charlsey, and all Charlsey wants is to go home to Cambridge. He makes an effective enough earl, but he could never detach himself enough from her problems to be king."

"So that leaves me?"

"Let's stop joking, Sir Jack. I'm willing to play along with you for a few minutes while you recline on that tree looking me over like I'm some amusing kind of snob. But now I've had enough of it!"

"Sorry, Marsha," I said, "and I don't underestimate you. But I frankly think your idea of making a king out of me is a big joke."

"Oh, you're far from perfect, I admit, and you'd need a lot of help, God knows! But the people would embrace you as their ruler without any fuss and that's very important. We could have a stable, smooth-running kingdom again."

"Marsha, why don't you save me the trouble entirely and just become king yourself?"

That seemed to please her. "In a way I would be king. There's a vast amount of trouble in managing a kingdom and you'd soon tire of most of it. But as far as running on my own ticket, so to speak, that would be the quickest way I know to start creating factions and divisions and controversy, which is the last thing we want. No, you are the natural choice, the organic choice, whether that pleases you or not."

I tried to take it all in. "What would happen to the Picts if you became the undercover king behind puppet-hero Jack?"

"As I see it, the Picts are a cult of Jo Mama's, and when he dies the Picts will evaporate. In the meantime they do no more harm than fairies or leprechauns."

"And where does Queen Jenna fit in? I don't think you can count on her to evaporate."

"It will probably be necessary for you to marry her. Ha, ha, Sir Jack! You ought to have seen your face! You must have some strong feelings about the queen. Does she attract you? Never mind, it's none of my business and it doesn't matter. It would be a purely political marriage, and as far as your private lives are concerned you can both do as you please. Of course, if she has a child, you'll have to acknowledge it and make it your heir."

"Renny is already the heir."

In the silence of the woods I could almost hear the glistening pink marbles of her brain revolving. "Renny," she said finally, "is a problem. Albert said all the correct things on his death bed. What else could he have said? But we who are left behind with all the problems of this real kingdom, we must interpolate. It would be an unusual boy who was ready to assume a king's power at eighteen, and Renny's just an ordinary boy, rather green, rather spoiled. Fortunately he's only turned fifteen, so we have a few years leeway to consider Renny's succession. A good deal could change in three years. What's more important right now is what will happen in the next three weeks, don't you think?"

Ben and Matt were bursting with curiosity, but I hardly said a word all afternoon beyond a few simple questions about the work at hand. Feeling hassled and overwhelmed, I sulked and refused even to think about my encounter with Lady Bennett. What I desperately wanted was for people to leave me be for a little while so I could get my feet on the ground. But when could I look forward to that? It was not until Ben and Matt had gone for the day that I was able to shake off my angry feelings.

"What did Lady Bennett want?" Mora asked me; and it took me a few moments to come up with an answer because I was concentrating on the two delicious smells in the cottage at that moment: supper and Mora.

"She wanted to go to bed with me, but I told her I was already in love with you."

"She better not come around here after you, because I will scratch her eyes out!"

I had meant it for a joke but I should have known better. "I'm sorry, honey. Sometimes I'm not as funny as I think I am. Lady Bennett was here about politics. She thinks Lord Hawke won't be running the show much longer, and they might need me in the government again."

"She is a spider. You should be careful of her."

"Why is that?"

She struggled for her words. "I can't explain what I feel about her, but . . . well, look at her husband. He isn't very happy, that's plain. And they say she wants every little thing her own way."

That evening I took the time to go carefully over everything that Marsha had said to me. By the time I had worked on my hand, and the dishes were done, and the baby had nursed, and we were ready for bed, I understood that whatever else might be true about Lady Bennett, she was certainly a fabulous manipulator. She was so skillful at it, I realized, that she could tell you right up front how she was going to twist you around her finger and at the same time convince you she was doing you a favor.

"That's twice in two days," I said to Mora as we were turning in, "that someone has come to recruit me. I could spend a pleasant winter just with you and the baby, but I don't think politics is going to let me."

"I don't know anything about politics. All I know is the land."

"Where I came from, politics meant millions of rats a-fighting. My inclination was usually to stay out of it."

"Yes, I wish you would," she said, snuggling up against me.

But I knew perfectly well I was going to be dragged into it, and what was so bad about that? What had become of my spirit? Guy Hawke had killed Albert. Didn't I want a place among the people who were going to drag him down? I was still quaking inside from what had happened to me in the dungeon, but mostly it was my useless hand that made me feel helpless and furtive. Without my own right hand to come to my aid in whatever life sent me, I had no confidence and no audacity. Over the last few days it had loosened up a bit, but it had ever so far to go, and I knew that circumstances were not going to give me the time I needed. Things were heating up too fast, and soon I was going to have to make a decision.

I thought of Leo and Gordon and the others out in the forest. *Goodnight, Leo. Goodnight, Gordon. Hope it doesn't rain.* There was a twinge of guilt but I shoved it away. Whatever was coming would be here soon enough.

Chapter Eighteen

The next morning it was chillier and the rain fell in buckets. Mora poked the thatch around with a pole in her expert way until she had it the way she wanted. Then she stood in the doorway looking out at the weather.

"How does it look to you?" I asked her.

"I think we have a little time yet. The rain is still pretty warm. My guess is it will clear tomorrow."

"I suppose a lot of people will be making bets on the weather today. How do you know when you have to start the harvest?"

"Everybody knows at the same time. You know because your neighbors know, and they know because you know. Everybody just feels it and then we don't stop working for days and days except to eat and sleep."

"That's what you do anyway."

"Oh, no," she laughed. "At harvest time we *work*."

"Then what do you call what you usually do?"

"Going to market and nursing the baby and making the dinner?"

"And chopping the wood and hauling the water and mucking out the pens and everything else that needs to be done."

"That's just life. That's the way we live. What else is there to do? Oh, I know a few people who'd rather just drink and sit around all day if they could. But they're not the happy ones. Would you be happy sitting around all day?"

"What do you do after the harvest is in?"

"Well, everybody has a good long sleep because we're all worn out. But then we cook and make presents and we go visiting, and there are decorations and costumes to make for the festivals and rehearsals and, well, life doesn't just stop."

"What about in the dead of winter?"

"The days are very short, so there's only so much you can do. I can spin by firelight and knit practically in the pitch dark, but I don't like to sew at night. We have some time on our hands in the winter, so we go visiting more and stay at people's houses and tell stories by rushlight. Mickey the smith is a great storyteller. His house is crowded all winter. And that's good for him because you have to bring something when you visit, even if it's just a little bit. There are lots of fun things to do in winter like sleigh rides and sledding and skating on the ponds. I love winter."

"You said you had cat for dinner last winter."

"We didn't have to eat the cat until just before spring thaw. Last winter was hard without Dad, but Mom and I had a lot of help from friends. This year I want to do much better."

The rain had stopped for about an hour when I saw five horsemen start up the path from the market road; one of the riders was Lord Hawke. He held up his hand and three of the riders remained in the road. They were all warriors, heavily armed. The other rider continuing up the path with the duke was my own darling Jenna, complete with a circlet of gold around her brow. She had a very guarded look about her. We looked right into each other's eyes but I found no clues there except that she was afraid.

The duke reined in a dozen paces or so from the cottage

door, and I went to meet him. Curiously, my guts weren't churning and my heart wasn't pounding the way they were the last time he paid me a visit.

Marsha Bennett was right. The duke was deteriorating. Even since our last meeting only days before, I could see the change. The circles went right around his eyes now, so he seemed to be staring out of deep pits. And though his eyes still glittered, it was dimly now, as if the fire was banked in the ashes of his fatigue. I almost felt sympathy for him, but not quite.

"You look right at home in your commoner's clothes," he said. "Unfortunately, I need your help at court. You can ride behind one of my men. If there's anything you want to bring, get it quickly."

"My lord wants me in court?"

"Yes, in court," he said impatiently. "Didn't you hear what I said? You can come back and muck in the dirt some other time if that's what you like to do, but right now I need you to play prime minister."

"Is this a game?"

"For you it's a game," he snapped. "What the hell do you know about this kingdom? You're coming back to court with me, and I'm going to tell you what to say and when to say it."

"My lord does me too much honor."

"Don't get cute with me, Darcey. This is an opportunity you won't get again."

"An opportunity to do what? Betray my friends?"

"What friends?" sneered the duke. "If you mean that little gang in the woods, the sooner they're rooted out of there the better for everyone."

"I'm really very sorry, my lord," I said, trying to sound

as polite and reasonable as I could, for I didn't feel the least bit safe arguing with this man with his crazy, glittering eyes staring out of two black holes. "I'll do anything within reason but I can't help you with that. Surely you can understand."

"Do you want to die?"

"No, my lord, I don't want to die," I said, "and I would think you'd had your fill of killing by now—the way you look. How many more people do you want sitting on your chest at night?"

It was not the right thing to say, of course. At worst it would get me killed. But for some reason I wasn't as afraid as I should have been. Feeling a hand on my arm, I glanced over to see Mora standing by my side. She dropped him a curtsy, but he just pursed his lips and gazed off into the forest for a moment or two before turning back to me.

"There are a great many rumors flying around right now, Darcey, but I wouldn't pay too much attention if I were you. I have had a touch of insomnia, but I assure you nobody is sitting on my chest. *You* talk to him," he said suddenly to Jenna, turning his horse and riding to the edge of the clearing where he sat glaring out into the forest. The three warriors had tensed in their saddles, but the duke made no sign to them and they settled again.

"Jack," said Jenna, "you must do as he says."

"Yesterday I probably would have," I said, still surprised at this new attitude. "Bad timing."

"You could come back to court and make an effort to work with him," she told me earnestly. "You could have an effect on what happens in the kingdom."

"Jenna, he killed Albert." I was immediately sorry; the words seemed to strike her like a blow.

"Yes," she said finally, "yes, I suppose he did." She put her hand up to her mouth and began to cry silently, her shoulders shaking. "Jack, what's to prevent him from killing you too? Please come back to court with us, Jack. I need you. I'm very frightened."

Mora's hand tightened on my arm. "I couldn't do it, Jenna," I said. "I couldn't keep my mouth shut. I'd just wind up back in the dungeon, and that would kill me this time sure enough."

"Jack," she said very softly, fighting to control her voice. "I'm in danger. Please don't leave me like this!"

"I'll find some way to help you, Jenna, I swear I will. But I can't come back to court and be the duke's mouthpiece. He just wants me to help him squash this rebellion he's got on his hands. That's plain enough, isn't it? What happens after that?"

"I don't know. I'm frightened."

"Jenna, do whatever you need to do to stay alive until we come for you. I understand what I have to do now."

"Come, come, what's all this whispering?" said the duke, riding into our midst. "You disappoint me, Darcey. I thought you had got some sense." Now he turned to Jenna with a chilling smile. "Swilling pigs is more his style, your majesty. We'll have to get along without him. Come, I think it's time we left. Goodbye, Darcey. Don't say I never gave you a chance."

He took hold of Jenna's bridle and turned her horse toward the road. "We're leaving now, your majesty."

Jenna cast me one imploring look before she tapped her horse with the heel of her boot. The duke rode out behind her and the three warriors fell into step behind them. Down the road they went at a trot in the direction of the duke's manor.

"Go get the baby and throw some food in a sack," I said to Mora without taking my eyes off the riders.

"Where are we going?"

"We have to get away from here right away. Is there a friend you can stay with while I go look for Sir Leo? Someone you can trust who'll hide you if need be?"

"Why do I have to go stay with a friend?"

"Mora, I want you to wait someplace safe while I find Sir Leo. Then I'll come get you and take you to the forest."

"Jack, I can't just go away and leave the farm like that. Who will look after it?"

"Mora, please hurry. The duke isn't going to ride away and let us be. We need to get away from here right now or it's going to be too late." I glanced back at the riders, and saw the duke take hold of Jenna's bridle. Suddenly there was a sickening sensation in my stomach and I knew exactly what it meant. It was already too late.

"Jack!" screamed Jenna. "Jack, look out!" The three warriors were wheeling their horses around, and now they came galloping back.

"Get the baby and hide in the woods!" I was running for the cottage and propelling her along with me. What was I going to do? I didn't even have a weapon. Yanking open the cottage door, I shoved Mora inside, and then raced for the tool shed. When the riders galloped into the yard, there I was with the scythe in my hands.

"Ride him down!" shouted one of the warriors.

"Ride him down yourself," said another.

"All right, all right, let's take our time and be careful," said the first one. "Somebody needs to get behind him."

Suddenly I saw Mora dash behind one of the horses with something smoking in her hand and then the horse was bucking and kicking, and it was a good thing she kept running because those slashing hooves would have been the end of her. The warrior couldn't keep his seat. He crashed awkwardly to the ground and only managed to get halfway to his feet before I clipped his head off and sent it rolling away into the bushes.

I heard Mora scream, and I was running even as I turned. My body was way ahead of my mind, for I had dropped the heavy scythe in order to run faster. Mora dodged around the big stump in the middle of the yard, and the rider pursuing her was forced to do the same. Right there I caught up with him, running up the stump and hurling myself through the air to land on the horse's back behind him. Ass over teakettle we went crashing to the ground.

Mora took a swing at his head with the poker, but it bounced harmlessly off his steel helm. He had lost his sword in our wild tumble, but it was yards away and no use to me. Snatching out his long dirk, he tried to slash at Mora, but I had him by the wrist before he could strike, and Mora hit him a blow on the shoulder that made him howl. I made a grab for his chinstrap, hoping to yank off his helm, but my hand closed around his Adam's apple instead, and when I felt that brittle cartilage bend and crack in my desperate grasp, I pried deeper with my fingers and squeezed and squeezed until my fingers met my thumb behind his windpipe.

Out of the corner of my eye, I saw the third rider dismount and draw his sword. "Mora, run!" I yelled. But she just held her poker out in front of her, pointing at the advancing swordsman as though she was planning to take him on with it. The man I was holding by the windpipe was pitching his body this way and that in the last stages of panic. I didn't dare let go of his wrist or his throat and I couldn't get to my feet.

"Jack!" screamed Mora, backing away from the oncoming soldier, but there was nothing I could do. Holding his sword in both hands like an axe, he threw the blade up over his head. Much as I needed to shield myself, I had run out of hands.

Another step and he would cleave me open like a chicken on the butcher's block.

But now the warrior looked puzzled. He seemed to have forgotten all about me. His sword hand dropped to his side, and the other hand was grasping at his chest. He looked down and there it was: the heavy triangular head of a war arrow and several inches of the shaft sticking out of his chest. He was trying to figure out where it had come from, I suppose, and so was I.

This time I heard the thump, and now there was another arrow sticking out beside the first. The sword dropped from his grasp and he nodded his head a couple of times, as though, just at the last moment, he had figured out what the matter was. Then he pitched forward on his face.

When I turned my attention to the man I was holding by the throat, I saw that he was also dead. His face was a reassuring shade of deep purple and his eyes had rolled back in his head. Gasping for breath, I clung to him while my heart bounced back and forth between my chest and my backbone. My head ached with the adrenaline and the rest of my body was throbbing with fatigue.

Leo and Gordon came bounding up. Leo had an arrow nocked and Gordon was swinging his great stick up as he ran, but when they saw the soldier's purple face, they let their weapons drop to their sides.

"I'm terribly sorry, my lord," gasped Leo between breaths. "Oh, God!" he cried, quite beside himself. "We almost lost him, Gordon!"

"It's all right, Leo, we came in time," said Gordon. "Are you all right, Mora?"

"Oh yes, I'm fine," said Mora, and then she fainted. Gordon caught her as she fell and lifted her up in his arms like a child.

"Is she hurt?"

"No, she's just having a nap like the good girl she is," said Gordon, gazing down on her as lovingly as any father. "You're a lucky man, my lord."

"Every time I turn around that girl is saving my life. Many thanks to you, Leo. Very nice shooting, very!" I was trying to disengage myself from the dead man but it was not that easy to do. My left hand seemed as rusty as an old iron clamp around the man's wrist; and my right hand, which had crushed out his life . . .

Staring at my hand in amazement, I slowly released my grasp, and the dead soldier slumped to the ground like a bag full of sand. The hand was stiff, and it tingled and prickled, but it was working.

"It works!" I'd just received the most wonderful gift in the world. With a real right hand, I was myself again. I was Sir Jack!

"You had a good fight for it here," said Leo. "This one has no head."

I was quite amazed that we were still alive. How could Mora and I have prevailed against so many armed men? But we made a good team and we were fighting for each other, and that had somehow pulled us through.

"We've all been due for some better luck," said Gordon.

"Here's his head," said Leo, lifting it out of the bushes by the hair. He laid it near the body. "We'll take their armor and weapons and lay them out side by side. With your approval, my lord, I would prefer to be safely in the forest before more company arrives. They all have families to claim them."

"Did you know these men, Leo?"

"Oh yes, I recognize them. They're just farmers in armor. This is a terrible time for this kingdom."

Looking at the bodies, I felt sad for my soul, for I felt no remorse for having killed two more men. We were at war now, but that wasn't what made the difference. No, the real reason was that I was getting used to it. I was adapting to my environment. I was developing a thicker skin.

"Put me down, Gordon," said Mora. "Did I faint?" She put her clothes to rights and shook out her hair.

Taking her hand, I said, "Come along, sweetie. We're off to our new home in the greenwood."

She took one long wistful look at her farm. "All right, Jack, I'm ready to go."

Chapter Nineteen

By the time we arrived at Sir Leo's camp in the forest, the story of the fight at the farm had traveled ahead of us along that uncanny gravevine. I could tell that everybody knew about it already by the way people looked at me, and particularly by the way they looked at Mora. Their eyes were shining with such luminous emotion that I knew I had been elevated to a new level in my legend and that Mora had been given her own glory as my warrior mate.

On the one hand it was pleasant to be greeted with so much admiration, but on the other hand it made me uncomfortable to see that I had become larger than life in their eyes and hence somewhat unreal. Mora didn't seem to be affected by the attention that was being paid her. She nodded and smiled and said hello to the people she knew without any trace of self-consciousness, though they were making her very special.

I was aware that even my gestures would be significant to these people who were watching my every move and who were expecting me to live up to the role that was being thrust upon me. So I raised my hand slowly with the fingers outstretched, made a fist high in the air, and then stretched my fingers out again. They responded with a pantomime cheer that shook their bodies but was utterly silent—the camp was a secret.

Sir Rudy Strapp was there, and Sir Bradley, and Sir Maynard, and the rest of Albert's knights, and Don the armorer and many other faces that I recognized, along with many that I didn't. We dismounted where the knights were gathered, and after many embraces, Sir Bradley said, "I think you'll look better in these." Much to my surprise I saw he was holding the clothes I had worn as a knight, all clean and mended after their rough treatment the last time I'd worn them.

"Where did you get these?" I asked Sir Bradley, who pointed into the crowd.

"Ask Kitchen John, who smuggled them out." John of the kitchen, who I barely knew in passing, nodded with a grin, happy to have played his part.

It took me only a few moments to change my clothes on the spot, and when I presented myself to the crowd as Sir Jack of old, there was another silent cheer. Then the crowd parted and out stepped Marya Mage with my very own sword. Didn't they all go nuts with silent happiness when she handed it to me.

I held the sword in its scabbard up over my head and called out very softly, "For Albert!" And the king's name, quietly but with a fierce energy, echoed throughout the crowd.

Next we had a meal, and none too soon either, for I was faint with hunger. The fare was venison, vegetable soup, bread and cheese, and we sat down to eat under the trees. Mora went to sit with some women friends who were making a fuss over her, and I was left with Marya and Sir Leo. When I had filled my gut, I leaned back against the roots of a tree and looked around.

Part of the camp was dug into the southern side of a hill, taking advantage of natural caves. There were crude shelters of cloth and skins on frameworks, and a large common area with three big firepits. Food was hanging from tree limbs in sacks and baskets, and there were several caches where weapons were kept close at hand. Simple as it might be, there was an orderly look to everything which I would have expected from Leo.

"I like the way you've organized this camp, Leo," I said. "But are you sure the duke doesn't know where it is?"

"No, my lord," said Leo. "There's no way we can be sure of that. But we have sentries posted against an attack, and people watching the castle too. This spot also has natural fortifications, like the ravine to the west and the rocky north side of this hill, which make it inconvenient to horsemen."

"What's the plan if we're attacked?"

"We melt into the trees with our provisions and weapons and rendezvous elsewhere."

"Can you do that smoothly and quickly with women and children?"

"We have a drill every day, my lord. Would you like to see?"

"No, Leo, I believe anything you tell me. But do you have to call me my lord so often?"

Leo sighed and looked away, and then there was a silence. I had said something wrong but I wasn't sure what.

"Wake up, Jack," Marya said; after a bit it dawned on me what she meant. Leo was a natural leader, and he already had everything well organized. What he needed from me was authority. Albert was dead, and if Leo went up against the duke, he was just a rebel leading a band of rebels. But Albert had made me prime minister and put me in charge of the kingdom in regency along with the queen. Looking at the situation from that point of view, it was actually Guy Hawke who was the rebel.

"Sir Leo," I said, "with the power vested in me by our late king, I hereby appoint you master-at-arms of all the royal forces and any commoners who support us in overthrowing the usurper and tyrant, Lord Hawke."

"Thank you, my lord."

"Please keep me advised in all matters, but you will have complete authority to act spontaneously if the situation demands it."

"Very good, my lord." Leo brought his heels together and gave me a short, formal bow with his arms at his sides. With a smile that contained both gratitude and relief, he left Marya and me alone.

"Good for you, bubber," said Marya. "That was just right."

"Okay, I'm willing to do anything I have to do for the time being, but I just want to tell you, Marya, that this hat doesn't fit me. I was terrible as a farmer, but at least I could kind of believe in what I was doing. But playing lord high muck-a-muck seems totally wrong and false. Listen to this. Marsha Bennett came to see me about being the new king; and she told me not to worry about a thing because she would be right behind me working the strings that made my head nod and my hands go up and down."

"I understand what you must be feeling, and it is a little crazy, isn't it? But listen to me, Jack. Everywhere you look you'll see someone who's a better farmer than you'll ever be. But there's only one Lord Jack, don't you see? That's who you really and truly are. You just need to get used to it. You'll be fine, Jack. I have complete faith in you."

Ben and Matt burst into the clearing, gasping for breath, and ran to where Mora was sitting. People nearby hurried to hear what they had to say. "We ran as fast as we could to tell you, Mora," said Ben, "but it's not a good thing."

"What is it, Ben?"

"Soldiers burned down your cottage, Mora."

"We didn't dare try to stop them," said Matt.

"They burned down my house?"

"They torched the field and trampled the gardens. They drove off the livestock too," said Ben. "It was a terrible thing to see."

"Then I've got no farm left," said Mora.

"We're very sorry, Mora," said Matt. "We didn't dare try to stop them."

Before this news had time to sink in, a tall man came out of the forest looking for Don the armorer. "Well, here I am, Lou," said the armorer. "What is it, man? Why do you look so pale?"

"Duke's soldiers burned your cottage, and they beat your wife, Don. Some others are bringing her along, but I ran ahead to tell you."

"They beat Dorothy? Is she all right?"

"She'll mend, Don, I've no doubt. But she's very scared and she needs you."

Don and the tall man scrambled off into the forest together and it wasn't long before they returned with his wife; her face and arms were badly bruised.

"Now, Dorothy, you're safe now, so dry your tears. There's a brave girl. Now tell us what happened," said Don.

"Oh, Don, they burned everything, and what they couldn't burn they stole. 'Tell that rabble they can eat twigs and leaves this winter.' That's what the soldiers told me. Oh, whatever will we do?"

"Do? Why, Dorothy, we'll just do whatever we need to do to get by as always," and he threw us a wink, but he looked scared and worried too.

"And the soldiers said they were doing the same for everyone who'd gone to the forest!" said the wife.

Well, that brought a roar from the crowd, and then

everybody was talking at once in a panicky way. Even the knights, I could see, were thinking about their holdings and wondering what to do. *If I were only at home now*, every face seemed to say, *I could protect what is mine!*

"Do something," said Marya to me.

"What should I do?"

"Do anything and make it quick. If these people head for their homes, it will be the end of our fight. The duke will pick them off one at a time."

"Sir Leo," I said, loud enough for everyone to hear. "Pull your people together and break camp. It's time we settled this once and for all."

"Stations and battle gear, smartly now!" roared Leo, and people scrambled to their tasks. Leo was everywhere at once, shouting orders, directing traffic, lending a hand where it was needed. If anything, it was happening too fast. In no time at all they would be ready to go, and where would I lead them?

"Leo," I said, pulling him aside, "I want to do a tour and pick up supporters just the way we did with Albert."

"Lord Griswold's manor house is very close by. From there we could go through the woods to get Lord Dugdale. Are we going to fight the duke today?"

"How long before the whole valley will know we're on the march?"

Leo snorted. "As long as it takes to boil up a pot of mush."

"Then I'm thinking the duke will have to rally his soldiers as quickly as he can, and there'll be no time for him to burn farms."

"To Griswold's then?"

"Yes, and we'll leave the womenfolk there."

No sooner had I said that than I was surrounded by Marya

and a half dozen other women who were already carrying bows and other weapons. Lord or no lord, I was kidding myself if I thought I was going to make *that* order stick. "Okay, okay," I had to shout because they were all talking at once. "Anybody who wants to go can go." And the women ran off to continue their preparations.

Soon our whole band was moving through the trees, and I was surprised to see a manor house just over the brow of the first hill. "Griswold's?" I asked Leo. "You weren't kidding when you said it was close."

"There's a forge at the manor, and that's where Don the armorer and his crew have been doing their work."

"You mean Harvey is mixed up in this?" I said, very impressed and pleased.

"This valley is too small for anyone not to be mixed up in it."

We were close enough now for me to see the defensive preparations, the sentries and the bowmen. When we approached the manor house, we had to thread our way carefully through a maze of sharpened timbers and ditches.

"Hello, Jack," said Harvey, coming to meet us in his armor. He still wore his cynical smile, but his eyes were shining with excitement; I realized for the first time that Harvey was actually a grown man and not the boy I had gone to school with.

"Harvey, I owe you an apology. I've had it in my mind that you were a scandalous wimp. What does the duke think of this?"

"He was here a few days ago foaming at the mouth, but he didn't try to come in past the stakes."

"It sounds like you're not too worried about him."

"Wrong. I'm very worried about him. I'm worried enough

to keep sentries and archers up all night and to make everybody else sleep in their clothes. I'm worried enough to keep two runners watching the castle. I wasn't kidding when I said he was foaming at the mouth."

"Okay, right; but what I mean is that you're not knuckling under."

"That's not new. I can't explain everything that happened in the early days, but this has always been the free-love fief. It's on the other side of the kingdom from Lord Hawke's fief. I run it my own way, and I've always let him know that if he didn't like it he could jump on a flagpole. I never cared much for armor and battle-axes and all that crap, but I have some of the finest archers in the kingdom here and we never have any trouble from him and his boys. That was the way it was when Albert was alive, and that's the way it is today. The only thing that's new is the stakes and the ditches."

I had to shake my head and sigh. "I never had time to get the lay of the land, Harvey. People still have to explain the simplest things to me. Yet at the same time I'm supposed to be the big leader and hero around here."

Harvey laughed. "So you are, so you are. Look, Jack, it's all crazy politics. The world is a crazy place and this kingdom isn't any different. But we're glad you're here and you made a big difference, see what I mean? Albert got killed and that was a terrible thing; now we have to rally around you and see if we can't get things straightened out again. We'll do the best we can. It doesn't have to make sense, and it's never going to."

"Okay, tell me about Dugdale. We're going there next."

"Well, Charlsey went hysterical for awhile," said Griswold. "Don't ask me exactly what happened, but that's Charlsey for you. Dugdale had his hands full trying to keep the top of her head glued on. Are you asking me if he's ready to go on the march?"

"Yes, I am."

"You haven't asked me if *I'm* ready to go on the march."

"Well, aren't you?"

"What happens if we get to the castle with four hundred people and the duke is sitting there all alone in front of the fire with the door wide open?"

"You know damn well that isn't going to happen."

"Yeah, but humor me, your lordship, because I want to know what we're planning to do this time *before* we get started."

"We'll stick him in the dungeon and try him for killing Albert."

"I don't think that's such a good idea. A couple of thousand people saw the king get stabbed by some Picts who disappeared into the woods."

It was a good point and I didn't know what to say.

"Also," Harvey went on, "the harvest is going to start soon. We don't have time for a big trial, even if there was any point in having one."

"So what do we do?"

"That's up to *you,* my lord."

I looked around at the faces of the people I knew and also the ones I didn't know who were all standing there listening, and I realized that they all knew what they wanted me to say.

But somehow it wouldn't do for them to come right out and tell me what it was. I myself, as the repository of dead Albert's authority, was supposed to come up with it.

"What you want me to say," I finally said, "is that we can't afford to take him alive." There was a low murmur from the crowd that was hard to interpret. Harvey nodded encouragingly, but it was clear from his expression that there was more to it than that.

"So even if he were to surrender, unlikely as that might be," I said, feeling like I was limping through rough and unfamiliar terrain, "then I suppose in that case we ought to take him to the nearest stump and chop his head off. Is that what you want me to say?"

Now there was such a silence and such a stillness that I might have thought time had stopped entirely except that the leaves were still rustling in the chilly wind. That was what they wanted me to say all right. The duke was history as soon as we laid our hands on him. No waiting for *this* haircut. Everything right off the top. No more chances. No rehabilitation. No excuses. No mercy. Snip! No more duke.

Could I really bring myself to do such a thing? I tried to imagine it. *Goodman Smith and Goodman Jones: tie Lord Hawke's hands behind his back, if you don't mind.* □Yes, my lord.—*Now bend him over this stump.*—Ready, my lord.— *Goodman Brown: since you happen to be standing next to the axe, would you be so kind as to strike off the duke's head?*— Who, me, m'lord? Oh, I couldn't do that, sir!—*Well, do we have a volunteer, then?* □Stillness. Silence.—*I suppose you would all just as soon have me do it myself, is that it?* □Low murmurs of approval . . .

And it wasn't really funny, because the possibility of such a scene actually happening was a real one.

"Jack," Marya said softly. "I know this is a hard moment for you, but if you're indecisive it's going to hurt our cause. For the sake of the whole kingdom we need a leader who will do what he has to do."

"But how can you ask me to do this," I whispered to her. "How can I just condemn a man to death?"

"I know that wasn't the way your mother raised you, Jack. But that was long ago and far away. Be a man, Jack. That's all you have to do."

"To be a man is to kill a man?"

"To be a man is to face what's ahead."

"Only the law can condemn a man to death." It sounded sententious to my ear, but it was all I could think of to say.

"You *are* the law."

"I am?"

"Well, think about it, but hurry up! Is Renny the law? Is Jenna? The two of them are locked in the tower for all we know. Is Lord Hawke the law? Will you settle for that? This is a little kingdom in the deep woods. If the common people attack Lord Hawke without legitimate authority, then the law in this kingdom falls apart and there is no law anymore. There would be no law, Jack!"

"I am the law."

"That's right."

"My word is law."

"It's the best we've got."

"And that's why I have to be on the spot."

"Thank you, Jack. I knew you would get it."

"All right, then. Off with his head."

"Tell the people. Tell your people."

There was a little platform nearby with two steps to the top, likely used to mount a horse. I climbed up and turned to the crowd. There was an extraordinary tingling sensation running through my whole body that was like nothing I had ever felt before. It wasn't like adrenaline and it wasn't like ordinary excitement or fear. It was a rippling pins and needles sensation, not unpleasant, quite the contrary, but very distracting, like the whole inside of me was getting scrubbed with diamonds. I wanted very much to give my attention to that amazing new feeling, but I couldn't stand there any longer in front of that expectant crowd and say nothing. So I opened my mouth and took a deep breath, hoping that whatever came out would be vaguely cohesive.

"My friends," I said, and then I had to clear my throat because my voice was croaking. "Friends," I tried again, "farmers, knights, soldiers, servitors, loyal subjects. The day of reckoning has come!" The crowd made a sound that was low and deep and full of power, like distant thunder. I felt like I must be on the right track.

"We once marched with King Albert, the finest man I ever knew, but now King Albert is dead, treacherously murdered on his wedding day." This time there was a growl that came from a mouth with about two thousand teeth in it.

There was a high scream, and then I heard the pounding hooves. Down the market road at a headlong gallop came Jenna and Renny, barely ahead of a troop of the duke's cavalry; suddenly we were all scrambling over the ditches and through the maze of sharp timbers to meet them.

Griswold's fortifications were designed to make it confusing and difficult for horsemen to approach the manor, but unfortunately the effect was the same for Renny and the queen. Turning their horses this way and that, frantically looking for an opening, they lost the slim lead they had and we were obliged to rush outside our own defenses to meet them. We were all still carrying the weapons we had brought with us, and with the addition of Griswold's men-at-arms and archers, we were a formidable force. But though we tried our best, we were not quick enough to surround Renny and the queen before the duke's troops caught up with them. Instead, we were packed together against the troopers with Renny and Jenna in the middle.

"The queen comes with us!" shouted one of the troopers who seemed to be in command, and with his mailed fist he grabbed Jenna's bridle. Renny tumbled out of his saddle and was shoved by a dozen hands to safety within the crowd. But Jenna was staring in horror at the soldier who had hold of her horse. In front of her the duke's men were unslinging crossbows, drawing their swords and axes, and urging their horses forward in an effort to surround her. Vastly outnumbered, I have no idea why those soldiers even took a stand. Maybe they were afraid to face the duke. Maybe it all just happened too fast.

"Hands off, trooper!" shouted Griswold. "Ready archers!"

"Archers, choose your marks!" shouted Leo.

"Jenna, jump down!" I shouted, thrusting my way through the crowd to pull her out of the saddle if I had to.

There was a thumping sound, and Jenna came hurtling backwards out of her saddle and into my arms with a crossbow bolt in the middle of her chest.

"Jack!" she screamed, clutching at me, but her body was twitching and would not obey her. "Jack!" Her voice was already weak and her eyes swirled with pain and confusion. "Oh no, please!" Then the blood came out of her mouth and she convulsed and was gone forever.

Around me there were screams and grunts and clashing and chaos, but it meant absolutely nothing to me. I didn't care what was happening and I didn't care what might happen to me. Now and again I was jostled in the melee that raged about me, but I paid no attention to it. I just cradled her body and gazed down into that face that would never again know fear or pain. Death had relaxed her, and her perfect beauty had returned. Her eyes were open and looked a little puzzled, as though she was trying to remember where she had put something, and as I reached up with my fingers to close them, I began to cry.

Through the translucent curtain of my tears I saw again,

one by one, all the episodes of our brief romance: the first moment I saw her in jeans and a sweatshirt as I stepped out of Albert's Rolls-Royce; bare-ass Jenna leaping the chasm of death, her fingers locked in her horse's mane; the candlelit dinner and our first magical night of love. Then a short string of passionate encounters, just a few of them really, but so wild and so beautiful.

I cried in my grief for all that was lost and gone, and I cried in my rage that the gods were so jealous and stingy. I cried in my fear and my guilt as though I myself had killed Jenna by neglecting to save her. I cried until I melted myself down into a kind of trance that was strangely orchestrated by the sounds of battle.

"My lord." A hand was shaking my shoulder. "My lord." I opened my eyes and there was Gordon with his great kindly face a little lopsided with the scar that ran across it, staring down at me. "Let me have her now."

I nodded, willing to do whatever I was told and grateful for the guidance. Unwrapping my arms from Jenna's body, I released her to Gordon, who lifted her lightly up.

It was much quieter now. The din of battle had been replaced with a low chorus of groans and weeping. Looking around, I found myself in the middle of a bloody mess of dead bodies which were lying just as they had fallen.

"I think you ought to stand up now, my lord," said Gordon. "People are beginning to arrive."

Gordon carried the queen a dozen yards and laid her body gently down on a raised platform that had been organized out of timbers and poles and cloth. Two women attended her, adjusting her limbs and crossing her arms, straightening her clothes and brushing her hair.

As I was getting to my feet, I found Jenna's little gold crown on the ground. Walking over to where she now lay in state, I gave it to the women and they placed it on her brow. Poor Jenna. From the moment of her coronation her luck began changing, first to bad and then to worse and now she was dead without one single day to just relax and get a kick out of being a queen, her life snuffed out by a clumsy soldier with a crossbow in his hand, nothing more than a stupid accident. How awful life was sometimes; how stupid and cruel it was!

People were indeed arriving: armed men and boys with their slings, and women and girls also. They stood off at a distance while the two women were preparing the queen; and when the women had finished, then the people began to file past her body. There was no hurry and no protocol. Some placed flowers or small gifts near her body, some stood and gazed at her, some knelt down to pray. Each made his farewell in his own way and in his own time moved on.

Most of the women gathered in groups and many wept and held each other. The men and women who had come to fight were gathered in their own groups with their crude weapons close at hand, and talked in low voices if they talked at all. When a new fighter arrived, he would silently show me the weapons he had brought, and I would nod in acknowledgement that he had pledged himself. Through our first battle I had done nothing but cradle the queen and weep; but that had not diminished my image as the warrior who had been sent to turn the tide against the duke. I was cast in that role the day I killed Mike and Mitch, and that was who I would be to these people forever.

Mora came to stand by my side, putting her arm through mine. "The duke may as well get a good night's sleep," she said, "because tomorrow is his last day on earth."

"Everybody knew what was going on between the queen and me, didn't they?"

"It doesn't matter. We loved her just the way she was."

I understood exactly what she meant. Jenna had placed herself a little bit outside the boundaries of ordinary life and the people had accepted her that way. I had been her lover but I wasn't the only one. It didn't make me special and it didn't seem to bother Mora. I didn't have to feel guilty and I didn't have to pretend. Everybody loved Jenna just the way she was.

"Stay with me now, Mora."

"Are you hungry?" she said. "Would you like me to find you something to eat?"

"I'm not hungry. Just stay with me."

People continued to arrive. The first few waves had come by foot. Now they were coming in carts and wagons from the far ends of the kingdom. Griswold's people had to start directing traffic and helping people to cooking and camping spots; but any resemblance to coronation day ended there. It was a deadly serious multitude that kept coming even after the sun had gone down. They brought only their food for the night, their blankets and their weapons. They found places for their wagons and animals and then they went to see the queen, whose body was lit by torches on the four corners of her bier. The crowd was pulsing with a violent and impatient energy. All I would have to do tomorrow morning was mount up and stay a few yards in front of the doom that would be headed for the castle and the duke.

Shortly after sunset Leo and Gordon came to see us. Leo looked tired and there was a bandage around his head with a bloody spot soaked through it. "Good evening, my lord," he said. "Good evening, Mora."

"Good evening, Sir Leo," I said. "Good evening, Gordon. I'm sorry I missed the battle. How did we do, all in all?"

"How did we do?" said Leo. "That was the wrath of the gods. When the queen fell, the people swarmed over those troopers and killed every one of them." He paused and a whole array of emotions passed across his face before he went on. "Of course we suffered on our side too. Lord Griswold's hall is a hospital tonight. Four of our people were killed in the fray and two more have died since. They would not have killed so many of us except for those crossbows. Curses on such cowardly weapons forever!"

"What's being done with the dead?" I asked Gordon.

"Well, sir," said Gordon, "the dead have been laid out as decently as possible to wait for their families to claim them. I never imagined that anything like this could happen in this valley, with people killing each other like cats. I'm hoping very much that it will all be over tomorrow so we can go back to being humans again."

"Thank you, Gordon," I said. "I share your sentiments. And thank you all for taking care of everything. I'm afraid I wasn't much use. Is there anything else I need to know?"

"Lord Hawke has been to see Lord Bennett as we expected," said Leo, "and between them they rounded up Bennett's peasants and herded them off to the castle to fight for the duke. Bennett is there, of course, and his three sons too."

"All three? One of them is very young."

"I believe they're all at the castle."

"Where's Renny?"

"He's asleep," said Gordon. "After the battle he began to shiver and shake and then he cried his eyes out. Lord Griswold put him to bed in the stables, for the hall is full of the wounded."

Mora stifled a yawn, and that made me realize how completely exhausted I was myself. "Well, let's get some rest. Any idea where Mora and I can bunk down?"

"I'll find you a place if you'll come with me, my lord," said Leo.

On our way I stopped to look at the queen, who lay peacefully among the simple tributes from her subjects. "We'll watch her all the night, my lord," said one of the women. "Flora and me and all these others as well. If it rains, we'll see she's properly cared for, don't you worry."

Jenna's face was a pale transparent color and cold to the touch. It made me want to howl with anger and frustration. Her death had been nothing but an idiotic mistake, a nervous finger on a little iron lever. Nobody had wanted to kill her. Other mistakes in life could be set to rights. Why not this? What was so special about death?

Near Jenna's bier, standing so silently and motionless in the shadow of a tree that I might easily have passed right by without noticing him, was Rudy Strapp. "Hello, Rudy," I said to him. "How goes it with you?"

"Since you ask, I am not feeling so good, my lord."

"Did you get hurt in the fight today?"

"I have not felt good since the king got killed. It was my job to look after him, but I let him down because I was enjoying myself when I should have been working."

"I know exactly how that feels, Rudy."

"Albert brought me in out of the cold and made something out of me. When someone does that for you, you're not supposed to let them down. But I did. And now the queen is dead and I feel like I let him down again. Look at her. Did you ever see anyone so beautiful? We should never have let any of this happen."

"Tomorrow we will finish this."

"Yes, I hope so," said Rudy. "But I don't have such a good feeling about tomorrow."

"Meaning what?"

"When we decided to guard the king we tried to plug up all the ratholes, but we missed one little one and look what happened. So I think about tomorrow and I'm asking myself what is it that we haven't thought of? We have plenty of people here, and I know just how they feel. We could tear the goddamn drawbridge right off the castle if that's what we need to do. But what is that one thing we haven't thought of?"

Chapter Twenty

I awoke in the predawn with everyone else, and by sunrise our army was on the move. As I had suspected, there was little I needed to do besides put on my armor and get on my horse. The energy I had felt from the crowd the evening before had become even more palpable, even more irresistible; if I had done nothing at all, they would have dressed me and placed me on my horse in the course of their impatient preparations.

Dugdale arrived at the last minute with only a handful of his retainers. "I had trouble breaking away this morning," he explained, "but the rest of my people are already here. Very sorry about the queen, Darcey. Very sorry indeed. She was a lovely lady, and she will be mourned by us all."

"Thanks, Dugdale," I said. "I appreciate your kind words. Sir Leo, would you find a place for Lord Dugdale in the cavalcade?"

"Just here in front of Sir Maynard if you don't mind, my lord," said Leo, and Dugdale steered his horse into line. "We are ready, my lord," said Leo.

Feeling very strange, and not in the least bit in control of what was happening that morning, but rather impelled by forces ever so much more powerful than I was, I raised my arm as I was expected to do, and after a dramatic pause swept it forward. With that, the entire multitude began to move. It seemed clear to me that it was the multitude that moved my arm rather than the other way around.

We had a strong turnout. About two thirds of the people who had arrived the day before had come prepared to fight, and the fighters numbered over five hundred souls, more even than had marched with Albert. Of the other people, the majority dispersed into the woods headed in the direction of the castle.

After we had gone about a quarter of a mile I looked around at the knights and the lords I was riding with and said, "Gentlemen, we are marching at the head of a lot of raw power. But so far we have not made any specific plans."

"The plan as I understand it, my lord," said Sir Bradley, "is to capture Lord Hawke and chop off his head."

It was an idea which I still couldn't get used to, but so what? If we succeeded that day in killing the duke, I would have plenty of time to get used to it. And what else was there to do?

"Thank you, Sir Bradley," I said, "but do you think we're going to find the drawbridge down and the gates open?"

"No," said Sir Bradley, "unless the duke makes a run for it."

"Is that a possibility? What do you think, Sir Leo?"

"Anything is a possibility."

"What do you think, Renny? Will the duke run away?" Renny hadn't said a word all morning, and he looked so serious that I wanted to draw him out.

"Aren't you supposed to call me your majesty?"

It took me a moment to get over my surprise. "What do you think, Dugdale? Am I supposed to call this young man your majesty?"

"Actually no," said Dugdale. "Since he is under your stewardship until he is eighteen, it would be more appropriate to call him your royal highness."

"I'll never get used to this," I said.

"We all had trouble with the titles at first," said Dugdale. "But since this is a kingdom that we created, the less confused we are about it, the less confused the people tend to be. That was our experience the first few years. It seemed easier for everyone when we were strict about titles. Am I right, Griswold?"

"Perfectly right," said Griswold. "The more I insisted that everyone call me my lord, the more the farm girls wanted to jump in the hay with me."

"Well, your royal highness," I said finally, "do you concur that the plan is to capture the duke and chop off his head?"

"Yes," said Renny. "He killed my father. He killed Queen Jenna. Other people are dead because of him. Now it's his turn."

"Well," I said, "that's it then. At least we know what we're going to do."

A couple of hours had passed by the time we finished lining up our army to its best advantage across the meadow from the duke's army, which was lined up in front of the castle. On the castle battlements Lord Hawke was standing next to that massive chair that Jenna had said was a symbol of his defiance of Albert. He must have had it lugged all the way from his manor house. Was he planning to sit in it while he watched the slaughter?

Close to a thousand people were ready to rush together and mangle each other; a few hundred more were spread around the edge of the forest. The time of handclasping and embracing was over. These last-minute exchanges were necessarily all too brief, and the message was always the same: *If we don't see each other again, it was good to know you.* Now there was nothing left to do but fight.

"I still don't like this," I said to Leo. "Why did he decide to fight us in the field when he could box himself up in that castle? We outnumber them, don't we?"

"Yes, my lord," said Leo. "We have the margin by well over a hundred."

"Those peasants," I said, pointing at their line, "are not eager for this fight. They would all go home if the duke's cavalry wasn't riding herd on them."

"I'm sure that's true," said Leo.

"Is there something we haven't thought of? Has he got people hidden inside the walls ready to attack us when the time comes?"

"I don't think so, my lord."

"Then how do you explain this?"

"I don't know what to say, my lord. Maybe he's too tired to think clearly."

I had been watching the duke, but at that distance he was just a shape that paced on the battlement, or sat in that ugly chair.

"My lord," said Leo, "I think it's time."

We exchanged a look that was eloquent with unanswered questions about the human predicament. "All right, Leo. Let's do what we have to do."

I lifted my arm in the air and looked up and down our line. Then I saw the lone rider approaching the field on her distinctive mare. Wearing a sedate riding costume and wrapped in her customary aura of self-possession and infallibility, she entered the meadow between the two armies at a dignified trot, and no one yelled, "Hey, lady, can't ya see . . ?" We all knew that Marsha Bennett knew exactly what she was doing, and we were obliged to wait to find out what it was.

When she came to the middle of the killing ground, she reined in her mare, and after pausing to make sure she had everyone's attention, she said in a voice which could easily be heard along both lines, "Peter, James, and Michael! Come along with me!"

Thousands of eyes now shifted to Lady Bennett's three boys and their father, who sat their horses together among Lord Hawke's cavalry. "Aw, Mom!" exclaimed the oldest boy, snatching off his helmet in a gesture of frustration and protest.

Lady Bennett nudged her horse to a walk and rode directly toward them. "You heard me, Peter," she said. "James, Michael, come out of there this minute!"

Lord Bennett looked shaky and ill and very much on the defensive. "Marsha, this is intolerable!" he cried, trying to draw himself up in an imposing manner. But there was neither force nor vitality behind his complaint.

"You ought to be ashamed of yourself, Terry," Lady Bennett told him. "I'll speak to you when we get home. Peter, James, Michael! I will *not* say it again!"

Furious and embarrassed but unable to resist her, the oldest boy clapped his heels to his horse and galloped off the field, down the road, around the bend, and out of sight. She paid no attention to him as he went by, instead keeping her focus on the other two boys, who rode out to meet her and reined in several yards away.

Turning her eyes one last time toward her husband, Lady Bennett shook her head. Everyone on that field was witness to that look of disappointment and dismissal. Lord Bennett was trying to look angry, but he was crumbling before our eyes. Finally he flicked the reins against his horse's neck and rode slowly away out of the press of the duke's cavalry, away from his wife, away from the crowd, away from his shame.

A scream of rage from the battlements: "Bennett!" But there was no response from the retreating figure. "Bennett!"

For just a second I thought I could see, even at that distance, the duke's eyes glowing bright red in their black sockets. "Bennett!" screamed the duke for the third time, his voice croaking from the strain. But Bennett gave no indication that he had heard. A dying man has his own priorities.

"Farmers!" announced Lady Bennett. "There is no need for you to stay and fight in Lord Hawke's lost cause. The harvest is beginning and there is work to be done. You are free to go to your homes!" Without waiting for a response, she urged her horse to a trot and ushered the two boys quickly out of the path between the two armies.

Now there was a chaotic jostling all through the ranks of the peasants in front of the castle. Lord Hawke leaned out over the battlements and bawled orders to the captains of his cavalry, who began yelling orders in their turn. Then the duke's cavalry began to press inward from the flanks to maintain the lines by penning the peasants between the horsemen. Marsha Bennett was standing up as high as she could in her stirrups, staring straight at me, and pointing with her outstretched arm at the center of the duke's unstable line. It was an eloquent message without any words. *Well, don't you see what I've done for you? What are you waiting for?*

If we could split that rebellious energy down the center and turn it outward toward the flanks . . .

"Forward now!" I shouted. "Quick step! Follow me! The center! The center!" Our army began to move, heavy at first, then faster and faster still.

"Lances now! Keep together! The center!" Down came our steel-tipped spears, all pointing right into the vortex of all that desperate energy. Glancing for a split second up at Lord Hawke, I had the fanciful impression that he was tearing that massive, carved chair in half with his bare hands, but I had no time to wonder about what I thought I had seen.

"Together now and charge!" I bawled at the top of my lungs and the army responded with a roar that must have echoed for miles with the vehemence of its pent-up anger as we hurtled across that meadow toward the castle. And the duke's line split just at the point where our lances were aimed; the two halves of the duke's line surged against the cavalry that sought to contain them. I was still shouting wildly, screaming and crying with all the feelings that had been stuffed inside me since Albert's death. It seemed as if all the frustrated feelings of my whole life were coming up at the same time; I was wailing like a banshee as our army charged.

To my left I saw Renny dashing ahead of the army at a full gallop with his sword waving high over his head. "Renny, stay with us!" I yelled after him, but he was already some twenty yards ahead of the charge; and little wonder he didn't hear me because everyone on that field was screaming. The duke's cavalrymen were screaming threats at the peasants who were screaming as they tried to make a run for it. We were screaming as we charged. All the people who ringed the field at a distance were screaming. The whole world was screaming. I lashed up my mount and took off after Renny.

Then Renny did a strange thing. He dropped his reins and his sword and both his arms went out to the sides in an odd, submissive gesture; he was falling backwards, relaxed and careless, and under him his horse was falling too.

Now my own horse was falling under me, and I hit the ground hard in my leather armor. I barely managed to roll with my fall and now I was running toward Renny and my brain was racing too, because I knew something had gone terribly wrong but I couldn't figure out what.

When I came up to Renny I could see right away that he was dead. His face was mangled and he was covered with blood. He didn't look like Renny or even like a boy anymore.

What could have done that to him? Looking over my shoulder I was amazed to see that our charging army was reeling and falling in impossible confusion, horses and people just tumbling to the earth like trees struck by lightning or wheat nipped off by the scythe.

Renny's horse was lying dead on its side and I was taking cover behind it even before I knew what I was taking cover from. There was an evil thumping under all that screaming that didn't belong in our kingdom and didn't exist in our time. It belonged to that time of the everlasting cacophony of the machines, and suddenly I recognized the thumping of that machine gun that was the sudden death of our entire cause.

Pulling my knees up, I tried to get my whole body behind the meatiest part of that dead horse. At the same time I was trying to get as flat to the earth as I possibly could. Peeking out from under my arm I could see our army in rout. Those who could run were running; those who could run no longer were crawling or kicking or just lying on the ground like rocks or logs. Our cheering section had fled into the woods. It was all over, and it had only taken a few moments.

"Darcey! Where are you? Come out and let's play!" The screaming had been replaced by the wailing of women and the groaning and crying of the wounded, and now I could hear the duke clearly, shouting in his triumph. "Where are you, Darcey? Don't you want to fight me? Is that you over there?"

Several puffs of dust showed me where the machine gun bullets were hunting along the ground for my flesh. The bullets slammed into one of the bodies on the meadow, flipping it rudely over. But it wasn't me. It was all that was left of Sir Maynard, his high spirits and his laughter gone, nothing now but bloody meat.

"You spoiled it, Darcey! This is all your fault, you know!" the duke shouted. "Can you hear me? Albert and I

341

were playing for the castle and the woman, and I was winning because I always win, Darcey! It was none of your business!" I wanted very badly to get a look at him. For all my fear of the bullets I wormed my way toward the front end of that horse and peeped out with one eye between the shoulder bone and the slope of the neck.

"Come out, Darcey! Let's have a little swordfight, you and I. Do you like my sword? I knew I would never need it against silly old Albert, but I kept it for a rainy day. Wasn't that prudent of me?"

There he was, all alone up on the battlements, crouching over the heavy weapon that had been concealed in his chair. It was some tripod-mounted monster that fed from a bullet belt that trailed down into the innards of the chair. Now he squeezed off a burst, but the bullets weren't aimed at me. If he had known where I was, he could have blown me to pieces, horse or no horse, for I was fairly close to the castle wall. For the moment I was safe, but I couldn't just lie there. His soldiers would surely be riding out soon to do the mopping up. They would find me, and off I would go to the dungeon or the chopping block.

"I don't see you out there, Darcey," bawled the duke. "But I'll find you, never fear. You're through making your little messes in my kingdom. No more chances now!"

I considered jumping to my feet and making a dash for the woods, but the odds did not appeal to me. I had no options. I couldn't run and I couldn't hide.

"I'll make you a deal, Darcey. Show your face and I'll kill you now. Otherwise you'll eat rats in the dungeon until you die, damn you!"

Should I just stand up and have done with it? I would join Albert and we could haunt him day and night until both his eyes turned into black holes of howling insanity.

"Anderson!" shouted the duke to one of his captains. "Take a troop and search the field. If Jack's dead, bring me his head. If he's not, bring me the man alive."

The peasants had all fled. Only the duke's cavalry remained, lined up near the wall. The captain who the duke had spoken to was a very large man with a face as big as a ham and close-cropped sandy hair. I had it in my mind that the duke's soldiers were all aggressive and cruel, but this man just looked shocked. He held his helmet in one huge hand that was gnarled and knotted from working in the soil; and rather than jumping to carry out his orders, he sat motionless on his horse.

"Snap to it, Anderson!" said the duke sharply. "Get out there and bring me what's left of Jack the Jester!"

But the captain wasn't paying attention to the duke. Now he was looking around at the other men, and they were looking around at each other. They all looked shocked, and they looked embarrassed too.

Now I began to hear again the terrified wailing of the women and the children on the outskirts of the battlefield, and the agonized groaning of the wounded. Anderson slowly dismounted. Bending over, he picked something up from the ground. I was just close enough to see that it was a brass casing from one of the machine gun slugs. The sun glinted on the metal as he put it up to his nose and sniffed at it. Finally, he dropped it on the ground, turned toward the duke, and said quietly, "I'm sorry, m'lord, but it's harvest time." Then he pitched his helmet away like a rotten melon.

"You dare!" screamed the duke, beside himself. "You're under arrest! Krystoff!" he shouted, pointing to another of his captains. "Put this man under arrest and then go and find Jack!" The duke's brow was beaded with sweat and his voice was cracking with tension.

Anderson and Krystoff exchanged a look. Then Krystoff

looked over his shoulder at the duke and said, "I would, my lord, but it's harvest time." He unstrapped his helm, and let it fall to the ground.

"It's harvest time," said a third soldier, brushing off his helm and unbuckling his harness. The words echoed down the line as the cavalry divested itself of arms and armor.

Snarling, the duke snapped the barrel of the machine gun around, but there was not enough space between the crenels of the parapet for him to bring the gun to bear on the men directly below him. "Damn you!" he shrieked. "You'll rot in the dungeon, every one of you!"

The men paid no attention to his threats. Before my astonished eyes his soldiers were turning back into the farmers they had been before falling under his spell so long ago, and soon the ground was littered with the iron paraphernalia of war. With a terrible howl of rage and hate, the duke ripped the heavy machine gun loose from its mounting in the chair and stumbled with it back away from the parapet, dragging the bullet belt behind until I could no longer see him.

Suddenly there was a horrible screech of iron on iron and I thought *Oh God, what now?* But it was the massive chains of the drawbridge as it came crashing down; and over the bridge swept a wave of women with their hands full of bandages and blankets and buckets and stretchers, running out onto the field.

With one eye on the battlements, I got to my feet. The peasants who had fled were returning, moving into the field to search for their loved ones. All the many different ways that men, women, and children can cry in sorrow and horror and sympathy and relief, all that crying rose in the air over the field. Mora too was crying as she ran into my arms.

The soldiers who were still alive and whole were picking themselves up off the field and soon a squad of very grim-looking men and women had gathered around me. Leo was wounded in the leg but insisted on going with us. "Never mind that," he said. "Tie me a strip around here, Gordon. Tie it tight. Give me a hand now. Do you think I'm going to miss this?" We moved warily across the drawbridge.

"Nobody knew he had any such a thing," said one of the duke's men who we met as we entered the courtyard.

"All right. Go in peace," I said.

"I feel ashamed now," said the man.

"Go help with the wounded. Where is the duke?"

The man pointed up a flight of stone stairs. Looking around I saw that the size of our squad had grown. "You people go around by the king's chamber," I said, splitting them up. "This group up the stairs by the stable. You all come with me. Be careful. Stay low."

We came upon the duke on the big balcony outside the royal suite with his back to the wall. He seemed to be talking to himself as he struggled to get the gun set up. There was no grip on the front of the gun except the hot barrel itself, and it burned him every time he touched it. Snatching at his cloak, he wrapped the cloth around his hand for a hotpad. Then I heard him say, "Go away, Albert."

Sir Leo was nocking an arrow, but I put out my hand and he paused. "Leave me alone!" cried the duke, yanking his shoulder away from nothing that I could see. "Get back in your grave."

The two other squads made their appearance, converging slowly on both sides of the balcony. I motioned them to take cover, and put my finger to my lips. "Let go! Let go of me, Albert!" cried the duke, jerking his body. "Can't you see I'm busy?"

More people were arriving; and taking the example from those who were already there, they crouched behind merlons

345

and peered around corners and hid themselves in shadows, silently watching the duke. "No, no, I don't want to! Stop smiling! Get away from me!"

Suddenly the duke yanked the barrel of the gun around and the air was full of fire and smoke and whistling slugs in a thunderous blast aimed at something he seemed to be seeing in the empty air. Cartridge casings fell rattling to the stones and then it was over. The fury of that last volley dissolved into the silence of the valley and the smoke melted away.

The duke was looking down at his empty weapon. His face was contorted and colorless, and he said so quietly that I could just barely hear it, "Look what you made me do."

Everyone understood that the gun was empty now and began moving from cover. By the time the duke looked up, the inner edge of the balcony and the battlements on both sides and above him were thronged with people. "This is all your fault, Darcey," said the duke, throwing down the gun and pointing a trembling finger at me. "All this killing, all this chaos! We had a nice peaceful kingdom before you arrived."

"Archers, ready now!" said Leo, raising his arm, and forty men and a dozen women nocked arrows.

"You dare!" snarled the duke, throwing a glance over his shoulder. Behind him was the stone railing of the balcony, and beyond that was nothing but a long straight drop to the stones of the courtyard.

"Archers," said Leo, "remember the positioning of your feet. I want to see every one of you with a rock solid base."

"You have no right to do this!" screamed the duke, turning this way and that. "Rebels! Outlaws! You have no right!"

"My lord?" said Leo, grimacing from the pain of his wounded leg.

"Sir Leo," I said, "kindly execute this villain in whatever

manner seems appropriate to you."

"Thank you, my lord," said Leo. "Archers, choose you marks. The mark is a magnet that reaches out for the steel of the arrowhead; a nest that beckons to the homecoming bird in flight."

"You're making a fatal mistake, Darcey. This kingdom will never hold together without me."

I was feeling as disembodied as Albert's ghost. I was Lord Jack, but I had no control over what was happening. The duke's death was wrapping itself around him like a glove on the hand of God. All I could do was to stand by and watch. I felt no joy and I felt no pity.

"Archers, draw your bows. Clear your minds. Feel the wind. See the path."

"In six months time you'll all be a gaggle of starving Picts with no farmers to steal from!"

"Inhale now, and hold your breath. Release at my signal."

"You'll be sorry!"

"Now!" cried Leo, and the duke was a changed man, with about as many arrows in him as his body could hold. For a few seconds he teetered, like a man up on roller skates for the first time, and then he crashed to the flagstones as dead, dead, dead as ever a man could be.

Chapter Twenty-One

"Don, I want that devil weapon to disappear completely from the face of the earth. Cut it up, melt it down, mix it with other iron and give it to the blacksmiths to make spades and hoes and horseshoes."

"Yes, my lord," said the armorer.

"Here is the brass from the cartridges," I said, handing him a sack. "I'm not sure we've found them all, so there's a bounty of a quarter bit of gold for every one that's turned in from now on. After two weeks, raise the bounty. I want every cartridge casing in this kingdom to cease to exist."

"I understand, my lord," said the armorer.

"Spread the brass around and mix it up so that nothing remains that can be traced to that gun. As time goes by I want people to forget what that gun really was. I want legend to turn it into some evil magic that the duke conjured up."

"Leave it to me, my lord."

Outside the armory Marya gave me a pat on the back. "Good job, my lord."

"Stop calling me that, Marya. I don't want this job. I'm just tying up a few loose ends and then that's it."

"But what are you going to do?"

"I'm going to join the Picts."

"Oh? What's Mora going to do?"

"She'll go with me. She and the baby."

"She will because she's in love with you, but I doubt it's what she wants. She's a green thumb farmer from a green thumb line, and her heart is in that farm."

"If that's her heart's desire, I won't keep her from it."

We continued to walk in silence toward the hospital in the great hall of the castle. There Marya conferred with head nurse Hélène while I went to see Leo. He'd had a bullet cut out of his thigh, and he was weak and pale.

"They say I'm going to be limping for a while and I believe them," said Leo. "Still I am a very lucky man. They say Sir Bradley will never make it through the night."

"I'm sorry, Leo," Marya said. "Everyone loved Sir Bradley."

"What's to be done with that cowardly and disgraceful weapon?" Leo asked. I told him and he nodded. "Good! And what about that chair?"

"It's already ashes blowing around on the mountain."

"Well, now you'll be king, and we'll have peace and be human beings again."

"No, Leo. I'm going to join the Picts."

"Psss! Don't say such a stupid thing! This has been a terrible shock to all our souls, don't I know it? Get some rest, man. Then you'll feel better."

As soon as I saw Sir Bradley, I could see by his papery appearance that he was very close to death. In my drifty life, I had seen little of death; now I was becoming an expert. Since I had come to Albert's kingdom I had dealt out death and led men and women to their deaths and died a death of my own; now I seemed to be surrounded by death on every side.

Sir Bradley barely managed to raise his right arm, and when I extended my hand to him, he gripped me weakly on the forearm. He made an attempt at a smile and said, "My liege."

Gazing into his eyes, I also tried to smile. If his dying wish was to salute his king, it was all right with me. That I would never be king wouldn't make any difference to him, and indeed, a few moments later, his arm fell limply to the blanket, and Sir Bradley was gone.

Through a film of tears I watched Marya close his eyes. Finally I turned to leave, but as I passed by the other beds, the hands of the wounded reached out to touch me. "My liege," they said. "My liege." It sounded like a prayer. They wanted my blessing and a promise of strength and solidity, but what could I give them? I let them touch me and I gazed into their eyes trying to give them something I didn't have myself.

By the light of the torches outside the castle, Marya laid a hand on my arm. "My liege," she said.

"I won't do it, Marya."

"Oh, Jack, don't play hard to get. Even the stars in the sky want you to be king. Can't you feel it?"

"No, I can't feel it, and I'm not going to do it. I don't want thousands of people looking to me for wisdom and justice, and I don't give a damn whose cows belong to who. I am not the man for that job."

"Jack, it doesn't matter whether you think you want the job or not. Life is much smarter than you are. Reach out and take what life is giving you for your growth and embrace it graciously as the gift that it is."

"Marya, all these deaths—Albert, Jenna, Renny, Maynard, Bradley, all the others—that blood is on my hands."

"Oh, to be sure, you're responsible, Jack. You could have run the duke through that day on the bridge, and I know how that must plague you. But everything that happened is my fault too. I made you appear out of a deck of cards. And let's not forget that Albert himself made Guy Hawke a duke and

350

then couldn't stand up to what he had made. The truth is that we're every one of us responsible for everything that happens, good and bad. If you want to try to hog all the blame, I can't talk you out of it, bubber, but it's just your foolish pride."

"I need to find Mora."

"Come on then, Jack. I'll help you look for her, and then I have to get back to my patients."

No one in the castle had seen Mora, so I took a horse and rode out to Mora's farm. There I found her sitting on that big stump in front of the ruins of her home.

I put my arms around her and she clung to me; in that moment I felt once again the majesty of the infinite, sparkling night sky above us and the awesome loneliness of the mountains and the wilderness that surrounded us. Together we watched the moon come up; and finally we burrowed into a pile of hay for shelter. Bundled together in our cloaks, and full of the warmth that we shared, we passed into a sleep that was deep and still and filled with the peace of centuries.

In the morning Mora collected her baby and we went to find the Picts. It was a breathless day with a stillness unusual even for the valley. Hand in hand we walked into the woods as unerringly as if we had been following a map.

They seemed to be expecting us. Jo Mama was wearing a garland around his brows and not much else, and his Picts were dressed in their elaborate masks of leaves and bark and flowers. There were some I recognized from my first encounter, and others who I hadn't seen before. There was even a family: momma, poppa and baby bat with their leafy wings folded around them.

They made a sound when we entered the clearing, and whether it was a greeting or a cheer or a growl or a ritual I could not tell. We continued toward Jo Mama as the semi-circle of Picts closed around us.

"We wish to join you," I said. There were other things I had planned to say, but the words seemed unnecessary now.

There was a long empty silence which did not seem encouraging. The god was gazing quietly at us, a trace of a smile flitting across his face. Finally he approached me and draped one arm over my shoulder. His eyes probed into mine, questioning me. He seemed to be waiting expectantly for my answer. But what was the question? What was the answer?

Finally the message came through. There were regrettably no positions open at this time. He was sure I would understand.

"But I don't understand, Jo Mama."

He smiled at me and waited. His eyes were clear and pleasant and he wasn't selling anything. He was just waiting for me to get it, and finally I did.

"I don't want to be king, Jo Mama."

He nodded. He understood. He felt that way sometimes himself. But it didn't matter. There were more important considerations than what you felt like doing or didn't feel like doing.

"But I guess I'm being called to it, eh?"

He shrugged. How would he know? Didn't I know? What did I expect him to tell me that I didn't already know?

I thought about the massacre, about the wounded and the dying. I thought about the harvest coming and so many people missing, of winter with its hardships and scarcities. I was the man who had been chosen according to the curious logic of circumstance, the man that people would welcome to the throne. With help from those I trusted, I could make decisions and learn the ropes. Someday I might get good at it. Maybe I would even grow to like it.

Others were entering the forest now. I felt them before I

saw them, and when I turned around, there they were. Marya was there, and Gordon. Marsha Bennett was there with her oldest boy, and Griswold with his arm around some wench. Émile and Hélène and Rudy Strapp were close behind. They had come to collect me and make me their king. I knew I had to go.

When I turned to say goodbye to Jo Mama, he had vanished with his Picts, leaving his garland of vine leaves swinging from a branch. There wasn't a bent blade of grass to show where they had been.

"Well, sweetie," I said to Mora, "would you like to be queen?"

"I want to rebuild my farm," she said. "And you'll need someplace peaceful to come to when you're fed up with all the problems at court. I'll always be there for you when you need me, Jack."

I placed the god's garland around Mora's brow. Then, surrounded by my subjects and with my arm around my lady, feeling a little woozy but still hanging in there, I started back through the woods toward my castle.

And as I walked along, I became more and more aware that Albert was there among us, very much alive and well in that kingdom he had created with his spirit of moral courage and abiding decency that was his lasting legacy and which had ultimately defeated Guy Hawke. I felt certain that I could count on his help, and that gave me hope.

"All right then, Albert," I said to him. "Let's make it happen." And Marya turned to me and grinned.